CUPCAKE DIARIES

This book is a work of fiction. Any references to historical events, real people, or real places are used fictitiously. Other names, characters, places, and events are products of the author's imagination, and any resemblance to actual events or places or persons, living or dead, is entirely coincidental.

SIMON SPOTLIGHT
An imprint of Simon & Schuster Children's Publishing Division
1230 Avenue of the Americas, New York, New York 10020
This Simon Spotlight bind-up edition March 2015
Katie and the Cupcure Cure, Mia in the Mix, Emma on Thin Icing, and
Alexis and the Perfect Recipe copyright © 2011 by Simon & Schuster, Inc.
All rights reserved, including the right of reproduction in whole
or in part in any form.
Text by Tracey West and Elizabeth Doyle Carey
Chapter header illustrations and design by Laura Roode
All rights reserved, including the right of reproduction in whole or in
part in any form. SIMON SPOTLIGHT and colophon are registered
trademarks of Simon & Schuster, Inc. For information about special
discounts for bulk purchases, please contact Simon & Schuster Special Sales
at 1-866-506-1949 or business@simonandschuster.com.
Manufactured in the United States of America 0215 FFG
2 4 6 8 10 9 7 6 5 3 1
ISBN 978-1-4814-5235-9
These titles were previously published individually by Simon Spotlight.

CUPCAKE DIARIES

Katie and the cupcake cure

Mia in the mix

Emma on thin icing

Alexis and the perfect recipe

by coco simon

Simon Spotlight

New York   London   Toronto   Sydney   New Delhi

Katie

and the

cupcake

cure

CHAPTER 1

Who's Afraid of Middle School? Not Me!

Every time I have ever watched a movie about middle school, the main character is always freaking out before the first day of school. You know what I mean, right? If the movie's about a guy, he's always worried about getting stuffed into a garbage can by jocks. If it's about a girl, she's trying on a zillion outfits and screaming when she sees a pimple on her face. And no matter what movie it is, the main character is always obsessed with being popular.

My name is Katie Brown, and whenever I watched those movies, I just didn't get it. I mean, how could middle school be *that* different from elementary school? Yeah, I knew there would be new kids from other schools, but I figured every-one from our school would stick together. We've all pretty much known one another since kindergarten. Sure, not everybody hangs out together, but it's not like we put some kids on a pedestal and worship them or anything. We're all the same. Back in third grade, we all got sick together on mystery meat loaf day. That kind of experience has to bind you for life, doesn't it?

That's what I thought, anyway. I didn't spend one single second of the summer worrying about middle school. I got a really bad sunburn at the town pool, made a thousand friendship bracelets at day camp, and learned from my mom how to make a cake that looks like an American flag. I didn't stress out about middle school at all.

Guess what? I was wrong! But you probably knew that already. Yeah, the cruel hammer of reality hit pretty hard on the very first day of school. And the worst thing was, I wasn't even expecting it.

The morning started out normal. I put on the tie-dyed T-shirt I made at day camp, my favorite pair of jeans, and a new pair of white sneakers. Then I slipped about ten friendship bracelets on each arm, which I thought looked pretty cool. I brushed my hair, which takes about thirty seconds. My hair is brown and wavy—Mom calls it au naturel. I only worry about my hair when it starts to hang in my eyes, and then I cut it.

When I went downstairs for breakfast, Mom was waiting for me in the kitchen.

"Happy first day of middle school, Katie!" she shouted.

Did I mention that my mom is supercorny? I think it's because she's a dentist. I read a survey once that said that people are afraid of dentists more than anything else, even zombies and funeral directors. (Which is totally not fair, because without dentists everybody would have rotten teeth, and without teeth you can't eat corn on the cob, which is delicious.) But anyway, I think she tries to smile all the time and make jokes so that people will like her more. Not that she's fake—she's honestly pretty nice, for a mom.

"I made you a special breakfast," Mom told me. "A banana pancake shaped like a school bus!"

The pancake sat on a big white plate. Mom had used banana slices for wheels and square pieces of cantaloupe for the windows. This might seem like a strange breakfast to you, but my mom does stuff like this all the time. She wanted to go to cooking school when she got out of high school, but her parents wanted her to be a dentist, like them. Which is unfair, except that if she didn't go to dental school,

3

she wouldn't have met my dad, and I would never have been born, so I guess I can't complain.

But anyway, in her free time she does the whole Martha Stewart thing. Not that she looks like Martha Stewart. She has brown hair like me, but hers is curly, and her favorite wardrobe items are her blue dentist coat and her apron that says #1 CHEF on the front. This morning she was wearing both.

"Thanks, Mom," I said. I didn't say anything about being too old for a pancake shaped like a school bus. It would have hurt her feelings. Besides, it was delicious.

She sat down in the seat next to me and sipped her coffee. "Do you have the map I printed out for you with the new bus stop location?" she asked me. She was doing that biting-her-bottom-lip thing she does when she's worried about me, which is most of the time.

"I got it, but I don't need it," I replied. "It's only four blocks away."

Mom frowned. "Okay. But I e-mailed the map to Barbara just in case."

Barbara is my mom's best friend—and she's also the mom of my own best friend, Callie. We've known each other since we were babies. Callie is two months older than I am, and she never lets me forget it.

"I hope Callie has the map," my mom went on. "I wouldn't want you two to get lost on your first day of middle school."

"We won't," I promised. "I'm meeting Callie at the corner of Ridge Street, and we're walking to the bus stop together."

"Oh, good," Mom said. "I'm glad you finally talked to your old bus buddy."

"Uh, yeah," I said, and quickly gulped down some orange juice. I hadn't actually talked to her. But we'd been bus buddies ever since kindergarten (my corny mom came up with "bus buddies," in case you didn't figure that out already), so there was no real reason to believe this year would be any different. I knew I'd see her at the bus stop.

Every August, Callie goes to sleepaway camp, which totally stinks. She doesn't get back until a few days before school starts. Normally I see her the first day she comes back and we go to King Cone for ice cream.

But this year Callie texted that she was busy shopping with her mom. Callie has always cared a lot more about clothes than I do. She wanted to find the perfect outfit to wear on her first day of middle

5

school. And since we only had a few days before school started I didn't think it was *that* weird that I didn't see her. It was a *little* weird that she hadn't called me back. But we had texted and agreed to meet on the corner of Ridge Street, so I was sure everything was fine.

I ate my last bite of pancake and stood up. "Gotta brush my teeth," I said. When you're the daughter of a dentist, you get into that habit pretty early.

Soon I was slipping on my backpack and heading for the door. Of course, Mom grabbed me and gave me a big hug.

"I packed you a special lunch, Cupcake," she said.

Mom has called me Cupcake ever since I can remember. I kind of like it—except when she says it in front of other people.

"A special lunch? Really?" I teased her. Every lunch she makes me is a special lunch. "What a surprise."

"I love you!" Mom called. I turned and waved. For a second I thought she was going to follow me to the bus so I yelled, "I love you too!" and ran down the driveway.

Outside, it still felt like summer. *I should have worn shorts,* I thought. There's nothing worse than sitting in a hot classroom sweating a lot and having your jeans stick to your legs. Gross. But it was too late to change now.

Ridge Street was only two blocks away. There were lots of kids heading for the bus stop, but I didn't see Callie. I stood on the corner, tapping my foot.

"Come on, Callie," I muttered. If we missed the bus, Mom would insist on walking me to the bus stop every morning. I didn't know if I could take that much cheerfulness before seven thirty a.m.

Then a group of girls turned the corner: Sydney Whitman, Maggie Rodriguez, and Brenda Kovacs—and Callie was with them! I was a little confused. Callie usually didn't walk with them. It was always just Callie and me.

"Hey, Cal!" I called out.

Callie looked up at me and waved, but continued talking to Maggie.

That was strange. I noticed, though, she wasn't wearing her glasses. She's as blind as a bat without her glasses. *Maybe she doesn't recognize me,* I reasoned. *My hair did get longer this summer.*

So I ran up to them. That's when I noticed they were all dressed kind of alike—even Callie. They were wearing skinny jeans and each girl had on a different color T-shirt and a thick belt.

"Hey, guys," I said. "The bus stop's this way." I nodded toward Ridge Street.

Callie looked at me and smiled. "Hi, Katie! We were just talking about walking to school," she said.

"Isn't it kind of far to walk?" I asked.

Maggie spoke up. "Only little kids take the bus."

"Oh," I said. (I know, I sound like a genius. But I was thinking about how my mom probably wouldn't like the idea of us walking to school.)

Then Sydney looked me up and down. "Nice shirt, Katie," she said. But she said it in a way that I knew meant she definitely didn't think it was nice. "Did you make that at camp?"

Maggie and Brenda giggled.

"As a matter of fact, I did," I said.

I looked at Callie. I didn't say anything. She didn't say anything. What was going on?

"Come on," Sydney said, linking arms with Callie. "I don't want to be late."

She didn't say, "Come on, everybody but Katie," but she might as well have. I knew I wasn't invited. Callie turned around and waved. "See you later!" she called.

I stood there, frozen, as my best friend walked away from me like I was some kind of stranger.

CHAPTER 2

The Horrible Truth Hits Me

*Y*ou might think I was mad at Callie. But I wasn't. Well, not really. For the most part I was really confused.

Why didn't Callie ask me to walk with them? Something had to be going on. Like, maybe her mom had told her to walk with those girls for some reason. Or maybe Callie didn't ask me to walk with them because she figured I would be the one to ask. Maybe that was it.

The sound of a bus engine interrupted my thoughts. Two blocks away, I could see a yellow school bus turning the corner. I was going to miss it!

I tore off down the sidewalk. It's a good thing I'm a fast runner because I got to the bus stop just as the last kid was getting on board. I climbed up the steps, and the bus driver gave me a nod. She was a friendly-looking woman with a round face and curly black hair.

It hit me for the first time that I would have a new bus driver now that I was going to middle school. The elementary school bus driver, Mr. Hopkins, was really nice. And I might never see him again!

But I couldn't think about that now. I had to find a place to sit. Callie and I always sat in the third seat down on the right. Two boys I didn't know were sitting in that seat. I stood there, staring at the seats, not knowing what to do.

"Please find a seat," the bus driver told me.

I walked down the aisle. Maybe there was something in the back. As I passed the sixth row, a girl nodded to the empty seat next to her. I quickly slid into it, and the bus lurched forward.

"Thanks," I said.

"No problem," replied the girl. "I'm Mia."

I don't really know a lot about fashion, but I could tell that Mia was wearing stuff that you see in magazines. She could even have been a model herself—she had long black hair that wasn't dull like mine, but shiny and bouncy. She was wearing those leggings that look like jeans, with black boots, and a short black jacket over a long gray T-shirt. I figured that Mia must be a popular girl from one of the other elementary schools.

"Are you from Richardson?" I asked her. "I used to go to Hamilton."

Mia shook her head. "I just moved here a few weeks ago. From Manhattan."

"Mia from Manhattan. That's easy to remember," I said. I started talking a mile a minute, like I do when I'm nervous or excited. "I never met anyone who lived in Manhattan before. I've only been there once. We saw *The Lion King* on Broadway. I just remember it was really crowded and really noisy. Was it noisy where you lived?"

"My neighborhood was pretty quiet," Mia replied.

I suddenly realized that my question might have been insulting.

"Not that noisy is bad," I said quickly. "I just meant—you know, the cars and buses and people and stuff . . ." I decided I wasn't making things any better.

But Mia didn't seem to mind. "You're right. It can get pretty crazy. But I like it there," she said. "I still live there, kind of. My dad does, anyway."

Were her parents divorced like mine? I wondered.

I wanted to ask her, but it seemed like a really personal question. I chose a safer subject. "So, how do you like Maple Grove?"

"It's pretty here," she answered. "It's just kind of . . . quiet."

She smiled, and I smiled back. "Yeah, things can be pretty boring around here," I said.

"By the way, I like your shirt," Mia told me. "Did you make it yourself?"

I got a sick feeling for a second—was she making fun of me, like Sydney had? But the look on her face told me she was serious.

"Thanks," I said, relieved. "I'm glad you said that because somebody earlier didn't like it at all, and what was extra weird is that my best friend was hanging around with that person."

"That sounds complicated," Mia said.

That's when the bus pulled into the big round driveway in front of Park Street Middle School. I'd seen the school a million times before, of course, since it was right off the main road. And I'd been inside once, last June, when the older kids had given us a tour. I just remember thinking how much bigger it was than my elementary school. The guide leading us kept saying it was shaped like a U so it was easy to get around. But it didn't seem easy to me.

We climbed out of the bus, which had stopped in front of the wide white steps that led up to the front door. The concrete building was the color of beach sand, and for a second I wished it was still summer and I was back on the beach.

Mia took a piece of yellow paper out of her jacket pocket. "My homeroom is in room 212," she said. "What's yours?"

I shrugged off my backpack. My schedule was somewhere inside. I zipped it open and started searching through my folders.

"I've got to find mine," I said. "Go on ahead."

"Are you sure?" Mia looked hesitant. If I hadn't been freaking out about my schedule, I might have noticed that she didn't want to go in alone. But I wasn't thinking too clearly.

"Yeah," I said. "I'll see you later!"

After what seemed forever I finally found my schedule tucked inside one of the pockets of my five-subject notebook. I looked on the line that read HOMEROOM . . . 216.

So I wouldn't be with Mia. But would I be with Callie? She and I had meant to go over our schedules to see what classes we'd have together. Now I didn't know if we had the same gym or lunch or anything.

Maybe we're in the same homeroom, I thought hopefully. I studied the little map on the bottom of the schedule and went inside. From the front door, it was pretty easy to find room 216. It looked like a social studies classroom, I guessed. There were maps of the world on the wall and a big globe in the corner. I scanned the room for Callie, but I didn't see her, although Maggie and Brenda were there, sitting next to each other. Almost all of the seats were taken; the only empty ones were in the front row, where nobody ever wants to sit. But I had no choice.

I purposely took the seat in front of Maggie— partly because I knew her from my old school, and partly because I wanted to get some info about Callie.

I set my backpack on the floor and turned around. Maggie and Brenda were drawing with gel pens on their notebooks. They were both tracing the letters "PGC" in big bubble print. When they saw me looking, they quickly flipped over their notebooks.

"Hey," I said. "Do you know if Callie is in this homeroom?"

"Why don't you ask her yourself?" Maggie asked, and Brenda burst out into giggles.

"Um, okay," I said, but I could feel my face getting red. Callie and I had never hung out with Sydney, Maggie, and Brenda at our old school, but they had always been basically nice. At least, they'd never been mean to me.

But I guess things had changed.

The bell rang, and for the first time, I felt a pang of middle school fear. Just like those kids in the movies.

It was a horrible thought, but I knew it was true.… Middle school wasn't going to be as easy as I'd hoped!

CHAPTER 3

Humiliated in Homeroom!

$\mathscr{L}$uckily, the homeroom teacher walked in before Maggie or Brenda could say anything else. Mr. Insley had dark brown hair and a beard and mustache.

"Welcome to homeroom," he said, smiling. "This room will be your first stop every morning before you head out to your classes. I can guarantee that this will be your easiest class of the day. On most days, we only have three things to do: take attendance, say the Pledge of Allegiance, and listen to announcements."

"Yeah, no homework!" a boy in the back of the room called out.

"You'll get plenty of that in your other classes," Mr. Insley said, and a bunch of kids groaned. I had to admit that it made me nervous. I had heard that there was tons more homework in middle school, but I hoped it wasn't true.

"Today is your lucky day, because you get to have homeroom with me for an extra ten minutes," Mr. Insley went on. "I'll be giving you some tips about how to get around this place."

There was a loud beeping sound over the intercom.

"Good morning, students! This is Principal LaCosta. Welcome to Park Street Middle School. Please stand for the Pledge of Allegiance."

We launched into the pledge, and after the principal made a few announcements, Mr. Insley took attendance. There were more kids from my old school than I realized, but no Callie.

As Mr. Insley started to explain about how to get around the school, I got this crazy urge to talk to Callie. I carefully reached for my cell phone in my backpack.

I know what you're thinking: *She can't use her cell phone in class!* And you're right. I knew that. But it was like some alien or something was controlling my hands.

Must . . . text . . . Callie.

I slipped the phone under the desk and flipped

it open. I glanced at Mr. Insley and then I quickly texted my best friend.

> What happened this morning? R u taking the
> bus home or walking again?

I sent the text and looked up at Mr. Insley again. He had his back to the class, pointing to a map of the school projected on the screen. So far so good.

I felt the phone buzz in my hands and checked Callie's reply.

> Let's talk after

After what? I wondered frantically. After homeroom? After school? My alien hands started texting again.

> Where r u now? Where is ur homeroom? Should
> we talk b4 class? Or I can meet u

"Miss Brown, is it?"

I looked up to see Mr. Insley standing right over me! I was so busted. I felt my face get hot.

"Um, yes," I managed to squeak out.

"I should probably remind you of the rule that there is no texting during class in this school,"

Mr. Insley said. "Normally, I'd have to confiscate your phone. But since it's the first day of school, consider this a warning."

I nodded and stuffed the phone in my backpack. I could hear kids laughing behind me.

"Bus-ted," Maggie sang in a loud whisper, then giggled.

Did you ever wish that you could blink your eyes and magically disappear? That's exactly how I felt. I'd even take a time machine—I could go back in time to the start of homeroom and leave my cell phone in my backpack. Or how about wings? I could unfurl them and fly out the window, far away from middle school.

But I was stuck with the awful reality of being humiliated in homeroom. There was nowhere to run.

Fortunately the bell rang. One good thing about being in the front row was that I could make a quick getaway. I dashed into the hallway.

Crowds of kids streamed through the halls. Callie had to be somewhere close by, right? I walked up and down, trying to find her.

Then I noticed that kids were opening their lockers and putting their backpacks inside. I had a feeling I was supposed to be doing that too. *Where*

19

was that schedule again? It had to be here somewhere. . . .
Found it!

I took it out and tried to find my locker on the map that was on the bottom of my schedule. I had locker number 213. Isn't thirteen supposed to be an unlucky number? But, luckily, it was just down the hallway.

The locker had a built-in lock. I spun the dial, searching for the combination numbers that were printed on my schedule.

26 . . . 14 . . . 5 . . .

The door wouldn't open the first time. The hallway was getting emptier by the second. Panic started to well up inside me.

I took a deep breath and tried again.

26 . . . 14 . . . 5 . . . Click!

The door popped open, and I shoved my backpack inside. I took out the notebook I needed for my next class, science.

I slammed the locker shut and checked the schedule again. Science was in room 234, on the left leg of the *U*. It should have been easy to find, except I wasn't sure what part of the *U* I was in.

I guess if I had been paying attention to Mr. Insley, I would have known where to go. I ran down the hall as fast as I could and turned the corner. Room 234 should have been the first door on the right.

I stepped in the doorway, breathless. I looked around for a seat.

That's when I noticed the chalkboard.

French—Bonjour!

Mademoiselle Girard

I was in the wrong room!

A girl with reddish hair in the front row saw me. "You look lost," she said.

"I am," I told her. "I'm trying to find science. Room 234."

She pointed to the doorway with her pencil. "Right across the hall," she said.

"Thanks!"

I raced across the hallway just as the bell rang.

I was going to be late for my very first class! Could this day get any worse?

CHAPTER 4

Abandoned at Lunch

Okay, so it turned out that I wasn't the only one who was late, and we weren't in any trouble. The science teacher, Ms. Biddle, waved us all in.

"Enter, enter, all you lost souls," she said.

I liked Ms. Biddle right away. She wasn't much taller than any of us students, and her blond hair was spiked on top of her head. She wore a bright blue T-shirt that said EVIL MUTANT SCIENCE TEACHER.

"Welcome to science," she announced. "I am Ms. Biddle, and this is my co-teacher, Priscilla."

She pointed to a plastic skeleton hanging from a stand in the front corner of the room. A bunch of us laughed.

"Based on the existence of Priscilla in this class-room, who can create a hypothesis about what we're going to learn this semester?" she asked.

I raised my hand. "The human body?"

"Excellent!" the teacher cheered. "What a bright bunch of students. I can tell this is going to be a great year."

My humiliating homeroom experience took a backseat in my brain. I really had fun in science class. Science has always been my favorite subject. And I had a feeling that Ms. Biddle could make any subject fun, even math.

When science ended, I resisted the urge to look for Callie in the hallway. I didn't want to be late again. My next class was social studies with Mr. Insley, back in homeroom.

I stopped at my locker and got my social studies notebook on the first try. I made it to the room before the bell rang.

"Hey, it's the cell phone girl," Mr. Insley said when he saw me, and I cringed a little. But I recovered quickly.

"Cell phone? What cell phone?" I joked, and to my relief, he gave me a smile.

Social studies went pretty smoothly too—but still no Callie.

I knew my next period was lunch, and I felt sure I would see her there. I had to. If I didn't talk with her soon, I knew I would go crazy!

I had to stop back at my locker to get my lunch. I swiftly spun the dial.

26 . . . 15 . . . 14.

Nothing happened.

"Okay," I told my locker. "We can do this the hard way or the easy way."

I tried the combination again, and it still didn't work. Frustrated, I pulled my schedule out of my notebook and checked it again.

26 . . . 14 . . . 5. I'd gotten the numbers mixed up.

"Sorry," I told my locker. "My bad."

I grabbed my lunch and raced to the cafeteria but, of course, I was one of the last people to get there.

The cafeteria was twice as big as the one in my old school. Kids sat at rectangular tables that stretched all the way to the back of the room. More kids were lined up in front of the steaming lunch counter along the wall to my right.

It didn't take me long to spot Callie in the crowd. She was sitting at a table with Sydney, Maggie, and Brenda.

Somehow I wasn't surprised. But I wasn't exactly prepared either. What was I supposed to do? Just walk up and sit with them?

Why not? I asked myself. *You and Callie have sat together at lunch every day for years. Why should today be any different?*

I took a deep breath and walked toward the table. There was an empty seat. Perfect!

"Hi," I said, moving toward the seat. But Sydney stopped me with just a few words.

"Sorry, Katie," she said. "This table is reserved for the PGC."

"What's the PGC?" I asked.

"Popular. Girls. Club," Sydney replied, saying each word slowly, to make sure I understood. "You have to be a member to sit here. And you are not."

I turned to Callie. "So, you're a member?"

"Yeah," she said. "It's no big deal, Katie, it's just—"

"Right. No big deal," I said quickly. I didn't want to hear what Callie had to say. I just needed to get away from that table. I felt like I couldn't breathe.

"Hey, Katie!" I heard Callie call behind me. "I'll call you later!"

I walked away and tried to find another seat. I could feel tears forming in my eyes. I could *not* cry in the middle of the cafeteria on my first day of school. I just couldn't.

I saw some kids from Hamilton at other tables, but I walked right past them. I headed for an empty table in the back of the room and sat down.

What had just happened? Callie had joined a club, and I wasn't invited. Fine. But couldn't she at least have warned me before today?

I opened my lunch bag. I didn't feel much like eating, but Mom would be disappointed if I didn't at least try the special lunch she made for me.

Mom had packed carrot sticks with ranch dip (my favorite) and a tuna fish sandwich, plus my aluminum water bottle filled with apple juice. Besides all that, there was a pink plastic cupcake holder, the kind that's shaped exactly like a cupcake. Mom had written on it with a glitter marker, "A cupcake for my Cupcake." Corny, yes, but I knew the cupcake inside would be delicious.

Suddenly I realized I was hungry after all. I unwrapped the sandwich and took a bite.

"Is anyone sitting here?"

I looked up to see Mia, the girl from the bus.

"No, unless they're invisible," I replied. Mia smiled and sat in the chair across from me.

"How's everything going so far?" Mia asked me. She was opening up her lunch bag and taking out a container of what looked like vegetable sushi rolls.

"Let's see," I began. "I got in trouble in homeroom for using my cell phone. My locker hates me.

26

I keep getting lost. And, oh yeah, my best friend would rather hang out with a bunch of mean girls than me."

Mia raised an eyebrow. "Really?"

"It's all true," I said solemnly. "How about you?"

Mia shrugged. "It's okay . . . just, different. Hey, did you have science yet? Isn't Ms. Biddle awesome?"

I nodded. "I know! I love her T-shirt."

As we were talking, two girls approached our table, carrying trays of food. I recognized one of them as the girl with the reddish hair who helped me find the science room.

"Hi," I said. "Do you want to sit down? There's plenty of room."

"Thanks," said the girl I recognized.

"I'm Mia," Mia said.

"And I'm Katie," I added.

"Hi. I'm Alexis," she replied. "And this is Emma."

"Hi," Emma said shyly.

Alexis's reddish hair was neatly pulled back in a white headband that matched her white button-down shirt. She wore a short denim skirt and ballet flats. I noticed everything matched.

Emma had big blue eyes and straight blond hair. She was really pretty. She had on a sleeveless pink dress with small white flowers on it and white sneakers.

"Did you guys go to Richardson?" I guessed.

Alexis nodded. "Right. Did you go to Hamilton?"

"I did," I replied. "But Mia's from Manhattan."

"Ooh, I always wanted to go there," Emma said. "I heard there's a museum with a giant whale that hangs from the ceiling, and you can walk right underneath it. Have you ever been there?"

Mia nodded. "It's so cool. It's amazing to imagine that something that big lives on the planet, you know?" she said. "You should go sometime. Manhattan's not that far from here."

"Maybe someday," Emma said wistfully.

"So has anyone had that math teacher yet, Mrs. Moore?" Mia asked. She shuddered. "Scary."

"Uh-oh," I said. "I have her next period."

"Me too. But I heard she's not so bad," Alexis told us. "My sister Dylan told me she's strict, but if you just do what she says, you'll be all right."

I finished my sandwich and dug into my carrot sticks. Mia, Alexis, and Emma were really nice, but I couldn't stop thinking about Callie. I glanced over at the PGC table. Callie was laughing at something Sydney was saying. Were they laughing about me?

I didn't realize it at first, but I was accidentally

ignoring the girls at the table, so I quickly tuned back in.

"Earth to Katie," Alexis said. "I was asking you if you had social studies yet."

"Oh, sorry," I said.

"Her best friend dumped her to hang out with some mean girls," Mia explained.

"Really?" Alexis asked. "Which ones?"

I pointed to Sydney's table.

"Oh, I know those girls from camp," she said, shaking her head. "You're right. They are mean. Especially that Sydney."

"I don't know what Callie's doing with them," I said with a sigh.

"Callie?" Alexis said. "I know her from camp too. She always seemed nice."

I reached into my lunch bag and took out my cupcake holder. For a second I forgot about the corny message my mom had decorated it with. I tried to turn it around so the other girls wouldn't see it, but it was too late.

"Aw, that's cute," Mia said.

"Thanks," I replied, relieved. I opened the cupcake holder and took out the sweet treasure inside.

"Wow, your mom packed you a cupcake?" Emma asked. "Lucky!"

The icing was a light brown color. I sniffed it.

"Peanut butter," I said out loud. "With cinnamon."

"What's inside?" Emma asked.

I took a bite, and a yummy glob of grape jelly squirted into my mouth.

"Jelly," I reported. "It's a P-B-and-J cupcake."

I took another bite, making sure to get the icing and the jelly in the bite at the same time. Like all of mom's cupcakes, it was superdelicious.

At least some things never change, I thought.

I realized that all of the girls were eyeing me a little bit enviously. I couldn't blame them. I mean, who doesn't like cupcakes?

"I've never heard of a peanut-butter-and-jelly cupcake before," Emma said.

"There's a cupcake shop in my dad's neighborhood that has fifty-seven flavors," Mia told us. "I bet they have P-B-and-J."

I thought about offering them a bite, but I already had my germs all over it, and the jelly was getting kind of messy.

"The next time my mom makes cupcakes, I'll bring some for all of us," I promised.

"Cool," Mia said.

"Thanks," said Alexis and Emma at the same time.

The lunch bell rang. It was time for my next class.

I stuffed my empty cupcake holder into my bag. My first day of middle school wasn't even half over, but I had a feeling that the only good part of it had just ended.

CHAPTER 5

The Cupcake Cure

So here's what happened the rest of the day:

• Forgot my locker combination after lunch.

• Was late to math class. Mrs. Moore gave me a sheet of math problems to do as punishment. Mia was right! She *is* scary.

• No gym until next week, so I hung out with Emma, who's in my gym class. (Okay, something went right.)

• Had English with Mia, Alexis, and Emma. Good. But left my summer reading report in my locker. Bad!

• Had art as my special class for seventh period. Found out that there's cooking, but I can't take that until January. Rats!

• Spanish is my last class of the day. Then it's *adios*!
• No Callie in *any* of my classes.

When the last bell rang, I stuffed all of my books into my backpack and went outside to look for Joanne's car.

Joanne works in my mom's office. When I was in elementary school, I went to an after-school program until Mom got off of work. But there's no after-school program for middle school. Mom doesn't think I'm old enough to go home by myself. So her plan was for me to hang out at the office every day. Doesn't that sound like fun?

Anyway, she told me Joanne had a small red car, so I started looking around for it. Then I heard Sydney's voice behind me.

"Looking for your former friend?"

I turned and saw Sydney, with Maggie and Brenda laughing behind her. At least Callie wasn't with them. I turned around without answering.

Then I heard a beep. Joanne was waving out of a car window down by the parking lot. I ran to meet her.

"Hey, Katie. How was your first day of middle school? Was it awesome?" Joanne asked.

"Sure," I said, sliding into the front seat.

I like Joanne a lot. She's really tall and has lots of blond hair that she piles on top of her head. She always talks to me like I'm a person, not a little kid. Not all adults know how to do that.

"Hmm. You don't sound so sure," Joanne said.

"It was fine," I told her.

I really didn't feel like talking about it. Not just now, anyway. Sydney had put me in a really bad mood.

Joanne seemed to understand.

"Cool," she said. "Your mom's been talking about you all day. She can't wait to see you."

When we got to the office, my mom was busy with a patient. Joanne set me up in my mom's personal office, where she has a desk and a phone and all of her books about dentist stuff.

"Gotta go," Joanne said. "Yell if you need me. But not too loud. Don't want to scare the patients."

"Thanks!" I told her.

Then I took out my cell phone and called Callie. The phone rang three times before she picked up.

"Hello?"

"Cal, it's Katie. Can you talk?" I asked.

"Of course," Callie answered, and for a second I wondered if the whole day had been some kind of weird dream. Callie sounded like she always did.

"Why didn't you tell me we weren't taking the bus together?" I blurted out.

"Listen, Katie, I'm sorry," Callie said, and she sounded like she meant it. "I became good friends with Sydney, Maggie, and Bella at camp. And they asked me to join their club. I wanted to tell you, but we never got together."

"Okay, but—wait, Bella? I thought her name was Brenda?" I asked.

"It was, but she changed it to Bella," Callie explained.

"Oh," I said. I'd never known anyone who actually changed his or her name before. But that wasn't important right now. "You could have called me. Or texted me," I said.

"I know, I know, but I was really busy when I got back. Honest," Callie said. "Please don't be upset."

"Are we still friends?" I asked. There was a lump in my throat when I said the word.

"Of course!" Callie assured me. "You're my best friend."

"But you won't walk to school with me or have lunch with me," I pointed out. I knew I sounded like a baby, and I really was about to cry. I was just so confused.

"It's not like that," Callie protested. "Katie, we're

in middle school now. Middle school is bigger than just the two of us. We're going to make lots of new friends. Both of us."

I thought briefly about Mia, Alexis, and Emma. Callie had a point—but I was too angry and hurt to admit it.

"Sure—right," I said lamely.

"And I'll see you this weekend," Callie said. "For the annual Labor Day barbecue."

"Okay," I said with a sigh.

"Hey, did you notice I got contact lenses?" Callie asked. "No more glasses for me!" So that explained why she wasn't wearing glasses today.

"Well, I already have homework to do. Plus I need to figure out what I'm going to wear tomorrow!" Callie said, and then we hung up.

I felt better after the call—not much, but just a little. I was glad Callie was still my friend. But the whole thing was weird. Callie was basically saying, "I'm sorry, but I'm still going to ignore you at lunch tomorrow."

I've heard "I'm sorry—but . . ." a lot in my life. Mostly from my dad. As in, "I'm sorry, Katie, but I can't come visit you this summer. . . ."

It doesn't feel good.

I took out my math assignment—my only homework assignment for tonight—and started working on the problems. Just as I was finishing, Mom opened the door.

"There you are!" she said, crushing me in a hug. She smelled like mint toothpaste. "I'll be ready to go in just a few minutes, okay?"

As you can probably guess, Mom was full of questions on the car ride home.

"Are your teachers nice?"

"Did you get any homework?"

"Did you find the bus stop okay?"

"Did you like your cupcake?"

"Is Callie in any of your classes?"

That one was the hardest to answer. I couldn't bring myself to tell Mom everything that had happened with Callie. How could I, when *I* wasn't even sure what was happening?

"We only have lunch together," I replied.

"Oh, that's too bad!" Mom said with a frown. "At least you get to sit together."

I just nodded and looked out the window.

"You must be tired," Mom said. "You've had a big day today. Try to relax when we get home. I'll call you when it's time to set the table."

Because it was the first day of school, Mom made my favorite food for dinner: Chinese-style chicken and broccoli with rice. (Yes, I'm a weirdo who likes broccoli.) It smelled so good!

"Would you like to do anything after dinner?" Mom asked. "It's nice out. We could walk over to Callie's."

Not a good idea! But I didn't tell Mom that.

"I was thinking," I said. "Can we make some pineapple upside-down cupcakes?"

Mom got a knowing look on her face. "Ah. So you need a cupcake cure?"

Once, when I was seven, I fell off of my bike and messed up my knee really bad. Mom made me pineapple upside-down cupcakes and gave them to me with a note: "Turn your frown upside down." Hey, I've been telling you she's corny. Since then, we make pineapple upside-down cupcakes together whenever one of us is feeling sad. We call it the "cupcake cure." It's hard to not feel better when you eat a cupcake.

I nodded. As we took out the ingredients and started measuring, I started talking—not about Callie, but about everything else. My evil locker. Being late for class all the time. Scary Mrs. Moore.

Mom listened while I talked. When I was done, she had a bunch of suggestions for how to make things better. Mom lives to solve all of my problems. Unfortunately, I didn't tell her about my biggest problem.

Pineapple upside-down cupcakes are not that hard to make. The trick is that you don't use cupcake liners. You spray the cupcake tins with that nonstick stuff. Then you fill the bottom of each cup with a mix of canned pineapple and some spices. You pour the batter on top and then you bake them.

When the cupcakes are done, you take them out of the pan and turn them upside down. Each cupcake has a beautiful golden pineapple on the top. To make them extra nice you can add a candied cherry on top like we do.

Mom and I each ate one with a glass of milk. They were still warm. So yummy!

As Mom packed one for me in my cupcake holder, I remembered what I'd told the girls at lunch.

"Can I bring in three more?" I asked. "For the girls at my lunch table."

"Of course," Mom said. "I have a small box we can use."

I found myself looking forward to tomorrow's lunch—even without Callie.

CHAPTER 6

The Perfect Plan . . . Almost

By lunchtime the next day, I was sure of one thing.

My locker is an evil robot in disguise, sent here to Earth to prevent me from finishing middle school. Or maybe it's from the future; I'm not sure.

But I'm sure its mission is to ruin my middle school career. Maybe one day I'll become president of the United States and save the Earth from the alien or robot invasion. But if I never finish middle school, I can't become president, and the robots will rule forever.

My mom had written my combination on an orange rubber band for me to wear around my wrist so I wouldn't forget. But even with the right combination the locker wouldn't open on the first try, or even the second try! How could that be?

I was late for science again, but Ms. Biddle didn't care. I knew that Mrs. Moore was another story, though. So I devised a plan: I would take my math book with me to lunch. Then I would walk to class with Alexis, who seemed to know her way around. That way, I'd be on time.

When I finally got my locker open before lunch, I spotted the white box of cupcakes on my top shelf. I couldn't forget those! I carefully picked them up by the string, eager to show them off to the girls.

I was a little nervous, of course. What if they all decided to sit somewhere else? But when I got to the table in the back of the room, Mia was already there.

Mia's eyes got big when she saw the white box.

"Ooh, are those cupcakes?" she asked.

"My mom and I ended up making some last night," I explained.

"That's really nice of you," Mia said.

Alexis and Emma came over and dropped their books on the table.

"We've got to get in line before it gets too long," Alexis said.

"Hurry back," Mia said. "Katie brought cupcakes."

Emma flashed me a grateful smile as she and Alexis headed off to the lunch line.

Soon we were all eating lunch together. Mom had packed me some leftover chicken and broccoli, which tastes even better cold.

"I can't believe it's Friday already!" Alexis said. "It's weird, starting school and then having three days off."

"I think they're trying to ease us into it—you know, like how you stick only your foot in a pool when it's really cold, and then slowly put the rest of your body in," I guessed.

"I always jump right in," Emma said. "Cold or not."

Mia shuddered. "You're brave!"

"I think we're going to the beach this weekend," Alexis said. "Last swim of the summer."

"I'm going to the city this weekend, to see my dad," Mia chimed in.

"Are your parents divorced?" Alexis asked, like it was no big deal.

Mia nodded. "Four years ago."

I didn't say anything about my own parents being divorced. To be honest, I was a little jealous that Mia was going to see her dad. I hadn't seen mine in years.

"We're going to my grandma's house for a pic-
nic," Emma spoke up.

"We're going to a barbecue," I said. "Over at . . .
Callie's."

I glanced over at the PGC table.

"Isn't that the friend who dumped you?" Alexis
asked.

"She didn't dump me," I protested. "We're still
friends. Best friends."

"Emma is my best friend," Alexis said. "If she sat
at a table with other girls, I'd sit next to her."

"But I wouldn't sit at a table with other girls,"
Emma said, and then she gave me an apologetic
look, like she was worried she'd hurt my feelings.

"Exactly," said Alexis. They both looked at me.

"Look, it's kind of complicated," I said. "They
formed this club. The Popular Girls Club. And you
can't sit at the table unless you're a member. It's a
rule."

"Are you serious? They actually named themselves the Popular Girls Club?" Alexis asked. "If
you're popular, do you really have to advertise it
like that? Plus, what did everyone do—take a vote
or something?"

Mia had an amused smile on her face. "It does
seem a little desperate," she admitted. "But I have all

of those girls in a lot of my classes. They seem nice."

"Callie is nice," I said. "Really. I'm just not so sure about the others."

There was a weird silence.

"So, Katie." Mia nodded to the white box. "When do we get to try those cupcakes?"

"Right now," I answered. I slipped off the string and opened up the top of the box. The cupcakes looked perfect.

"They're so pretty!" Emma cooed.

"What is that golden stuff?" Alexis asked.

"It's pineapple," I explained. "These are like pineapple upside-down cake, except they're cupcakes."

Mia shook her head. "Where do you get all these amazing cupcake ideas?"

"It's my mom, mostly," I admitted. "She's cupcake crazy."

Mia laughed. "My mom is shopping crazy."

"You're lucky," said Alexis. "My mom is cleaning crazy."

Emma shrugged. "My mom says me and my brothers make *her* crazy."

"She has three brothers," Alexis told us. "They're all monsters. Emma is the only normal one."

Emma blushed.

"Less talking, more cupcakes," I joked, and each of us picked one up.

It was quiet for a second as we took a bite of golden goodness.

"These are absolutely delicious," Mia said.

Alexis nodded. "The pineapple is supergood."

"I love the cherry on top," Emma said.

I was happy that everyone liked them.

"I'll bring in cupcakes every day if I can," I offered.

"That might be cupcake overload," Alexis pointed out. "Even for your cupcake crazy mother. How about one day a week? Like every Friday?"

"Cupcake Friday," I said. "I like it."

I liked it for a bunch of reasons. Making cupcakes is fun. But it also meant my new friends wanted to sit with me—for at least another week.

The bell rang, and I turned to Alexis. "Can I follow you to math? I don't want to be late."

"Of course!" Alexis replied.

We got to math in plenty of time. Mrs. Moore was already there.

"How nice to see you on time, Miss Brown," Mrs. Moore told me.

I felt fantastic. My plan had worked.

When the bell rang, Mrs. Moore asked us all to

take out our math books. I looked down at my desk. I had my notebook with me, but not my math book! Had I left it at lunch?

Then I remembered. I had grabbed the cupcake box instead of my math book! It was still in my locker.

With a sigh, I raised my hand. "Excuse me, Mrs. Moore . . ."

She gave me *two* worksheets that night!

CHAPTER 7

Just Like Old Times . . . Almost

The morning of Labor Day I woke up with a huge knot in my stomach. I didn't know what it would be like with Callie at the barbecue. And this year I wanted everything to be especially perfect.

Unfortunately, my need for perfection made me argue with my mom about what kind of decorations to put on the cupcakes we were bringing. The night before, we made vanilla cupcakes with vanilla icing, which are Callie's dad's favorite. That's a pretty boring cupcake, so we always add some decoration on the top. Sometimes it's candy. But lately, Mom's been into using this stuff called fondant. It's like a kind of dough, but it's mostly made out of sugar. You can color it, roll it out, and cut shapes out of it just like cookie dough. But you don't have to cook it. Then you can put the shapes on top of your cupcakes and they look amazing. It's a little hard to make, but as I said, Mom is like Martha Stewart. She could make a house out of fondant if she had to.

Mom and I were looking through the tin of mini cookie cutters for shapes to use. I wanted to use a sun and color the fondant yellow. Mom wanted to use a leaf shape and color the fondant orange.

"But it's still summer," I whined. "It's, like, a hundred degrees out there."

"Eighty-five," Mom corrected me. "And summer is over. School's started."

"But the first day of autumn isn't until September twenty-third," I said. "That's a fact. A scientific fact."

"Technically," Mom agreed. "But as soon as I see school buses driving around, I think of fall."

I frowned. I didn't want summer to end just yet. Mom looked at me. She knew something was wrong and I didn't want to tell her what it was. I sighed and gave in.

"How about half suns and half leaves?" I suggested.

Mom smiled. "Perfect! The orange and yellow will look nice together."

By noon we were pulling into the driveway of

Callie's house. It's easy to find because it's the only house on the block painted light blue. From the sidewalk you can tell which room is Callie's—it's the window on the second floor on the left with the unicorn decal on it. I have one just like it on my bedroom window.

We walked through the white wood gate and headed right for the backyard. Callie's dad was standing by the grill on the deck.

"Hey, Katie-did!" he called out. He wiggled his eyebrows when he saw the cupcake holder in my arms. "I hope that is filled with lots of vanilla cupcakes!"

"Of course!" I replied. "With vanilla icing."

Mr. Wilson gave me and my mom a hug. He's got kind of a big belly, so his hugs are always squishy.

"It's Barbara's fault. All that good cooking," he'll say, patting his stomach, and everybody always laughs.

I've known Mr. Wilson—and Callie's whole family—since even before I was born. My mom and Callie's mom met in a cooking class while they were pregnant. In a way, the Wilsons are like my second family. Mrs. Wilson is like my second mom. Callie's like a sister. And Mr. Wilson's like a dad. And since I never see my dad, he's the closest thing to one that I've got.

Then it hit me as I was standing there on the deck. If Callie and I stopped being friends, what would happen to my whole second family?

I didn't have much time to think about it because Callie and her mom came out onto the deck. Callie's mom and my mom gave each other a big hug. Callie and I nodded to each other. Things definitely felt a little weird between us.

"Where's Jenna today?" Mom asked. Jenna is Callie's older sister. She's a junior in high school. Callie has an older brother, too, named Stephen. He just started college this year.

"She's with her *friends*," Mrs. Wilson said, rolling her eyes. "When you're sixteen, a family barbecue is apparently a horrible punishment."

Mom looked at me and Callie. "Well, we've got a few more years left with these two, don't we?"

I hate when parents talk like that. Like when we're teenagers we're going to turn into hideous mutants or something. It kind of made me nervous, in a way. What if they were right?

"So how do you like middle school, Katie?" Callie's mom asked me.

I shrugged. "It's only been two days. It's kind of hard to tell."

"I'm so glad the girls are on the same bus route,"

my mom said. "Middle school can be pretty scary. It's nice that they have each other to navigate through it."

Mrs. Wilson looked confused. "Callie told me she's been walking to school. Aren't you two walking together?"

Callie looked down at her flip-flops.

"It's no big deal," I said quickly. "I like to take the bus. Callie likes to walk."

I just didn't want to get into a whole big discussion about it. Not in front of our mothers, anyway. I saw Mom biting her bottom lip. She looked at Callie's mom and raised her eyebrows.

"Callie, why didn't you mention this?" her mom asked.

Before Callie could answer, Mr. Wilson stepped into our circle.

"Hey, it's going to be about a half hour before the food is ready," he said. "I inflated the volleyball this morning. How about a game of moms against kids?"

That sounded good to me. I'm terrible at volleyball, but I still think it's fun. Besides, anything would be better than standing around talking about why Callie and I weren't taking the bus together.

"Kids serve first!" I yelled, and I ran into the yard

and grabbed the ball. I tossed it to Callie. "You'd better start. You know I usually can't get it over the net."

Callie laughed, and we launched into the game. Let me explain what happens when I play volleyball: I will chase after any ball that comes over the net. I will hit it with everything I've got. The problem is I have no idea how to aim it. Sometimes the ball goes way off to the side. Sometimes it goes behind me, over my head. If I'm lucky, it'll go right over the net. But that doesn't happen a lot.

Pretty soon Callie and I were cracking up laughing. We kept bumping into each other, and once we both tumbled onto the grass. It was really hilarious. And the funniest thing is that even though I am terrible at the game, we still beat the moms!

"That's game! Katie and Callie win!" Mr. Wilson called up from the deck.

"Woo-hoo!" Callie and I cried, high-fiving each other.

"And that's perfect timing," Callie's dad added. "Lunch is ready!"

Mr. Wilson might blame Callie's mom for his big stomach, but he is a great cook too. After I drank two big glasses of lemonade (volleyball makes me thirsty) I dug in to the food on the table. There were hamburgers, hot dogs, potato salad, juicy tomatoes from the garden, and of course, corn on the cob. I put a piece of corn on my plate before anything else.

"Katie, remember the time you ate six pieces of corn on the cob?" Callie asked, giggling.

"I was only six!" I cried.

"I can't believe we weren't paying attention," my mom said, shaking her head. "Six pieces. Can you imagine that?"

"And I didn't even get a stomachache," I said proudly.

"I love corn on the cob, but I could never eat six pieces," Callie added.

The rest of lunch was like that. We told funny stories, and we laughed a lot. It was just like last year's Labor Day barbecue. Like nothing at all had changed.

"Want to go to my room?" Callie asked when we were done.

"Sure," I said.

"I might eat all the cupcakes while you're gone!" Mr. Wilson warned.

I hadn't been in Callie's room in more than a month. Some things were the same, like the unicorn decal and her purple walls and carpet. And the picture of me and Callie from when we went to an amusement park and had our faces painted like tigers. Callie with her blond hair and blue eyes, me with my brown hair and brown eyes. Totally different—but the tiger paint made us look like sisters.

Other stuff was new. Like now she had lots of posters on her walls—lots of posters of boys. Most of them were from those vampire movies.

When did she start liking those? I wondered.

"You've got to see my pictures from camp," Callie said. "I have so much to tell you."

"I know," I said. "This is, like, the first time we've been together."

Callie held up her cell phone so I could see it and started scrolling through the photos. As they whizzed by, I saw lots of pictures of her and Sydney and the others. She stopped at a photo of a boy on a diving board.

"That's Matt," she said. "Isn't he cute? He was a lifeguard at camp."

I squinted at the photo. Matt had short brown hair and he was wearing a red bathing suit. He looked like a regular boy to me. But he didn't have tentacles or antennae or a tail or anything, so I guessed that was a good sign.

"He's in eighth grade," Callie said. "I pass him in the hallway every day between fifth and sixth period. The other day he actually said, 'Hi, Callie.' Isn't that amazing?"

Wow, he can put two words together, I thought. But out loud I said, "Yeah, amazing."

Callie's cell phone made a sound like fairy bells. The photo faded and a text message popped up on the screen.

"No way!" she cried. "*Teen Style* magazine has posted the best and worst fashion from the music awards last night. You have got to check this out!"

It was easy to guess who the text message was from—Sydney. It had to be.

Callie grabbed her laptop and started typing away. A page popped up on the screen.

"That's hilarious," she said. "They divided the page into 'Killer Looks' and 'Looks That Should Be Killed.' Ha!"

I briefly wondered what kind of weapon would be used to kill an ugly dress. Maybe some robo-scissors?

"Oh my gosh, that is *awful!*" Callie squealed. She grabbed her cell phone and started texting.

Any fuzzy feelings I'd had before were evaporating. Callie was supposed to be hanging out with me today. It was like I wasn't even in the room.

"Hey, Callie," I said.

"Yeah?" She looked up from her phone.

"I know we're still friends," I said. "But the other day you said we were still best friends. I'm just wondering about that. I mean . . . *best* friends sit together at lunch. They talk to each other during school."

"I know," Callie said. "But it's complicated. I still wish we could be best friends, but . . ." She sighed and looked away.

That's the moment I knew there was no going back. Callie had changed over the summer.

"But what?" I asked.

"You're still my friend, Katie. You'll always be my friend."

"Just not best friends," I said quietly.

Callie didn't answer, but she didn't have to.

"I don't under—"

Then I heard my mom's voice in the doorway. "Girls, it's cupcake time."

Mom had a kind of sad look on her face. I wondered how long she'd been standing there.

I figured Mom would be full of questions on the ride home. But for once, she wasn't. I stared out the window, thinking.

Tomorrow I'd start my first full week of school. There would be no more barbecues. No more swimming. Just day after day of middle school.

Maybe Mom was right. It wasn't September twenty-third yet, but summer was officially over.

CHAPTER 8

Just Call Me "Silly Arms"

*T*uesday wasn't just the start of my first real week of school. It was also the first day of gym.

I knew gym was going to be different from how it was in elementary school. For one thing, we have to wear a gym uniform: blue shorts and a blue T-shirt that says PARK STREET MIDDLE SCHOOL in yellow writing on it. I wasn't too worried about the changing-into-the-uniform thing. I just put my favorite unicorn underwear in a different drawer so I won't accidentally wear it during the week. Nobody needs to know about my unicorn underwear.

I also knew that the gym would be bigger, and the teachers would be different. But what I didn't count on was that the kids in gym would be different too. I'm not just talking about the kids from other schools. Kids I've known all my life had completely changed. Like Eddie Rossi, for example. Somehow he grew a mustache over the summer. An actual mustache! And Ken Watanabe—he must have grown a whole foot taller.

The boys were all rowdier, too. Before class started they were running around, wrestling, and slamming into one another like they were Ultimate Fighting Champs or something. I moved closer to Emma for safety.

"They're gonna hurt somebody," I said, worried.

Emma shrugged. I guess having three brothers, she's used to it.

Our gym teacher's name is Kelly Chen. She looks like someone you'd see in a commercial for a sports drink. Her shiny black hair is always in a perfect ponytail, and she wears a neat blue sweat suit with yellow stripes down the sides.

She blew a whistle to start the class.

"Line up in rows for me, people!" she called out. "We don't do anything in this class without warming up."

We did a bunch of stretches and things to get started. That was easy enough. Then Ms. Chen divided us into four teams to play volleyball.

You can probably see what's coming. I didn't—not right away. We always played volleyball in elementary school. Everybody had fun, and most kids were pretty terrible at it, just like me. So I wasn't too worried.

My first warning should have been when I got my team assignment. Ms. Chen put me on a team with Sydney and Maggie! Ken Watanabe was on our team too, along with two boys I didn't know named Wes and Aziz.

On the other team were a bunch of kids I didn't know and George Martinez from my old school. Emma was on a team playing on the other side of the gym, so George was the only friendly face in sight.

"All right, take your places!" Ms. Chen called out.

Everyone scrambled to get in line. For some reason, I was in place to serve the first ball. Ken tossed it to me.

My hands were starting to sweat a little.

"What are you waiting for?" Sydney called out.

I took a deep breath and punched the ball with my right hand.

It soared up . . . up . . . and wildly to the right, slamming into the bleachers. It bounced off and then bounced into the basketball pole, ricocheting like a pinball in a machine. Then it rolled to Ms. Chen's feet. She tossed it to the other team.

"Nice serve," Sydney said snidely, and Maggie giggled next to her.

My face flushed red. The only good thing about messing up the serve was that I got to move out of serving position. I wouldn't have to serve again for a while.

I was safe while I was in the back row. Ken was in front, and he was so tall that no ball could get past him. The other kids were all hitting the ball pretty well too. It was like everyone had suddenly become volleyball experts over the summer. Why hadn't I acquired this amazing skill?

But then it was time for us to switch positions, and I was in front of the net. My hands started to sweat again.

Sydney served the ball, and George volleyed it back. It was one of those balls that kisses the top of the net and then slowly drops over, like a gift. It should have been easy to hit.

Not for me. I swung my arm underhand to get to it, and the ball went flying behind me. Aziz tried to get it but it bounced out of bounds.

George was grinning. "Katie, you look like that

sprinkler in my backyard, you know, Silly Arms? The one with all those arms and they wave around and sprinkle water everywhere?"

George started spinning around and waving his arms in a weird, wiggly way. Everyone started laughing.

I was laughing too. George and I have been teasing each other since kindergarten. I knew he wasn't trying to hurt my feelings.

But then Sydney and Maggie had to take the fun out of it.

"Do you guys want Silly Arms on your team? We'll trade you," Sydney called out.

"Yeah, we'll never win with this one on our team," Maggie added.

I couldn't wait for gym to be over. For the rest of the game, George wiggled his arms like the Silly Arms sprinkler every time the ball came to him. If I wasn't so mad at Sydney and Maggie, I would have thought it was funny. Instead, I was miserable. As soon as I got back to the locker room I changed fast and ran out.

I had English class next. It's the one class I have with Mia, Emma, and Alexis. George Martinez is in that class too. He walked past me on the way to his seat.

"Hey, Silly Arms," he said with a grin.

"What's that about?" Mia asked.

"Gym class," I said with a sigh. "We were playing volleyball, and George said my arms look like the Silly Arms sprinkler."

"That's so mean!" Mia said.

"But it's true," I told her. "I think I hate gym now."

"Tell me about it." Mia rolled her eyes. "Gym was so much better in my old school. We got to bring in our iPods and dance to the music we brought in."

I noticed that Mia was wearing another model-worthy outfit: a belted gray sweater vest over a blue-and-black striped T-shirt dress, tights, and short black boots with heels. That gave me an idea.

"Hey, do you know anything about the *Teen Style* website?" I asked her.

Mia's eyes lit up. "Of course! They are the best with all the new fashion trends. Why?"

"Just wondering," I said. Honestly, though, I was thinking that if I knew more about it, maybe Callie and I would have something to talk about sometime.

"I know," Mia said. "Why don't you take the bus home with me today? We can check out the website at my house."

The bell rang. "I'll text my mom and let you know," I whispered as Mrs. Castillo took her place in front of the room to begin today's class.

I know what you're thinking, but I did *not* text my mom in class. I had learned my lesson in homeroom. I waited until the bell rang and texted her before my next class.

Can I go to my friend Mia's after school?

The answer came back quickly. My mom may be an adult, but she is a superfast texter.

Not until I talk to Mia's parents. And what are you doing texting during school? I will take your cell phone privileges away next time.

See? Even when I try to do the right thing, I get in trouble.

I knew there was no point in replying, or I'd lose my phone. Mom is pretty strict that way.

It's not fair. I fumed as I stomped down the hall. I lost my best friend. How was I supposed to make new ones if my mom wouldn't let me?

CHAPTER 9

Teen Style and Two Tiny Dogs

I was embarrassed to tell Mia that I couldn't go until our mothers met, but she was cool about it. She quickly took my phone from me.

"Hey, why fight it?" She laughed. "My mom is the same way. I'll enter my number in your address book," she said. "Your mom can call me tonight, and I'll put my mom on the phone. Maybe we can do it tomorrow. Don't stress it."

I really admire the way Mia handles things. She's pretty cool about everything. *And* she's down to earth, too. She's totally not snobby or anything. I realized how much I liked Mia. I was starting to feel really glad that her mom had moved to our town.

So that night, I decided to play it cool, like Mia would. I gave Mia's number to Mom and told her I wanted to go the next day after school. I didn't give her a hard time about not letting me go. I couldn't resist arguing about the cell phone, though.

"You know, texting between classes doesn't count," I said.

"It's still in school," Mom countered. "And your cell phone is for emergencies *only* while you're in school, whether you're between classes or not."

It's very hard to win an argument with Mom.

But the good news is that she talked to Mia's mom, Ms. Vélaz, and they both said it was okay for me to take the bus to Mia's house after school. My mom agreed to pick me up on her way home from work. She was laughing on the phone with Mia's mom, so I figured she liked her. That was a good sign.

I was pretty excited to go to Mia's house the next day. Even gym couldn't bring me down. Ms. Chen mixed up our teams, so I didn't get stuck with Sydney and Maggie again. Even better. But I did get stuck with George, who kept calling me Silly Arms even though I was on *his* team this time. Go figure.

Mia's house was one of the last houses on the bus stop route. That's because it's in the part of town where the houses are really big and far apart. The bus stopped in front of a white house with a perfect green lawn in front. The lawn at our house is usually filled with dandelions, but Mom and I think they're pretty so we let them grow.

Mia let us in through the front door, and the first thing I noticed was the noise. Loud heavy-metal music was blasting through the whole house. Two tiny white dogs were barking on top of it. They ran up to Mia and me and started sniffing my sneakers.

"That's Milkshake and Tiki," Mia told me. "If you don't like dogs, I can put them in their crate."

"No, I love dogs!" I said. "I want one so bad, but Mom's allergic. Can I pet them?"

"Sure," she replied. I reached down to touch them, but the skittish dogs wouldn't stand still. I could barely feel the fur under my fingers.

"Follow me," Mia instructed. We went down a hallway and through one of the doors there.

A woman with black hair like Mia's and headphones on was sitting at a desk, typing on a computer.

"Mom, can you please tell Dan to turn down the music?!" Mia yelled.

But Ms. Vélaz didn't see or hear us. Mia walked over and took the headphones off her mother's ears. Ms. Vélaz smiled.

"Oh hello, Mia." She nodded to me. "And this must be Katie."

"Nice to meet you," I said.

"Mom, can you *please* tell Dan to turn down the music?" Mia pleaded.

"Would you mind asking him yourself?" her mom asked. "I'm IM'ing a potential client, and I can't leave the computer right now."

Mia sighed. "All right. But I bet he won't do it."

"Please get a snack for Katie too!" Ms. Vélaz called out to us.

We left the office, and Mia grabbed a bag of cookies before we headed up the gleaming wood staircase. Mia told me her story as best as she could over the loud music.

"Mom used to work at a fashion magazine in New York, but then she met Eddie, who already had a house out here," she explained. "So now she works out of the house. She's starting her own consulting business."

We stopped in front of a door on the second floor.

"This is Dan's room," Mia shouted. "He'll be my stepbrother when Mom and Eddie get married in a few months."

Mia pounded on the door. It slowly opened, and

a teenage boy with dark hair hanging over his eyes stood behind it.

"Too loud?" he asked.

"What do you think?" Mia shouted back.

Dan closed the door and a few seconds later the music was much quieter. Mia shook her head as we walked to her room.

"He's a junior in high school," she said. "Two more years and he's out of here. I hope."

I wondered if he knew Callie's sister, Jenna. Callie was always popping up in my head.

We stepped into Mia's room. I was kind of expecting it to be as neat and stylish as Mia. The rest of her house looked like something from a magazine. But her room was a little messy, which was fine, just kind of a surprise.

"My old room in Manhattan was *so* much nicer," she said, pointing to the wallpaper. "Can you believe those flowers? I think some old lady must have lived in here before. Eddie keeps promising that we'll paint it, but he and Mom are always so busy."

I forgot who Eddie was for a minute until I realized Mia was talking about her almost-stepdad. I have never called an adult by their first name before, except for Joanne at my mom's office, but she's not like a real adult anyway. I tried to imagine calling my mom by her first name, Sharon. Weird!

Mia pushed aside some clothes on the bed and opened up her laptop. "You want to check out *Teen Style*?" she asked.

"Sure."

"It's pretty fun," Mia said as she typed away. "They have a whole section of celebrities, and you can rate the outfits they're wearing."

She clicked a few times, and a photo of a thin, blond actress came on the screen. She was wearing a red dress with feathers on the bottom.

"What do you think?" Mia asked me.

I shrugged. "It's nice, I guess. I mean, if she likes it, then what's the difference?"

"I think it's too long," Mia said. "Take a few inches off of it and it would be perfect." She clicked on the number "7" and then a new picture popped up.

I really didn't get it. I had no idea why one outfit was better than another. But Mia had a definite opinion about everything.

We did that for a while, and then Mia clicked on another page. "This is *really* fun," she said. "You create an avatar of yourself and then you get to try on different outfits to see how they would look."

Mia made my avatar: skinny, medium height,

wavy brown hair, brown eyes. Then she started clicking on clothes, and they appeared on my avatar's body.

I couldn't tell what was wrong with other people's clothes, but it was cool to experiment and see what different stuff looked good on computer me. I had to admit that part was pretty fun. Well, for a while. Then it got a little boring. After I tried on a leather skirt, flowered dress, and five different pairs of boots, Mia looked at me.

"Want to play with the dogs?" she asked.

"Yes!" I answered gratefully.

The dogs were completely adorable. Mia said they were Maltese dogs. They could both roll over and sit. Then Mia did this trick where she sneezed and the one called Tiki ran to the tissue box and took a tissue out of it.

"That is truly amazing," I said.

Before I knew it, Mom came to pick me up. On the drive home, she asked me the usual questions about how things went. Then she sneezed.

"That's odd," she said. "My allergies usually don't bug me this time of year."

I knew the dog hair on my clothes was probably making her sneeze, but I didn't say anything.

I wanted to be sure I could go back to Mia's.

CHAPTER 10

The Best Club Ever

The next night I made a batch of cupcakes for Cupcake Friday. I remembered that I hadn't made chocolate cupcakes in a while. They're one of my favorites, and I don't even need Mom to help me make them.

I thought I knew the recipe by heart, but while I was adding the ingredients to the big mixing bowl, I realized that I didn't know how much baking powder to add. So I took the big binder of cupcake recipes from the kitchen shelf and looked up the chocolate cupcakes.

Recipes amaze me. If you follow the directions exactly, you can make something completely awesome.

There should be a recipe for middle school, I thought.

Follow the steps, one by one, and you'd have a perfect middle school experience.

So far, my middle school experience had been kind of a mess. If I had been following a recipe, it probably would look something like this:

Mix together:
1 evil locker
1 confusing best friend
3 mean girls
1 strict math teacher
2 silly arms
Bake until it hardens. If you overbake, go directly to detention.

Luckily, the recipe for the chocolate cupcakes is much better. Soon the whole house smelled like chocolate. After the cupcakes baked and cooled, I spread chocolate icing on them. Then I used a white icing tube to write a name on each cupcake: Katie, Mia, Emma, and Alexis.

Mom came into the kitchen as I was icing.

"Are these the girls you eat lunch with?" she asked.

I nodded.

"You forgot one," Mom said.

I counted again. "No," I said, and then I realized where she was headed.

I froze. Was she going to start asking me about Callie again?

Mom picked up the icing tube and started writing on one of the cupcakes: M-O-M. I relaxed.

"This is going in my lunch bag tomorrow," she said. "Hey, would it be okay if I decorated some for everyone who works in the office?"

"Sure," I said. "I'll help. We can both do Cupcake Fridays."

That's one of the best things about cupcakes. When you make them, there's always a lot to share.

At lunch the next day, I hadn't even sat down yet when everyone started asking about cupcakes.

"So, did you bring them?" Mia asked.

"What kind are they?" asked Alexis.

"I bet they're delicious," added Emma.

"I went for the classic chocolate today," I announced. I opened the lid, and everyone started to ooh and aah.

"We should save them for after lunch," Alexis said.

"Are you kidding? I can't wait!" Mia took hers out of the box.

"I'll wait," Emma said. "I like to save the best

74

for last—especially in this case. They smell delicious though."

Mia bit into her cupcake. A slow smile came across her face. "You don't know what you're missing."

Alexis and Emma headed to the lunch line. When they got back, Alexis looked agitated.

"You will not believe what those so-called popular girls just did!" she said, fuming. "Emma and I were waiting in line, and Marcus Ridgely was standing in front of us, and that girl Sydney came up with those other girls, and Sydney was like, 'Hey, Marcus, we're behind you, okay?' and then they cut right in front of us!"

"Right in front of us," Emma echoed.

"Did you say anything?" Mia asked.

"Well, no," Alexis admitted. "But what's the point? It's not like they were going to move. They think because they're in some club, that gives them special privileges or something. It's annoying. I can't stand them!"

I looked down at my sandwich. I totally understood why Alexis was upset. But still—she was talking about Callie.

"Alexis, Katie's friend is one of them," Emma said quietly.

Alexis's face turned red. "I know. I'm sorry. I mean, I'm sure your friend is nice. Maybe you get brainwashed or something when you join the Popular Girls Club."

"Not all clubs are bad," Mia said. "At my old school we had a Fashion Club. And a club for kids who like movies. Stuff like that."

"Well, that makes sense," Alexis said. "Those clubs are about something *real*. Not something made-up, like being popular."

I picked up my cupcake. "You know what would be the coolest club ever? A Cupcake Club!" I was mostly kidding around. "You don't have to be popular to join. You just have to like cupcakes."

Alexis grinned. "Now *that* is a club I could like!"

"The Cupcake Club," Emma repeated. "It sounds like fun."

"We should totally do it," Mia said.

"Really?" I asked.

She nodded. "Why not? This school needs more clubs."

I was getting into the idea. "We could have our meetings every Friday at lunch. That's when I bring cupcakes in anyway."

"I like to make cupcakes too," said Emma. "I could bring them in sometimes."

"Maybe we should take turns," Alexis suggested. "I could make up a schedule for all of us."

"Good idea, except I've never made a cupcake before in my life," Mia told us.

"Not even from a mix?" I asked.

Mia shook her head. "We always got them from the bakery down the street. They were soooo good."

"But ours will be better," Alexis said confidently. "Although I don't have a lot of cupcake-making experience either. I know mine won't be as good as yours, Katie."

"It's easy," I assured her. "You just have to follow a recipe."

Then I thought about the first few times I made cupcakes by myself. Mom was always there to help me. She taught me some tricks that weren't in any recipe. "You guys should come to my house this weekend," I blurted out. "We can have a cupcake-making session."

"A cupcake lesson," said Mia. "That sounds like fun."

"I just need to ask my mom," I said. "I'll call everyone tonight, okay?"

I was really excited about the Cupcake Club. Still, I found myself looking over at Callie. Callie loved to make cupcakes as much as I did. It was weird to think of being in a Cupcake Club without Callie.

Would Callie leave the Popular Girls Club to become a member of the Cupcake Club?

Somehow, I didn't think so.

CHAPTER 11

It's Time to Make Some Cupcakes!

So, how many girls are in the club?" my mom asked me as we ate our pizza that night.

"Four," I said. "Me, Mia, Emma, and Alexis."

Mom nodded. "Did you invite Callie to join?"

"I was thinking about it," I said honestly. "I just don't . . . I don't know if she wants to. She kind of made other friends this year."

There, I said it. It was the first time I'd told my mom about what happened with Callie. I felt relieved.

"That happens sometimes," Mom said gently. "People grow up, and they change sometimes. It happened to me in fifth grade. A new girl came to our school, and my best friend, Sally, suddenly became best friends with the new girl instead. I was really, really sad. But then I met new friends."

It was hard to imagine my mom as a little girl. I pictured her going to school in her dentist coat. But I knew what she meant.

"Callie and I said we'd still hang out sometimes," I told my mom. "I think I'm going to text her."

I sent the text after dinner.

Hey Cal. Making cupcakes tomorrow at 2. Wanna come?

Callie texted me back.

Sounds like fun! Wish I could go but I'm going to the mall. Maybe next time?

I texted back.

Sure.

I was a little disappointed, but not too much. I knew tomorrow was going to be fun, even without Callie.

"Callie's not coming," I told my mom. "Can we call the other girls now?"

"Of course," Mom replied. "I was thinking we could do simple cupcakes—vanilla with chocolate icing. I think we're out of sugar, but we can shop in the morning."

"Let's do something different on top," I suggested. "What about those little chocolate candies covered with white candy dots? That would be cool with a vanilla and chocolate cupcake."

Mom grinned. "Perfect!"

"And, um, Mom?" I said. "We might, you know, need some help, but I'm thinking that if we're going to be a Cupcake Club, we should learn to make them on our own."

"Oh!" Mom said, and I was afraid I hurt her feelings. "Well, I'll have to be home, of course, but that sounds right to me. You can just yell if you need me."

Sometimes Mom surprises me. For someone so corny, she can sometimes be very cool.

By two o'clock the next day, we were ready for the first official meeting of the Cupcake Club to begin. I helped Mom wash the yellow tiles on the floor and scrub the kitchen table until there wasn't a crumb on it. We got out our cupcake tins, the flour sifter, Mom's big red mixer, the glass measuring cup, and the little cup with the bird on it that holds the measuring spoons.

Finally, the doorbell rang. Mia was standing there.

"Hi," she said when I opened the door.

Then a blue minivan pulled up in front of the house, and Emma and Alexis got out, along with the woman driving the van. She was short, with blond hair that she wore in a ponytail. She was wearing a sweatshirt with a hummingbird on it, jeans, and sneakers.

"You must be Katie," she said, holding out her hand to shake mine. "I'm Wendy Taylor, Emma's mom. I was hoping I could meet your mom."

My mom magically appeared in the doorway. "Wendy, nice to meet you in person. I'm Sharon. Please come inside."

The moms walked in ahead of us, and Emma gave me an apologetic look.

"Sorry," she whispered. "My mom is really over-protective."

I smiled. "I know how you feel. My mom's the same way."

I led the girls into the kitchen.

"Whoa. It's like cupcake central," Mia remarked.

"We bake a lot of cupcakes," I admitted. "So we've got all the stuff."

We have a big closet in our kitchen that Mom calls the pantry. One whole shelf has all the stuff we need to bake cupcakes, cakes, and cookies: icing tubes, sprinkles, plastic decorations like balloons and flowers that you can stick into the top of a cupcake—stuff like that.

I opened the door to show the girls. "Everything we need is in here," I said. I started grabbing things and handing them to everyone. "Flour. Baking powder. Sugar. Vanilla."

"Don't you use a mix?" Alexis asked.

"Mom says it's just as easy to do it from scratch, and at least you know what's going in it," I said.

I got two eggs out of the refrigerator and picked up the butter that had been softening on the counter.

"That should do it for now." I nodded to the sink. "Before we start, we should all wash our hands."

"Wow, you are a strict teacher," Mia joked.

I laughed. "Can you imagine if Mrs. Moore taught us how to make cupcakes?" I did my best to imitate her voice, which was kind of deep and a little bit musical. "Concentration is the key to succeeding in this class, students! Without concentration, you won't be able to make your cupcakes."

Alexis and Emma started giggling like crazy.

"That is too perfect," Alexis said. "Can you do Ms. Biddle?"

I thought for a minute. Ms. Biddle had an upbeat

voice, like a cheerleader. And she always made everything about science.

"Who wants to make a hypothesis about how these cupcakes will taste?" I asked.

Mia raised her hand. "Delicious!"

"Wait, I can do Ms. Chen," Alexis said. She made her back really straight. "Look alive, people! It's time to make some cupcakes!"

By then I was cracking up so hard, my stomach hurt. That's when Mom walked in.

"I never knew cupcakes were so funny," she said.

I went back into my Mrs. Moore voice. "You are late, Mrs. Brown! Detention!"

That just made everyone laugh even harder. Mom shook her head and smiled.

"Emma, your mom will be back for you and Alexis at four," she told us. "So, girls, get started. I'll be in the den if you need me."

I kind of led the cupcake demonstration. First we mixed the eggs, butter, and sugar together in the mixer. We added the vanilla. Then we sifted the dry ingredients together in another bowl: the flour, baking powder, and salt. Everybody took turns measuring. When it was Alexis's turn to sift the flour, it puffed up like a cloud and settled on her face like powder.

"No flour in this classroom! Detention!" I cried out in my Mrs. Moore voice, and we all laughed again.

Then we slowly mixed the dry ingredients and wet ingredients together using the mixer. When it was all done, Mom popped in to check on us and showed us how to use an ice-cream scoop to put the perfect amount of batter into each cupcake cup, which is good because I always forget that part and they kind of get big and explode. Then we had to wait while the cupcakes baked. That was okay, because we had to clean up the whole mess we made. When the cupcakes were cooling, we used the mixer again to make chocolate icing.

I've always thought that icing the cupcakes is the hardest part. Mom got us special flat knives to use, but it's still kind of hard.

Alexis and Emma were struggling with the icing, just like me. But when Mia put it on, it was smooth and perfect.

"I thought you never did this before?" I asked.

"I haven't," Mia said. She looked really happy. "I guess I have a hidden talent for icing cupcakes."

"Mine looks like a very sad cupcake," Emma said, holding hers up.

"I know what will make it happy," I told her. I

took out the bag of chocolate candies Mom and I had bought and put one right in the middle. "See? Perfect!"

"It does look better," Emma agreed.

Everyone dug into the bag and we decorated the top of each cupcake. Emma, Alexis, and I put a single candy in the middle of each one. Mia got really creative. On one, she put the candies all around the edge of the cupcake. It looked really cool. She also made some look like flowers.

"You're a natural," I told her.

Mia beamed. "Can I try making the cupcakes for lunch next Friday? I really think I can do it."

"Sure," I said. "You can always call if you need help."

Before we knew it, it was four o'clock. Mom had small boxes for everyone so they could take some cupcakes home. Emma took home the most: one for each of her parents and her brothers.

There was some stuff to clean up after the girls left, but I didn't mind. Mom helped.

"It looks like the Cupcake Club got off to a good start," she remarked.

I smiled at her. "I think you're right!"

CHAPTER 12

Middle School Roller Coaster

Something happened after we formed the Cupcake Club: Middle school got a little bit easier.

Honest! For example, my locker started opening up on the first try. Coincidence? I don't think so. Alexis says I probably just loosened up the insides of the lock so it opens more easily, but I don't believe it. I'd rather think that the superpowers of the Cupcake Club defeated my evil alien locker.

Now, take math class. I wish I could say that Mrs. Moore was suddenly nicer, but I can't. What happens now is that every time Mrs. Moore says something serious, or threatens to give us all detention, I write down what she says so I can use it the next time I do an impression of her. She's not so scary anymore.

Not that everything is perfect. Take gym class. On Tuesday we were picking teams for flag football, and Sydney said, "Don't pick Katie unless you want to lose!" She said it really loudly, and a bunch of kids laughed. Sometimes I feel like saying something, but I don't. I keep waiting for the time when we have races outside on the track. I've been a faster runner than Sydney ever since third grade.

Then something happened in English class on Wednesday. It didn't happen to me, exactly, but to another member of the Cupcake Club: Alexis.

Here's what happened. At the beginning of class Mrs. Castillo told us she was giving us a vocabulary worksheet for homework. But she didn't hand it out. Then, right before the bell rang, Alexis raised her hand.

"Mrs. Castillo, what about the vocab worksheet?" she asked.

Everyone groaned. Everyone except for me, Mia, and Emma.

We know that Alexis is just like that. She likes to do things exactly the way you're supposed to. She especially likes to make teachers happy.

As you can guess, nobody was happy with Alexis.

"Thanks a lot, Alexis," Eddie Rossi said from the back of the room.

"Yeah, what, are you in love with homework?" added Devin Jaworski.

"Please settle down," ordered Mrs. Castillo. "You're lucky Alexis reminded me. Otherwise you'd have double homework tomorrow night."

But of course that didn't make anyone feel better. When the bell rang and we poured into the hallway, a lot of the boys were still giving Alexis a hard time.

"Teacher's pet!"

"Thanks for the homework!"

Alexis started to look like she might cry. I felt bad for her.

"Leave her alone," Mia said bravely, and we all hurried off to our lockers.

That was pretty much the worst thing that happened all week—until Cupcake Friday.

Mia came into the cafeteria carrying a really pretty pink bakery box. She opened the lid to reveal four perfect cupcakes with chocolate icing dotted with chocolate candies.

"They're so pretty," Emma said.

"I hope they taste good," Mia said with a small frown. "We didn't have any vanilla. And I lost count when I was putting in the teaspoons of salt. I might have put in an extra amount."

89

Alexis pounded her fist on the table. "Let the second meeting of the Cupcake Club begin!"

That's when Sydney and Brenda—I mean, Bella—walked by. Sydney stopped cold.

"Cupcake Club?" she asked. "Are you serious? What is this, third grade?"

"Yeah, that's so lame!" Bella added, making a big deal out of rolling her eyes.

"Not as lame as a Popular Girls Club," Alexis said under her breath.

Sydney raised an eyebrow. "Excuse me? Did you say something?"

Alexis, Emma, and I were all kind of afraid of Sydney. But not Mia.

"Maybe I'll bring some next time for you to try," she said coolly.

Sydney snorted. "No thanks," she said, and then she and Bella walked away.

"Well, that was fun," I said.

"Who wants a cupcake?" Mia asked.

We all reached for one, but I had a little knot in my stomach. I watched Bella and Sydney slide into their table with Callie. They were all reading some magazine. I tried not to look.

The cupcakes were good. They tasted a tiny bit weird because of the extra salt, but not too weird.

Plus the icing was especially delicious.

"Nice job," I told Mia, and she smiled at me. I could tell she was proud.

That same day, when the eighth-period bell rang, I was walking to my locker and I saw Mia talking to a bunch of girls from her class. They were all laughing.

For a second I got a strange feeling. Then it hit me. Not that I care about how "cool" people are or anything, but Mia is a lot cooler than me. What if she got bored with the Cupcake Club? What if she found other friends, like Callie had?

"There's no use in worrying about what might happen," Mom always says. "Concentrate on how things are right now."

I remember a lot of stuff Mom tells me, usually because she says it over and over again. Also, it's just me and her most of the time, so I guess she's a pretty big part of my life.

Anyway, I'm glad I remembered that. Because right now, Mia was my friend. She rode the bus with me every day and ate lunch with me every day. She invited me to her house and baked cupcakes for the Cupcake Club.

Maybe in the future that would change, just like things had changed with Callie over the summer.

But for now, everything with Mia was all right.

Mia saw me standing there and waved.

"Hey, Katie! See you on the bus!"

See? Sometimes Mom is right.

CHAPTER 13

Alexis Has an Idea

$\mathcal{I}$ did see Callie a few times over the next few weeks. One night my mom invited the Wilsons over for Italian food night. It's kind of a tradition between our families, like the Labor Day barbecue. My mom makes tons of pasta and salad. She lights candles on our dining-room table, puts out a red-and-white-checkered tablecloth, and goes all out, of course. But it's actually usually a pretty fun night.

Then another night Callie called and invited me to come over and watch the first episode of *Singing Stars* on TV. It's our favorite show. I had a good time, even though Callie kept getting texts on her cell phone the whole time.

Mostly I hung out with the Cupcake Club. Everyone came over one Saturday, and Mom showed us how she makes her P-B-and-J cupcakes. And one night Mia invited me over for dinner. Her mom got takeout food from an Indian restaurant. I'd never eaten Indian food before, and it was good—and spicy. Mia's mom and stepdad were nice, and her stepbrother, Dan, seemed nice too. Which was kind of a surprise, because Mia is always saying what a beast he is.

Oh, and I got detention from Mrs. Moore. Twice. But the whole class had it, so it wasn't so bad.

And the best thing was that I could talk to Mia, Emma, and Alexis about it. That's mostly what the Cupcake Club did. We baked cupcakes; we ate cupcakes; and we talked about stuff.

Things were not perfect, but they were good.

One Monday we were eating lunch, and everyone was talking about the announcement that Principal LaCosta had made that morning after the Pledge of Allegiance.

"This morning your homeroom teacher will be distributing permission slips for the first dance of the year," she said. "Please hand them in by next Monday if you're going to attend. This year's dance will be bigger than ever. That afternoon, we'll be holding a special fund-raising event for the school. Check your flyer for details."

Now we were sitting around the lunch table, looking at the flyers.

"I always heard we had dances in middle school," Alexis said. "I just didn't think it would be so soon."

"Do you think we actually have to *dance* at the dance?" I asked. My mom loves the movie *Grease*, and in that movie the high school kids twirl and throw one another in the air and stuff like that. I didn't think I could do that in a million years.

"We had dances at my old school," Mia informed us. "Sometimes people danced. Mostly everyone just hung around and talked."

"Did boys and girls dance together?" Emma asked. She sounded a little worried.

"Sometimes," Mia replied.

We were quiet for a minute. I think all of us except for Mia were feeling nervous about the dance.

"Did you see the part about the fund-raiser?" I asked. "It's going to be in the parking lot of the school. If you have an idea to make money for the school, you can set up a booth. The booth that makes the most money will get a prize."

"I heard the basketball team is doing a dunking booth with all of the gym teachers," Alexis reported. "I bet that will make a lot of money."

"Maybe we could have a dunking booth for math teachers," I joked.

Over at the PGC table, Sydney was talking in a loud voice on purpose.

"Our club is going to have the best booth at the fund-raiser," Sydney bragged. "That's why we have to keep it top secret."

Alexis rolled her eyes. "This is supposed to be for the whole school, not just the Popular Girls Club," she said. "Only Sydney can turn a good cause into something about herself."

"I wonder what their top secret idea is?" Emma asked.

Alexis had that look on her face where you know the wheels of her brain are spinning faster than a car's.

"You know, I bet we can raise a lot of money just by selling cupcakes," she said. "Who could say no to a cupcake for a good cause?"

"That's not a bad idea," Mia agreed. "But we'd have to make a lot of cupcakes, wouldn't we?"

Alexis took out her notebook and started scribbling numbers.

"There are about four hundred kids in the school," she said. "Let's say half of them go to the dance. That's two hundred. Then there are teachers. And parents, and younger brothers and sisters. So let's say that's another two hundred people, for a total of four hundred. Now let's say that half of those people buy cupcakes—"

"We'd need two hundred cupcakes," I said, and then gasped. "Oh no! I did math. Mrs. Moore must be getting through to me."

"That sounds like a lot of cupcakes," Emma said.

"Not really," Alexis said. "It's about seventeen dozen. We could bake a few dozen at a time over four or five days. Since it's for the school, I bet we can ask our parents to donate the ingredients. If we sell each cupcake for fifty cents, we'd make a hundred dollars."

"Fifty cents?" Mia asked. "At the cupcake shop in Manhattan, they charge five dollars a cupcake. Katie's cupcakes are just as good as theirs."

Alexis's eyes were wide. "Who would pay five dollars for one cupcake?"

"Maybe we could charge two dollars a cupcake," Emma suggested.

"That could work," I chimed in. "If we sold all of the cupcakes, we'd make four hundred dollars. We might even win the contest."

"We should definitely do this," Mia said, her eyes shining with excitement.

"I'm sure this is better than whatever Sydney is planning," Alexis said smugly.

I looked over at the PGC table. I wasn't really thinking about beating Sydney. I was thinking about Callie. She wasn't too interested in the Cupcake Club when I talked about it. But if we won the fund-raising contest . . . maybe Callie would be convinced she was in the wrong club.

"I'm in," I said. "So how exactly are we going to make two hundred cupcakes?"

CHAPTER 14

The Mixed-up Cupcakes

We should have a meeting so we can figure this out," Alexis suggested. "We could do it at my house this time. How about Saturday?"

"I'm going to my dad's this weekend," Mia said.

"Next weekend should be fine," Emma said. "It's a month until the dance, anyway."

"We need to figure out what kind of cupcake to make," I reminded everyone.

"We can do that next week," Alexis said. "We'll work out a schedule, too."

So the following Saturday I showed up at Alexis's front door with a whole bunch of recipes and enough ingredients for a couple dozen. If we were going to decide on a cupcake, we would have to do some research.

Alexis lives in a brick house with a very neat front lawn. The bushes on either side of the white front steps are the kind that are trimmed into a perfect globe shape.

Alexis looked surprised when she answered the door.

"Hi, Katie," she said. "What's all that?"

"It's for our meeting," I explained. "So we can experiment with cupcake flavors."

"Oh," she said. "I thought we were just going to talk about it."

"Why just talk when we can taste?" I asked.

Alexis led me into the kitchen. I've been in her house a few times so far, and I'm always amazed how clean it is in there. For example, there is nothing on the kitchen counter, not even a toaster. Our counter has a toaster, the big red mixer, a cookie jar shaped like an apple, Mom's spice rack, and usually a bowl of fruit.

Alexis's mom was at the kitchen table, setting up a pitcher of water and glasses for our meeting, along with a bowl of grapes. I noticed there was a piece of paper and pencil at each of the four places around the table.

Mrs. Becker was wearing a button-down light blue shirt and dark blue dress pants. I've never seen her wear jeans, not even on a Saturday. Her hair is auburn like Alexis's, but it's cut short.

"Hello, Katie," she said when she saw me. She noticed the bag I was carrying. "Did you bring snacks? How nice."

"It's actually supplies, so we can make test cupcakes," I told her.

"You mean you'll be baking?" she asked. "Oh dear. I didn't know you'd be baking today, Alexis."

"We'll clean up when we're done, Mom," Alexis said. "Promise."

"It's true. We clean up all the time when we bake at my house," I added.

Mrs. Becker gave a little sigh. "All right. But let me know when you are ready to turn on the oven!"

She hurried out of the kitchen.

"Mom doesn't like it when the plan changes," Alexis explained. "Especially when there's a mess involved."

"I promise we won't make a mess," I said. Then I remembered what my kitchen usually looks like when I bake cupcakes. "Well, not too much of a mess, anyway."

Emma and Mia arrived next, at the same time. Alexis neatly piled up the pencils and paper, and

I took all of the ingredients I'd brought out of my bag. Besides the basic cupcake-making stuff, I had mini marshmallows, chocolate chips, nuts, sprinkles, red-hot candies, tubes of icing and food coloring, and a jar of cherries—just about everything I could grab from the pantry.

"Mmm, everything looks so yummy," Mia said.

"Well, I was thinking that we have to make a really *incredible* cupcake if we're going to sell a lot," I said. "Something we've never done before."

"How do we do that?" Emma asked.

"We experiment," I said. "Mom and I do it all the time. That's how we came up with our famous banana split cupcake. Only I didn't have any bananas, so we'll have to come up with something else."

I turned to Alexis. "Do you have a mixer?" I asked.

"Not the kind you have," she replied. "It's the one you hold in your hand."

"That's fine," I said. "First we need to make a regular vanilla batter."

I had made so many vanilla cupcakes over the last few weeks that I didn't need a recipe at all. Pretty soon we had a perfect bowl of batter ready.

"Now we just have to figure out what to add in," I said.

"Everyone loves chocolate chips," Mia suggested. We stirred some in.

"Marshmallows go well with chocolate," said Alexis.

Emma nodded. "Definitely."

We added some mini marshmallows to the batter.

"What about nuts?" Emma asked. "It might be good to have something crunchy in there."

"Some people are allergic to nuts," Alexis pointed out.

"That's true," I said. "But sprinkles are crunchy too. Maybe we could put sprinkles in."

Alexis wrinkled her nose. "You mean put them *in* a cupcake instead of on top?"

"Why not?" I asked.

Nobody had a good argument. I dumped in half a bottle of rainbow sprinkles.

"They look good," Mia said. "And I don't think there's room in the bowl for anything else."

We scooped all of the batter into the cupcake tins Alexis put out for us. Because of all the stuff we mixed in, there was a lot of batter left over.

"I don't have any more pans," Alexis said.

"No problem," I told her. "We can always bake more when the first batch cools."

Mrs. Becker came in to preheat the oven for us.

She raised her eyebrow when she saw our cupcakes.

"My, those look interesting," she said.

"Wait till you taste it, Mom," Alexis told her. "You're going to love it!"

While the cupcakes baked, we whipped up some plain vanilla icing.

"Should we add anything into the icing?" I asked.

"I think the cupcakes have enough inside them," Mia said.

"Good point," I said.

We cleaned up our mess while we waited for the cupcakes to bake. When the timer rang, Mrs. Becker helped us with the oven.

"Do you take them out now?" she asked.

"We need to test them first," I said.

Mom had taught me how to stick a toothpick into the middle of a cupcake. If it came out clean, it was done. But if it had batter on it, the cupcake needed to cook more.

I stuck a toothpick into the middle of one of our mixed-up cupcakes. When I took it out, it wasn't clean. But it didn't have batter on it. It had gooey marshmallow, chocolate, and a sprinkle stuck to it.

I frowned. "I'm not sure if it's done or not," I said.

Alexis looked over my shoulder. "They look

done. They're a little brown on top, see?"

I realized there would be no sure way to tell if the cupcakes were done. We might as well take them out. Besides, I was dying to try one! The delicious smell of baking cupcakes was taking over my brain.

We put the cupcakes on a rack to cool. Normally, we talk a lot when we're waiting for cupcakes to cool off. But that day we stared at our cupcakes, like we were going to cool them off with the amazing power of our minds alone.

Finally Mia blurted out, "Maybe we should try them without icing. You know, to get a true sense of how they taste."

"That sounds very logical to me," I said.

We each picked up a cupcake. They were warm, but cool enough to handle. I unwrapped the paper and took a bite. A hot, gooey mess of chocolate and marshmallow exploded in my mouth.

"Mmmmmm," was all I could say.

Alexis had a weird look on her face. "It's too sweet!"

"There's no such thing as too sweet," I told her, and Emma nodded in agreement.

Mia had another complaint. "They're kind of messy," she said, wiping her hand on a napkin.

"Let's see what my mom thinks," Alexis said.

She left the kitchen and returned with both parents. Mr. Becker was tall and skinny with curly hair and glasses like his wife.

"I think you girls have a great fund-raising idea," he said. "Everybody loves cupcakes!"

Alexis handed one to each parent. "They're not iced yet," she said. "They might taste different when they're iced."

We held our breath as Mr. and Mrs. Becker bit into their cupcakes. Mrs. Becker made the same weird face that Alexis had.

"My, they're very sweet!" she said.

"They're tasty," said Mr. Becker. "But I'll tell you something. I'm not a big fan of marshmallows. Never liked them. You know what makes me happy? A plain vanilla cupcake. Mmm."

I thought of Callie's dad. "I think that's a parent thing. Parents like vanilla cupcakes."

"And don't forget, parents are a big part of our sales," Alexis reminded us.

I was starting to feel discouraged. "But plain vanilla cupcakes are boring! We need our cupcakes to be extra special so everyone wants them."

"Well, maybe they could *look* special," Mia said.

"What do you mean?" I asked.

"Well, this is a school fund-raiser, right? Maybe

they could be in the school colors or something," she said.

I immediately knew what she was talking about. "Mrs. Becker, can we have another bowl, please?"

I scooped half of the vanilla frosting we had made into the new bowl. Then I put a few drops of blue food coloring into one bowl, and a few drops of yellow into the other. Emma helped me stir them up.

"Make that one bluer," Mia said, pointing.

After a couple of more drops, we had the perfect blue and yellow—the official colors of Park Street Middle School.

"Mia, do your magic," I told her.

Mia expertly iced one cupcake with blue frosting and another cupcake with yellow frosting. Then she used an icing tube to write "PS" in yellow on the blue cupcake, and "PS" in blue on the yellow cupcake.

"Just imagine there are plain vanilla cupcakes inside," Mia said, holding them out to us.

"They're just right!" said Mrs. Becker.

"I bet you'll sell a hundred of those," agreed Mr. Becker.

"*Two* hundred," Alexis cheered.

"We will," I said confidently. "We are definitely

going to win this contest. We just have to do one thing."

"What?" Alexis asked.

"We have to *bake* two hundred cupcakes!"

CHAPTER 15

How to Bake
Two Hundred Cupcakes

Even though I was disappointed that we were making plain vanilla cupcakes, I loved Mia's cupcake design. And the next Cupcake Friday, Emma brought in cupcakes for us that she made herself.

When I bit into one, I tasted chocolate chips and sprinkles!

"I left out the marshmallows, so they wouldn't be too sweet or too sticky," she said. "What do you think?"

"I think they're amazing," I said.

Emma blushed a little. "Well, I really did like our mixed-up cupcakes."

That made me feel better. At least Emma liked them!

As we ate our cupcakes, we went over our plan

for the next week. Our parents had agreed to let us bake cupcakes once a day for four days before the contest. We would start baking on Tuesday and finish baking on Friday night. Then Saturday morning, we would ice and decorate every single one. We had to promise to get all of our homework done right after school.

Mom said we could do all the baking at our house. Each one of us would take turns bringing the ingredients and cupcake liners.

Alexis had the whole thing mapped out on a chart.

"Tuesday night, Katie will provide the supplies," she said, reading out loud. "I'll bring them Wednesday, Emma can bring them Thursday, and Mia will do Friday. Then Saturday, we'll all chip in for the icing. We'll have to make four dozen cupcakes every night, and do an extra dozen on Friday. Then we'll have four left over."

I leaned across the table to get a better look at the chart. Alexis had worked out a whole system with stickers. One cupcake-shaped sticker equaled a dozen cupcakes. It all looked very complicated.

"It looks a lot harder to bake two hundred cupcakes than I thought," I said.

I heard a laugh. When I turned around, I saw

Sydney and Maggie standing by the table.

"I saw the sign-up sheets for the fund-raiser," Sydney said. "You're doing a bake sale? Now *that's* really original."

"Bake sales are so boring!" Maggie added.

You know what's boring and unoriginal? I thought. *Following Sydney around and repeating everything she says like a parrot.*

I thought it, but I wasn't brave enough to say it. As usual, though, Mia wasn't afraid to speak up at all.

"Everybody likes cupcakes," Mia said. "So, what are you guys doing? On the fund-raising sheet it just says 'Popular Girls Club.'"

"It's top secret," Sydney said. "Nobody has ever done what we're planning. We're going to blow everyone away."

"Not everyone," said Alexis under her breath.

But Sydney and Maggie didn't hear her and walked away.

"I wonder what they're planning?" Emma asked worriedly. "I bet it's really good."

"I bet they haven't even thought of it yet," I said. "Otherwise, they wouldn't be bragging about their idea to everyone."

Alexis laughed. "You're probably right."

After Sydney's comments, I wanted to win that contest more than ever. We had a recipe. We had a plan.

Now we just had to make it happen.

Our first baking night was the Tuesday night before the fund-raiser. I could tell Mom was really excited too. She even bought extra cupcake pans for us to use.

Mia, Alexis, and Emma all got to my house right at seven o'clock. Mom gave us a little pep talk—and some instructions.

"There are enough pans here for four dozen cupcakes," she said. "But I wouldn't make a double batch of batter. Baking is tricky. Make one batch first, put it in the oven, and then start the second batch. Then you'll end up with perfect cupcakes."

"Thanks, Mrs. Brown," Mia said.

"Now, how about a huddle?" Mom asked.

Oh, Mom. . . . To make her happy, we all put our hands on top of one another's. Mom led the cheer.

"Goooooooo Cupcake Club!"

Then we got to work. By then, we were getting into a cupcake groove. Emma liked sifting the flour, Alexis liked measuring things, Mia liked mixing things, and I liked cracking the eggs. We had the first batch of two dozen cupcakes done in record time, and then the phone rang.

I wiped off my hands and picked it up. "Hey, Katie." It was Callie. "I tried texting you. Are you watching *Singing Stars*? Ryan just advanced to the finals. Can you believe it?"

I realized that I totally forgot it was time for *Singing Stars*. "Uh, I'm not watching it," I said. "We're making cupcakes for the fund-raiser."

"Hey, Katie, how many eggs is it again?" Mia called out.

"Oh," Callie said. "You have company. Sorry to bother you." There was a little silence. "Well, I'll talk to you tomorrow."

"Text me with the results, okay?" I asked.

"Sure," she said, and then she hung up.

I felt a little sad for a minute. Callie belonged in the Cupcake Club. She could be having so much fun with us if she wanted to.

"Earth to Katie. How many eggs?" Mia asked.

"Oh, sorry. Two," I replied.

By the time Alexis's dad came by to pick up everyone, we had four dozen cupcakes in boxes stored safely in our freezer.

"Forty-eight down, one hundred and fifty-two to go," Mia said as they were leaving.

"Actually, it's one hundred and fifty-six, since we're making two hundred and four cupcakes," Alexis pointed out.

"One hundred and fifty-six?" I cried. We had worked really hard tonight. Yet it didn't seem like we'd done much, after all.

After my friends left I flopped on the couch—for about five seconds.

"Time to jump in the shower, Katie," Mom told me. "I don't want you getting to bed late."

I rolled over onto the floor. "You'll have to drag me."

"Hmm," Mom said. "Maybe all this cupcake baking is too much for you."

I jumped to my feet. Mom always knows how to get me.

"Nope. I'm fine!" I told her. Then I ran to the bathroom.

As I drifted off to sleep that night, I thought about what the instructions would look like for someone making two hundred cupcakes.

How to Make 200 Cupcakes:
1. Do homework in a dentist office.
2. Eat dinner.
3. Clean up after dinner.

4. Make four dozen cupcakes.

5. Clean up after making four dozen cupcakes.

6. Shower.

7. Rinse.

8. Sleep.

9. Repeat.

10. Repeat.

11. Repeat.

CHAPTER 16

The Purple Dress

"Two hundred one, two hundred two, two hundred three, two hundred four!"

We counted together as the last cupcake—the last of seventeen dozen exactly—went into its box.

"We did it! Woo-hoo!" I cheered. Everyone kind of jumped around.

"You know, it's funny that there are exactly four cupcakes left over," Alexis pointed out. "One for each of us."

"I think that's a sign," Mia said. "We need to eat those four to make it an even two hundred."

"But four cupcakes equals eight dollars," Alexis reminded us.

"I know," I chimed in. "But maybe it's, like, a good luck thing."

That satisfied Alexis. "Good point. We should probably taste them anyway, to make sure they're okay."

The vanilla cupcakes were delicious, even without the icing.

"So we'll meet here tomorrow at eight to ice them," I reminded everyone. "The fund-raiser starts at noon."

The doorbell rang, and Alexis's mom came to pick up her and Emma. Then Mia's stepbrother beeped his horn outside.

"Mom and I will pick you up after dinner," Mia told me.

"Okay. I'll be ready," I said.

I forgot to mention that on Friday we baked the cupcakes right after school because we didn't have to do our homework right away. The night before, Mia had had an idea about how we should spend Friday night.

"What is everybody wearing to the dance?" she wanted to know.

Alexis shrugged. "I don't know. What I always wear."

"I was thinking about wearing my favorite dress," Emma said. "The one with the pink flowers."

"I didn't even think about it," I admitted. "Do

we have to get dressed up to go to the dance?"

"Well, no," Mia admitted. "You don't *have* to. But it's fun. I was thinking that tomorrow night we should all go to the mall and look for dresses to wear."

"I can't," Alexis said. "We're going to my aunt's for dinner."

"I'll probably just wear the dress I have," Emma said.

Mia looked at me. "Come on, Katie. What do you say?"

"I have to ask my mom," I said. Honestly, I don't like shopping at all. But I think Mia could make anything fun. "But yeah, why not?"

My mom agreed (after talking to Mia's mom, of course), and so Ms. Vélaz and Mia picked me up at seven.

The Westgrove Mall is really big, with a lot of buildings all connected together. It reminds me of a big maze. When we walked through the doors, Ms. Vélaz turned to us.

"What store are we going to first?" she asked.

Mia looked horrified. "Mom, seriously?"

"Of course! This is a big mall," her mom pointed out. "Besides, I promised Mrs. Brown that I'd stick with you girls."

I felt like sinking into the floor. My mom sticks to me like glue when we go to the mall. She used to make me wear one of those kid leashes until I was five. Here I was, in middle school, and I could still feel the invisible leash tugging at me.

Ms. Vélaz must have seen the look on my face. "You know, you girls are lucky to have an expert fashion consultant accompanying you!"

Mia grabbed me by the arm. "Come on. There's a supercute store right around the corner."

Mia's mom walked slowly behind us as we raced into the store. Loud dance music blared through the speakers. The store was pretty crowded with girls looking through racks of dresses, shirts, skirts, and jeans.

Mia skidded to a stop in front of a black dress with a zipper down the front.

"This is so cute," she said. "Katie, you should try it on."

"I don't know," I said. "It's black. Black clothes remind me of vampires."

Mia looked me up and down. I was wearing a pair of old jeans with a rip in the knee and a red T-shirt with a peace sign on it.

"So you like bright colors," she said. "What else do you like?"

I shrugged. "I don't know. I don't know what's in style and what's not. When I go shopping with my mom, we get some jeans and then I pick out whatever shirts I like."

"So you can do that with a dress, too," Mia said. "Just look around and see what you like."

That sounded easy enough. I started looking through the racks of clothes with Mia. At first I was just confused. There were so many dresses! And even though they were different colors and different styles, they kind of all looked the same to me.

Then a splash of purple caught my eye. I walked over to a display with a headless mannequin wearing a purple dress. It was *really* purple. Grape jelly purple. But I liked it. It had short sleeves and a straight skirt with a black belt around the middle.

I took one off the rack. "I kind of like this," I told Mia. "It looks good on the mannequin. But she doesn't have a head, so anything would look good on her, I guess."

"No, I like it!" Mia said. I could tell she was excited. "Try it on!"

The dressing rooms were lined up on the side wall. A salesperson used a key to open up one of the silver doors for me. I stepped inside and tried on the dress.

I looked at myself in the mirror. "Not bad," I had to admit.

Then I heard Mia's voice outside. "Katie, come out! I am dying to see how you look!"

I cautiously stepped outside the dressing room. Mia's eyes got wide when she saw me.

"Ooh, it's perfect! Turn around!" she ordered.

I felt like the world's worst fashion model as I turned in a circle for Mia's inspection.

"You have got to get it," she said. "Wear it with some short black boots and it'll be fabulous."

"What if I don't have short black boots?" I asked.

"Then you can borrow mine!"

I looked at the price tag. It cost less than the money Mom had given me to spend. "I think I'll get it," I said. "That was easy!"

Then I heard a familiar loud voice nearby. "That dress is gross, Mags. I wouldn't wear that to gym class."

Sydney! I had to get inside that dressing room before she saw me. I turned to run, but it was too late.

"Isn't it a little too early for Halloween, Katie?"

There she goes, I thought. If I couldn't escape, I might as well face her.

I spun around. "What do you mean, Sydney?"

"Well, that's a grape costume, isn't it?" she asked. "No, wait—you're that purple dinosaur."

She made me so angry! I wished I had some great comeback to give her. But as usual, she left me tongue-tied.

"You know, Sydney, violet was a hot runway color this fall," Mia said in that supercool tone of hers. "I was just reading about it in the color trends column in *Fashion Weekly*."

Now it was Sydney's turn to get tongue-tied. But she managed to recover. "Violet or not, it's an ugly dress."

For the first time ever, I thought of something to say to Sydney. And I wasn't afraid to say it, either. Maybe Mia was rubbing off on me a little.

"I don't care if *you* think it's ugly," I said. "I like it."

Then I marched back into my dressing room and out of the corner of my eye I saw Mia smirk. My heart was pounding. Something about that dress made me feel good. Good enough to tell stupid old Sydney to shut up.

And that's why my purple dress is still my favorite dress to this day. And as it turns out—it's my lucky one, too.

CHAPTER 17

PGC's Secret Is Revealed!

Saturday morning was, as the skateboarding dudes in my school say, intense. Mom and I got up super-early and started mixing batches and batches of icing. The girls came over, and Emma's mom came over to help too.

It took hours, but we got everything done. My mom and Emma's mom iced the cupcakes with me. Mia wrote the letters on them with her perfect handwriting. Alexis and Emma made a big card-board sign for the table that said CUPCAKES $2.00. Then they helped us with the icing.

By eleven o'clock we had two hundred perfect cupcakes. We carefully transferred them to Emma's mom's minivan, and she drove them to the school. My mom and I brought the sign, a cash box, one blue and one yellow tablecloth, and plastic trays for the cupcakes.

The day was perfect for a fund-raiser—sunny but not too hot. When we got to the school, the big parking lot was roped off with police tape. There were a bunch of canopies set up in a square all around the lot. Blue and yellow balloons tied to the canopies waved and wiggled in the air. We searched around until we found a table with a note that said CUPCAKE CLUB on it.

We started setting up. We spread out the blue tablecloth and then draped the yellow one over it in another direction so you could see both colors. Alexis and Emma taped up their sign. We put about half the cupcakes on platters. Then we stood back and checked out our table.

"Not bad," I said.

"It's a little flat," Mia said, turning her head sideways. "Maybe next time we could put the platters on pillars or something so that some are high and some are low."

Mom walked up behind us and put her arm around me.

"Well, *I* think it looks perfect!" she said. "Why don't you girls go stand in front of the table? I'll take a picture."

We quickly lined up: me, Mia, Alexis, and then Emma.

"Say 'cupcake'!" Mom called out.

"Cupcake!" we shouted.

Alexis glanced at her watch. "We still have fifteen minutes. Let's check out the competition."

"Good idea," I agreed.

We walked around. There must have been about a dozen tables besides ours. The basketball team was still setting up their dunking booth at the end of the parking lot. The girls' soccer team had a booth where they would take your picture, print it out, and put it in a frame. Then you could decorate the frame with shapes like stars and soccer balls. Then we walked past the Chess Club's table.

"Oh, no!" Emma cried. "A bake sale!"

The table was covered with paper plates topped with cookies, brownies, and yes—cupcakes.

"I think our table stands out more," Mia whispered to us. "And they don't have special Park Street Middle School cupcakes, either."

"Besides, they have mostly cookies," Alexis pointed out. "And they're only charging fifty cents each for those."

Mia and Alexis made me feel better. I think Emma felt better too.

Then we heard loud music coming from the other side of the parking lot. It was dance music, just like I'd heard in the clothing store the night before. We all turned our heads at the same time.

The PGC had set up their booth!

"Let's get a closer look," Mia suggested.

We walked across the parking lot. I hated to admit it, but the PGC booth looked really cool. The table was covered with a black cloth with silver stars dangling from it. There were glittery makeup cases all over the table. They had a banner (the printed kind you order from the store) tied to the canopy up above. It read PGC'S MAKEOVER MAGIC.

"What exactly are they doing?" I wondered out loud.

We walked even closer. Sydney and Bella were busy spreading out makeup and brushes and stuff on the table. Bella had a small sign on the table in front of her that said, GOTH MAKEOVERS ARE MY SPECIALITY. She was wearing a black dress with a poufy skirt. Her reddish-brown hair was pulled back in a sleek ponytail, and her face looked kind of pale. Smudgy dark makeup ringed her eyes.

Next to her, Sydney wore her long blond hair straight and sleek. She was wearing a long white T-shirt over a gray tank with black leggings and boots. It reminded me of an outfit that Mia might wear.

Callie was sitting at a tiny round table set up next to them with a cash box behind her. I noticed that she was dressed exactly the same as Sydney.

So was Maggie. She looked as perfect as Sydney and Callie, except that a long lock of frizzy brown hair was hanging over her eyes. She darted through the crowd, handing out "Makeover Magic" flyers.

"Flyers! Why didn't we think of that?" Alexis said with a frown.

"We don't need flyers to sell cupcakes," Mia said. "Cupcakes sell themselves."

The PGC booth worried me. I mean, it looked really good, a lot better than our table with its cardboard sign. Maybe Sydney had been right all along—they were going to win the contest with their secret weapon.

"Speaking of selling cupcakes, we should get back to the booth," Alexis said.

That's when Maggie bumped into us.

"Oh, hi," she said, shoving a flyer into my hand. "When things get slow at your cupcake stand, stop by for a makeover."

"We'll try, but I don't think things are going to get slow," I said.

We walked away, determined more than ever to sell every last one of our cupcakes.

"The PGC might have music and flyers and glitter, but we have delicious cupcakes!" I cheered. "Let's go win this contest!"

We ran back to our cupcake booth just as the fund-raiser officially opened. A bunch of people came in all at once. We were right by the front entrance, which was a good thing. Almost everybody stopped to check us out. They said nice things like "Wow, it's the school colors!" and "What nice cupcakes!"

But for the first few minutes, nobody bought one.

Then Mrs. Moore, my math teacher, came to the table.

I almost didn't recognize her. When she's teaching us, she wears skirts and blouses and dark colors. Her hair is mostly gray and she always has it pulled back.

But today she was wearing a sweatshirt with a teddy bear on it and jeans. Her hair was loose and went down to the top of her shoulders. I thought it looked nice that way.

"Hello, Miss Brown," she said. She looked at the table. "It must have been a lot of work to make all of these cupcakes."

"There are more in boxes," I told her. "We made two hundred. Well, two hundred and four, actually. That's seventeen dozen."

I was hoping my math would impress her, and maybe it did.

"I'll take one, please," she said, and handed me two dollars in exchange for a cupcake. She took a bite right in front of me.

"Vanilla!" she said. "My favorite."

Then she walked away.

I couldn't believe it. "It's our first sale!" I cried. Everyone let out a cheer. I turned over the money to Alexis, who was in charge of the cash box.

Mrs. Moore must have brought us good luck, because we started selling cupcakes like crazy after that. Some people asked for blue, some people asked for yellow, but most people didn't care which ones they got.

We were so busy selling cupcakes that I forgot about the PGC booth—until a friend of Mia's came to our table. I recognized her as one of the girls Mia talks to in the hallway.

"Hi, Sophie," Mia said. Then she gave a little gasp.

I turned away from the cupcakes to see what had startled Mia. Then I noticed—Sophie's face looked really strange. Her skin had so much white makeup on it that she looked like a clown. The dark makeup around her eyes was smudged everywhere.

"I know," Sophie said, noticing Mia's face. "It's terrible, isn't it? And it cost me five dollars!"

That's when I realized—Sophie was a victim of the Makeover Magic booth!

"It's not so bad," Mia said.

"I was hoping to look pale and mysterious, but this is too much." Sophie sighed. "You should see what's going on over there. It's more like Makeover *Tragic* than Makeover Magic."

Mia and I looked at each other. Then I turned to Emma.

"Can you and Alexis handle things for a minute?" I asked.

Emma nodded. "No problem."

We quickly made our way to the PGC booth. A big crowd had gathered around.

"Maybe Sophie just got unlucky," I said. "It looks like they're doing great."

We inched our way closer so we could get a better view. I realized that most of the crowd wasn't in line to get a makeover. Instead they were watching the action at the booth.

Sydney swiped a brush across the face of a girl sitting across from her.

"There," she said. "You're ready for the runway!"

The girl turned around, and a few people giggled. I tried not to laugh myself. Sydney had put so much fake tanner on the girl that her face looked like a tangerine. Glittery blue eye shadow covered her eyelids.

"I don't know much about fashion, but that doesn't look right to me," I said to Mia.

"That shouldn't look right to *anybody*," Mia whispered back.

"Okay!" Sydney called out. "Who's next?"

Nobody stirred. Then the girl with the orange face nudged her friend. "You promised you would get one if I got one."

The friend looked terrified, but she knew she had to go through with it. She slowly walked up to Callie and handed her five dollars.

"Thanks," Callie said with a smile. But I know Callie really well, and behind that smile I knew she wasn't really happy. I felt just a little bad for her.

The crowd thinned out, and Callie noticed me and Mia standing there.

"Hey, Katie," she called out. "Do you want a makeover?"

"Um, you know I don't wear makeup," I said. "Sorry. You should come check out our cupcake table. I bet your dad would like one. They're vanilla."

A woman I didn't know tapped me on the shoulder. She wore sunglasses and her brown hair was swept back in a tan scarf with designs on it.

"Did you make the cupcakes with the school colors?" she asked.

"Yes—I mean, we did," I said. "We have a club. The Cupcake Club."

"They were beautiful *and* delicious," she said. "Made from scratch, I could tell. I would love to have you make some for the PTA luncheon this spring. We'd pay you, of course."

Mia and I exchanged glances. Someone wanted to pay us to make cupcakes. Just like professionals. How awesome was that?

Maggie flew up to the woman. "Mom! The Cupcake Club is a *rival* booth! You're consorting with the enemy."

"Calm down, Maggie," her mom said. "It's all for the school. I was just coming to get my makeover."

Maggie glared at us, but I didn't care. I was feeling pretty good.

Then Callie stood up. "Maggie, can you work the cash box for a minute? I'm going to get a cupcake."

Sydney dropped the makeup brush she was holding. "Callie, you absolutely *cannot* buy a cupcake. Do you want to win this contest or not?"

"It's just a cupcake," Callie said quietly.

Callie walked over. We smiled at each other.

Maybe Callie was right. Maybe it was just a cupcake.

But to me, it felt like so much more.

CHAPTER 18

The Icing on the Cupcake

The fund-raiser ended at three o'clock, and by then we had sold almost every single cupcake. Then Mia's stepdad, Eddie, came to pick her up.

"Hey, girls," he said, smiling big. "How did the cupcake sales go?"

"Great," Mia told him.

Alexis counted the remaining cupcakes. "We sold one hundred and eighty-three," she reported.

"So that means you have seventeen left?" he asked.

Alexis nodded.

"Tell you what," Eddie said. He took his wallet from his pocket. "I've got a big meeting on Monday. I bet everyone at work would like some cupcakes. I'll take everything you have left."

"Wow, thanks!" I said.

"That will be thirty-four dollars, please," Alexis said matter-of-factly.

Mia smiled. "Thanks, Eddie," she said, and she looked really happy. "You didn't have to do that."

"I did," said Eddie. "I'm making them all work late, but they don't know it yet!" He laughed. I still couldn't tell how Mia felt about Eddie, but he seemed nice enough to me. I wondered what it would be like if Mom got married again. That would be weird. Too weird to think about.

Thanks to Eddie, we sold every single one of our cupcakes. We turned over our four hundred dollars to Principal LaCosta. Then we headed home to get ready for the dance that night.

I put on my new purple dress and Mia's black boots. I checked out my reflection in the mirror. I still didn't feel like I could be in a magazine or anything. But I thought I looked pretty good.

Mom got teary-eyed when I came downstairs.

"My baby's first dance," she said, gripping me in a hug. "Oh, you look so glamorous!"

"Mo-om," I said in a complaining voice. (But to be honest, I kind of liked it.)

We picked up Mia, who of course looked great, and then Mom dropped us off. The gym was

135

decorated just like you see in the movies or on TV. There were more blue and yellow balloons and streamers, and a DJ was set up over by the basketball hoop. I was happy to see that Alexis and Emma were there already, over by the food table.

"Wow, you look nice," Emma said.

"So do you guys," I replied. "So, what's to eat?"

"There's punch, some vegetable platters, and cupcakes," Alexis reported.

Emma groaned. "I don't think I can look at another cupcake today."

"I can *always* look at a cupcake," I said, examining the trays. They looked normal—chocolate with chocolate icing, and I could tell the icing came from a can.

"Speaking of cupcakes," Alexis said. "I talked to my parents at dinner about our PTA cupcake order. You know, they're accountants, so they can help us figure out what to charge so we make a profit. They said they could even set us up as a business if we want."

"Our own business?" I asked. I hadn't thought about our little Cupcake Club as anything more than . . . well, making and eating cupcakes. But making money, too? That couldn't be bad. "I like it!"

"I could design the logo!" said Mia.

"I bet I could make more than I do babysitting my brother!" said Emma excitedly. "I'm in!"

"Then," proclaimed Alexis, "we are officially the Cupcake Club. Open for business!"

"Yay!" We all laughed and went in for a group hug. It felt good. For the first time in a while I wasn't really worrying about anything. Not Callie. Not middle school. Not even math.

Then some girls I didn't know came up to us.

"Those cupcakes you made were sooo good," one of the girls said.

"Yeah," said her friend. "How did you make them?"

"It's easy," I said. "You just follow the recipe."

Then a funky beat blared through the gym. "Hey, I love this song!" Mia said. Before I could say no, she grabbed my arm and dragged me onto the dance floor. Alexis and Emma followed us. We danced to the whole song, and then the next one.

George Martinez was dancing by himself. He pointed at me.

"Hey, Silly Arms!"

I started waving my arms around like the Silly Arms sprinkler. George cracked up. Then Mia started doing it too.

"Hey, that's pretty fun!" she said.

Then the gym got quiet. Principal LaCosta walked up to the DJ and took the microphone from him.

"Students, welcome to Park Street's first dance of the year!" she cried, and a bunch of people cheered and whistled. "Now it's time to announce the winners of our first contest. The winning table today raised four hundred dollars for our school."

Alexis gasped. It still wasn't sinking in with me, though. Not until Principal LaCosta called our name.

"Let's hear it for the Cupcake Club!"

Emma let out a loud squeal. Then I realized I was squealing too. We won! We actually won! It was like the sweet icing on top of a delicious cupcake.

The four of us ran up to the DJ booth and Principal LaCosta handed us our prize. "Congratulations, girls! You've each won a Park Street Middle School sweatshirt!"

Everyone clapped. I still couldn't believe it. Then the DJ started to blast the song, "Celebrate!"

Mia draped the sweatshirt over her shoulders. "Victory dance!" she yelled.

Just then Callie ran up to me and gave me a big hug.

"Katie, that's so awesome!" she said.

Then we both stopped, stared at each other, and

started to laugh. We were both wearing the same dress! I had forgotten that purple was Callie's favorite color.

"You look great!" she said.

"You do too!" I laughed. I wondered if Sydney told Callie she thought the dress was ugly.

Mia, Alexis, and Emma were running out to the dance floor. I didn't know I was doing it, but I must have been following them with my eyes. A kind of sad smile crossed Callie's face.

"Go dance with your friends," she said.

Callie was the one who said we should make new friends in middle school. When she first said that, I was hurt. But she was right. It felt good to have new friends, but it felt good to have old friends, too.

"Come dance with us," I said.

Callie shook her head. "No, you go. I'll call you tomorrow, okay?"

"Okay," I told her, moving toward the club. Then I looked back. I saw her walking toward Sydney, Maggie, and Bella. Sydney did not look happy.

"Hey, Callie!" I called. She turned around. "I'm glad we're friends!" I yelled. I said it loud, so she could hear it over the music. But I also said it so Sydney could hear me.

"Me too!" Callie called back, and then walked toward the PGC.

I ran off to dance with the Cupcake Club. As I waved my silly arms in the air, I realized something.

The first day of middle school had been awful. Callie had let me down. I got into trouble. Things did not go the way I planned at all.

But the weird thing was that middle school was not a total disaster. Everything had worked out, somehow.

Maybe it was time for a new recipe.

Mix together:
One purple dress.
One corny mom.
Two hundred and four cupcakes.
Three new friends.
One old friend.
Stir gently until they're all blended together.
Then dance.

Mia
in
the
mix

CHAPTER 1

An *Interesting* Remark

My name is Mia Vélaz-Cruz, and I hate Mondays.

I know, everybody says that, right? But I think I have some very compelling reasons for hating Mondays.

For example, every other weekend I go to Manhattan to see my dad. My parents are divorced, and my mom and I moved out to a town in the suburbs, an hour outside the city. I really like living with my mom, but I miss my dad a lot. I miss Manhattan, too, and all of my friends there. On the weekends I visit my dad, he drives me back to my mom's house late on Sunday nights. So it's weird when I wake up on Monday and I realize I'm not in New York anymore. Every two weeks I wake up all confused, which is not a good way to start a Monday.

Another reason I don't like Mondays is that it's the first day of the school week. That means five days of school until I get a day off. Five days of Mrs. Moore's hard math quizzes. And I have to wait all the way till the end of the week for Cupcake Friday. That's the day that either I or one of my friends brings in cupcakes to eat at lunch. That's how we formed the Cupcake Club. But I'll tell you more about that in a minute.

Lately I've been looking over a bunch of journal entries, and I've realized that when annoying things happen, they usually happen on a Monday. Back in May, my mom told me on a Monday night that we were moving out of New York. When I ruined my new suede boots because of a sudden rainstorm, it was on a Monday. And the last time I lost my cell phone, it was Monday. And when did I find it? Friday, of course. Because Friday is an awesome day.

Then there was that bad Monday I had a few weeks ago. It should have been a good Monday. A *great* Monday, even, because that was my first day back at school after the Cupcake Club won the contest.

Remember when I mentioned Cupcake Club? I'm in the club with my friends Katie, Alexis, and Emma. It started because we all eat lunch together, and on the first day of school Katie brought in this amazing peanut-butter-and-jelly cupcake that her mom made. Katie is a fabulous cupcake baker too, and she and her mom taught us all how to make them, so we decided to form our own club and make them together. Fun, right?

A little while after we formed the club, Principal LaCosta announced there was going to be a contest the day of the first school dance. There would be a big fund-raising fair in the school parking lot, and the group that raised the most funds would win a prize at the dance.

We hadn't really planned on participating in the fund-raiser, but then this other group in our class, the Popular Girls Club, kept telling everyone they were going to win. The leader of the group, Sydney, bragged that they had some "top-secret" idea that was going to blow everyone away. It's not like we're rivals or anything, but once we heard that, we decided to enter the contest too. Our idea was to sell cupcakes decorated with the school colors (that part was my idea).

The PGC's big secret ended up being a make-over booth, which would have been a cool idea except they weren't very good at doing makeovers. In fact, they were terrible at it. But we were very good at baking cupcakes. We sold two hundred cupcakes and won the contest. At the dance that night, Principal LaCosta gave us our prizes: four Park Street Middle School sweatshirts.

I know it's not a huge deal or anything, but it felt really good to win. Back at my old school, things were really competitive. Just about every kid took singing lessons or art lessons or violin lessons or French lessons. Everyone was good at something. It was hard to stand out there, and I never won a prize before. I was really happy that we won. It made me think maybe it wasn't bad that we moved out here.

Just before my mom picked me up the night of our big win, Alexis had an idea.

"We should all wear our sweatshirts to school on Monday," she said.

"Isn't that kind of like bragging?" Emma asked.

"We should do it," Katie said. "All the football guys wear their jerseys when they win a game. We won. We should be proud."

"Yes, definitely," I agreed. I mean, Katie was right. We should be proud. Making two hundred cupcakes is a lot of work!

Except for one problem. I don't do sweatshirts. I'm sorry, but the last time I wore one I was five, and it made me look like a steamed dumpling. They are all lumpy and the sleeves are always too long.

Even though I wanted to show how proud I was of winning, I also knew there was no way I could wear that sweatshirt on Monday. I really care about what I wear, probably because my mom used to work for a big fashion magazine. So fashion is in my blood. But I also think clothes are a fun way to express yourself. You can seriously tell a lot about a person by what they choose to wear, like their mood for instance. And so to *me* a sweatshirt just says "I'm in the mood to sweat!"

I told Mom about my sweatshirt issue on the drive home.

"Mia, I'm surprised by you," she said. "You're great at transforming your old clothes into new and amazing creations. Think of your old school uniform. You made that look great and like you every day. If you *had* to wear a sweatshirt, I'd bet you could come up with something really cool and great."

Mom was right, to be honest, and I was a little surprised I hadn't thought of it first. Our old school uniform was terrible: ugly plaid skirts with plain white, itchy tops. But you could wear a sweater or a jacket and any shoes, so you could get pretty creative with it and not look gross on a daily basis. That's one of the good things about my new school—you can wear whatever you want. Inspired, I sat at my sewing table the next day and cut up the sweatshirt. I turned it into a cool hobo bag, the kind with a big pouch and a long strap. I added a few cool studs to the strap and around the school logo to funk it up a little. I was really proud of how it looked.

On Monday morning I picked out an outfit to go with the bag: a denim skirt, a blue knit shirt with a brown leather belt around the waist, and a dark-gray-and-white-striped-blazer. I rolled up the sleeves of the blazer, then put the bag over my shoulder and checked out my reflection in the long mirror attached to my closet.

Too much blue, I decided. I changed the blue shirt to a white one, then changed the belt to a braided silver belt and checked again.

Better, I thought. I pulled my long black hair back into a ponytail. *Maybe a headband . . . or maybe braid it to the side . . .*

"Mia! You'll be late for your bus!" Mom called from downstairs.

I sighed. I'm almost always late for the bus, no matter how early I wake up. I decided to leave my hair down and hurried downstairs.

Taking a bus to school is something I still need

to get used to. When I went to my school in New York, I took the subway. A lot of people don't like the subway because of how crowded it is, but I love it. I like to study the people and see what they're wearing. Everyone has their own distinct style and things that they're into. And there are all kinds of people on a subway—old people, moms with little kids, kids going to school like me, people from the suburbs going to work. Also, on the subway, nobody whispers about you behind your back like they do on the bus. Nobody makes loud burping noises either, like Wes Kinney does every single day in the back of the school bus, which is extremely disgusting.

The best thing about the bus, though, is that my friend Katie takes it with me. That's how we met, on the first day of school. Her best friend was supposed to ride with her, but she walked to school instead, so I asked Katie to sit with me. I felt bad for Katie, but it was lucky for me. Katie is really cool.

When Katie got on the bus that morning she was wearing her Park Street sweatshirt with lightly ripped jeans and her favorite blue canvas sneakers. Her wavy brown hair was down. She has natural highlights, as if she hung out every day at the beach.

151

If I didn't know Katie, I would have guessed she was from California.

"Hey!" Katie said, sliding into the seat next to me. She pointed to her sweatshirt. "I still can't believe we won!"

"Me either," I said. "But we did make some really fabulous cupcakes."

"Totally," Katie agreed. Then she frowned. "Did you forget to wear your shirt?"

"I'm wearing it," I told her. I showed her the bag. "What do you think?"

"No way!" Katie grabbed it to get a closer look. "Did your mom do this?"

"I did," I replied.

"That is awesome," Katie said. "I didn't know you could sew. That's got to be harder than making cupcakes."

I shrugged. "I don't know. It just takes practice."

Braaap! Wes Kinney made a big fake burp just then. His friends all started laughing.

"That is so gross," Katie said, shaking her head.

"Seriously!" I agreed.

This Monday was starting out okay (except for the part when I didn't get to wear my headband). But it got annoying pretty fast in homeroom.

None of my Cupcake Club friends are in my

homeroom, but I do know some kids. There's George Martinez, who's kind of cute and really funny. He's in my science and social studies classes too. There's Sophie, who I like a lot. But she sits next to her best friend, Lucy, and in homeroom they're always in a huddle, whispering to each other.

Then there is Sydney Whitman and Callie Wilson. Sydney is the one who started the Popular Girls Club. Callie is in the club too, and she's also the girl who used to be Katie's best friend. I can see why, because she's nice, like Katie.

Katie, Alexis, and Emma all think Sydney is horrible. They say she's always making mean comments to them. She's never said anything really mean to me. And to be honest, I like the way she dresses. She has a really good sense of fashion, which is something we have in common. Like today, she was wearing a scoop-neck T-shirt with a floral chiffon skirt, black leggings, and an awesome wraparound belt that had a large pewter flower as the buckle. So sometimes I think, you know, that maybe we could be friends. Don't get me wrong—the girls in the Cupcake Club are my BFFs, and I love them. But none of them are into fashion the way I am.

Sydney and Callie sit right across from me. Callie gave me a smile when I sat down.

"Those were great cupcakes you guys made on Saturday," Callie told me.

"Thanks," I said.

I thought I saw Sydney give Callie a glare. But when she turned to me, she was smiling too.

"That was a really *interesting* dress you wore to the dance, Mia," Sydney said.

Hmm. I wasn't sure what "interesting" meant. I had worn a minidress with black, purple, and turquoise panels, a black sequined jacket, and black patent leather peep toe flats. "Perfectly chic," my mom had said.

"Thanks."

"Very . . . red carpet maybe?" Sydney went on. "Although, I was reading this really *interesting* article in *Fashionista* magazine all about choosing the right outfit for the right event. You know, like how being *overdressed* can be just as bad as being underdressed."

I knew exactly what Sydney was doing. She was insulting me, but in a "nice" way. Sort of. I know my outfit might have been a little too sophisticated for a middle school dance, but so what? I liked it.

"There's no such thing as being overdressed," I replied calmly. "That's what my mom taught me. She used to be an editor at *Flair* magazine." Then

I opened up my notebook and began to sketch. I don't normally brag about my mother's job like that, but I didn't know what to say to Sydney.

"Wow!" said Callie. "*Flair*? That's so cool! Isn't that cool?" She turned to Sydney, who looked uninterested. "We read that all the time at Sydney's house. Her mom gets it."

Sydney opened her math book and pretended to start reading.

"You looked really great!" said Callie, like she was trying to make up for Sydney. I honestly didn't really care if they liked it or not. I thought I looked good and that outfit made me feel great.

I wasn't mad at Sydney—just annoyed. Which is not a fabulous way to start the day.

But what can you expect from a Monday?

CHAPTER 2

Meat Loaf Monday Continues

So, the next Monday-esque thing happened at lunchtime. I sit at a table with Katie, Alexis, and Emma. Katie always brings her lunch, like me, and Alexis and Emma always get lunch from the cafeteria.

When I got to the table, Katie was already eating her sandwich. I opened up my new bag and realized I'd forgotten to put my lunch bag inside this morning.

"This is seriously disappointing," I said with a sigh. Luckily, I always carry a few dollars around in case of an emergency. I looked at Katie. "Forgot my lunch. I'll be back in a minute."

Katie's mouth was full of peanut butter, so she nodded in reply. I walked over to the line and found myself right behind Alexis and Emma. They're best friends, but they're both really different. Alexis has reddish wavy hair and likes to talk a lot. Emma was taller, with straight blond hair and big blue eyes. She's a little bit shy, and definitely quieter than Alexis. They're both supernice though.

Today they were both wearing their Park Street sweatshirts. Alexis wore hers with a white denim skirt and a white headband in her hair, and Emma had on cute blue denim leggings.

"I forgot my lunch," I told them. "What are they having today?"

"Monday is meat loaf day," Alexis told me. "With mashed potatoes and string beans."

"Oh," I said. I am not a big fan of meat loaf. Of course, Monday would have to be meat loaf day.

"It's not bad," Emma said, noticing my face. "You can get a salad instead if you want."

That cheered me up. "I'll do the salad, definitely!"

"So, did you forget to wear your sweatshirt?" Alexis asked me.

"No." I held out my bag. "I transformed it, but I'm still wearing it, see?"

I wasn't expecting Alexis's reaction. "You cut it up?" She sounded a little upset.

"Well, I had to, to make the bag," I explained.

Alexis frowned. "It's just, I thought we were going to wear them together, like a team," she said.

"Oh!" I said, because I didn't really know what to say. Was she mad at me?

"But it's a nice bag," Emma said, giving Alexis a look.

"Thanks," I said. "And we are a team. It's just, I don't like sweatshirts. It's hard to look good in a sweatshirt, you know? They're so puffy and lumpy."

I felt bad as soon as I said the words. "I mean, you guys look great, I just don't like how I look in them," I said quickly.

Alexis turned away. "Time to order."

I felt really terrible as I took my salad from the cold shelf. The three of us were quiet as we walked back to the table.

"I've been so alone!" Katie said in a funny, dramatic way. "Thank goodness you're here at last! Hey, did you check out Mia's bag? Isn't it cool? Maybe you could make one for me, too. This sweatshirt is *hot*!"

And just like that, everything was all right. Katie is like that. She's so sweet and funny, it's hard to be in a bad mood when you're around her.

But I still felt bad about what I said. And there was a part of me that wished Alexis, you know,

158

got me better. Like my best friend, Ava, who lives in Manhattan. All I'd have to do is say the word "sweatshirt," and she'd know what I was talking about: steamed dumpling.

I think that's the biggest problem I have here at Park Street Middle School. I don't feel like anyone really gets me. Not like Ava does, anyway. The Cupcake Club is great, but Ava has known me since first grade. She knows everything about me. I try not to think about it too much, but it can be a bit lonely sometimes.

The Monday madness continued after school. When I got home, my dogs, Tiki and Milkshake, ran up to greet me like they always do. They're little, fluffy, white dogs with black noses, and I think they are perfectly adorable. Mom and I adopted them after the divorce when we went to live in a new apartment, one that allowed dogs. After I petted them both, I went over to my mom's office to talk to her.

Mom's starting up her own fashion consulting business, so she works out of the house, which is nice. I see her a lot more now.

But Mom wasn't there. Then I heard Eddie's voice behind me.

"Sorry, Mia. Your mom had to go into the city

for a meeting. She won't be home till late," he said.

Eddie is my soon-to-be stepdad. Mom and I live in the house with him and my soon-to-be stepbrother, Dan. Eddie is a lawyer whose law firm is over in the next town. When my mom left her job to start up her consulting company, Eddie asked her to marry him. They're getting married this spring.

"How late?" I asked.

"I'm not sure," he said. "But there's good news! I'll be cooking tonight. You're in for a real treat. It's my famous mystery meat loaf!"

It looked like I was not going to escape meat loaf, no matter how hard I tried. "Why is it a *mystery* meat loaf?" I asked.

"Because the recipe is very mysterious," Eddie said in a fake mysterious voice. Then he made spooky noises. *"Oooh, whooo . . ."*

Eddie is always trying to make me laugh. Sometimes I do, but it's not easy. His jokes can be pretty awful at times.

"Just let me know when it's time to set the table," I told him.

I walked up the stairs to my room, and Milkshake and Tiki followed me. Before Mom and I moved in with Eddie and Dan, the room was supposed to be a guest room, but it was mostly filled with boxes of stuff that Dan had when he was a kid. It has weird flowery wallpaper, like something you'd find in an old lady's house. Eddie keeps saying he'll paint it, but he's always busy. So is Mom. Between getting ready for the wedding and starting her new business, she doesn't have a lot of extra time.

So for now, I'm stuck with the room with the weird wallpaper. My room at my dad's apartment is much more me. We decorated it with a Parisian Chic theme. The walls are pale pink with black-and-white accents. My headboard is this twisted flowery iron, and my bedspread and pillows have a cool black-and-white pattern on them. I have a really pretty white vanity where I can keep all my hair stuff, and I can actually sit down to do my hair in the morning. One day I can put makeup in there . . . if my mom ever lets me wear anything other than lip gloss.

In *this* room the bed has a green quilt and the curtains are blue and they don't match at all. My old quilt doesn't fit because this bed is big—a double bed—which is nice, but the quilt is ugly. There's no vanity, but there's an old wooden dresser, which is *brown*, and a desk for my computer and a small table for my sewing machine in the corner. My table with my sewing machine on it is the only piece of furniture from my mom's old apartment. Since everything is so much bigger at Eddie's house, Mom said it was a perfect chance for us to leave my old furniture behind and update and redo my bedroom. Which she promises to do soon. But until that happens, I've just been covering up the wallpaper with fashion spreads that I tear out of my favorite magazines. It's not great, but at least it covers up most of those ugly flowers.

The one good thing about this room, though, is the closet—it's three times the size of my closet in New York. Which is good, because I keep most of my clothes at this house anyway.

The way my room is decorated isn't the only thing I don't like about it. The other bad thing is that it's next to Dan's room. And Dan loves heavy metal music—the loud kind, where the lead singer screams like there's a fire or something. He listens to it all the time.

Like right now. The loud music (if you can call it music) blared from behind Dan's door, shaking the walls and the floor. All I wanted to do was call Ava, but I'd never be able to hear her on the line.

I knocked on Dan's door. "Dan, can you turn it down, please?"

It was no use. He couldn't hear me. So I went into my room, sat on my bed, and stuck in my ear-buds. I pressed play on my iPod, and a song by my favorite singer filled my ears—but I swear I could still see the walls shaking.

Tiki and Milkshake curled up in the purple dog bed I keep for them in my room. Then I texted Ava.

FabMia: Miss you! How's ur Monday going?
Avaroni: Not good. U know those boots I got last week? The heel fell off rite in the middle of school! I almost fell.
FabMia: Oh no! U okay?
Avaroni: :(I hate Mondays!
FabMia: Me 2!
Avaroni: Hey, gotta go. Me n Delia r going to that xhibit at the Met.
FabMia: Jealous!
Avaroni: Peace out.
FabMia: Talk soon. Bye.

I clicked off the phone with a frown. I was happy for Ava, but I was jealous too. If I were still living in Manhattan, I would be going to that exhibit. I didn't even know who Delia was, either. I think Ava told me she met her in French class or something.

So . . . no Mom. No Ava. And mystery meat loaf

in my near future. I couldn't wait until Monday was over.

I took off my shoes and searched for my sketchbook, which I found under a pillow at the foot of my bed. I opened it up and started to sketch an idea for a dress I'd been thinking about. As I moved the pencil across the page, I didn't notice the shaking walls or the mysterious smell of meat loaf wafting up the stairs.

That's how it always feels when I sketch. The whole world melts away. And that is a nice feeling, especially on a Monday.

CHAPTER 3

We're in Business!

For the record, let me just say that "mystery meat loaf" probably got its name because it's a mystery why anyone would eat it. But I didn't want to hurt Eddie's feelings, so I didn't tell him that. Instead I managed to sneak most of it to Tiki and Milkshake, who always hang out under the table while we're eating, hoping to get some scraps.

Thankfully that was the last annoying thing that happened on Monday. And the next day, Tuesday, was much better, of course.

To start with, even though Mom got home late, she still packed me a lunch, and I didn't forget it this time. My mom made my favorite: a turkey and Brie wrap with a side of red grapes. Yum!

While we were eating, Alexis started talking

about the school fund-raiser. People were still talking about it.

"You won't believe what just happened in French class," she said, sticking a fork into her spaghetti. "Before class, Mademoiselle Girard came up to me and congratulated me on the Cupcake Club winning the contest. Sydney was standing right there, and she gave me *such* a nasty look!"

"I kind of feel bad for them," said Katie. "I know they worked really hard on that makeover booth."

"It's a shame that their makeovers were so terrible," I added. "Remember when Sophie showed us what Bella had done to her? She had on so much white makeup that she looked like a clown."

Alexis shrugged. "Well, I think their problem was that they didn't work out the numbers first. Each makeover must have cost five dollars if you add up all the makeup they bought, but took twenty minutes to finish. That's only fifteen dollars an hour. But our cupcakes cost two dollars each, and we could sell one every minute. Do the math."

"Do I have to?" Katie groaned.

I've never known anybody who loves numbers as much as Alexis. It's probably because her parents are accountants. Actually, that's something we have in common, in a way. My mom works in fashion, and

I love fashion. I wondered if I would be like Alexis if my mom had been an accountant. . . .

"I hope the girls in the PGC don't feel too bad," Katie said, and I knew she was thinking about Callie. "At least they tried."

While we were talking, Ms. Biddle came up to our table. She teaches science, and we all agree that she's the best teacher in our grade. She's really funny, and she has cool blond hair that she spikes up with gel. Every day she wears a different science T-shirt. See? Her clothes tell me she likes science! Today she was wearing a shirt with the periodic table of the elements on it.

"Hey there," she said. "Do you young entrepreneurs mind if I talk to you for a minute?"

I know what "entrepreneur" means because my mom is one. It's somebody who starts their own business.

"Sure," Katie said.

Ms. Biddle slid into the empty chair at the end of the table. "Next Saturday—not this one, but the next one—I have to throw a baby shower for my sister. She loves cupcakes. And I have never made a cupcake in my life that wasn't burnt or dry as toast. So I was wondering if the Cupcake Club would like the job."

"We would love it!" Katie said quickly. "I mean, if everyone agrees."

"Isn't baking cupcakes just like chemistry?" Alexis asked. "I thought you'd be good at making cupcakes."

"You're right," Ms. Biddle admitted. "Baking is a lot like science. It's a total embarrassment. I can make anything in a science lab, but put me in a kitchen and I lose all of my mojo."

"We should definitely do it," I said.

"I think so too," Emma chimed in.

Alexis took a small notebook out of her backpack. "Can you please give us the details? Time? Place? Number of cupcakes?"

Ms. Biddle gave Alexis the address. "I think four dozen should do it. How much do you charge?"

"Two dollars per cupcake is our normal price," Alexis answered. "But you qualify for the teacher discount. That's half price at one dollar each."

"Perfect!" Ms. Biddle said with a grin. She stood up to leave.

"One more thing," I said. Alexis is good with numbers, but she'd forgotten the most important detail. "What kind of cupcake do you want? And do you want any special colors?"

"We don't know yet if the baby is a boy or girl, so

the decorations are going to be yellow and green. I guess the cupcakes should match," said Ms. Biddle. "But you can make any flavor you want, as long as it's delicious."

"They will be!" Katie promised. "Thanks so much."

After Ms. Biddle walked away, Katie let out a happy squeal.

"This is amazing!" Katie said. "Our first paying job!"

"Don't forget we're doing the PTA luncheon in the spring too," Emma added.

"This will be good practice," I pointed out.

"I hope you don't mind me offering the teacher discount," Alexis said. "I thought it might help us drum up more business."

"No, that was a good idea," Katie told her.

"And it's a nice thing to do for teachers," Emma added.

Alexis tapped her pencil on her notebook page. "We should still be able to make a nice profit. I'm still working out how much it costs per cupcake. Our parents donated the ingredients for the fund-raiser, but we'll have to start paying for our own now."

"How will we buy the ingredients if we don't

have any money to start with?" Emma wondered.

"Maybe my mom could lend it to us," Katie suggested. She always has good ideas for how to solve problems. "Then we could pay her back when Ms. Biddle pays us."

"That could work," Alexis agreed.

I had been thinking about what Alexis said about profit. I was excited because making cupcakes is fun, but the idea of making some extra money was pretty nice. I could finally buy that great pair of jeans that Mom said were too expensive.

"So what will we do with our profits?" I asked, thinking about how those jeans would look really good with my favorite shirt.

"We should probably save some to make more cupcakes, and then divide up the rest," Alexis replied. "But we should talk about it."

"Can we have a meeting tomorrow?" Katie asked.

"Good idea," I said. "Maybe we could meet at the food court at the mall. Then we could go window-shopping afterward."

I'll find any excuse to go to the mall. It makes living in the suburbs a lot more bearable.

But Alexis wrinkled her nose. "The food court is too noisy for a meeting, don't you think?"

"Why don't we meet at my house? We haven't met at my house in a long time," Emma said.

Alexis rolled her eyes. "Your little brother is *way* noisier than the mall."

"No, let's go to Emma's!" Katie said.

I was disappointed we weren't going to the mall, but I was out-voted.

"Cool," I said.

Katie turned to me. "Joanne's picking me up tomorrow. I'll ask my mom if she can take us to Emma's house."

"Sounds good," I said. I was feeling pretty excited about the whole thing.

The Cupcake Club makes living out here a whole lot easier.

CHAPTER 4

Emma's House

After school the next day I met Katie on the school steps. Park Street Middle School is a big concrete building with two sports fields in the back, a little kids' park on one side, and trees on the other side. There's a big, round driveway in front where the school buses line up. If someone is picking you up in a car, you have to follow the sidewalk down to the street.

"I think I see Joanne," Katie said, pointing to a shiny red car.

Katie's mom is a dentist, and Joanne works in the office there. Most days, Joanne picks up Katie from school and brings her back to the dentist's office until Mrs. Brown gets off work. Katie's mom is really nice, but she's really overprotective, too.

"I'm so glad we have a meeting today," Katie told

me as we walked. "Otherwise I'd be stuck in a dentist's office."

"That does sound really boring," I admitted.

"It is," Katie said. "But you know what I hate the most? That dentist's office smell. I don't think I'll ever get used to it."

"I know what you mean," I told her. "Every time I smell it, it reminds me of that time I got my cavity filled. That was seriously painful!"

"You should go to my mom," Katie said. "Her patients all say it hardly hurts at all when she works on them. Although you should hear her lecture about the importance of flossing. Now *that's* painful."

Joanne stuck her head out of the car window when she saw us approach. "Hey, girlfriends! How are you doing today?"

"Good," Katie and I answered at the same time.

We got into the backseat together. Joanne's red car is really sporty, and she always plays good music. It's much better than taking the bus.

"So what's going on at Emma's today?" Joanne asked.

"A Cupcake Club meeting," Katie replied. "We got hired by Ms. Biddle to bake cupcakes."

"Is that the cool science teacher you told me about?" Joanne asked.

Katie nodded. "Yeah, she's really nice."

Joanne sighed. "I wish I was going to a cupcake meeting. Instead, I've got to go back to the office and try to explain to Mr. Michaels why he can't put his false teeth in the dishwasher."

Katie and I giggled. Then Joanne pulled up in front of Emma's house. "Have fun," she said. "Katie, your mom will get you on her way home."

Katie and I thanked Joanne and walked up to Emma's front door. She lives in a two-story white house with a porch that wraps all the way around it. It's a really pretty house, except for the big pile of sports equipment in the driveway. There were bats and gloves and basketballs, even a lacrosse stick. There's also a basketball hoop in the driveway, and Emma's two older brothers, Matt and Sam, were shooting baskets with their friends.

The ball bounced on the walkway in front of us, and Sam, who's a junior, ran up to get it.

He stopped when he saw me. "Hey, aren't you Dan's little sister?"

"I'm going to be his *step*sister," I replied. Katie kind of gave me a look. But I wasn't really Dan's sister. Or Dan's *real* sister. I don't know, it's all confusing. It was a lot simpler when I was an only child.

"Yo, Sam! Over here!" one of the boys called.

Sam ran off without another word. Then Emma opened the front door.

"Come on in. Alexis has us set up in the kitchen," she said with a smile.

We walked through the living room, stepping over a giant city of blocks surrounded by plastic dinosaurs. Emma's little brother, Jake, was standing in front of the TV, watching a cartoon. I think he's completely adorable.

Emma turned off the TV. "Jake, come into the kitchen with us."

Jake frowned. "I wanna watch TV!"

Jake is completely adorable—when he's not crying and whining. Emma says that happens a lot, but he'll grow out of it.

Emma gave us an apologetic look. "Mom's at work," she explained. "She'll be back soon. I said I didn't mind watching him since we're not baking today. He'll be good."

"I wanna watch TV!" Jake demanded.

Emma took his hand. "Later, Jake. We're going to color now."

That seemed to satisfy him. Emma led us all into the kitchen, where Alexis had a bunch of papers spread out on the table.

"Hey," she said. "So I've worked out how much

it will cost us to make each cupcake if we use basic ingredients. We need to figure out what we're making in case we need to add other stuff."

That's Alexis for you. She loves to get right down to business. We all sat down at the table, and Emma sat next to Jake. She gave him a banana and opened up his dinosaur coloring book.

"I was thinking about that," Katie said. "Ms. Biddle said the decorations will be yellow and green. So maybe the cupcake flavor could sort of match. You know, like a banana or a lemon cupcake."

I glanced over at Jake. Gooey banana was smeared on his face. At that moment the thought of eating a banana cupcake didn't sound too appetizing.

"How about lemon?" I asked. "Lemon is nice."

Alexis started writing in her notebook. "I'll have to check on the price of lemons and add that to our cost. How many will we need, Katie?"

Katie shrugged. "I'll have to look at the recipe."

"And what about the icing?" Alexis asked. "Should we make the icing green and yellow too?"

"I don't know about the green," Katie said thoughtfully. "It's a fun color for Easter, or to make monster cupcakes. But it might not be good for a baby shower."

"Yellow is pretty," Emma said.

Jake tugged on her shirt. "Color with me!"

"Sorry he's so loud," Emma said apologetically, and she picked up a crayon to color with her brother.

"Hey, he's way quieter than Dan, and Dan is sixteen," I said.

"Thanks," Emma said with a smile. "I sometimes feel like an alien or something around all these boys. Like I never fit in . . ."

"Tell me about it," I said. "Living with boys is hard!"

Katie shrugged; she was an only child. And Alexis had an older sister who had really nice clothes, so that had to be good for her.

"It's not easy," said Emma. She smiled at me. Maybe Emma could help me learn to deal with Dan.

"So, I googled baby shower themes last night," I said, pulling out pictures from my backpack. "I printed out some pictures."

I put my favorite picture on the table. It showed a green and yellow baby shower. Everything was set up on a white table sprinkled with real yellow flowers. There were no cupcakes, but in the center was a white layer cake decorated with yellow flowers and green leaves.

"Ooh, that's so pretty!" Emma said, and Alexis and Katie nodded in agreement.

"So maybe we could use white icing, and decorate it with flowers and leaves on top," I suggested.

Katie looked closely at the picture. "Cream cheese icing would be nice with the lemon. But how would we make the flowers?"

"I did some research," I said. Decorating the cupcakes is my favorite part. "There are so many amazing websites that sell cupcake decorations. I saw some pretty flower molds. You melt chocolate in any color you want, and then you get a little candy flower. Or we could get flowers made out of sparkly sugar. Those could be pretty."

Jake put down his crayon. "I want a cupcake!" he cried. Emma ignored him and kept coloring.

"Mia, you can be in charge of the flowers," Alexis said. "And Katie, can you shop for the ingredients? Your mom's going to lend us the money, right?"

Katie nodded. "She said it's no problem. She said it's okay to bake at our house, too, if we want. We should probably do it next Friday night so the cupcakes are fresh on Saturday."

"We could bake at my house this time if you want," I suggested. "We have one of those double ovens in our kitchen. We might be able to fit all four cupcake pans in at once. Then it won't take so long."

"Awesome!" Katie said.

"Mia, will you be home next Friday, or will you be at your dad's?" Alexis asked.

"I'm going to my dad's this weekend," I replied, "so I'll be here." I thought about it for a second; yep, that was right. Sometimes even I can't keep track of my own schedule.

Katie got a weird look on her face. She always does whenever I mention I'm seeing my dad. I know her parents are divorced, because Alexis told me once. But Katie never gets to see her dad like I do, though I'm not sure why. When I heard that, I tried to imagine what it would feel like if I didn't get to see my dad every other weekend. It'd really hurt.

"It looks like we have a plan, then," Alexis said, scribbling some more in her notebook.

Then a squishy piece of banana flew through the air. It landed right on the notebook page!

"Jake!" Emma scolded.

"Sorry, Lexi," Jake apologized. "It's slippery!"

Everyone laughed—even Alexis. I told you that kid was cute!

CHAPTER 5

A Surprise at the Mall

We hung out at Emma's house for a little while, playing dinosaurs with Jake. Then I got a text from my mom.

Be there in 5. Ready for a girls' night out?

I texted back.

Always ready.

Whenever we can, my mom and I go out to dinner—just the *two* of us. Eddie and Dan do not get to come. Tonight Mom suggested we go to the mall and then eat at the Italian restaurant there. Of course, I was happy to agree.

Mom texted me when she pulled up out front,

and I said good-bye to Emma, Katie, and Alexis. Then I ran outside and climbed into the front seat.

"It smells good in here," I said.

"New perfume," Mom told me. "One of my clients gave it to me. It's called Blue Mystery. What do you think?"

"It smells better than Eddie's mystery meat loaf," I replied.

"Oh, no. Did he make that for you Monday night?"

I nodded.

"Then you definitely deserve dinner out tonight," Mom said. "You poor thing!"

I can't figure Mom out sometimes. She agrees with me that Eddie's cooking is sometimes terrible, and so are his jokes. But she still wants to marry him. *What's up with that?* I mean, she could have stayed with my dad, who tells good jokes and makes really good chicken in tomato sauce.

When we got to the Westgrove Mall, Mom looked at her watch. "We have an hour until dinner," she said. "I was thinking we could stop in the candle shop first."

"Seriously?" I asked. "Mom, you have every flavor of candle that place makes."

"You mean scent, not flavor," Mom corrected

me. "And you're wrong. They just released their Midnight Jasmine collection."

I sighed. "Do we have to? All those *scents* make me dizzy."

"Isn't that clothing store you like a few doors down?" Mom asked. "Why don't you go there, and I'll catch up with you."

"Yes!" I cheered.

We rode the escalator up to the second floor. Katie says the mall is like a big maze, but it didn't take me long to figure out how to get around. My favorite clothing store, Icon, is three doors down from the candle shop, right between the Japanese pottery shop and the place that sells skater clothes.

My mom dropped me off by the entrance, and I walked inside. Before I got a chance to look around, I heard a familiar voice.

"Oh my gosh, oh my gosh, oh my gosh, this sweater is soooooooo cute!"

It was Maggie Rodriguez, one of the girls in the Popular Girls Club. I don't know Maggie that well, but it's easy to see that she has *a lot* of energy. She's always rushing around the hallways, late for class, and her frizzy brown hair is always flying around her face.

Maggie was holding up a really cute sweater. It was red, but not a bright red, more like a muted red, which was really nice. There were white designs on it, so it looked kind of like a ski sweater, but it wasn't big and bulky, like a sweatshirt. Plus it had a cool zipper down the front.

She was showing the sweater to Bella, another girl in the PGC. Bella is into the whole vampire thing. I think she uses a straightener on her auburn hair, and she wears pale makeup and a lot of dark colors. Katie told me her name used to be Brenda, but she changed it to Bella like the girl in that vampire movie. I think she made a good choice—Bella is a great name.

I walked up to them. "Hey, that's a really cute sweater," I said.

Maggie whirled around. "Isn't it? I can't believe they have the winter clothes out now. I haven't even started planning my winter wardrobe yet. This is terrible! I have to start, like, right now!"

Callie stepped out from behind a clothing rack. "Calm down, Maggie. There's plenty of time," she said with a smile.

Now I could see that Sydney was nearby, looking through the jeans stacked against the wall. It's hard to miss Sydney—she's tall, has blond hair that's perfectly straight and glossy, and teeth so sparkling white, she could star in a toothpaste commercial.

She must have seen me, too, but she didn't say anything just then.

"Where'd you find the sweater?" I asked Maggie. "That would look so good with these jeans I'm dying to get."

"Over here," Maggie said, rushing off. I followed her, and Bella and Callie came with us.

"Does it come in black?" Bella asked.

"I think so," Maggie said.

I pulled one of the sweaters off of the rack and held it up to me. "So cute," I said. "Last week I saw a spread in *Teen Style* that had tons of sweaters like this. It's the must-have for winter. They showed how you can wear it all these different ways, like even with flowy skirts. It was really amazing."

"I saw that too." It was Sydney. "With big furry boots, right?"

I nodded. "Yeah, that's the one!"

"It looked really great!" said Sydney. "Only the furry boots looked a little like a big gorilla or something."

I laughed. "They totally did!"

Maggie whipped out her smart phone and started frantically searching for the article online. "Seriously! Nobody tells me anything!"

"I saw some layered skirts back there," Callie said.

"Thanks," I told her. "I have got to check this out."

I grabbed the sweater and headed to the back of the room to find a skirt that would match.

Maggie started freaking out. "Oh wow, that is so supercute! You have to try it on!"

I didn't argue. I went into a dressing room and started trying on the outfit. As I was zipping up the sweater, it hit me.

I was having fun—with the Popular Girls Club!

Back in Manhattan, Ava and I would go into stores and try on clothes all the time. We didn't always buy something, but it was just fun to try on different styles. Sometimes we went into really fancy stores for inspiration. We would look at the displays and see what different designers were doing for each season. Then we'd go home and try to figure out how we could create the same look with the stuff we already had. Some of the stuff we came up with was pretty crazy and looked ridiculous, but sometimes we came up with something really cool.

I stepped out of the dressing room with the outfit on.

"What do you think?" I asked.

"I really like it," Callie said.

"It looks just like the magazine," Sydney said. "Without the gorilla part."

Bella nodded. "Just like the magazine," she echoed.

That's when my mom walked in, carrying a bag from the candle shop.

"Nice outfit," she said.

"Mom, this is Callie, Sydney, Maggie, and Bella," I said.

"Nice to meet you," Mom said.

Maggie ran over to Mom's bag and started sniffing the air. "Is that the new Midnight Jasmine collection? I have been dying to smell that."

"I'd better go change," I said. "Mom, isn't this the *perfect* outfit for winter?"

Okay, so I was hinting big-time. Mom doesn't always give in. But it was worth a try.

"Hmm, I saw something like that recently in a Damien Francis show," Mom said. "I wonder if I could get some samples from him. He owes me one. Who knows, maybe he has your size?" she said with a wink.

In the fashion industry, designers make samples of their clothes that they can show to shoppers for the big stores that want to buy them. Sometimes they sell them really cheap at things called sample sales, and sometimes they give them to friends—like my mom. Okay, so it wasn't a total yes or definite about the outfit, but I'll take it!

"No way. You know Damien Francis?" Maggie asked.

"He's an old friend of mine. I've worked with him a lot," Mom replied.

"That is sooo completely awesome!" Maggie gushed.

"When you worked at *Flair*?" Callie asked. I was kind of surprised she remembered.

"Yep," said Mom. "But I work with him a lot now that I'm a stylist, too."

Sydney didn't say anything, but I could tell from the look on her face that she was impressed. I was impressed too. Sometimes I forget that my mom knows famous designers.

"Okay, Mia," said Mom. "It's time for dinner."

I quickly got changed. When I got out, the PGC girls were still looking at clothes.

"See you around," I said, waving good-bye.

Mom and I left, and I felt a tiny bit guilty for having fun with Sydney and the girls from the PGC. I knew Katie, Alexis, and probably even Emma would think it was weird. But why should that matter? I could be friends with anyone I wanted to, *couldn't I*? It was all pretty confusing.

CHAPTER 6

The Same, Only Different

The next day at lunch, I didn't mention to Katie, Alexis, and Emma that I had run into the PGC girls at the mall. It wasn't like I was hiding anything. I just didn't want to make a big deal out of it.

Other than that, Thursday and Friday went by seriously slow, maybe because I knew that I'd be seeing my dad on Friday. I couldn't wait, and when I'm really excited about something, it feels like it takes forever to happen.

My mom picked me up at school and drove me to the train station. She always insists on parking the car and waiting with me on the platform until the train comes.

"Mom, I know how to get on a train," I told her. I say the same thing every time.

"Of course you do," Mom replied. "But I'm your mom, and I get to stay with you if I want to. That's one of the perks."

With a loud roar, the big silver commuter train came to a stop in front of us. I hoisted my purple duffel bag over my shoulder, and Mom gave me a huge hug and a kiss.

"Be good," she said. "Call me if you need me. I'll see you Sunday."

I climbed onto the train. The nice thing about being so far from the city is that I can always get a seat. The closer you get to Manhattan, the more crowded the train gets.

I found a window seat in the middle of the car and settled in, with my duffel bag across my lap. I waited until the conductor came and took my ticket, and then I got out my sketchbook and pushed in my earbuds. I listened to music and sketched for a while, but pretty soon I put down my pencil and just looked out the window. There are a lot of stops between my town and Manhattan, and sometimes I feel like I'll never get there.

It wasn't always this way. When my parents got divorced four years ago, their lawyers suggested they go to a judge to figure out who I would live with. They said it was the fairest way to decide. The judge said I should live with my mom full time and my dad every other weekend.

But when I lived in Manhattan, I saw my dad a lot more than that. I could always hop on a bus or a taxi and be at his apartment in less than twenty minutes. My mom used to work late at the magazine a lot, so I ended up hanging out with my dad a few nights a week.

That all changed in June when we moved in with Eddie and Dan. I hardly ever see my dad during the week anymore. The weekends I spend with him fly by. It just doesn't seem fair.

When the train finally pulled into Grand Central Station, I made sure to put my sketchbook back in my bag (I left one on the train once, which was seriously depressing) and made my way down the crowded car to the exit.

Dad was waiting for me on the platform, as usual. I ran up to him and gave him a big hug.

"Hey there, *mija!*" Dad said. (In case you didn't know, *mija* means "my daughter" in Spanish, and it's pronounced MEE-ha. Which is actually how I got my nickname, Mia. My full name is Amelia. But Dad kept saying *mija*, and Mom joked that it sounded like he was saying "Mia." And then Mia just stuck.)

"Hey," I said. "Where are we going for dinner tonight?"

"Hmm, I don't know," Dad said. "I was thinking . . . sushi?"

I smiled. Dad and I always have sushi on Friday nights. It's a good thing we both love it. So we made our way outside and took a cab to our favorite downtown sushi restaurant, Tokyo 16.

I love the taste of sushi—the cool fish, the salty seaweed, the dark taste of the soy sauce, and the spiciness of green wasabi paste, all in one bite. The other thing I like about sushi is that sushi restaurants are always beautiful. When you walk into Tokyo 16, the sounds of the city melt away behind you. There's a waterfall running on the back wall and the sound is very soothing. I love the shiny black chopsticks and the adorable tiny bowls that hold the soy sauce.

"So you and your friends won that contest last week," Dad said as we dug into our sushi rolls. "I'm really proud of you."

"Thanks," I replied. I dunked a roll of tuna and avocado wrapped in rice into the soy sauce. "We actually made two hundred cupcakes! I've never made that many cupcakes in my life."

"I bet they were really delicious," Dad said.

"You'll have to bring me one sometime."

I nodded yes because my mouth was full of sushi.

"I'm glad you're making new friends," Dad went on. "What are their names again?"

"Katie, Alexis, and Emma," I replied. "They're all nice." I thought about telling him about the PGC, but it was all kind of new.

"That reminds me," I said. "Ava invited me to her soccer game tomorrow morning and then out for pizza for lunch. Can I go?"

Dad made a pretend sad face. "You mean you don't want to spend all day with your dad?"

"You can pick me up in the afternoon," I told him. "Then we can do something."

"Actually, I made plans for us," Dad said. "My friend Alina is having an art opening. I think it would be fun to go."

I frowned. "Alina? Who is Alina?"

Dad cleared his throat. "We've been dating. She's really nice. You two are a lot alike. She's an amazing artist. It'll be fun."

I popped another piece of sushi into my mouth so I wouldn't have to say anything just yet. Dad had never talked to me about any of the women he dated before. Why was Alina different?

"It's our weekend together," I said. "Can't you

see her art show some other time?" I know I just told him that I was spending time with Ava, but that was different.

"It's opening night," Dad explained. "It's a big deal. There will be food and music and everything. You'll like it, I promise."

"Okay," I agreed. An art show sounded like fun, and Dad seemed really excited.

That night Dad and I watched a movie together before we went to sleep. The next morning, he took the subway with me to Ava's soccer game. He dropped me off with a wave, and I ran to meet Ava and her mom over by the bleachers. Ava was wearing a red and white soccer uniform with her team name, The Soho Slammers. Her straight dark hair was pulled back in a ponytail. Her mom was a few inches taller than Ava. She wore white leggings and a red T-shirt to match Ava's team colors.

"Mia, you are growing so big!" Mrs. Monroe said, hugging me. "What are they feeding you out in the suburbs?"

"Mystery meat loaf," I replied, and Ava burst into giggles.

"This is going to be an awesome game," Ava promised. "We're playing the girls from Riverside. Remember last year, we tied them?"

I nodded. Ava and I had played on the same soccer team since we were six years old. "You think you can beat them this year?"

Ava grinned. "I know we can!"

Ava's coach blew a whistle, and Ava ran off to join her team. I climbed up onto the bleachers with Mrs. Monroe.

It felt weird, sitting in the bleachers instead of being on the field. A big part of me really wished I was out there playing. But I couldn't because I didn't live in Manhattan anymore. I couldn't even play soccer in my new town, because I would have to miss every other game. It wasn't fair, but there was nothing I could do about it.

Mrs. Monroe and I cheered for the Slammers. Ava was right—it was an exciting game, and in the end, the Slammers won 3–2. We all went out for pizza after that, and I was with all my old friends again: Ava, Jenny with freckles, Tamisha, Madeline.

"Mia, we need you back on the team," Tamisha told me. "Nobody can make those long passes like you can."

"I wish," I said. "But you guys don't need me. You did great today."

Everyone let out a whoop. Then the talk turned from the game to gossip.

"Mia doesn't know yet," Ava announced.

"Know what?" I asked.

"Big news," Ava said. "Angelo got caught passing a note in class, and Mr. Tyler, our math teacher, read it out loud. You won't believe what it said!"

Everyone started laughing.

"Tell me! I can't stand the suspense!" I begged.

"It said that he has a crush on Madeline!" Ava shrieked, and everyone started laughing.

Madeline turned bright red. "The whole thing is seriously embarrassing," she said.

I started laughing really hard. Angelo thinks he's supercool. He's been slicking back his hair with gel since fifth grade. Poor Madeline.

I had a lot of fun at lunch. In a way, things were the same as always with me and my friends. But in another way, a big way, they were really different. I didn't get to beat Riverside. I wasn't there when Angelo got caught with the note.

It's a weird feeling—like I'm missing out on half of my life!

CHAPTER 7

The Friendship Police

That afternoon I dumped the contents of my purple duffel bag out on my Parisian Chic bedspread.

"I wish Dad had told me we were going to an art show before I packed," I muttered. He had said it was a big deal, but I didn't bring any "big deal" clothes with me—not even a single skirt. I kept rearranging the clothes I had and trying stuff on. Finally I decided on a pair of black leggings, a long white button-down shirt, and a cropped green cardigan over it.

I looked in the mirror. *Needs some sparkle,* I thought, so I added this cool vintage necklace with a green and blue crystal flower pendant that used to be my mom's.

When I went into the living room, Dad was busy putting on his tie. He looked really nice. My dad is tall, with jet-black hair and wire-rimmed glasses. He was wearing black pants, a black button-down shirt, a black tie, and black shoes. I don't like the all-one-color thing personally, but Dad can make it work.

"You look beautiful, *mija*. I've always loved that necklace," Dad told me. He glanced at his watch. "Let's go catch a cab."

"So what's Alina's art like?" I asked as we rode downtown.

"It's hard to describe. But you'll love it when you see it. I know you will," Dad promised.

The taxi pulled up in front of the gallery, which was on the first floor of a brick building. There were huge glass windows out front so you could see inside.

When Dad and I walked in, the first thing I noticed was the music. At least, I think it was music. It sounded like someone banging a stick against a metal garbage can over and over again while a remote control plane zipped through the air. It wasn't as loud as Dan's heavy metal, but it was just as annoying.

A tall, thin woman with short black hair walked

up to us. She was wearing all black—a sleeveless, short black dress, black tights, and black heels. That's when it hit me—she and Dad were dressed alike! Maybe this dating thing with Alina was more serious than I thought.

Alina gave my dad a hug and a kiss on each cheek.

"Alex! You made it!" Then she smiled and held out her hand to me. "And this must be Mia. I'm Alina. It's nice to meet you."

"Nice to meet you, too," I said, to be polite. Inside, I wasn't sure yet.

"Your father tells me you're an artist," she said.

"Yes, she's always drawing in that sketchbook of hers," Dad said, patting my shoulder.

"Fashion designs, mostly," I told her. "I want to work in the fashion industry someday. Like my mom."

"The worlds of fashion and art are intertwined," Alina said. "Come, let me show you my work."

First she led us to a big white wall. There was a hole in the middle of it.

"I call this piece 'Rage,'" Alina said.

"It looks like someone punched a hole in the wall," I remarked.

"Exactly!" Alina looked really happy. "I encapsulated a moment of sheer rage and froze it in time."

"Hmm" was all I could manage.

But Dad was acting like it was the greatest thing in the world. "Brilliant, Alina. I love it!"

We moved to the next piece, a white canvas with some black blotches on it.

"This one is 'Rage, Part Two,'" Alina explained.

From what I could tell, she had gotten angry and thrown some paint against a canvas. But you won't believe what Dad said about it.

"Fascinating." He adjusted his glasses, like he was trying to see better. "You can feel the anger emanating from the piece."

The rest of the art was just like that. It was all weird, and Dad was acting like it was the best stuff in the world. I didn't say much, because I didn't want to hurt Alina's feelings.

When we were done looking at the art, some guy came up and whispered in Alina's ear.

"Got to go," she said. "A big art buyer walked in the door."

"Let's get some food," Dad suggested.

There was a food table in the back, but all they had were glasses of wine for the adults and some cucumber slices with pink glop on top. I was feeling pretty hungry, and the music was giving me a headache.

"So," Dad asked. "What do you think?"

"It's um, *interesting*," I said, and I realized I sounded like Sydney. "It's not really my style."

"That's art for you," Dad said. "Everyone has an opinion."

Luckily we didn't stay much longer, and Dad took pity on me and we picked up Chinese food on the way home. Later when I was sketching in my room, I started thinking about what Dad had said yesterday.

"You two are a lot alike."

I mean, seriously? First of all, I never wear all black—I leave that to the vampires like Bella. And I would never play music like that, and I *definitely* would not punch a hole in something and call it art. And when I have my first runway show, I plan on having a sushi buffet. Who wants to eat pink glop, anyway?

It was like Dad didn't really know me. The thought bothered me a lot.

As I stared at my pink and black walls, a thought crossed my mind that bothered me even more. When Mom and Eddie decided to get married, we moved in with Eddie. What if Dad and Alina got married? Would we move in with her?

I could just imagine her apartment—bare white

walls, all-black furniture, and that screechy music playing nonstop. I bet there are holes in the walls too.

I sank back into my pillows.

Don't panic, I told myself. *They're only dating.*

But I didn't sleep well that night at all.

Sunday was a pretty normal day with Dad—sleeping late, getting bagels, biking in the park, and Dad making his famous chicken in tomato sauce for a late lunch. Then it was the drive back home and sleep. My same old every-other-Sunday routine.

I woke up the next morning for school feeling really confused. First I was confused as always about where I was, then I kept thinking about Alina and Dad, and missing out on things with my friends from Manhattan. It took me forever to pick out an outfit for school. I kept wondering what an outfit would look like if you felt confused. Mixed patterns—plaid with stripes? I finally settled on some skinny jeans and a T-shirt with a graphic design of New York on it. It wasn't great, but it was the best I could come up with.

I was glad to see Katie on the bus.

"How was your weekend with your dad?" she asked.

"Pretty nice," I said. "Except he has this weird

girlfriend, Alina, who's an artist who punches things."

It felt good to talk about Alina out loud. I hadn't told my mom, of course. But talking to Katie is really easy—I feel like I can tell her anything.

Katie raised an eyebrow. "I hope she doesn't punch people."

"Only walls," I said. "And then she hangs it in a gallery."

"I'm glad my mom doesn't go on dates," Katie said. "That would be totally weird."

"It is totally, seriously weird," I assured her.

Braaaaaaap! Wes Kinney made what was probably his loudest fake burp yet. Katie and I shook our heads. Another Monday had begun.

After homeroom, my first class of the day is math, which is always painful even on non-Mondays. Bella and Callie are in that class too, so I waved when I came in and sat down.

Mrs. Moore hadn't arrived yet, so I took out my sketchbook and began to draw. I had been trying to come up with a sweater/skirt combo like the ones I'd seen in the magazine.

Callie sits behind me, and I noticed her looking over my shoulder. "That's really cute," she said. "I wish I could draw like that."

"You probably can," I told her. "I wasn't very good until I took lessons. Then I learned some ways to do things that I never thought of before."

"Can you show me sometime?" Callie asked.

I was about to answer her, but the bell rang just then. So I waited until after class. Callie and I both have science together second period, so I walked with her down the hallway.

"So Callie, if you want to draw together sometime, just let me know," I said.

"That would be nice," Callie replied. "I should give you my cell phone number. Come see me before you get on the bus and we can exchange, okay?"

"Okay," I said.

That's when I noticed Katie walking toward us. Her class was in the opposite direction.

"Hey!" I said with a wave. Katie waved but had a puzzled look on her face. I didn't understand why until I saw her later at lunch.

"So, what were you and Callie talking about?" Katie asked.

I thought it was kind of a strange question to ask. I mean, I can talk to whomever I want, can't I? For a moment I felt like I was being quizzed by the friendship police.

Then I remembered that Katie and Callie used to be *best* friends. So maybe Katie was just interested.

"Callie liked a drawing I did," I said. I left out the part about us maybe getting together. "I was sketching a sweater and a skirt."

Alexis rolled her eyes. "Is that all those PGC girls think about? Fashion and makeup?" she asked. "What about all of the problems in the world? Don't they know that the rain forest disappears bit by bit every day? And what about all those polar bears up north? All their ice is melting and they have nowhere to live! Doesn't the PGC care about that?"

Emma shook her head. "Alexis, you worry too much."

"You can't be serious *all* the time," I pointed out. "Besides, those PGC girls aren't all that bad."

"That's your opinion," Alexis said. "When I see them do something to help the polar bears, then maybe I'll change my mind."

Katie looked really worried and unhappy. I wasn't sure why. Maybe she was worried about the polar bears too. But I had a feeling that something else was bothering her—me.

CHAPTER 8

Sweet and Sour

The rest of the week was pretty normal, except that I spent every night cleaning the kitchen to get ready for the Cupcake Club meeting on Friday. Mostly it was Dan's mess. He is addicted to tortilla chips and cheese sauce, and so there are always piles of dried-up orange cheese all over the counters and the table. But if you try to talk to him about it, it goes like this:

Me: "Dan, can you please clean up that cheese all over the counter?"

Dan: "You mean that little orange dot?" (He takes a paper towel and moves it once over the cheese.) "Done."

But, of course, the cheese is still there.

I also had to figure out how to do the yellow and

green flowers for the top of each cupcake. I spent some time looking online. There are a lot of cool sites that sell cupcake and baking supplies.

Finally I found a site that sold these beautiful yellow flowers made out of sparkly sugar. Each flower had two little green leaves sticking out of it. They were so pretty! I showed them to Mom, and she ordered four dozen of them for me. She said we could pay her back after Ms. Biddle paid us.

Mom had a meeting in the city on Friday, and Dan had a basketball game, so Eddie got pizza for the two of us. I put Tiki and Milkshake up in my room because they go nuts when a lot of people come to the house.

Katie, Alexis, and Emma all showed up at seven. Emma's mom was standing behind them.

"I'll be back later to pick everyone up," she said. "What time do you think you'll be done?"

Katie spoke up. "If we can bake all four dozen at once, we'll probably be finished by nine," she said.

"Sounds good," Mrs. Taylor said. "I'll see you girls later."

Everyone came inside, and Eddie walked up with a big smile on his face.

"So, what kind of cupcakes are we making tonight?" he asked.

"*We* are making lemon cupcakes with cream cheese icing," I told him.

Eddie made a goofy frown. "Aw, don't I get to help?"

"You can be the official oven-turner-onner," Katie suggested.

"I can do that," Eddie said. "I'm an expert at that."

"We'll call you when we need you," I said. Then I nodded to my friends. "Follow me."

"Your stepdad is really funny," Emma remarked once we got inside the kitchen.

"*Almost* stepdad," I corrected her. "And you wouldn't say that if you spent more time with him. Most of his jokes are awful."

"Yeah, my dad thinks he's much funnier than he really is too," Emma said. "But I'd rather have that than some grumpy old dad."

Hmm, Emma had a point. I'd take Eddie's humor over Alina's anger issues any day!

Katie put the shopping bag she was carrying on the kitchen table, and Alexis took out her notebook.

"If we divide the tasks, we can get things done faster," she said. "Katie, since you're the best baker you can start mixing together the cupcake batter.

I'll squeeze the lemons for you. Emma, you can make the frosting. And Mia, you can work on the decorations for the cupcakes."

"It's going to be easy this time," I told her. I picked up the package of sugar flowers on the counter. "We just need to stick one on each cupcake, see?"

"Ooh, they're so pretty!" Emma said.

"Ms. Biddle's going to love them," Katie added.

"Okay, good," Alexis said. "Then Mia, you can help Katie with the batter. That should cover everything."

"Not everything," I said. I unclipped my iPod from the waistband of my skirt and plugged it into the player on the kitchen table. "We need some music."

I always work better with music in the background (unless it's Dan's heavy metal music), and pretty soon we were dancing around the kitchen as we worked. Katie and I measured out the flour, baking powder, and salt, and sifted them together. Then we melted some butter and put that in a bowl. We added some eggs, sugar, and vanilla. Alexis gave us a measuring cup with fresh lemon juice inside, and we dumped that into the rest of the wet ingredients. After we mixed those together, we slowly started adding the flour mixture. After doing two hundred cupcakes for the fund-raiser, we knew the steps pretty much by heart.

"Eddie! It's time to turn on the oven!" I called out.

Eddie came running into the kitchen like a football player running onto the field from the sidelines. "Okay, what temperature do we need?" he asked.

"Three hundred and fifty, please," Katie told him.

While the oven was heating up, we used an ice cream scoop to plop some batter into the lined cupcake pans. Katie had picked out yellow cupcake liners to match the flower on top. The batter was a pretty yellow color too.

"These are going to look so nice," Emma said as we slipped them into the oven.

I nodded. "Wait until we put the flowers and icing on top."

We set the timer for twenty minutes. That's one of the great things about cupcakes—they don't take long to cook. While the cupcakes baked, I washed the bowls we'd just used, and Katie dried them. Alexis took a spoon and took a taste of Emma's cream cheese frosting.

"Mmm, that is sooo good," she said. "It's going to go great with the lemon."

The timer buzzed, and Eddie came running into the kitchen.

"Better leave this to me, ladies," he said. "Hot stuff coming out!"

I rolled my eyes at Katie, and she smiled back. I knew she could appreciate how corny Eddie can be—she always says how corny her mom can be too.

Eddie removed the pans from the oven, and we showed him how to carefully tip over the pans onto the cooling racks. The cupcakes looked golden yellow and perfect, and they smelled super lemony.

We sat and talked while the cupcakes cooled off. Then I heard the front door bang shut. Dan was back.

"What's that smell?" he asked, walking into the kitchen. He was wearing his red and white basketball uniform, and he was pretty sweaty.

"Please do not get sweat on the cupcakes," I told him, and I heard Emma giggle behind me.

Dan ignored me. "I am so hungry. Mind if I take one?"

But he didn't wait for an answer. He just picked one up, broke it in half, and stuffed it in his mouth.

"Dan!" I shrieked. "Those are for a baby shower tomorrow. We're being *paid* to make those!"

Katie, Alexis, and Emma all looked as horrified as I felt.

"Maybe it's not so bad," Emma said. "We're only one short."

Then Dan made a face. "Whoa, what kind of cupcakes are these? They're supersour!"

"They're lemon cupcakes," Katie said. "They should taste like lemon, but also be sweet."

Dan handed the uneaten half of his cupcake back to me. "I don't know. It doesn't taste sweet to me."

"You just don't know a good cupcake when you taste one," I said. I broke off a piece and popped it into my mouth. The sour taste of lemon stung my tongue.

"Uh-oh," Katie said. "Is he right?"

I nodded. "It's really sour. Not sweet at all."

I handed each girl a piece of cupcake. Each one made a face as she tasted it.

"So, how much lemon did you put in these anyway?" Dan asked.

"I measured it myself," Alexis replied. "One and a half cups, just like the recipe said."

Katie frowned. "One and a half cups? I thought the recipe said one half cup."

"I don't think so. I'm pretty sure it was one and a half cups," Alexis said, but her voice didn't sound so sure.

Katie looked in the recipe book. "Nope. It says

right here, one half cup of lemon juice. That's probably what happened."

Alexis's face turned bright red. "Oh, no! I'm so sorry!"

I felt bad for her. "I should have checked when you handed me the measuring cup," I said. "It's my fault too."

"Looks like you guys need to make some more cupcakes," Dan said.

I looked at the clock. It was already after eight o'clock.

"I'll do it," Alexis said. "I'll stay up all night if I have to, but I'll finish them."

"Of course you won't," Emma said. "We're all in this together."

Katie grinned. "Don't sweat it, Alexis. You've got so many numbers in your brain, you were bound to get them mixed up sometime."

Alexis shook her head. "I still can't believe it. I thought I checked it, like, three times."

"You know, you guys should *thank* me for eating that cupcake," Dan told them. "Otherwise, whoever's paying you would have been pretty disappointed."

I hated to admit it, but Dan was right.

"You can be our official cupcake taster," Katie said.

"I don't know," Dan said. "It could be dangerous."

Everybody laughed. Even though we had to start
from scratch, it wasn't terrible, because we were all
in it together, just like Emma said.

And that, unlike our cupcakes, was pretty sweet.

CHAPTER 9

Sadness at the Smoothie Shop

It was a night that would go down in cupcake history. First Katie, Alexis, and Emma had to call home to make sure they could stay late. Then we had to get to work on making the cupcakes from scratch again.

This time, we all watched closely as Katie measured each ingredient. After Alexis squeezed more lemons, she took the measuring cup to each of us to check it. It was exactly one half cup.

"Alexis, your flair for perfection has returned," Katie kidded her.

We filled the cupcake tins, stretching out the batter just a little bit so that we had two extra cupcakes with which we could do a taste test. Mom walked in just as we were putting the second batch in the oven. Even though she looked a little tired, she still looked fabulous. She wore a ruffled ivory shirt with sleek trousers, a gold necklace and bangle bracelets, and, of course, her favorite black high heels.

"Eddie says you had a cupcake emergency," she said. "Anything I can do to help?"

"We've got it under control," I told her. "When the cupcakes are done, we'll wait until they cool, then ice them and decorate them."

I noticed that Alexis was standing six inches from the oven, staring through the glass window that showed the cupcakes baking inside.

"Alexis, what are you doing?" I asked.

"Making sure they don't burn," she said. "We don't have time to make a new batch if this goes wrong."

"Whoa, I didn't think of that," Katie said. She stood next to Alexis and peered through the window.

"Seriously, you can't look through that thing for twenty minutes, can you?" I asked.

"Oh yes we can," Katie replied.

"Well, I'm going to do the dishes," I replied.

Emma grabbed a dishtowel. "I'll help."

Katie and Alexis stayed glued to the oven until the timer went off. Eddie came in to take them out again.

"You know what they say. Second time's the charm!" he said cheerfully.

"Where's Dan?" Katie asked. "We need our official cupcake taster."

"In the family room, watching TV," Eddie replied.

Katie ran out of the kitchen and came back a minute later, dragging Dan by the arm.

"I don't know if I want this job," he said. "It's risky."

"Very funny," I said. I handed him a cupcake. "Now taste."

Dan took a bite. He made a face, just like before.

"Oh, no!" Alexis wailed. "Is the cupcake sour again?"

We were all staring at him. Even Eddie looked nervous.

Dan smiled. "JK! No. It's good." We all sighed with relief. Dan hung out in the kitchen a little bit watching us with Eddie, but he didn't get in our way. I think it's the first time there were ever that many girls in their kitchen. I wondered if it was a little weird for them.

But we still weren't finished. By the time we let the cupcakes cool, iced them, and added the flowers, it was almost eleven thirty. Yawning, we began to put the cupcakes in the special boxes we had.

Emma's mom walked into the kitchen with my mom. They were both yawning too.

"Are you girls ready to go?" Mrs. Taylor asked.

I snapped the lid on the fourth cupcake box. "All done."

"I'll drive tomorrow," my mom told Emma's mom. "We'll be by to get Emma around eleven."

"I'll be at Emma's house," Alexis said.

"Thanks for letting us use your kitchen, Ms. Vélaz," Katie said.

"No problem," my mom told her. "Now go home and get a good night's sleep!"

The girls left, but I still had one thing to do before I went to bed. I wrote "DO NOT EAT" on a piece of paper and taped it to the cupcake boxes. Dan might have helped us out, but I still didn't trust him.

Luckily, Dan didn't touch the cupcakes, and they were beautiful and perfect when we dropped them off at Ms. Biddle's house the next morning.

I'd never been to a teacher's house before. I was kind of expecting her to live in a mad scientist's lab, with test tubes bubbling over or something. But she lived in a cute little red house with no test tubes in sight. A fat orange cat was lazing in the sunny window when we rang the bell.

Ms. Biddle was happy to see us. She wasn't wearing a crazy science shirt. Instead, she had on a yellow button-down shirt and linen capris. Today Ms. Biddle's outfit said to me that she was happy and calm. Yellow is known to be a very happy color.

"Wow, you guys are professional," she said. "Come on in."

The living room and the dining room were decorated with pale yellow and green streamers and matching balloons. She pointed to a skinny table in the dining room with a pile of yellow plastic plates on it.

"I thought we could put the cupcakes here," she said.

"Perfect!" I said. "We'll set them up so they look nice."

We arranged all of the cupcakes on the yellow plates and lined them up on the table. It all looked really pretty.

"My sister's going to love this," Ms. Biddle said. "Thanks so much."

She held out a white envelope, and Alexis reached for it. "I'll take that," she said. "Thanks a lot."

We waited until we were back outside, and we gave one another a high five.

"We did it!" Katie cheered. "Our first paying job!"

"I'm really proud of all of you," my mom said. "Let's go to Sal's Smoothies. My treat."

Fifteen minutes later we were sitting in a booth at Sal's. It's a fun place, with pink walls and lime green cushions in the booths. We each got a different flavor. Katie got banana berry, Alexis got ginger and peach, Emma got strawberry, and I got mango with passionfruit.

Alexis opened up the envelope and counted out the money. "Forty-eight dollars," she announced. "One dollar per cupcake."

"We still need to pay back my mom," Katie said. She dug into her pocket and handed a crumpled receipt to Alexis. "All the ingredients came to sixteen dollars, but we can use the leftover flour and sugar the next time we bake."

Then I remembered about the sugar flowers. "Mom, do you have the receipt for that?" I asked.

"I think so," Mom replied. She searched through her purse and came up with a piece of white paper. She handed it to Alexis.

Alexis slurped on her smoothie as she studied it. "No way," she said. "Those flowers were seventy-five cents a piece?"

"Um, I guess so," I said. "I thought that was pretty reasonable. Seventy five cents isn't a lot of money."

"But seventy-five cents times forty-eight is thirty-six dollars," Alexis said. "That means we spent fifty-two dollars making these cupcakes—that's four dollars over budget!"

I felt awful. "I'm sorry, really."

"Don't worry about the flowers," Mom said quickly. "Think of it as a donation for your start-up business. We businesswomen need to stick together."

"That's really nice of you," Emma said.

Alexis was shaking her head. "This is why we need to do a budget every time. We can't make mistakes like this."

"It's our first paying job, remember," Katie said. "We're going to make lots of mistakes starting out. Like putting in too much lemon juice."

Alexis blushed. "You're right. I didn't mean to get upset. Thanks, Ms. Vélaz."

"I think we should save the money we made and use it for our next order," Katie said. "Then we won't spend any more than we have."

"That sounds like something Alexis would say," Emma kidded her.

Katie grinned. "What can I say? She must be rubbing off on me."

"I'm sorry, Mia. I didn't mean to make you feel bad," Alexis said.

"It's okay," I said.

After that, nobody talked about the cost of the flowers again. But I still felt really bad. I didn't say much after that, and I didn't even finish my smoothie.

CHAPTER 10

An Invitation

$\mathcal{M}$om, can we go to the mall?" I asked. We had just dropped off the girls and were heading home, but I needed a serious mall experience.

"Why not?" Mom asked. "I need a new charger for my cell phone anyway."

Soon we were walking through the doors of the Westgrove Mall. "Are you going to Icon again?" Mom asked.

"I was thinking Blue Basics," I said. It's a great shop that sells every kind of jeans you can think of, plus classic shirts and sweaters. I love jeans because everything goes with them. Plus I grew, like, a foot over the summer, so all of mine were too short.

Mom must have been reading my mind. "Good

idea. You need some new jeans anyway. I'll meet you there in a little bit. Cell phone on?"

"And charged," I told her.

Mom turned the corner, and I headed to Blue Basics, which is on the first floor. I hadn't gotten far when I saw Sydney, Maggie, Bella, and Callie walking toward me.

"Hi!" I said.

"Wow, I can't believe we ran into you again!" Maggie gushed.

"It's like destiny," Bella said in a serious voice.

"Or maybe it's just that we all like to look at clothes," Callie pointed out.

I smiled. "I don't know. I think fashion is my destiny, sometimes."

"Well of course it is, with a famous mother like that." Maggie brushed a stray lock of frizzy hair out of her face. "It's in your blood."

"She's not famous, exactly," I replied.

"But she knows famous designers!" Maggie said. "I still can't believe she knows Damien Francis. Have you ever been to his house?"

"It's not like that," I tried to explain, but I don't think Maggie was interested in the boring truth. So I changed the subject. "I'm going to Blue Basics. Do you guys want to come?"

"Ooh, the Double B!" Maggie said. "I could use some new jeans."

Then Sydney spoke up for the first time. "We'll go with you," she said, and I got the feeling that the decision was hers to make.

Sydney walked beside me as we made our way to the store. "Maggie can get soooo starstruck," she said. "Once she spent a whole day outside Dave's Pizza in Manhattan because she heard that Justin Bieber liked to eat there when he came to New York."

"That was such a lie!" Maggie said with a pout. "But at least the pizza was really good."

"So, does your mom know any other designers?" Sydney asked casually.

"She knows a lot of them," I said truthfully. "She was in charge of choosing the clothes for the magazine's photo shoots. So any designer who wanted to get into *Flair* had to get friendly with my mom."

"So you must get a lot of free clothing samples, then," she said.

I shrugged. "Sometimes."

"But your mom doesn't work at *Flair* anymore?" Sydney asked.

"No, she started her own consulting business," I replied. "So she's still in fashion."

Sydney was being nice, but I was starting to feel like I was being interviewed or something.

Thankfully, the questions stopped once we got to Blue Basics. We must have spent an hour trying on different pairs of jeans. I was really glad the PGC girls were there because they stopped me from buying a pair of bleached-out jeans that were too "eighties," even for me. I ended up with two pairs of skinny jeans that my mom paid for when she got there.

Before I left, Sydney came up to me. "So, Mia, why don't you eat lunch with us on Monday?"

I hesitated. "Um, I don't know. I have friends that I sit with already."

"Your cupcake crew won't miss you for one day," Sydney said.

"Come on, Mia," Callie urged. "Let us share you with your other friends."

I liked the way Callie put it. I wasn't ditching the Cupcake Club, just sharing my time with other friends I liked. There was nothing wrong with that. It was just one lunch, after all.

"Okay," I said. "I'll see you on Monday."

Mom and I each got a big salad from the make-your-own-salad place on the way out of the mall. When we got home, I was anxious to try on my new jeans and plan some new outfits with them.

"Mom, where's my white button-down shirt?" I asked, after I'd finished petting Milkshake and Tiki.

"I thought I saw it in the laundry basket," Mom replied.

"Oh, right." I headed for the laundry room, which is right next to the kitchen. But the laundry basket was empty.

"Mom! It's empty!" I called out.

Eddie poked his head into the laundry room. "Dan did a wash this morning. Check the dryer."

I opened up the dryer and saw a bunch of colored clothes. I started to panic. Dan wouldn't have put my white shirt in with the colors, would he?

But that's exactly what he did. I pulled out my white button-down shirt, only it wasn't white anymore. Now it was streaked with pink.

"It's ruined!" I wailed.

I stomped into the kitchen where Mom and Eddie were sitting and drinking coffee. "Look at this! It's ruined! It's all Dan's fault!"

Usually I can stay pretty cool when something goes wrong. But for some reason, the ruined shirt was making me furious.

"Calm down," Mom said. "Dan didn't mean to ruin it, Mia."

"I'll buy you another shirt," Eddie added.

"That's not the point!" I fumed. "This *never* happened when it was just you and me, Mom. Why can't things just be the way they were?"

"Oh, Mia," Mom said sadly.

I felt like I was going to cry, so I ran up to my room. Tiki and Milkshake were so scared of me that they hurried out of my path. When I got to my room, I slammed the door shut behind me. Then I flopped onto my bed and put a pillow over my head.

I wished we had never left Manhattan. I wished Mom had never met Eddie. I wished a lot of things were different.

I also knew that my wishes didn't mean anything, and that's what hurt the most.

CHAPTER II

I Finally Get It

A few minutes later, Mom knocked on my door.

"Come in," I said.

I quickly wiped away my tears and sat up as Mom walked in.

"Mia, can we talk?" Mom asked. "I understand that you're upset. Honestly I do. I also know that there's a lot more than a pink shirt that's bothering you."

I nodded. "Living here is hard sometimes."

"I know it's a big change," Mom said. "For all of us, really. But Eddie and I are trying really hard to make it good for you here. And you know I wanted to move away from Manhattan even before I met Eddie. I love Manhattan, but it's too fast there. I needed to slow down, you know?"

I nodded. "I know."

"And I thought you liked Eddie?" Mom asked. "You were the one who told me I should keep dating him."

I realized that was true. When Mom first introduced me to Eddie, I thought he was supernice. He still is.

"I do like him," I said. "But I miss Manhattan. I miss my friends. I miss being close to Dad."

I started to cry again. I couldn't help it. It was like the floodgates had opened and everything kept pouring out.

"I feel like an alien here sometimes. Even my room doesn't feel like me—I mean look at this room!" I said.

Mom was quiet for a minute and looked around my room. It was like she was looking at it for the first time.

"I guess I've been so busy lately I hadn't noticed. I'm sorry," Mom said. "You're right, this room is kind of depressing. Wow, look at that wallpaper. . . . I bet Eddie picked it out."

We both started to laugh. Mom hugged me and we sat there laughing about the room for a bit.

"Here's the thing," she said finally. "I love Eddie, and I think being here is a good place for us. But

I'll do what I can to make things easier, okay? For example, I'll get you your own laundry basket with your name on it. Then you can do your own laundry just the way you like it. And we'll redo your room over the next few weeks."

"That sounds good," I said.

"And *maybe* when I have meetings in the city in the afternoons, you can come along," Mom said. "You could have dinner with your dad or see your friends. But only if you have little or no homework!"

"Oh yes, yes! Thanks, Mom!" I squealed with delight.

Mom kissed me on the head. "I love you, Mia."

"I love you too, Mom."

"And Mia?" Mom said. "It's a little hard for Dan, too. Just try to remember that, okay?"

I thought about Dan watching us in the kitchen. It was just Dan and Eddie before we moved in. Just like it was just Mom and me before.

"Okay," I said.

I felt better after that. But I had one more thing to worry about. I would have to tell Katie, Alexis, and Emma that I wasn't eating lunch with them. And I really did not want to do that. Of course, I had to do it on a Monday.

I tried to tell Katie on the bus ride, but I chickened out. Then I tried to tell Alexis in the hallway, but I chickened out again.

Then it was time for lunch. I had no choice. I *had* to tell them. I walked up to our usual table before Alexis and Emma got in the lunch line.

"Hey," I said. "Um, listen, guys, today I'm sitting with Sydney and Callie and those guys. Just for today."

A hurt look crossed Katie's face, and I felt terrible.

"You mean the PGC?" Alexis asked. "Why on earth would you sit with them?"

"It's just—we keep meeting at the mall, and we like to talk about fashion and stuff," I said. "They invited me to eat with them today, and I didn't want to be rude or anything."

"If you want to talk about sweaters and skirts for forty minutes, then be my guest," Alexis said.

"Yeah, have fun," Emma said.

"It's cool," Katie said, but I could tell it was definitely not cool with her.

"Okay then. See you in English class," I said.

When I got to the PGC table, there was an empty seat between Callie and Maggie. I sat down.

"So, did the cupcake crew give you clearance to sit with us?" Sydney asked.

"It's not like that," I said. "I mean, I can sit where I want."

"I'm glad you're sitting with us," Callie said. "You know, my sister, Jenna, has known your stepbrother since kindergarten. She says he's really cute and nice."

"She must be confusing him with someone else," I said. "I mean, I guess he's cute. And he can be nice sometimes. But mostly he's seriously annoying."

"So is Jenna," Callie said. "No wonder they get along!"

Sydney rolled her eyes. "I'm an only child, thank goodness!"

"You can have my little sisters if you want," Maggie chimed in. "They drive me crazy!"

"I wouldn't mind having a brother or a sister," Bella said. "Sometimes it can be really lonely being an only child."

"Bella, you have said some ridiculous things before, but that might be the most ridiculous," Sydney told her, and I quickly looked at Bella. Were her feelings hurt?

But it didn't seem to faze her. "One day someone will recognize the beauty of my lonely soul," Bella said. "Until then, I will suffer alone."

Callie laughed. "Bella, you need to go to drama school, seriously."

"So, did anyone else take Mrs. Moore's quiz today?" Maggie asked. "It was superhard, I swear!"

"Oh, great," Callie moaned. "Not another one!"

"I've got a better one," Sydney said. "Did anyone see that outfit Sophie's wearing today? A plaid skirt and a top with a matching plaid collar? It looks like she's wearing a school uniform or something."

I happen to like Sophie a lot, so I wasn't happy with Sydney's comment.

"I loved the skirt," I said. "Maybe the top isn't a great match, but she's got the right idea."

"Yeah," Callie agreed. "She definitely gets points for that skirt. It's adorable."

Sydney just rolled her eyes.

The rest of the lunch went kind of like that. Maggie chattered on a mile a minute. Bella occasionally said something weird and dramatic. Sydney made slightly mean comments, and Callie and I had a completely normal conversation.

I wonder what Callie's doing with the rest of these girls? I found myself thinking. *She's really friendly and cool.*

Then it hit me. That's what Katie had been upset about since the first day of school. I tried to imagine if Ava stopped hanging out with me and hung out with other girls instead. It would be totally weird, and I wouldn't like it one bit. And now here I was doing kind of the same thing Callie had.

Katie wasn't trying to be the friendship police. She just didn't want to lose another friend. (You probably figured that out already, but what can I say? I really didn't get it until just then.)

When the bell rang, I walked up to Katie as she was leaving the cafeteria.

"How was your lunch?" she asked, and I noticed that she wasn't looking directly at me.

"Fine," I said. "But you know, it wasn't a permanent thing or anything. Tomorrow it's back to normal."

"Cool," Katie said.

I'm not sure if that made her feel any better, but I hope it did. Katie was one of the nicest things about Park Street School, and I didn't want to lose her as a friend.

CHAPTER 12

Not a Good Mix

At dinner that night it was Mom, Eddie, Dan, and me all at the same time. That doesn't happen a lot because of Eddie's work or Mom's meetings or Dan's basketball. I still felt a little bad about my freak-out in front of Eddie, but he hadn't said anything to me about it.

Eddie, as usual, was in a happy mood.

"Mmm, this is delicious, Sara," he said, swallowing a bite of food. "What is this called again?"

"Chicken *piccata*," Mom replied. "*Piccata* means 'larded' in Italian but there's no lard in this, just a sauce of butter and lemon juice."

"What are these little hard round things?" Dan asked.

"Capers," Mom said. "It's a pickled flower bud."

"They taste kind of weird," Dan said. "But the chicken's really good."

"I always pick the capers out," I said, and then it hit me—I was agreeing with Dan. Double weird!

"Well, I love it, capers and all," Eddie said, taking another bite.

Mom put down her fork and smiled at us. "So, I have some good news. I'm going to hold a fashion show to launch my new business. Right here in town!"

"That's wonderful news, honey!" Eddie said. "When will it be?"

"Two weeks," Mom said. "Yes, I know that's not a lot of time. But I made friends with a woman who owns the big banquet hall downtown, and they have an opening, and the space is terrific. . . . I couldn't resist."

"I'll help!" I offered.

"I was hoping you would," Mom said. "Especially backstage, styling the models. But I'll also need help from the Cupcake Club."

"Really?"

"Really," Mom said. "The show's going to be on a Sunday, so you'll have all Saturday to bake. And you'll need it. I'm going to need eight dozen cupcakes."

"If we bake them here, we can do four dozen at a time," I said, thinking quickly. "So that's about four to six hours together. We could do that in a day."

"Nice math, Mia!" said Eddie, and I smiled. Eddie sometimes had to help me with my math homework.

"The whole theme is going to be how to spice up your look with key pieces and accessories," Mom said. "So maybe you can use that idea for your cupcakes somehow. I'll pay you for the ingredients plus a dollar per cupcake. How does that sound?"

"I've got to tell everyone, but I'm sure it'll be okay," I said. I was starting to feel excited. "This is going to be really fun."

After dinner I grabbed my cell phone and texted Katie, Emma, and Alexis at the same time.

Mom's got a big job for us! Must talk at lunch tomorrow.

Yay! Katie replied.

Can't wait! texted Emma.

I hope she doesn't want lemon lol, was Alexis's response.

Another text came in. I figured it was from someone in the Cupcake Club, but it was Sydney.

Lunch 2morrow?
Can't, I texted back. Maybe next time. Thanks though!

I knew that probably meant I'd never be asked to sit with the PGC again, but I couldn't worry about that now. The Cupcake Club had a lot of planning to do!

The next day at lunch we got down to business. Alexis had her notebook, of course, and Katie had brought a book full of cupcake recipes.

I told them what details I knew—how much Mom was paying us, how we'd have a whole Saturday to do it, and about the whole "spice up your wardrobe" theme.

"There are lots of recipes for spiced cupcakes in here," Katie said, flipping through the recipe book. "Like zucchini spice cupcakes, and chocolate spice cupcakes, and tea spice cupcakes, and applesauce . . ."

"How can we pick just one?" Emma wondered aloud.

"Maybe we don't have to," Alexis said. "We're baking two batches of cupcakes anyway. We might as well bake two different flavors."

"That's a great idea," I said. "That way if somebody doesn't like one flavor, they can choose a different one."

Alexis looked at her notebook and frowned. "We have so much to do. We have to figure out what we're making and make an ingredients list and figure out how to decorate."

"We probably need to think of how to display them too," I said. "This is going to be a pretty classy event. We can't just put the cupcakes out on paper plates."

Katie looked excited. "I saw a cupcake show on TV where they made cupcakes for a party at an amusement park, and the display looked like a roller coaster with all these cupcakes on it."

"So you think we should make a roller coaster?" Alexis asked.

"Of course not," Katie said. "But I bet we could come up with something just as awesome."

"We should meet this weekend," I said, and then I remembered. "Oh wait, I can't. I'm going to Dad's this weekend."

"How about after school?" Katie suggested. "Mom gets home early on Wednesdays. We could do it at my house."

"That would be great," I said, and Alexis and Emma agreed.

After lunch, Callie came up to me in the hallway.

"Hey, we're going to the mall after school," she said. "Maggie's mom is driving us. Do you want to come?"

"Sure," I said. "I need to get there soon anyway. My mom's doing a big fashion show in a few weeks, and I'm going to help style the models."

I hadn't told Katie and the others this part of it all, but I was really excited to talk to Callie.

"Oh, wow, that sounds really awesome," Callie said. "I've never been to a fashion show before. I've always wanted to go to one. I bet Sydney would love to go too."

I was about to blurt out to Callie that she and the PGC could come, but I stopped myself. It was Mom's show for her business, and I didn't know if she had any extra tickets or not. Besides, even though it was a fashion show, it was still a Cupcake Club thing, you know? And one thing I've figured out is that the PGC and the Cupcake Club are not a good mix.

"Yeah, it's really amazing to see them in person," I said. I didn't want to promise Callie anything just yet.

I had some thinking to do.

CHAPTER 13

General Sydney

After school I texted Mom and asked if I could go to the mall with Callie and the others. She made me get the number of Maggie's mom so she could make sure an adult was going with us. But then she said it was okay.

I realized I was a little bit nervous when Maggie's mom pulled up in her blue minivan. Before, I'd only met the PGC at the mall by accident. But now I was going with them, as part of the group. I've never felt nervous about going out with friends before in my life. So why was this different?

We climbed into the van. Maggie sat in front with her mom, Sydney and Bella took the second row, and Callie and I sat in the last row. I didn't see a crumb or speck of dirt anywhere, and everything smelled like vanilla.

Maggie's mom had brown hair, like Maggie, but hers was superstraight. She wore a large pair of sunglasses that were half as big as her face. I know all the celebrities wear those big sunglasses, but whenever I see them on someone it always makes me think of bugs.

"Mia, I spoke to your mother on the phone," Mrs. Rodriguez said, looking in the rearview mirror so she could see me. "What a lovely woman."

"Thanks," I said.

Callie leaned forward. "Mia's mom is holding a fashion show for her new business! Can you believe it?"

Maggie turned around so fast, I thought her head might fly off. "Oooh, a real fashion show! When is it? Where is it? Will Damien Francis be there?"

"It's in two weeks, at the banquet hall downtown," I replied. "I'm not sure who's going to be there yet. It's all happening so fast."

Maggie, Bella, and Callie started chattering with excitement.

"I wonder what kind of clothes the models will be wearing," Bella wondered.

"And where is she getting the models? From

here in town?" Maggie asked. "Ooh, maybe there'll be a model competition."

"I'd love to take photos during the show," Callie said.

Sydney was the only one who remained cool about it. But when the talking died down, she turned and looked right at me.

"Of course we can go with you, right?"

And of course, I didn't know what to tell her. "Um, I'm not sure," I said. "I'm going to be backstage helping Mom, so . . ."

"But she must have extra tickets she can give out." Sydney wasn't giving up. "We could go, even if you're backstage."

"I have to ask her," I said honestly. "I don't know how many tickets she has."

"Well, it all sounds very exciting," Maggie's mom said as we pulled into the mall. "Now, let's meet back up at five o'clock. Where should we meet?"

"We'll be at the smoothie place at five," said Sydney. I thought it was kind of interesting that Sydney was the one who answered, not Maggie.

"We have to go to Forever Young first," Sydney said as we walked through the door. "I saw some dresses on their website that I just have to try on."

That sounded good to me. The clothes in Forever

Young are really cute. They blast really loud dance music, though, so it's hard to have a conversation.

After about twenty minutes in there I was ready to leave. But Sydney tried on dress after dress after dress. I noticed that Maggie and Bella always said the same things each time.

"That one's fabulous!"

"You look sooooooo cute!"

"You *have* to get that."

Callie and I were definitely more honest. For example, I thought the blue dress with the bubble skirt was way too short, so I said so.

Sydney looked in the mirror. "Wow, you're right, Mia."

"That *is* way too short," Maggie quickly agreed.

"Definitely," Bella added.

We finally left Forever Young. Then we went up to the second floor and I saw the sign for Icon, which, as you know, is my favorite store there.

"I think they've got new jackets," I said, heading for the door.

Sydney grabbed my arm. "We can't go in there. It's Tuesday."

I was puzzled. "So?"

"Tuesday is the day that this salesgirl named Denise works there," Maggie explained for Sydney.

"She is, like, so totally rude. Once Sydney wanted to take ten items into the dressing room, and she was like, 'Sorry, it's store policy.' Can you imagine? Like, what's the big deal?"

"Oh," I said. "Okay. Fine." But it seemed like a silly reason not to go into the store.

"We're going to Monica's next," Sydney said. Then she marched off toward the store without waiting to hear if anyone else liked the idea. We all followed right behind her. For a second I got an image in my mind of Sydney in an army general's uniform, leading the troops.

Monica's is this store that sells accessories, like jewelry, hair bands and barrettes, bags, and stuff like that. I was actually happy we were there because I could get some ideas for the fashion show.

I found this cute red beret and clipped a rhinestone pin to it. I gave it to Callie.

"Here, put this on. I want to take a picture."

Callie put it on. "Hold on. I'll give you my supermodel look."

She tilted her head and got this totally fierce look on her face, just like a model in a magazine. I laughed.

"Perfect!" I snapped some photos with my cell phone.

I started looking at the necklaces next. I saw some cool-looking chokers and some really long chains with different stones linked in. I started wondering how the chokers and the long chains would look together, so I ran up to Maggie and draped them around her neck.

"Ooh, that's pretty!" Maggie said.

"Okay, hold still," I told her. Maggie smiled as I snapped a few more pictures.

I was really having fun. I was looking through the handbags when Sydney spoke up in a loud voice.

"I am so done here. Let's go to Basic Blue."

"Could we stay a little bit longer?" I asked.

Sydney was firm. "Maggie's mom is picking us up at five, remember? I don't want to spend all our time in one place."

But it's only been fifteen minutes! I wanted to say. *And you spent, like, an hour in Forever Young!* But somehow I knew it was useless to argue with Sydney.

So we all went to Blue Basics, and I was bored because I was just there on Saturday. This time, Callie and I hung out and talked while Maggie and Bella oohed and ahhed over Sydney's outfits. I found out that she has an older brother in college and that she became friends with the PGC when she went to summer camp. I told her all about Ava and my dad's apartment in New York. She's really easy to talk to.

Then Sydney appeared in front of us. "We're going to Sal's Smoothies," she informed us.

Sal's Smoothies is pretty popular in this town—there's a store downtown and one in the mall, too. We got in line to place our orders.

"We will have five ginger peach smoothies," Sydney told the girl at the counter.

Five? "Can you make mine a mango and passion fruit instead, please?" I asked the counter girl.

Sydney looked at me. "We always order ginger peach."

"I like ginger on my sushi," I said. "But not in my smoothie. It's weird."

"So, four ginger peach and one mango passion?" the girl asked.

Sydney didn't answer.

"Yes," I said.

I was kind of quiet when we sat down to drink our smoothies. To be honest, Sydney's bossiness was really getting to me.

I started thinking about my other friends in the Cupcake Club. Alexis can be a bit bossy, I guess, but she's just trying to organize complicated things, like schedules and budgets. And she's never mean. Then there's Katie. When it comes to recipes and stuff, she's usually the one to come up with ideas first. So she's like a leader in that way. But she's always interested in hearing everyone else's ideas too.

I tried to imagine Katie in a general's uniform, ordering everyone around the kitchen—"Crack those eggs now! Measure that milk! Sift that flour!"—but I couldn't.

Sydney, on the other hand . . . well, that was how she was. Mom always says that you can't expect people to change. You either accept how they are or stay away.

I wasn't sure how I was feeling, exactly. I liked hanging out with the PGC, especially Callie, and trying on clothes and talking about fashion. I absolutely didn't like Sydney's bossiness. Why do things always have to be so complicated?

CHAPTER 14

A Spicy Afternoon

*T*he next day after school I had a completely different experience. I got off the bus with Katie for the Cupcake Club meeting. Katie lives in a small white house. There are orange flowers planted in pots on either side of the front door. When we got inside, Katie's mom called to us from the kitchen.

"Hello!" she said cheerfully. "How was school today?"

"Good," Katie answered. "Unless you count Mrs. Moore's daily quiz of death."

Mrs. Brown was shaking her head when we walked into the kitchen. "She can't be that bad, can she?"

"Oh yes, she can," Katie said. "Right, Mia?"

"True," I agreed. "But she did buy a cupcake from

us at the fund-raiser, so maybe she's not *all* bad."

Katie sighed. "Maybe not."

"So I picked up all the ingredients for your first test run," said Mrs. Brown. She kind of looks like Katie. They have the same big brown eyes and brown hair, only Katie's is long and Mrs. Brown's is shoulder length. Mrs. Brown is always either wearing her dental smock or an apron. So trying to guess what she's into isn't that hard. "I like your idea of doing spiced cupcakes. Very clever," she said.

Katie's kitchen table was loaded with everything we needed to make the cupcakes. Her kitchen looks really fun all the time. The walls are yellow, and there's this really cute cookie jar shaped like an apple and salt and pepper shakers that look like two blue birds in a nest.

The doorbell rang, and Katie ran to get it. She came back in followed by Alexis and Emma.

"Wow, we have a lot to do," Alexis said, looking at all the ingredients. "I still need to work out the budget for everything, and we need to think of a display."

"You can do the budget while we mix," Katie suggested. "And we can talk about the display while the cupcakes are cooling."

"That sounds good!" Alexis agreed. She sat down

at the table and opened up her notebook.

Katie, Emma, and I got to work on the applesauce spice cupcakes, which we'd decided to test first. We used applesauce, cinnamon, and nutmeg in the batter, and the kitchen quickly began to smell fabulous. Alexis had finished her budget by the time the cupcakes were in the oven, so we had a chance to talk while we did the dishes and worked on the frosting.

"Mia, do you think you can decorate the cupcakes for twenty-five cents apiece?" Alexis asked me.

"Sure," I said. "I've been looking at a bunch of different things online, and they're all cheaper than the sugar flowers."

"Great," Alexis said. "Then we should make a profit this time."

I winced a little bit and looked at Alexis, but she was scribbling numbers. Did she mean that as a jab at my last mess up?

"Cool," Katie said. "Now we just have to figure out how to display them."

"I was thinking about that," I said. "It might be cool to have something that's raised above the table, so people can really see them from a distance. They'll be easier to pick up, too."

I walked over to the table. "Alexis, can I borrow a page in your notebook?"

Alexis nodded, and I started to sketch my idea: a pole with a round plate on the bottom, another plate about ten inches above that one, and a third plate about another foot higher.

Katie, Alexis, and Emma gathered around while I sketched.

"Very cool," Katie said. "I bet we'd need two of them to hold all eight dozen cupcakes."

"They are cool," Alexis agreed. "But how will we make them?"

"My dad and I make stuff all the time," Emma spoke up. "He's got lots of spare wood in the garage, and I know we have wooden poles we could use."

"That would be awesome!" I said. "I was thinking we could paint them red, but I'll check with my mom tonight and let you know at lunch tomorrow."

"That reminds me," Alexis said. "I never asked how your lunch went with the PGC. Did Sydney spend the whole time insulting everyone in school?"

I thought about what Sydney had said about Sophie. "Well, not everyone," I replied. "But mostly we talked about normal stuff. Like Mrs. Moore's math quizzes. And brothers and sisters. It wasn't so different from stuff we talk about."

"Right. Because we are *so* much alike," Alexis said sarcastically. "I'll believe that when Emma comes to school dressed like a vampire, and Katie dyes her hair blond."

"Now you're starting to sound like Sydney," Emma said.

Alexis blushed. "Sorry. Those girls bug me, that's all. I survived three years of their torture at summer camp. It's hard to get over."

"I don't think being blond is Sydney's problem." I added.

"Right. Your hair color has nothing to do with your personality," said blond-haired Emma.

"All right, all right, I'll drop it," Alexis said. "Isn't it time to frost these cupcakes now?"

We started putting the vanilla cinnamon frosting on the cupcakes. We spread the frosting on with a special knife Mrs. Brown uses. It makes the icing look smooth and shiny.

"You know, I was thinking," I said. "I've seen it in some of Katie's books—how you put the icing in a pastry bag and then pipe it out onto the top of the cupcake. You can do swirls or little dots, stuff like that."

"Mom has pastry bags," Katie said quickly. She ran into her big pantry and came out with plastic bags shaped like triangles and two metal tips. Then she showed us how to slide the tip into the bag so it poked through the hole in the point of the triangle. Then we stuffed the bag with icing.

"So, you kind of push the icing from the top down while you squeeze," Katie explained. She put some on top of one of the cupcakes in a swirl pattern. It looked really nice.

"Can I try?" I asked.

I tried squeezing some out but I squeezed too hard the first time, and it came out in a big glop.

"Just a little squeeze," Katie told me, and I tried again.

This time I did it better, and a perfect dollop of white icing came out. I covered the top of the cupcake with icing circles, and that looked really nice too.

"We should definitely do this for the show on Saturday," Emma said, and everyone agreed.

"But you mean Sunday," Alexis said.

"Sunday!" Emma cried. "I thought it was Saturday! Sam is in this big basketball tournament on Sunday, and we're all going out of town to cheer him on."

"It's okay, Emma," I said, thinking Dan would probably be there too. Eddie was going to be at the fashion show though. Who would cheer on Dan?

"Ugh, brothers!" Emma said, shrugging at me. "Promise you'll take pictures and text me so I know how it goes?"

"Of course," I said.

"What about the display?" Alexis asked.

"I'll make sure we finish by Saturday," Emma said. "We can work on it this weekend."

Soon we had all the cupcakes finished. Because it was right before dinner, we unwrapped one and cut it into four pieces.

"Mmm, really good," Alexis said.

"I'm thinking a little more nutmeg?" Katie said.

I nodded. "Definitely. They're good, but they need a little more kick. Then they'll be *fabulous*."

Right about then, Eddie came by to bring me home for dinner. I had a small box of our test cupcakes with me for dessert later.

"Did you have a nice time?" Eddie asked when I got in the car.

"It was seriously fantastic," I told him. "The cupcakes came out great, and we're going to make this fabulous display that Mom will love, and we tried a new icing technique."

"That's great," Eddie said. "I bet you girls are going to have a terrific time at the fashion show."

Eddie's remark reminded me—the PGC wanted to go too. I still hadn't figured out what to do about that, but I knew I couldn't put things off much longer. I would have to decide soon and hope nobody got hurt.

CHAPTER 15

It's Complicated

Friday I took the train to see my dad as usual. We went to Tokyo 16 and then watched a movie when we got home.

The next morning Dad made us omelets and toast. We ate sitting on high stools at the counter that separates the kitchen from the living room. Dad's apartment is big for Manhattan, but the place is pretty small compared to a house in the suburbs. Everything in the kitchen and the living room is either black, silver, or made of glass. My dad's bedroom is like that too. The only color in the house is the pink in my Parisian bedroom.

"So, what are we doing today, *mija*?" Dad asked me as we ate. "Are you going to Ava's soccer game?"

"I've got a big social studies project to do," I replied. I know I haven't mentioned this yet, but besides shopping at the mall and baking cupcakes, I've been doing tons of homework. It seems like there is way more homework now than at my old school. "I don't know if I'll get to see Ava this weekend."

"Why don't we invite her to dinner tonight?" Dad suggested. "I know she loves my chicken."

"What about Alina?" I asked. "Do we have plans with her again?"

"I don't know if I'll be seeing Alina anymore," Dad said. "She and I didn't have as much in common as I thought."

"Hmm. That's too bad," I said. What I really wanted to say was *Hooray! No new stepmom for me! And our walls will be safe too!* But I didn't want to hurt Dad's feelings.

I picked up my dish and put it in the dishwasher. "I'll text Ava about dinner. Then I've got to start on my project. I've got to make this color-coded map showing the most populated countries in the world. It has to have a map key and everything."

"Well, that's right up my alley," Dad said. He's an architect who helps design office buildings, mostly. Dad had a big roll of paper I could use for the map, and he even let me use his special set of colored pencils that I always drool over.

It took me all afternoon to finish the map, but when it was done, it looked great. Mr. Insley, my social studies teacher, would have to give me an A, I just knew it.

Things got even better when Ava came over. Dad made his chicken in tomato sauce, like he promised he would, and we talked and laughed all through dinner.

After we ate, Ava and I went to my bedroom to listen to music. We both flopped down on the floor, and Ava grabbed my sketchbook and started looking through it.

"These are really nice, Mia," Ava said, turning the pages. "I really like the plaid mixed with the flower pattern."

"Thanks!" Ava's always been my biggest fan.

My cell phone beeped, and I flipped it open. There was a text from Sydney.

Want to hang out at my house Monday?

"Who's that?" Ava asked.

"It's Sydney," I replied. "She wants me to hang out at her house on Monday."

"Sydney? I don't remember you talking about her. Is she in the Cupcake Club?"

"No." I propped up a fluffy pink floor pillow against the side of the bed and leaned back. "It's complicated. Sydney formed this club called the Popular Girls Club."

Ava rolled her eyes. "Seriously?"

"I know, but the girls in that club are basically pretty nice," I explained. "And they love to go to the mall with me and talk about fashion. None of my friends in the Cupcake Club are into that."

"So why is it complicated?" Ava asked. "Can't you just be friends with everybody?"

"It's not so easy," I told her. "You see, Katie used to be best friends with Callie, and then Callie dumped Katie to hang out with the PGC. And Alexis kind of hates Sydney, because Sydney's really mean to her, and Emma . . . I think she doesn't like them because she sticks up for Alexis."

"Yeah, things get complicated in middle school." Ava closed the book and sat up. "Like our friends on the soccer team. I love them, but I'm also friends with girls from my dance class. It's not like we all hang out together."

"But it's different," I said. "It's not like the girls

on the soccer team and the girls in your dance class are enemies."

"Maybe not, but I always feel like I'm splitting my time. So are you going to hang out with Sydney?" Ava asked.

I quickly looked at the schedule I keep on my phone. "It doesn't matter if I want to or not, 'cause there's a big math test on Tuesday."

I texted Sydney back.

Math test on Tuesday. Have to study.

I wasn't expecting her reply.

We can study together.

Are u sure? I asked. It's a big test.

Sydney texted back.

Do u want to come or not?

Ava was looking over my shoulder. "Just go. What's the big deal?"

I sighed.

OK. See u Monday.

"It was so much easier when I lived here," I said, flopping backward.

"Well, if you think I've got it easy here, you're wrong," Ava told me. "I have to go halfway across town to get to school. It takes forever. I hardly know anybody. You have, like, a hundred friends already. You're lucky."

I thought about it. Ava might be right. I think I'd rather have too many friends than none at all, even though it can get seriously confusing.

But that didn't make it easier on Monday, when I knew I would see Katie on my way out of school. Katie was waiting for Joanne on the school steps, like she usually was. (I wanted to tell her during lunch, but I just couldn't do it, somehow.)

"Hey!" Katie said. "Joanne's running late today. I wish my mom would just let me take the bus with you."

"Um, I'm not taking the bus today," I said. "I'm going to Sydney's house to study."

Katie looked hurt, but as usual, she tried to act like she wasn't. Right then, Joanne's red car pulled up down the street.

"Okay, cool," she said. "I'll see you tomorrow."

I felt kind of bad. Then I heard Sydney calling me.

"Mia!"

Sydney was on the corner with Bella and Callie. I ran over to meet them.

"Hey," I said. "Where's Maggie?"

"She goes to ballet class on Mondays," Sydney replied. "Her mom thinks it will make her more graceful."

Bella giggled. "I went to her last recital. Poor Maggie. She's hopeless!"

Now that's the difference between the PGC and the Cupcake Club right there. In the Cupcake Club, nobody talks behind anybody else's back.

"I always wanted to take dance lessons," Callie said. "But I was afraid I wouldn't be good at it."

"I like to dance for fun," I said. "Like when we have parties at my aunt's house. We crank up the music and everybody dances—in the kitchen, on the porch, wherever."

"Did you ever go dancing in the dance clubs in New York?" Bella asked.

"No," I said. "You have to be older to do that." Bella looked disappointed.

"So, are you guys studying with us?" I asked Bella and Callie.

"Mom's taking me to the eye doctor for a follow-up," Callie said. "And then I'm studying tonight."

"And I have . . . other plans," Bella said a little nervously. Sydney was glaring at her. I got the feeling that maybe Sydney had ordered Bella not to hang out with us.

Callie's house was first on the walk home, and then Bella lived a few blocks away. That left me and Sydney. We talked about the new movie starring Ann Harrison that was coming out this weekend. We both think she's gorgeous and seriously talented.

Finally we came to a block that had a lot of old houses like the one Emma lives in. But one house on the block looked brand-new. It was twice as tall as the other houses and it was made of these pinkish-brown smooth stones. There was a big window over the front door and you could see a huge chandelier glimmering through it.

You've probably guessed by now that it was Sydney's house. She took a key from the key chain hanging from her backpack, unlocked the front door, and opened it up.

"Magda! We'd like two sparkling lemonades, please!" Sydney called out.

We walked through the big front hallway (I think it's called a foyer, right?) into a dining room with a gleaming wood table. Another smaller chandelier hung in that room. There was a big cabinet with glass windows with fancy plates and glasses inside. The whole place was sparkling clean.

Sydney dumped her backpack on top of the table and sat down. I sat down across the table from her just as a slim woman with pale blond, pulled-back hair hurried in, carrying two glasses of lemonade. Without a word, she placed them on the table in front of us.

"Thanks!" I said, but Magda quickly left without responding.

"She's not much of a talker," Sydney informed me. "The last housekeeper we had just talked and talked and talked. Mom couldn't take it anymore, so we had to get a new one."

I opened my backpack and took out my math book. "I seriously hate dividing fractions," I said. "It's never made any sense to me. Why do you have to turn the numbers upside down? What's the point?"

Sydney sipped her lemonade. "Yeah, I know. So, tell me about your mom's fashion show. Did she choose the designers yet?"

"I think so," I said. "We're supposed to go over that tonight. I was at my dad's all weekend so we haven't had a chance to talk yet."

"Be right back," Sydney said. She returned a minute later carrying a laptop.

Okay, I thought. *We're going to start studying.*

She typed on the keyboard and turned the screen toward me to show me an image of a model in a long red coat.

"This is perfect for winter, isn't it?" she said.

"It's nice," I agreed. "But we should really study for math now, shouldn't we?"

"One more minute," Sydney said. "We have to check out *Fashionista's* website first. They had a whole spread about Ann Harrison and all her different styles. You have got to see it!"

I was fed up with Sydney's bossiness. I really wanted to study for my math test so I could talk with Mom about the fashion show later. So I did something I wouldn't normally do.

I slipped my math book back into my backpack and stood up. "Listen, Sydney, thanks for inviting me over and everything, but I seriously need to study."

"But it only takes, like, five minutes to go over the review sheet," Sydney said.

"Maybe you only need five minutes, but I need more time," I said. "I'm really, really sorry."

"Okay, whatever." Sydney sounded annoyed.

Great. Now I had hurt two friends in the same day.

As I walked home, I realized I was in the neighborhood where Alexis and Emma lived. I checked the time on my cell phone and saw it wasn't even three thirty yet. So I walked over to Alexis's house and knocked on the door.

Alexis looked surprised to see me. "Hey, Mia. What are you doing here?"

"Well, I was in the neighborhood, and I was wondering if maybe we could study for the math test together," I said.

"Sure. I was just starting," Alexis told me. She motioned for me to come inside.

"Mom! Mia's here! We're studying for math!" Alexis called out. She led me into her kitchen, which was sparkling clean and very, very white. She had her math book and a pad of graph paper spread out on the kitchen table.

Mrs. Becker walked in. She has short hair and glasses and likes to wear mid-length skirts with comfortable-looking shoes. I'd love to give her a makeover some day. She's naturally pretty, but with a makeover she could be a totally hot mom!

"Nice to see you, Mia," she said. "There are bananas and apples on the counter if you're hungry."

"Thanks, Mrs. Becker," I said.

Alexis and I got right down to business. By four thirty, I was almost an expert in dividing fractions. I even knew what a "reciprocal" was. Amazing.

"You should become a teacher," I told Alexis. "I actually feel like I understand this stuff."

Alexis blushed. "Yeah, I think about that sometimes. Want a banana?"

I nodded, and she went to the counter and grabbed a banana for each of us.

"Thanks so much for studying with me," I said as I peeled my banana. "Mom's going crazy getting ready for this fashion show, and we're supposed to meet to talk about it today."

"What's making her crazy?" Alexis asked.

"There's just so much to be done," I said. "Getting the food, making the seating chart, hiring the models, deciding which model will wear what look . . ."

Alexis started sketching on a piece of graph paper. "Why don't you make a flowchart? That's what I always do when I have a lot to do."

I looked over her shoulder. "That is pretty awesome. Can I show my mom?"

"Sure," Alexis replied. "Or how about this? I can do a blank one on the computer and send it to you."

"Oh my gosh, that would be fabulous!" I said. "Alexis, you are the best!"

Alexis grinned. "Let me know if you need any help at the fashion show, okay? I don't know anything about fashion, but I'm good at organizing things. I could always stay after we set up the cupcakes."

"Thanks. I'll ask my mom," I said.

As I walked home, I thought about how different Alexis was from Sydney. If I were having a friend contest, Alexis definitely would have won the prize today.

Maybe things weren't really as complicated as I thought.

CHAPTER 16

A Big Deal

$\mathcal{M}$om was thrilled with the flowcharts Alexis e-mailed me.

"Alexis did these?" she asked in disbelief. "I should hire this girl as my assistant."

"Hey, I thought *I* was your assistant," I said.

"You're my number one *fashion* assistant," Mom promised. "But I do need someone to help keep me organized."

"Alexis said she would help out if you wanted," I told her.

"Maybe," Mom said. "But fashion first! Let me show you the outfits and accessories I've got so far."

Mom had gotten a lot done over the weekend. In her office were two racks filled with clothes and a few large plastic bins filled with shoes, bags, and jewelry. Mom and I spent two hours matching dresses and jackets, shirts and skirts, pants and tops, and picking out accessories for each look. We still hadn't finished when I started yawning.

"Sorry, sweetie, I didn't realize how late it was getting," Mom said. "I'll finish up here. You need to rest for that big math test tomorrow."

I don't know what I was more nervous about— my math test or facing Sydney after walking out on her. But I shouldn't have worried. When I saw Sydney in homeroom, she flashed me that toothpaste-commercial smile of hers.

"Hey, study nerd," she said. "Were you up all night getting ready for the test?"

"No," I admitted. "But I think I'm ready for it."

"Of course you are," Sydney said. "So, you owe me after yesterday. Sit with us at lunch, okay?"

I could picture the hurt look on Katie's face if I accepted, but it was hard for me to refuse after everything that happened.

"Cool, thanks."

I ended up acing the math test, thanks in part to Alexis. She was really a good teacher. Either that or math was starting to make sense.

I got to lunch early so I could talk to Katie. I caught her by the front door.

"Hey, Katie," I said. "I need to tell you something."

"Let me guess," Katie said. "You're sitting with the PGC today."

"You're right," I said. "I kind of have to. I was sort of rude to Sydney yesterday and left her house like five minutes after I got there. But I'm not changing tables permanently or anything."

Katie didn't look directly at me, and I knew she was upset. She doesn't like to say how she's really feeling, though.

"You're the best friend I've made since I moved here," I told her.

Katie smiled a little bit. "Okay. Have fun talking about boring clothes." She rolled her eyes in a funny way, and I knew she was teasing.

"Thanks," I said. "I'll talk to you later."

The rest of the PGC girls were sitting down when I got to the table. Maggie rushed over to me.

"Oh, Mia, Mia, Mia!" she said. "Say it isn't true!"

"Say what isn't true?" I asked.

"My mom told me that tickets to your mom's fashion show are all sold out," she said. "But that can't be true, can it?"

"Maybe—I mean, I'm not sure," I said. "She didn't say anything."

"But we can still go, right?" Sydney asked.

"I still have to find out," I said. I had put off asking my Mom last night, because I still didn't know what to do.

Callie changed the subject. "So, how was the math test?"

Thankfully nobody mentioned the fashion show again for the rest of lunch, so that was good.

With the math test off of my mind, I was able to concentrate on cupcakes. I had no idea how to decorate the tops of the cupcakes for the fashion show. After school I went up to my room and started looking online for ideas.

Somehow I came across this site for a baking supply store. They had tons and tons of stuff, and two things caught my eye. They had these little pieces of candied ginger that would look just like jewels on top of the chocolate cupcakes. They also had red cinnamon-flavored sugar that looked like glitter. How cool would that be on top of the white frosting on the applesauce cupcakes? And perfect for Mom's spicy theme too.

But it was already Tuesday, and there was no way they would get here in time if I ordered them—at least, that's what I thought. When I checked the contact page, I saw that the store was in

Springfield—right over in the next town!

I ran downstairs as fast as I could. Dan was at the kitchen table doing homework, and Mom was chopping vegetables for dinner.

"Mom, I found this awesome baking supply shop in Springfield," I said. "It's got the perfect decorations for the cupcakes for your show. Can you take me there tonight? They're open till eight."

"Oh sweetie, I've got to go to the banquet hall tonight to work out the floor plan," Mom said. "I'm so sorry. I know Eddie would take you, but he's working late tonight."

Dan looked up from his book. "I'll take you," he said.

I was surprised. "Really? You don't mind?"

Dan shook his head. "We can go after dinner."

Mom gave him a huge smile. "Dan, that's so sweet of you. Thanks!"

So right after dinner I was driving to Cake Sensations in Dan's red sports car that used to belong to his uncle. He'd been driving it around ever since he got his license last month. I was sure that's why he agreed to drive me.

But as we rode along, I figured out he had another reason.

"So, I'm sorry I ruined your shirt," he said. "I

didn't mean to. I'm just used to dumping everything in the laundry basket into the machine at once. It's just everything's you know . . . different now."

He didn't sound mad when he said that last sentence, or sad, either. But something about how he said it made me think again that it must be weird for him, too. I guess we were all adjusting to the changes.

"It's okay," I said. "It's just a shirt."

It didn't take long to get to Springfield.

"The directions say to take a left onto Main Street," I told Dan.

Dan slowed down and put on his blinker. "Hey, I know this place," he said. "It's right next to the doctor where I get my shots."

"Shots? What shots?" I asked.

"You know, for the dogs," Dan said. "I'm allergic to them, so I have to get shots."

Why hadn't I heard this before? "Seriously? I didn't know that. You mean you have to get shots because of Tiki and Milkshake?"

Dan shrugged. "It's okay. They don't hurt. Besides, I like those dogs."

Dan parked the car in front of Cake Sensations, and when we got out, I walked over to him and gave him a hug.

"Uh, thanks," Dan said. "But it's just a short ride. It's no big deal."

But I wasn't hugging him just because of the ride.

"It *is* a big deal," I said. "Thanks."

CHAPTER 17

Mixing It Up

I bought a jar of the glittery cinnamon sugar and a container of small pieces of candied ginger at the Cake Sensations store. Dan used the calculator on his cell phone to divide the cost between eight dozen cupcakes, and I came in at nineteen cents per cupcake. Alexis would be so proud of me!

When we got home, Dan went into his room and blasted his music, but I didn't mind it as much as I usually do. I put on my headphones and did a little sketching before bedtime. I was about to change into my pajamas when Mom opened the door.

"Well, that went smoothly, thank goodness," she said. "Those charts Alexis made really helped. Please thank her for me."

"You can thank her tomorrow," I said. "Everyone's coming over after school to do a test batch of the chocolate spice cupcakes, remember?"

"Oh, right!" Mom said. "Hey, that reminds me. I saved three front-row tickets for you to give to your friends."

Mom looked through her purse and came up with three tickets printed on red paper, which she handed to me. "They're the last three tickets I've got."

"Thanks, Mom," I said. I got up and gave her a hug.

Mom kissed my cheek. "Get a good night's sleep, sweetie."

She left, and I looked at the three tickets in my hand. I knew how badly Sydney wanted to go. But if they belonged to anyone, it was the Cupcake Club.

Katie, Alexis, Emma. I wrote their names down in my sketchbook. Then I remembered that Emma wasn't going to be there.

Katie, Alexis . . . Sydney? Yikes. That would never work.

I tried thinking another way. Katie and Alexis had never once asked me for tickets to the show. They probably didn't even want to go.

Sydney, Maggie, Bella, Callie. That was one girl too many. But which girl would I leave out? I liked Callie, so she could stay. Sydney would be furious if I left her out. That left Maggie or Bella, and I didn't want to hurt either of their feelings. They'd always been nice to me.

And then, how would Katie and Alexis feel if I didn't even offer them the tickets? Maybe they didn't ask because they just assumed they were going. . . .

Frustrated, I closed the sketchbook. I didn't want to think about it anymore. Maybe the decision would come to me in a dream. . . .

It didn't. I still hadn't made any decisions by the time the Cupcake Club came over the next day after school. Katie brought the ingredients with her, and I was really excited to show everyone what I had found at Cake Sensations.

"See this glittery sugar? It's cinnamon flavored," I said. "I think it will look so pretty on the apple-sauce cupcakes, and it matches the red display."

"It's perfect!" Emma agreed.

"And these are little pieces of candied ginger." I picked up one of the little orange jewels. "I thought they'd be good for the chocolate spice cupcakes, since there's ginger inside."

"That's going to look really cool," Alexis said. "Hey, can I crack the eggs this time?"

"The eggs are all yours," Katie said, handing her the carton.

But before we started baking, Mom came into the kitchen holding some papers in her hand.

"Hi, girls," she said. "I thought I'd show you where the cupcake table's going to be set up on Sunday."

She spread out the papers on the table. They showed a floorplan of the banquet hall.

"See, there's the runway," she said. "And these are the seats. And the refreshments will be over here."

"Where does everyone check in?" Alexis asked.

"What do you mean?" Mom asked.

"You know, like where they turn in their tickets and get their seat assignment," she replied.

Mom turned pale. "Oh, no! I didn't think of that."

Alexis pointed to the layout. "I think right here's the perfect spot for it. I'm sure the banquet hall can set up one more table for you."

Mom hugged Alexis. "You are a genius! Mia said you'd be willing to help out during the show. Would you work the check-in table for me?"

Alexis looked thrilled. "I would love to! That would be fun."

"Thank you, thank you, thank you!" Mom said. She quickly picked up the papers. "I need to go call the banquet hall right now."

"I wish I was going," Emma said after Mom left.

"I'll text you photos, I promise," I told her.

"Stupid game," Emma muttered. That reminded me about Dan. But just then Katie leaned over the counter.

"I was meaning to ask you," Katie said. "Can I stay and watch the show after we set up the cupcakes?"

"Um, I just need to find out if Mom is going to give me tickets," I lied.

Katie shrugged. "Cool. It sounds like fun, but as long as the cupcakes are perfect, I'll be happy."

My mind was racing. Alexis didn't need a ticket. I really needed to give Katie one. That left two. *Katie, Callie, Sydney?* Way awkward.

Katie measured the flour and dumped it into the bowl.

"Okay, now we need a teaspoon of powdered ginger and two tablespoons of cocoa powder," she said. "And then we need to mix them up."

Emma added the spices, and Katie started

stirring the ingredients with a whisk. She did a groovy dance. "Oh yeah. Mix it up, mix it up," she sang.

Then it hit me. *Mix it up.* When you mix the wrong ingredients together, the result can be a disaster. But when you mix the right ingredients together, everything comes out delicious.

Suddenly everything was clear.

I knew exactly who to give the three tickets to.

CHAPTER 18

A Little Sweetness in the End

Ninety-five, ninety-six," Alexis counted, placing the last cupcake on top of the display.

Katie, Alexis, and I took a step back and admired our work. It had taken all of us (plus Emma) all day and part of the night on Saturday to make all ninety-six cupcakes. They looked beautiful. And the displays Emma and her dad made were really cool, just like I imagined them. The two red towers were simple, but they were the perfect accent for the colorful tablecloths Mom had chosen for the refreshment tables.

"Let me get a picture for Emma," I said, taking a quick shot with my phone and sending it to her.

The displays are perfect! U r the best!

Thanks! Emma texted back. Miss u guys! I'll text
you the pictures on this end too!

Katie started gathering up the empty cupcake
carriers.

"I'll help you," Alexis offered.

"Cool." Katie nodded to me. "See you later!"

It was just two hours before the fashion show,
and things were getting pretty crazy in the banquet
hall. The DJ was setting up his equipment in the
back corner, and Mom was on the runway talking
to a guy about the lights. She climbed down when
she noticed that we had finished the display.

"Wow, Mia, that's fabulous," Mom said. "These
look delicious."

"Thanks," I said.

"Listen, the models are starting to arrive. Can you
start helping them get dressed? I'll be back there in
a minute." She handed me a clipboard with Alexis's
charts on it.

"Sure, Mom," I said. I've been backstage with
Mom at fashion shows since I can remember, but
this was the first time she was actually letting me
help. I didn't want to let her down.

I headed to the curtain behind the runway. It
separated the banquet hall into two spaces—the

show area and the backstage area. The models would be getting changed in the room behind the curtain.

Thankfully, the charts made things pretty easy. As soon as I walked backstage, a model with long, glossy black hair walked up to me.

"Is Sara Vélaz here?" she asked.

"I'm her daughter, Mia," I said in my most professional voice. "Can you please give me your name?"

"It's Lori," the model told me.

I found her name on the chart and started walking to the racks of clothes. Each model had a picture of the outfit she'd be wearing under her name on a wall. And each model had a rack with all the outfits hung on them. I found "Lori" on the card taped over one rack. "Here are the clothes you'll be wearing," I told her. "The red dress is your first outfit. Please head to the makeup room first."

I pointed toward the large ladies' room, where Mom had the makeup artists set up.

"Thanks, Mia," Lori said. "You know, you're a lot like your mom."

The next two hours went by really fast. The models started coming in, and Mom and I helped each one get ready. There were all kinds of problems: One shirt was too big, one skirt was too short, one model had on the wrong earrings—stuff like that.

In the middle of it all Ray, the DJ, came backstage.

"Sara, one of the outlets just lost power," he said.

Mom looked at her watch. "Oh, great. The show starts in twenty minutes." She turned to me. "Mia, can you go to the main office and ask for Ernie? He should be able to help with this."

"Sure, Mom," I told her. I ducked out a nearby door that led into a hallway that bypassed the main room because I knew it would be faster and less crowded. I could see the check-in table up ahead. Alexis had her back to me and was talking with three guests.

Then I heard Sydney's loud voice. "But I'm *sure* Mia put us on the list."

My heart pounding, I ducked behind a big pillar and listened to what was going on.

"Sydney, I'm sorry, but your name isn't on this list," Alexis said. "Or Maggie or Bella, either."

"That's impossible. Mia told us all about the show," Sydney said. She sounded really mad. "And where is Callie, anyway?"

"There's nothing I can do for you. The show is sold out," Alexis explained patiently.

"Of course you can do something. You can go find Mia for me," Sydney insisted.

"Give me a second," Alexis replied.

My cell phone buzzed in my pocket. I quickly shut it off. Like it or not, I would have to face the music. I stepped out from behind the pillar and walked up to the check-in table.

Sydney was done up to the max, wearing a black dress with a bubble skirt and black heels. She had her hair swept up on her head and had tons of perfume on.

"There she is!" Sydney said, pointing at me.

"Mia? I just tried to reach your phone," Alexis said, looking confused. "Anyway, Sydney and Maggie and Bella keep saying you put them on the list." Alexis looked at me.

"I know," I said. I felt awful. "Listen, I'm really sorry about this, but I just didn't have enough tickets for everyone who wanted to come," I said weakly.

Sydney just stared at me.

"But you promised we could come!" Maggie wailed.

"I didn't promise anything," I replied. "But I should have told you about the tickets earlier. I'm so sorry. I really am."

287

Then I had an idea. "Hey, why don't you come backstage and help out? I can ask my mom if it's all right. It's a really cool way to see the show."

Sydney looked horrified. "We came to watch the show, not *work* it," she said, with a disgusted look in Alexis's direction. "Mia, I don't know how you could do this to a friend. We were seriously considering you for a membership in the PGC, but we're going to have to reevaluate your membership status now."

"Well, my friends don't *evaluate* one another," I shot back.

Sydney stormed off without another word, with Maggie and Bella following behind.

I turned to Alexis, embarrassed. "Don't worry about it, everyone makes mistakes . . . even me!" Alexis said. She was trying really hard not to laugh. "Hey, shouldn't you be backstage helping your mom?"

I slapped my hand on my forehead. "Oh, no! I've got to find Ernie!"

Luckily, Ernie was in his office, and he quickly followed me backstage. I helped Mom with the rest of the models, and a few minutes later Ernie came back.

"You're all set, Ms. Vélaz," he told Mom.

Mom turned to me. "Deep breath," she said, and we both took a deep breath at once. "Okay. I'm on."

Mom stepped out onto the stage and the noisy crowd quieted down. I walked to the end of the curtain and quietly slipped through so I could watch.

"Thank you so much for coming, everyone!" she said. "I'm Sara Vélaz, and today you're going to see some of the latest fashions from top designers. We've carefully crafted the looks today to show you how you can add some key pieces to spice up your wardrobe."

Everyone clapped.

"And after the show, please stay for a little sweetness, courtesy of the Cupcake Club," Mom said, pointing to the refreshments table.

I realized then that my mom could have hired anyone to cater her first big event, but she chose us. I guess it was her way of including my latest hobby and new friends. Mom was really trying to help everything fit in together.

I looked out to the side and saw Eddie standing in the back. He looked really proud. He was taking pictures and videos of everything. Which reminded me . . . I turned on my phone. Sure enough, there was a picture from Emma of her brother Jake holding the sign I made: GO, DAN GO! And there was a text from Dan:

Thx sis. Save me a cupcake.

I couldn't help but smile at being called "sis."

I looked out at the front row and gave a little wave to my three friends sitting there: Katie, Callie, and Ava. My best friend from the Cupcake Club, my best friend from the PGC, and my best friend from New York. The perfect mix.

I still haven't totally figured out how to mix *every-thing* from my old life and my new life together, but that's okay. This is good enough for now, and so far, the results are pretty sweet.

Emma
on
thin
icing

CHAPTER 1

Everything Is Better with Bacon

$\mathcal{M}$y name is Emma Taylor, and my life can be pretty hectic sometimes. I have three brothers, four goldfish, a guinea pig, and two jobs. Yup, two businesses. The first is a dog-walking job I have after school. My other job isn't really a job. It's a club with my best friends—Alexis, Katie, and Mia. Together we're the Cupcake Club. We bake and sell cupcakes for different people and events. It's totally fun, but we don't earn that much money . . . yet.

Between my brothers, chores, and the club, things can get pretty crazy. Most of the time, though, being in the middle of all this craziness can mean getting some pretty great inspirations. Like the one I had about bacon. Bacon cupcakes. Trust me, they're great. They're salty with the bacon and sweet with the sugar and the combination is really the best. It just *sounds* gross. I had been waiting to bring it up until just the right time, so finally, at our club meeting, I decided to see how it would fly. We were talking about new ideas because we're always trying out new things, depending on the event. I was a little nervous, but I decided to float the idea.

"Okay, ready? How about . . . bacon cupcakes?" I asked.

I spread my arms wide in an arc—like "ta-da"— as I announced my idea. I wasn't sure how the others would react to it, but I thought it was pretty neat. And original. That was for sure. I just hoped they didn't think I was nuts.

"Ewwww!" cried Katie, with a full-body shudder.

"Are you kidding me?" Alexis looked so horrified, you would have thought I had suggested roadkill cupcakes.

I just shrugged. I knew better. "My brothers loved them. I made them last week. Actually, they're delicious. Kind of salty and sweet. Think about it."

Unlike the other members of the Cupcake Club, Mia was quiet, and she looked like she was actually considering the idea. Finally she said "I love bacon *and* cupcakes, but I've never thought about them together. Bacon is kinda in right now. There's bacon gum, bacon mayonnaise, bacon ice cream, bacon-shaped Band-Aids. It would be pretty cool to have bacon cupcakes."

Mia was pretty hip. She had long, straight, dark hair and really cool outfits, and was from Manhattan. I have no idea how she knew what was "in" or what wasn't, but we all pretty much listened when she said something was in. So Katie and Alexis stopped their dramatic groaning and belly-clutching and listened.

Seeing that I was making headway with my idea, I forged on. "I was thinking, maybe for the groom's cake. You know how they do that? Have a special cake on the side for the men? It's kind of a Southern thing. The bride has her own cake and the groom has his."

"Like an extra order?" asked Katie.

I nodded and looked a little guiltily at Mia. "Not that I want to make money off your mom or anything."

"Emma, you may have just doubled our revenue!" said Alexis, ever the businesswoman. She raised her glass of Gatorade in a toast. I smiled and raised my glass back at her. Alexis actually did look like a businesswoman right now with her red hair up in a bun and a sensible button-down shirt, holding a calculator and a pad of paper.

The Cupcake Club was meeting in Mia's cozy room to brainstorm about upcoming jobs. One of our next big events was Mia's mom's wedding to Eddie, her supernice fiancé. We were all excited for Mia because Eddie was great and her mom was really happy. But we were also excited for ourselves because Mia's mom had placed an order with the club for cupcakes for the wedding! She had given us the green light to do whatever we thought was appropriate. And I thought bacon cupcakes were appropriate. Best of all, she would pay us for the order.

Alexis was taking notes. "Okay, let me just read this back to you. One idea is a circular cupcake wedding cake built with three sizes of cupcakes to make up the tiers—our medium, large, and jumbo sizes building out the cake, with a few minis on top. The cake would be white, the frosting white buttercream. Decorations would be white flowers molded from edible fondant. Cupcake papers would be shiny and white." She looked up at the other Cupcake Club members for confirmation. We all nodded, and she looked back at her notes.

"Another idea is to do all minis laid out in a large sheet, mostly white cake and white frosting but with select cupcakes frosted in pink raspberry frosting and placed to form the shape of a heart in the middle of the layout." Again, we nodded. The mini cupcakes were very popular; they were not much bigger than a quarter and they could be consumed easily in vast quantities.

Alexis continued. "We will also submit a bid for a groom's cake made of . . . um, bacon cupcakes. These are . . . what kind of cake?"

"Caramel cake," I said. My mouth was watering just thinking of it. "And the frosting is just a standard buttercream with flecks of real bacon in it. It comes out sort of beige."

Alexis shuddered. "Okay. Beige cupcakes. I will do an analysis on head count and budget and come up with a cupcake count so we can submit our bids to your mom by the end of the week. I'll e-mail it to everyone for approval first. Especially the bacon cupcake part. Then we can meet and go over it again."

We nodded in agreement.

"Next on the agenda is—"

"Wait!" interrupted Mia, her eyes shining with excitement. "I have great news." She clasped her hands together.

I restrained myself from looking at my watch.

I didn't want to be rude, but I prided myself on being extremely punctual and organized and I had to be at the Andersons' to walk Jenner, their retired greyhound rescue dog, at four o'clock. It had to be almost three forty-five now. I really hated to be late. I also didn't want to lose the dog-walking job. In fact, I couldn't afford to.

Meanwhile Mia had paused for effect. Then taking a deep, dramatic breath she announced, "My mom wants us all . . . the four of us . . . to be junior bridesmaids at the wedding!" Mia jumped up on the couch and started to hop up and down with excitement, swinging her arms.

"Oh my gosh!" cried Katie, jumping up after her. "I've never even been to a wedding, never mind *in* one!" She jumped up and down too.

"Me neither!" I cried. I jumped up on the couch, since it appeared that was how we were celebrating. I caught a glimpse of Katie's watch in midair as her arm sailed past. Three forty-nine. *Could I leave now? No, that would be rude.* I had to stick it out for five more minutes to enjoy the news with the other girls. And it *was* good news.

"That is excellent," said Alexis definitively. She was not the couch-jumping type, but we loved her anyway.

"Your mom is so cool," I said. Then I felt bad. My mom was cool too, but she'd been distracted and out of touch the past couple of weeks because she'd gotten furloughed, or suspended, from her job at the town library due to government cutbacks. Basically they'd told her to go home until they could come up with some money to pay her. Last week she'd finally had to take a part-time job at the bookstore at the mall just to have some extra income. But the hours were terrible and our family's routines and schedules had been turned upside down. This was bad because I love a schedule, and I get really jumpy and grumpy when my schedules get messed up. My dad had given me and my three brothers a pep talk about how we had to stick together and pitch in and not worry Mom or put any pressure on her. It was hard. But I was nothing if not dependable. "I know I don't have to worry about you, Emma," Mom would always say. And I made sure she really didn't have to worry about me now. But I missed seeing Mom and having her there when I got home after school. She was always running around these days. To be honest I wasn't sure my mom even remembered what the Cupcake Club was, let alone how important it had become to us.

It had all started on the first day of middle school, when we sat together at lunch, and we stared at Katie's delicious homemade cupcake. The next day she brought in cupcakes to share and they were good. Really good. It was Alexis's idea to bring cupcakes every Friday, and we all took turns. We all banded together then. We stuck together when Sydney Whitman formed the Popular Girls Club and none of us were in it. We started to bake together and then formed a business. The Cupcake Club took off, and we began making cupcakes for events all over town. It was sometimes a lot of work, but it was also a lot of fun.

"So what are we going to wear?" asked Katie.

Mia's mom worked in fashion, so the question of the bridesmaid dress was sure to get a great deal of discussion. "Well, we just started talking about it, and we didn't get too far before she had to leave for work," said Mia. "She's going to pick up some bridal magazines for ideas, and we can all look at them. Then we might go to the bridal salon where she got her dress and try stuff on."

"Fun!" said Alexis. "Have you ever been?"

"Yes, I was there when my mom went to try on her wedding dress for the first time . . . ," began Mia, warming to the topic.

I wanted to stay and listen, but I started getting antsy. I had not budgeted time for this and now I was stuck here for another ten minutes at least, discussing the various types of wedding dresses and junior bridesmaid dresses. And worse, I knew that if we had to buy dresses for the wedding, it would be a big expense. Since my mom had lost her job, there hadn't been any money for extras. There was hardly enough money for clothes or sporting goods. (In a house with three brothers, sporting goods were as much of a basic necessity as food. Things were always getting lost or being outgrown.) We had to earn extra spending money for movies and pizza and things like that, which is why I started walking Jenner. I tried to save most of my dog-walking money, though. I had been saving up for so long for a pink KitchenAid mixer I'd seen in the Williams-Sonoma catalog. We were the only ones who didn't have a fancy mixer, and baking at our house was such a pain when someone had to use the old hand-held one we had. Oh no. Would I have to spend all the money on a bridesmaid's dress?

"What do you think?" asked Mia, turning to me.

"Huh?" I said. I had been thinking about my savings account.

"Earth to Emma! You've been such a space cadet

lately!" chided Katie with a smile. "Are you bored of us?"

I could feel my face get red. "I guess I should be eating more cupcakes to keep my energy up," I joked. It was just that I had so much to keep track of: school, flute practice (I'm in the school orchestra), Cupcake Club, my new job walking the neighbors' dog, and babysitting my younger brother. It was getting to be a lot. I hadn't told anyone about my mom's job or how I had to babysit Jake more or how many conversations we had about saving money at my house.

"Oh no! Am I rambling on too much?" asked Mia, embarrassed. "You know I could talk about fashion all day!"

I instantly felt rotten about putting any kind of damper on what should have been a great moment for Mia. I didn't want her to think I wasn't excited.

"No, you're not rambling at all! And I am so psyched about your mom's wedding. I think it's so cool that we get to do the cupcakes, and I am so excited about us being junior bridesmaids. It's so amazing." I really did mean it. It was great news.

Mia smiled. "Thanks! I can't wait!"

"It's just . . ." I wanted to tell my best friends about our money troubles, but I just couldn't. It would be embarrassing, not to mention kind of disloyal to my family. And anyway, I didn't want to lay it all out and then have to run out the door and potentially leave them all talking about me and feeling sorry for us Taylors. "It's just that I have to go home and watch Jake. And I'm worried I'm going to be late for his bus! But I don't want to run out on all this great news! I want to talk about all the dresses, but then I'll be late!"

Well, it wasn't a total lie. I did have to watch Jake, but not until tomorrow, when my brother Matt had basketball practice. It was his turn to watch Jake after school today. Running out on them for Jake sounded more legitimate than running out on them for a dog, that's all.

"Oh no! Go! We're totally done," said Mia sweetly.

"What about the Garner job? The four-year-old's birthday party? We need to submit a bid for that . . . ," said Alexis.

I froze. I was halfway to standing up, and I plunked back down on the couch. The club rule was that we all had do to the planning together so no one got stuck with it (even though I secretly thought Alexis would totally be okay doing all of it).

But Mia waved. "Go, go. You can't be late! We'll

e-mail you what we come up with, okay?"

I was torn. I hated feeling like this. "Really?" I knew I was biting my lip.

"Go! It's fine!" said Katie nicely. "Really!"

I looked at Alexis, and she nodded.

"Okay," I said. "Sorry." I gave Mia a big hug. "Just let me know the details . . ." Then I grabbed my backpack and hustled out.

I am going to be so late, I thought as I dashed out of Mia's house, which I loved. Everything here was so stylish and neat and clean in contrast to my house, where everything was sturdy enough for three boys and slightly trashed and of question-able cleanliness. Just yesterday I had to kick three pairs of Matt's disgustingly stinky socks off the sofa before I sat down.

I clipped my bike helmet on and hopped on my bike. Well it was mine now. It was a hand-me-down from Sam, my eldest brother, by way of Matt, the next one down. It was a boys' bike, with a bar, and it was gray and a little too big for me. But it was in decent shape and totally reliable. I pumped hard for the seven blocks home, standing up on the pedals almost the whole way, and taking the most efficient route.

I passed Jake's bus, which was stopped on the

block before our house. Flying by at top speed, I just waved at all of the windows. One of them had to be Jake's. I turned up the driveway, ditched my bike in the rack so I didn't get yelled at for leaving it out, ran into the mudroom and dumped my backpack and flute case into my locker (yes, we actually have lockers at home; it is the only way to contain the madness, my mom says), and was about to dash back out to get Jenner for his walk.

"Where have you been?" Matt screeched. He went flying past me out the door, dressed in his basketball uniform with his jacket over it, the jacket flapping open in his haste. His light, curly hair was smushed under a baseball hat and his blue eyes flashed with impatience.

"What?" I asked, not comprehending. I followed him out to the driveway.

"They changed my practice time!" yelled Matt, hopping on a bike. *My bike!*

"Wait, that's my bike!" I yelled. "And what about Jake?"

"He's all yours! Mom said! And it used to be my bike so I still can claim it!" And Matt went sailing off.

The bus pulled up, and Jake shuffled out. His shaggy blond hair was all messed up and his blue eyes looked tired. He had on jeans and his favorite T-shirt; it was blue and said NYPD.

"Bye, buddy!" called Sal, the driver. Sal waved at me. I sighed and waved back. This was not what I bargained for.

"Hi, Emmy," said Jake as he trudged up the driveway. His backpack was bigger than his whole back. I couldn't imagine what he carried in it besides his lunch.

"Hi, pal." I sighed again and took a deep breath. I didn't want to snap at him. It wasn't Jake's fault Matt had ditched him. It wasn't his fault that Mom had a new part-time job so she couldn't be home to meet him after school.

I thought about how I was going to negotiate this. Jake requires careful planning. "I'll grab you a quick snack while you use the bathroom and then we'll go walk Jenner real quick, okay?" I said, trying to keep my voice light. Jake could be a bit of a tyrant, and if he wasn't in the mood to do something, there was no way he'd do it. It was a little like taking care of a puppy.

"But I'm tired!" whined Jake, his shoulders drooping. "I just wanna stay home and watch TV!"

I could see the Jenner walking job slipping away, and I couldn't let that happen. I had to think fast.

"You can bring your scooter and . . . we'll go to Camden's, and I'll buy you a piece of candy!" It would cost me, but it would be worth it.

Jake paused as if weighing his options: tantrum or candy. I held my breath. Finally he spoke. "Two pieces."

Phew. "Two pieces it is, mister, but hustle now. Poor Jenner is crossing his little doggy legs, he needs to pee so badly!"

This sent Jake into peals of laughter, and I knew I had him. And it was only 4:10.

One problem at a time conquered with a little planning. *That's how we roll, baby,* I said to myself as I hustled us out the door. *That's how we roll.*

CHAPTER 2

Dogs and Brothers Don't Mix

Jenner leaped excitedly behind the Andersons' door as I got the key from its hiding place and put it in the lock at 4:20. Jake watched the dog closely through the window with wide eyes. Jenner could be as much of a handful as Jake sometimes.

"You stay here, Jakey, while I go in and get his leash on, okay?" I said. Once he was on his leash Jenner would be fine.

Jake nodded. He didn't hate dogs, but he wasn't crazy about them either. Especially big, excited ones.

Sliding my knee through the opening in the door, I forced Jenner gently backward, then pulled the door shut. He was a good dog, but a little energetic at first.

"Hey, boy! Hi, buddy!" Jenner jumped up and tried to put his two front paws on my shoulders. I grabbed him firmly by the collar and spoke to him in a soothing voice and patted his head. It had taken a few tries, but I learned that you just had to be very calm with him. Kind of like when you were talking to Jake on the verge of a meltdown. Sure enough, Jenner stopped jumping, and I grabbed the leash from the hook and clipped it to his collar. Then I picked up the pooper-scooper Baggies holder and put it in my pocket. All set.

I looked around before I left. The Andersons' mudroom was so neat, with everyone's shoes in individual cubbyholes and the Anderson girls' jackets and sporting equipment neatly aligned. I loved organization. I inhaled deeply. Something smelled really good. *Mmm,* I thought. Beef bourguignonne—a savory stew. Mom used to make it a lot. Mrs. Anderson worked full time at an insurance agency so, because of her schedule, she was a big Crock-Pot aficionado. A Crock-Pot cooked all day, and every time you came into the house you smelled dinner. Lately we ate mostly microwave stuff. It didn't smell nearly as good.

Jenner gave a short bark, and I realized I had been standing there for a minute. "That's a good boy, now. Time for your walky," I said. Poor guy. He probably really had to go.

I opened the door, and Jenner charged out, yanking on the leash. "Easy, boy," I said. Then I turned to find Jake, but he wasn't standing where I had left him.

"Jake?" I called. Where could he have disappeared to so quickly?

Jenner pulled on the leash toward the sidewalk where we usually go, but I thought Jake must be in the Andersons' backyard. They had a swing set and that would have captured his attention. I pulled Jenner along and peered over the low, white picket fence into the backyard. No Jake. Uh-oh. He could only have headed down the driveway to the sidewalk. Now I felt a little nervous.

"C'mon, Jenner," I said, and we trotted quickly down the driveway to the street. I looked left. No Jake. Then I looked right and there, way off in the distance about two blocks ahead, was Jake, motoring along on his scooter. "Oh no!" I cried, and we took off. How long had I been in the house?

Jenner needed little encouragement to run. Greyhounds can reach a top speed of forty-five miles per hour, which is why people use them for racing, and Jenner must've been a champion in his day. I was in pretty good shape from volleyball at school, but I could barely keep up with him. Up ahead, Jake was nearing a busier street, and since he had already crossed the two quiet cul-de-sacs that intersected the Andersons' street, I knew he'd have no qualms about crossing the next street. I had to reach him fast.

"Jake!" I screamed. He looked back at me over his shoulder and kept on going. He could be so bad! All I could think about was that my mother was going to kill me. Jake was still halfway up the next block, scootering at full speed. "Jake! Stop!" I cried, louder this time. But he didn't even turn around.

Jenner strained at his leash. Jake was nearing the corner, with only thirty feet to go. Jenner and I crossed the final cul-de-sac—I looked both ways first—and we were only about half a block behind Jake. "Jake!" He looked back one more time and his scooter swerved a little, but he straightened it out and kept going. He was headed right for the busy main street. I froze. Then, in a split second, I just let go of Jenner's leash. He took off at double the speed we'd been running and reached Jake in about fifteen long strides.

Jake was so spooked by the big dog chasing him

that he jumped off his scooter sideways, landing with a thud on a soft mound of lawn just before the corner.

I ran as fast as I could and flopped down next to him, gasping, and grabbed his shirt, just in case he hopped back on. Jenner was licking Jake maniacally, and Jake was crying. I grabbed Jenner's collar, too, so I was hanging on to both of them.

"Jenner! Sit!" I said. "Stay," I said firmly, holding my palm out flat toward him. I still had one hand on Jake. "Jakey, are you okay? Are you hurt?" I asked. "Don't cry."

Jake was more scared and mad than anything else. "That doggy tried to bite me!" he accused, pointing a finger at Jenner. Jenner looked at him and whimpered but didn't move.

"Good dog," I said. "Jake, he didn't try to bite you. He saved you! You can't just take off like that. It's dangerous, and dumb, and . . . illegal!" Jake was into law enforcement big-time, so I knew to throw that in.

That got him. Jake stopped crying. "It is not!" he said.

I nodded, knowing I had him now. "Yes. Kids aren't allowed to scooter alone on the sidewalk until they're eight. It's a law."

Jake looked at me skeptically. "I don't believe you."

"Well, it's true. If we see a police officer on the way to Camden's, we can ask. Now come on, let's go. And don't ever take off on me like that again, or I'll have to turn you in at police headquarters." I tried to make my voice sound stern. I didn't even know where the headquarters was.

I picked up Jenner's leash and helped Jake back onto his scooter. I let out a big sigh of relief. Everything was under control again. Jenner stepped off the curb to do his business.

"I still get my candy. Two," said Jake stubbornly. It wasn't a question but rather a statement.

"Well . . . ," I said. Mom was always talking about not rewarding bad behavior. And Jake was definitely bad, taking off like that.

Jake's lower lip began to tremble. "You said!" he accused.

I knew I was in rough territory, but suddenly I was mad too. "Well, that was before you took off, mister!" I said. The aroma of Jenner's business at the curb was unpleasant. I fished in my pocket for the Baggies clip.

"I hate you!" accused Jake.

I sighed and bent to pick up Jenner's poop,

standing on his leash so he didn't wander away. Jake was being a pain and now I had yucky dog doo. Nothing was going according to plan. It couldn't get worse. But as I stood up, I found myself face-to-face with Sydney Whitman, neighborhood resident, founder and president of the Popular Girls Club, and all-around mean girl, and her hench-lady Bella. *Well,* I thought, *I guess my day can get worse.*

I never ran into Sydney except at the worst possible moments. Weeks could go by without seeing Sydney. Then I'd go outside to get the mail in my pajamas on a Saturday and she would walk by, saying, "Oh, Emma, are you sick?" I really didn't like her. I looked at Jenner's poop bag and Jake's tear-streaked face, and my heart sank.

"Pee-yoo!" said Sydney, waving her hand in front of her nose. "Is that the kid's or the dog's?" she asked, giggling. Bella snickered appreciatively.

I rolled my eyes and said nothing.

"I didn't know you had a dog," said Sydney, tossing her long, Barbie-blond hair from one shoulder to the other in a pointless way.

"He's our neighbors'," I said. It wasn't like Sydney knew anything about me, so why should she act like she did?

"Oh good, because he's so ugly, I was going to

feel sorry for you. But I guess I just feel sorry for your neighbors!" She laughed a kind of fake laughter, and Bella joined her.

Poor Jenner, I thought. Greyhounds were funny-looking, but Jenner was a good dog, and he had just saved my little brother. "He's a good dog, aren't you, puppy?" I reached down and gave Jenner a loyal pat, and he licked my hand.

"Gross. I hope you wash that hand before you make cupcakes," said Sydney.

"Yeah!" agreed Bella unoriginally.

Jake stood up. "I hope you wash your face before I take you down to headquarters!" he said loudly, his hands on his hips and his scooter resting at his side. I laughed.

Sydney and Bella turned to look at him. "Isn't he cute?" said Sydney in a sweet voice.

"What's your name, little boy?" asked Bella.

Jake puffed up his chest and refused to answer. *Good boy,* I thought. He might be a pain, but he's my brother. "That's Jake," I said, trying to sound light and breezy. "And he has a date at the candy store. Let's go, buddy." Then I turned my back on Sydney and Bella and lifted Jenner's leash out from under my shoe.

"So long!" said Sydney.

"Later," I said. *Like, much later.*

Bella and Sydney continued walking along the sidewalk, and we headed off to cross the street.

"Thanks for sticking up for me, Jake," I said after a minute.

"Two pieces, right?" said Jake, grinning. Well, the kid was smart. I started laughing.

"Right," I agreed. "Two pieces for you!" Little brothers were a pain, but sometimes they weren't too bad.

CHAPTER 3

Home, Not-So-Sweet Home

After we went to Camden's we took a good long scooter ride around the neighborhood, and Jenner got an extra-long walk. Jake had eaten one Air-Heads and saved another for later. Jenner was tired out and, after a long drink of water, went straight to his doggy bed in the Andersons' kitchen and curled up for a nap. Mrs. Anderson had left an envelope marked "Emma" on the kitchen island, and I picked it up and opened it, then smiled at the five-dollar bill inside and left, closing the door behind me to lock it.

At home Jake went right for the TV, and I grabbed my backpack and flute case to head upstairs to my room. I never really had a problem getting my work done and my flute practice in each day. It was all a matter of scheduling and maximizing my time. I loved making schedules. It felt good to be able to check things off. Plus I liked knowing exactly what was happening when. That way there were no surprises. I hate surprises more than anything. They make me nervous.

After a while I heard my older brother Sam come home from basketball practice, so I went downstairs and found him wolfing down a chicken Parmesan sub at the kitchen sink. He worked nights at the movie theater and didn't usually have time to eat with us.

"Hey, Sam," I said.

"Hey, kiddo," he said. He wiped his mouth with a paper towel and took another bite.

Sam was handsome. There was no denying it. Girls called the house all the time and hung up, giggling, when I answered. I usually just rolled my eyes. It didn't really bother me that they called, but it bothered me that Sam seemed to like it. I can't explain why. I guess I should just get used to it because all my friends have huge crushes on him. Besides being handsome, he was also pretty nice. At least as far as brothers go. He was just so busy between schoolwork (he had to make honor roll to get a scholarship to a Division One college); playing varsity football, basketball, and lacrosse; and his job at the movie theater that he was kind of like a ghost in our family. You'd see signs that he'd been home—a dirty plate, a small pile of laundry on top of the machine—but rarely spy the actual Sam. I was glad to see him.

"What's new?" I asked, reaching for a cookie. Before I could grab it, though, I went to the sink to wash my hands. I couldn't help thinking about Sydney and her dog poo comment.

Sam stepped aside and took a long drink straight from the quart of milk on the counter. "Gross," I said. It was kind of automatic. Honestly, my brothers do so many gross things, I should be used to it by now.

He tipped back the container and finished it. "Mom texted me to say she got taco stuff for you guys. It's in the fridge."

"Okay," I said. At least tacos were easy. I could make them if my dad didn't get home in time. He was trying to leave work earlier now that Mom had to work evenings, but he didn't always make it out early enough to make dinner. Usually Jake and Matt were so hungry and whiny that I ended up making it.

"Anything good on this week?" I asked hopefully.

Sam's job at the movie theater meant sometimes he could get me discounts.

"New Will Smith coming. I can get you half-price passes," he offered. "Four good?"

I smiled, thinking of Mia, Alexis, and Katie. And saving money. "Perfect. Thanks," I said.

"Got any cupcakes in exchange?" asked Sam.

I shook my head sadly. In a house with three boys, cupcakes went fast. "All out. Sorry. I'll make more tomorrow. I promise I'll save you one." I started to go back upstairs. "Have fun at work!" I called.

"Always do," said Sam, and he burped a long, loud belch.

"Gross," I said. Automatic again. There is seriously a lot of burping in my house. "But impressive. Maybe you can get on varsity burping."

I flopped down into the fluffy armchair in my room. I pulled out my music stand, flipped open to the piece I was working on, opened the flute case, and just sat for a minute with my flute in two pieces in my lap. I love my room. It's pink, first off, which is my favorite color. Right before I started middle school my mom told me that we could redo it so it wasn't so babyish. I was really glad to get rid of the Barbie sheets, since I was embarrassed every time I had a friend over. My mom and I worked really hard to get it just right. We went through all these magazines to find just the right look. It took months and months.

We bought a wooden bedroom set—a desk, twin bed with a trundle, a dresser with a tilting mirror on top, and a bedside table—at a yard sale and spray painted it a shiny pale pink. Then we took an old armchair from my grandmother's attic, and Mom had it reupholstered with white fabric that has a pattern of tiny, pale- and hot-pink flowers with green stems so it looked so pretty.

The pièces de résistance, as my mom calls them (which kind of means the "big deal"), are the walls. We copied a project we had seen on a TV design show where they'd covered the walls in panels of fabric with this kind of foam behind it, so now my room is totally cushy, soundproof, and quiet. It's like my own little nest.

After a half hour of practice I dashed off a quick e-mail to the club, asking if anyone wanted to go see the new Will Smith movie on Friday night, and then I cracked open my book bag to start my homework. But the computer called to me again, and I gave in. Just one quick peek, I told myself. I logged on to the Williams-Sonoma website, and there it was. The pale pink KitchenAid mixer. All $250 of it.

I thought about how much faster and easier it would be to turn out delicious cupcakes if I had that mixer. Not to mention breads, muffins, cookies, and more. And I knew I would get a jolt of happiness every time I saw it on the counter. It was that pretty. I pulled open the bottom drawer of my desk and took out the dustcover I'd already bought for the mixer on eBay. It had a pink quilted background with a pattern of cupcakes repeating across it—red velvet, white buttercream, and double chocolate with a cherry on top. I hadn't been able to resist it and only twenty-three dollars, it had been easy to hand the cash over to Mom and convince her to charge it, even though I didn't yet have the machine it would cover. Dad would have refused, being the more practical of the two parents, but my mom understood the importance of dreaming big. She even bought it for me in the end and wouldn't take the dog-walking money I gave her. *One day,* I thought, *that mixer will be mine.*

Just then, there was a knock on the door. "Emma!" came Jake's muffled voice. All the boys knew they had to knock on my door. It was a girls-only zone. Luckily my parents strongly enforced the rule.

"Come in!" I called, and Jake opened the door.

"I'm hungry," he said.

I looked at my watch. Six thirty. "Is Dad home?"

Jake shook his head. I looked at my pile of homework and sighed. Well, I had to eat too.

"Let's go, officer," I said. "I'll make some tacos, okay?"

Jake nodded happily and skipped down to the kitchen.

Tacos are really easy. My mom taught us all how to make them, but I make the least mess in the kitchen, so I try to get there before Matt or Sam does. The family rule is that whoever doesn't cook helps clean up, and if my brothers are in the kitchen, the cleanup goes to a whole other level. I sautéed the ground beef and set out the condiments while Jake set the table (that's his job, and he's okay at it as long as you remind him that you need forks and knives and not just spoons). Matt rolled in midway through and I told him he was on cleanup duty. He nodded. He'd bailed on babysitting Jake today, so he owed me, big-time. He ran up to shower while I finished the cooking.

"Hello, everybody!" Dad's voice echoed through the front hall, and the door clunked shut behind him. I heard his keys drop on the tray on the console. Sam had left, Matt was in the shower, and a bomb couldn't take Jake's interest from the TV.

"Hey, Dad!" I called in reply. "I'm in here!"

Dad walked in, loosening his tie. He was tall and athletic, like Sam, with the same curly hair and the same twinkly blue eyes. He worked at a bank downtown so he had to wear a suit, but to me it always looked like a costume. He looked most like himself when he was in sweats and a T-shirt with a whistle around his neck. He'd coached many of our teams over the years and also played in a men's soccer league at night once a week with his friends.

"Hi, honey!" Dad crossed the kitchen to hug me, and he lifted me up and spun me once, then kissed the top of my head. I knew I was getting a little big for it, but that's what he always did when he came home. At least he'd stopped saying "Hello, my little princess."

Dad sniffed, looked around, then looked relieved. "Thanks for making dinner. You're a star."

I shrugged. "Gotta eat," I said, but I smiled. My parents could depend on me. They always told me that, and I never wanted to disappoint them. Anyway, I liked doing things myself.

Dad rolled up his sleeves and washed his hands in the sink. Then he grabbed a bag of chips and a bowl and some salsa. "I had hoped to get out early so you wouldn't get stuck with dinner, but we had a couple of new deals to process, and I couldn't leave," he said. "How was your day?"

I thought back to school, then the Cupcake Club meeting. "Oh! Mia's mom asked us to be in her wedding!" I said. It was exciting, even if it might be too expensive.

"Wow!" said Dad, reaching for a chip. "That's neat. What do you have to do?"

"We're going to be junior bridesmaids. Actually, I'm not sure what we have to do!" I laughed. It had all been about the dresses, not the actual responsibilities. "I'd better find out."

"You probably just walk down the aisle ahead of the bride. You just have to make sure you smile," said Dad. "That shouldn't be too hard for you." He winked. I was just relieved that he was so clueless about clothes and weddings that he didn't think to ask what we would need to wear; that kind of stuff just wasn't on his radar unless someone spelled it out for him. I wasn't going to tell him about the dress.

"What else happened today?" he asked.

I thought over the rest of the day and decided not to say anything about Matt leaving me with Jake or

Jenner saving Jake's life. But gosh, was it hard to keep what felt like secrets from Dad. I wasn't used to it. Changing the subject was easier. "Hey, can I go to the movies with the Cupcake Club girls on Friday night? Sam's getting us passes."

"Sure," said Dad. Then he started to talk about carpools, and I kind of tuned him out and finished making the tacos. Matt and Jake came in and we all sat down at the table to eat. Except Sam. And Mom of course.

"A doggy saved my life today," said Jake out of nowhere. I felt my face get really red.

"Oh, ha-ha, Jakey. You're such an exaggerator!" I said, laughing a fake laugh.

Dad's eyebrows lifted. "Really. That's pretty interesting. What happened?"

"Well, I was going superfast on my scooter—"

"Hang on, back up," I interrupted. If the story was going to be told, all the details needed to be in place. "I had to walk the Andersons' dog, Jenner, after school, and Mr. Disorganized"—I gestured at Matt—"bailed on Jake because he had practice all of a sudden, so I had to take Jake."

Matt burst in, taco pieces spraying out of his full mouth. "Hey! It's not my fault! The coach changed it last minute, and I called Mom and she said to ask

Emma! I can't miss that stuff, or I'll get benched!"

"Matthew, don't talk with your mouth full. And while you're at it, get your elbows off the table." Dad looked irritated. "Is it true that you bagged Jake today?" he asked.

I smirked at Matt and he gave me a dark look. "Yes, but . . ."

"But what if Emma hadn't come home?" asked Dad.

"Well, obviously I wouldn't have gone and left Jake. I waited until she got here, anyway," said Matt.

Dad sighed. "Listen, guys, the logistics of your mom's new job are tricky, there's no denying it. Three to nine are hard hours for anyone and I know it puts a lot of responsibility on you guys. But we're a family. And families chip in and help out and look out for one another." He looked around the table.

Jake was drooping in his chair. It was past his official bedtime of seven thirty. Matt looked miffed. I tried not to look upset. I missed Mom. It was so much easier when she was here and Matt and I didn't have to babysit every day. I knew it wasn't Mom's fault that she'd been "downsized," or whatever they called it, from her job at the library. And I knew Mom wasn't thrilled about working at the bookstore at the mall. Sure, the discounts were great, but the hours stank and she was on her feet all day for not that much money.

"Here's the deal. If you can't babysit on your assigned day," Dad said, looking at us in that Dad-like way, "then you have to let the other person know as soon as possible. And you owe that person a day. It has to be even. Do you understand?"

We nodded.

"Can I go to bed?" asked Jake.

"Run on up, take off your clothes, and get out your PJs, and I'll come run your shower in one minute," said Dad. Jake scraped back his chair and took off.

"Clear your plate!" I called, but Jake was gone. I turned to Matt. "Okay, you owe me, so you have Friday."

"What? No way!" protested Matt. "I have plans!"

"Me too, and you owe me a day. I can stay with him until five. After that, just take Jake with you," I said. "That's what I did."

"What was all that business about Jake and the 'doggy,' anyway?" asked Dad.

Oh no. "Oh, I had to walk the Andersons' dog, Jenner, and Jake was, uh, going too fast on his scooter, and Jenner, um, stopped him for me," I said. I really did hate to lie. But it was either that or not be able to dog walk on the days I had Jake, and I couldn't afford to lose any jobs.

Dad gave me another look. "Just make sure that Jake is your number one priority when he's with you, okay?" he said sternly, but not really like he was mad.

I nodded.

"And you, too, buddy," he said to Matt. "I'm going up to start Jake's shower and get him to bed. If you can get your dishes in the sink and make a quick plate for Mom, I'll come back down and clean up, okay?"

Matt smiled a gloating smile that he was off the hook for cleanup. I rolled my eyes at him as we all stood up.

"And kids?"

We looked at him.

"Thanks. Thanks for pitching in. You're great kids." He smiled a tired smile and started to leave the kitchen. "I'll have a chat with Mom when she gets home tonight, and we'll work out a better schedule, okay?"

We nodded at Dad and then turned and gave each other dirty looks. The battle was over, but not the war.

CHAPTER 4

Burned

I was so busy with school, flute, babysitting Jake, and walking Jenner that the week flew by. Alexis had sent around our cupcake proposals for approval by e-mail, and after reaching a consensus, she had e-mailed them on to our clients (Mia's mom being one). Friday came quickly, and after a quick pit stop at the grocery store for supplies after school, the Cupcake Club came over for a meeting and to bake up a few samples of a new recipe of Katie's. The plan was that after we baked we would head downtown for a slice of pizza and the movie.

Alexis called the meeting to order and said that Mia's mom would like to sample the bacon cupcakes for the groom's cake before she placed her final order for the wedding cupcakes. Alexis coughed and shot me a look. "She'll love it once she tastes it!" I promised.

We agreed to meet next Friday to bake them; Mia would take them home afterward. Next Mia confirmed the timing for the club's outing to the bridal store the next morning. My stomach turned over as the reality of the dress set in. I hadn't really paid attention to the e-mails about the plan because I didn't want to. I still didn't want to ask Mom for money for it, and I wasn't sure I was going to have enough from dog walking or cupcake making. Finally, we discussed some leads we had for other jobs. Then it was time to bake.

On the menu today were raspberry swirl cupcakes with a pink cream cheese frosting. I was beating the frosting with a hand mixer, having to pause and rest the mixer on its back while I added ingredients. I couldn't help fantasizing about the hands-free pink stand mixer. Someday. Soon!

Mia had brought three bridal magazines, and the others were all flipping through them while the cupcakes baked in the oven. Tomorrow were going to The Special Day bridal shop at the Chamber Street Mall, and Mia wanted us to get some ideas before we went.

"Here's a really cute one!" declared Katie. I

peered over Katie's shoulder to see the dress she was pointing at. I looked at the price first. All the prices were a lot more than I thought. I had never really paid attention when I went shopping with Mom before, and lately there hadn't been much shopping. I couldn't remember how much a dress was supposed to cost, but the ones in the magazines were a lot of money.

"Ooh! Look at this one!" said Alexis. She handed the magazine across the room to Mia, and I leaned over to see it. It was a white, shin-length dress with a sash. It was beautiful. It was also $350! I gulped and prayed Mia wouldn't like it.

"Oh, that is pretty!" said Mia. "I love it! But three hundred and fifty dollars! No way!"

Whew, I thought. *I love my friends.* "That is crazy!"

"That's business for you, baby," said Alexis, reaching out her hands to take the magazine back. "They want to suck every possible dollar out of the big day."

The back door opened and shut with a bang. "Emma!" It was Sam.

Mia, Alexis, and Katie sat up straight and adjusted their outfits and hair, trying to look good for Sam. It was kind of funny and kind of not. "In here!" I called.

Sam walked into the kitchen. "Yum! Did you save any for me?"

Mia flipped her hair. "We will," she said with a big smile.

"They're not ready yet," I said.

Katie and Alexis stopped talking. And for Alexis that was a big deal. She just looked at Sam and smiled. Katie couldn't even look at him. She stared at her sneakers.

Sam smirked. I think he thought it was cute that all my friends had crushes on him. "Here are your passes for the movie. Have fun!" He slid them across the counter.

"Thanks," I said.

"Have you seen it?" asked Mia.

"Part of it. It's killer," said Sam. "Gotta go!"

The back door opened and slammed closed again.

"He is really cute," said Katie.

"Totally," agreed Mia. "And so nice!"

"Depends on the day," I said. But Sam was pretty nice. Nicer than Matt.

"Such a hard worker . . . ," said Alexis dreamily, and we all roared with laughter. All Alexis thought about was business.

Katie stood and went to peek in the oven at the cupcakes. "Almost," she said.

"Don't overbake them!" warned Alexis, picking up the timer and glancing at it. "Remember our bottom line!"

We'd wasted a whole batch last week because we'd gotten distracted by a reality TV show. We'd had to toss them all and start over; it had been a total waste of money and time.

The phone rang. I checked the caller ID and saw that it was Jenner's owner, Mrs. Anderson, calling from work.

"Hi, Mrs. Anderson," I said. Had I done anything wrong? Mentally I reviewed my last visit to the Andersons'. I was sure I'd locked up.

"Hi, honey. Ooh, that caller ID still gives me a start! Anyway, I was wondering if I could ask a favor?"

"Sure," I said, relieved.

"Any chance you could give Jenner a quick run around the block today? The girls have a birthday party, and I'm going straight from work to meet them there. I totally forgot. The poor guy won't make it. . . ."

I looked at my watch. I had to meet Jake at the school bus in fifteen minutes. The cupcakes would have to come out in a few minutes, then cool before we frosted them. Then we absolutely had to leave for pizza by five, when Matt got home. The movie was at 6:20. But Mrs. Anderson depended on me, and I hated to say no. Plus, if I was going to have to buy a bridesmaid's dress, then I needed the money. I planned it out in my head.

"Hang on just one second while I check something." I covered the phone. "Would you guys meet Jake's bus for me while I run over to the Andersons'?"

The others looked surprised but readily agreed. "Jake's so cute!" said Katie, who didn't have any siblings of her own.

"Let's hope so," I said. Then, returning to the call, I said, "Sure. No problem!"

"Great! I'll just double up on the money for the next time you come, okay?" asked Mrs. Anderson.

"That's fine. Don't worry. Bye!" I hung up and took off my pink apron.

Mia was looking at me strangely.

"What?" I asked. "Mrs. Anderson needs me to walk Jenner. I'll just be a second. The frosting's almost ready. It just needs vanilla and one more whip. Then we'll have to wait until the 'cakes are done to frost them anyway. I'll be back in no time."

"Don't worry! Take your time. It's no problem.

Really." Mia stood to assume the role of chief frosting officer. She smiled, but she seemed . . . well, something was wrong. Was Mia annoyed?

I couldn't think about it long. I had to run. "Okay. Thanks! Be back in less than half an hour. Jake will be here in ten minutes."

I ran down the block to the Andersons'. Jenner jumped up, happy to see me, and I took him out. It took him forever to do his business (probably because he was off schedule), but he finally did, and then I ran him around the block a couple of times for good exercise.

I miscalculated how long that would all take—it had been about forty-five minutes. I glanced at my watch and ran home. When I got there, I saw Jake's backpack flung on the driveway and the back door standing open.

"Hello?" I called, entering the house. But there was no reply. Only the smell of very burnt cupcakes. They were sitting on the counter, dark brown as pretzels and just as hard. "Bummer," I said.

"Guys?" I walked through the downstairs, listening for my friends and little brother. They could hardly be this quiet. I opened the door to the basement rec room. Maybe they were playing video games?

Then I heard a "Hello?" from behind me. It was Matt, just arriving.

I walked back to the kitchen. "Uh . . . are you just getting here?" I asked.

"Yeah, but I'm ten minutes early! Give me a break!" said Matt, bristling. Mom had read him the riot act for ditching Jake on me the other day, and he'd been conscientious about his two turns since then.

"No, no, I'm not annoyed at you. It's just . . ."

"Where's Jake?" asked Matt. My heart sank.

"Uh, I'm not sure."

"Was he here before? I saw his backpack. . . ." Matt headed out to the driveway and I followed him.

"I know, but I had to go walk Jenner . . . so I wasn't here. . . ."

"What?" exploded Matt. "You mean he came home to an empty house?"

"No, my friends were here. I'm sure they met him. I asked them to, but now I don't know where they are."

"You left your friends in charge? Those cupcake girls?" Matt knew that it drove me crazy when he pretended not to know my friends' names.

"Yes, Alexis, Mia, and Katie," I said, trying not

to get angry. "They're very responsible."

"I'm telling Mom!" gloated Matt. "You shirked your duty!"

"Never mind that," I said, starting to get a little panicky. "Where did they go?"

"Well, they couldn't have gotten far. They weren't driving, were they?" he teased.

I didn't answer. He thought it was funny, but I knew something could be wrong. "I'll check the park. Why don't you go check—"

"I'm not checking anything," said Matt happily. "This is your problem. I'll be in here relaxing. Good luck."

"You're a jerk," I said.

I walked quickly to the park, but it still took about five minutes and there was no sign of them there. Where else could they be? The duck pond? I hustled over, but there was no sign of them there either. Oh, why oh why wouldn't my parents let me have a cell phone? (Well, I knew why: It was expensive. Mom and Dad had taken them back as a cost-saving measure. But it was so worth it! I decided to ask for mine back again when Mom got her old job back.)

Ice cream? Camden's? Could they have gone that far? But there was no sign. Now I had been searching for more than twenty minutes, and it was five fifteen. I decided to run home and check to see if they'd returned. By now I realized that my friends would take care of Jake, so nothing bad probably happened. But where were they?

When I turned up my block, I could see that Jake's backpack was no longer in the driveway. And there was certainly no way he'd picked it up himself. One of the girls must have done it. Phew. They were home. I slowed down and sauntered up the driveway, relieved.

But Dad flung open the back door angrily. "Emma! Where is your little brother?"

Oh no! "Isn't he . . . here?" I asked, cringing. Obviously not, since Dad was so mad.

Matt appeared in the doorway behind him, grinning through a mouthful of burnt cupcake.

"I'm going out in the car to look for them," Dad said harshly.

"I'll come," I said readily.

"No, you stay here and call my cell in case they come back while I'm gone." He dashed out and backed the car out of the garage.

"You know these things aren't half bad if you load on the frosting," said Matt as he helped himself to another cupcake.

"Shut up," I said, and went to wait on the back stoop.

Twenty minutes later, which seemed like about four hours later, Jake and the girls returned. I ran in and dialed Dad's cell as soon as I saw them coming. "Good" was all he said, and then hung up. Oh, boy. I ran back outside.

Jake was covered in ice cream, and he held two large candy bars, one in each hand. He was laughing and joking, and the girls were laughing at him. No one seemed hurt or mad or frustrated. Except me.

"What happened?" I demanded, coming down the sidewalk to meet them.

Mia rolled her eyes. "This one sure doesn't like babysitters, do you, pal?" She ruffled Jake's hair.

"I like you!" said Jake winningly. The girls all laughed.

"*Now* you tell us," said Alexis.

"Where were you?" I asked, trying not to yell.

The girls explained how Jake had been upset that I wasn't there to meet him. So he'd had a temper tantrum and taken off down the street. They'd chased him and caught him, at which point he became hysterical and demanded candy.

"He said you buy him two pieces from Camden's

every day!" said Katie incredulously. "Is that true?"

"No, it's not," I said icily. I was glaring at Jake, and he ducked his head guiltily.

"Anyway, we figured we'd better bribe the kid, so we took him around . . ."

"And bought him some stuff," finished Mia.

"Clearly," I said.

"The cupcakes burned while he was having the temper tantrum."

"Luckily, Katie remembered and ran back to turn them off, before they burned down the house."

"That is lucky," I said, thinking that would have really made Dad mad. I looked at my watch. It was 5:40. There was no way we were going to make it for pizza, but we could still make the movie. I was really mad. And really tired. Then I looked up at my friends. They had tried to help me out. It wasn't their fault that Jake was such a pain. I just messed up with the timing. I'd just have to plan better next time, that's all.

"Guys, I'm so sorry. Thank you for dealing. I really appreciate it." I smiled at them. They were such good friends. And I was grateful. "But you!" I said, turning to Jake. "You are in trouble with me, mister! No candy for you next week, not on my watch!"

Jake hung his head. "Okay, sarge," he said.

"Let's go. Matt's waiting for you, and we have to leave. Sorry about the cupcakes, you guys. They were looking good."

"It's okay," said Mia. "How was the dog walking?" she asked.

"Good," I said.

"How much do they pay you?" asked Alexis.

"Five bucks a walk," I said proudly.

"Wow," said Katie. "Pretty good, considering if you had your way, you'd have your own dog and be walking it for free."

I smiled. "Yeah, a dog is definitely not in the budget for our family right now." I felt badly about saying it as soon as it came out of my mouth.

Mia was quiet. We went back to the house and hustled to clean up the kitchen. Then Dad came in.

"Hey, buddy!" he said to Jake as Jake ran to greet him.

"Emma's going to the movies with the baby-sitters!" said Jake.

"Not yet, she's not," said Dad. "Emma, may I see you in here for a minute, please?"

I felt my face get hot and put down the cupcake tin I was drying. I followed Dad into the living room. I felt my friends' eyes on me.

"Emma," he said quietly. "I know you've got a lot on your plate right now. We all do. But you have taken on way too much. When your brother is in danger because of your decisions, it's time for you to take a look at your priorities. And it sounds like this was the second time this week there was an incident that involved dog walking."

I put my head down, thinking of Jake and Jenner and the scooter ride the other day. "Jake wasn't in danger, though," I protested weakly. I knew Dad was right.

"Your primary responsibilities are to your family and to taking care of yourself. I think it's wonderful that you are so entrepreneurial with the Cupcake Club and the dog walking. I know it's terrific to earn your own money, and . . . well, I know you need it right now for some of the little extras we've cut back on. And I understand that you are trying to incorporate Jake, too, which Mom and I appreciate. But I just think you are getting stretched a little too thin right now. Do you understand?"

I nodded. Visions of expensive bridesmaid dresses swam in my head. Without the cupcakes and the dog walking, there was no way I could afford that dress.

Dad tipped my chin up to look him in the eye.

"You are a very capable young lady. You're just like your mom—organized, energetic, and kind—and we're proud of you. I know Jake can be a handful, but we're all trying to get by the best we can. I just don't want to see you make the wrong decisions or mix up your priorities."

I nodded. I didn't think I was making wrong decisions. I was getting things done. I was walking Jenner and doing my homework and practicing flute and contributing to the Cupcake Club and helping out as much as I could at home. I even made dinner a lot. Jake was the only thing that was a problem. I knew that was mean, but it was true.

Dad sighed. "You're a good kid, sweetheart. And I hate to say this, but if there's another incident with Jake . . . we're going to have to make some hard decisions about what you can and can't spend your time on, okay? And that includes the club and dog walking."

"It's okay, Dad. I understand," I said, but I really didn't. *I would just do better,* I thought. I didn't want anyone to worry about me. And I could take care of myself pretty well.

Dad hugged me and patted me on the head. "Now it's time to go."

"I can still go to the movies?" I said, kind of surprised.

Dad laughed. "Yes, you should go have fun with your friends."

"Thanks, Dad!" I said, and flung my arms around him. Then I ran into the kitchen.

Katie, Alexis, and Mia were waiting, having finished cleaning up the whole kitchen.

Matt smirked at me from the TV room, where he and Jake were watching *SportsCenter*. I could tell he was happy I was in trouble. And that he thought I was grounded. "Have fun, kids!" Matt said.

"We will!" I called back with a big smile on my face.

Matt looked like he couldn't believe it. I felt good. Things were getting better already.

"The pizza's on me," said Dad, glaring at Matt. "You still have time, and I'll drop you off."

We all climbed into the minivan and off we went. I just hoped the Will Smith movie had nothing to do with cupcakes or dogs. Or brothers.

CHAPTER 5

The Dress That Takes the Cake

$\mathcal{M}$om was making her specialty—banana chocolate-chip pancakes—for breakfast on Saturday morning. I could smell the bananas and warm, melting chocolate all the way up in my room, even with the door closed. I lay in bed thinking about them until I could taste them. Then I couldn't wait anymore and scrambled downstairs to the kitchen.

"Hi, Mama!" I called, using my babyish, private name for Mom. In public, of course, she was Mom. And in public I was Emma.

"Good morning, lovebug!" Mom said back, using her babyish, private name for me. Mom was already dressed in khakis and a cute lavender sweater. Her blond hair was tied back in a short, bouncy ponytail with a pink ribbon, and she had Keds on her feet. Mom got dressed within five seconds of getting up. I only saw her in her pajamas when she was sick. People always joked that she looked like she could be my sister, but when you got close, you could see from her smile lines that she was definitely mom age.

Mom came around the island to give me a big squeeze and a kiss on top of my bed head. I hopped up on a stool, tucking my legs up under my nightie.

"Yum. Thanks, Mama, for making these."

"I've been craving them myself," Mom said. "But I'm really making them as a thank-you to all you kids. I know what a bumpy week this has been, and I really appreciate all your help. I'm very proud of you all."

I wasn't sure Mom should be too proud of Matt the Brat or Jake the Snake, or even me (Emma the . . . ?), but I didn't say anything. Late last night, when everyone had come home and was relaxing in the TV room (everyone except Jake, who had been fed and bathed and put to bed at a reasonable hour by Mom), everyone agreed that Mondays and Wednesdays were Matt's days to meet Jake, and Tuesdays and Thursdays were mine. Sam would meet him on Fridays. Everyone was happy with the solution for now, and there was a temporary peace in our house.

"So how's your new job?" I asked, propping my chin in my hand. "Give me all the deets."

Mom started filling me in on all the details of the characters she worked with, and the sections of the store that she managed (cooking and fiction), and where she went on her breaks. She told me that she saw a few cookbooks that had some cupcake recipes I might like. It felt good to just be relaxing in the kitchen. I wasn't worried about babysitting Jake or walking Jenner or how much things cost. I was just happy to be with my mom, eating pancakes. It was like it used to be.

"So today's the day I'm going to the mall with Mia and her mom and all the CC girls to look for the dress," I said. I wasn't sure where I was headed with this. I had filled Mom in on the exciting junior bridesmaid news already.

"Ooh! What fun!" said Mom. She was quiet for a moment, then she bit her lip. She had that worried look on her face that she seemed to get a lot these days.

"What?" I asked, but I already pretty much knew.

"Oh, nothing. I was just thinking," said Mom.

"Are you wondering how much the dress will cost?" I asked quietly. "Because I have . . ." I gulped. "I have money saved up that I can use."

"Oh no, sweetheart. It isn't that at all! Really. And I don't want you to use your savings on something like that. Not when you've worked so hard. That's for the mixer! Look, we'll just cross that bridge when we come to it, okay? You just find a pretty dress today, and then Dad and I will figure it out."

But what if I found a dress that was too expensive? I was worried. I guess I'm a lot like Mom because the same worried look must have showed on my face. Mom wiped her hands on the worn apron she was wearing and then leaned over, putting her arms around me.

"I love you, muffin, and I don't want to see you taking the weight of the world on your shoulders. Dad and I can make things work. Okay? It's not all up to you. Though I appreciate your sensitivity and your work ethic, the most important thing is that you have fun at the store today and on the wedding day. The rest will fall into place, all right?"

I smiled to make her feel better, but I felt awful. I hated seeing Mom so worried. And all for a silly dress. I would just pay for the dress myself. I'd take my cupcake and dog-walking money and use my mixer-fund money to pay for the rest. The mixer could wait. It wasn't that bad to use the handheld one. I felt a lot better.

Mom turned back to the stove and loaded up another plate of gooey, sweet pancakes. "Hot off the press!" she said. "Enjoy!" and she handed it to me.

"Yum!"

"Now let's talk about your trip to the bridal store today! What fun!" Mom said. "What color dress do you think you'll buy?" Mom was excited and suddenly I was too. And we talked about colors and long or short dresses and sashes and bows, and I finished a third plate of pancakes before Matt came downstairs and yelled, "Hey, save some for me!" and Mom got up to get him some too.

The ride to the mall was giggly. We were squished into Mia's mom's Mini Cooper, but we didn't mind. But because of the tight space and the squishing and the fact that we were really excited, we couldn't stop laughing. Sometimes that happens a lot with us, and we just laugh so hard that we can't stop.

"What did you cupcake girls eat for breakfast today? Frosting?" asked Mia's mom with a grin, and this made us all laugh harder. We finally got it together as we walked through the mall and into the store.

The Special Day bridal store made us all quiet. There was a big white door and as soon as you stepped inside, it was like another world. There was thick, plush white carpeting and big white sofas and chairs and pretty roses all over the store, in big pots, in vases, and even hanging from a gleaming chandelier. Everything was quiet, and there was soft music playing. It was the prettiest store I had ever seen.

"Isn't it incredible?" Mia whispered to me.

"To die for!" I said, using one of Mom's favorite expressions. And it was.

"Like a fairy tale," Katie said breathlessly.

"Is this a franchise?" asked Alexis, looking around. I rolled my eyes and laughed. Alexis didn't have a romantic bone in her body.

Inside, the tall, elegant manager came to the front of the store to meet us with her hands out-stretched in a friendly greeting. "Call me Mona," she declared. She kissed Mia's mom on each cheek, and then Mia's mom took a moment to properly introduce each of us. Mona made a special effort to greet each of us, complimenting our looks or outfit and saying how happy she was to have us in her store. I wasn't used to salespeople being so nice. Usually they just rang me up or opened the dressing room door with one of those little keys.

"Follow me, ladies," said Mona. "Let's go back where we can be comfortable and talk about what you are looking for."

"Wow," whispered Katie as we followed Mona's trim, stylish figure across the white wall-to-wall carpeting. "This is superfancy."

I got a little nervous. It was fancy. And fancy meant expensive.

There were gorgeous wedding dresses on mannequins and on racks on the walls, and more beautiful chairs and sofas and coffee tables with Kleenex boxes and oversize white binders that Mia pointed out as "look books." Because they'd been here before to select her mom's dress, and because her mom worked in fashion, Mia was very comfortable in the fancy setting. I noticed that all the salespeople were really pretty (prettier than most of the customers, which was kind of funny) and everyone spoke in hushed and ladylike tones. Like "indoor voice," as we told Jake. I stood up straighter, and I was glad I'd taken Mom's advice and dressed up for the occasion in a skirt and my ballet flats. This was not the kind of place to wear sneakers.

We settled into sofas and chairs around a table. There was a plate piled high with delicate sugar cookies, and there was a silver tea service. My grandmother had a tea set like that, but I had never seen her actually use it. I noticed there were a lot of tissue boxes around. I pointed at them.

"Oh," said Mia, "that's because the brides are so beautiful, everyone cries a lot."

Mona assigned one assistant to dole out snacks to us, and another was sent to round up the rack of junior bridesmaid dresses. I noticed there was an entire row of mirrors so you could see yourself in all directions.

Mona's assistant handed me two cookies and tea, and it was a little weird to eat while I was staring at myself in all the mirrors. Mia was so excited, she was jumping around. She went to help her mom put her dress on in the changing room and the three of us were left alone for a moment.

"Can you believe this?" whispered Katie.

"I'm never leaving," I said, nibbling on a cookie.

"Hey, I wonder where they buy these cookies?" said Alexis, inspecting hers as if it would have a label on it. "We should ask Mona if they'd like us to supply them with cupcake minis—white cake with white frosting, of course."

I laughed. "Look out, Bill Gates, there's a new mogul in town."

"Seriously," said Alexis.

"Actually, it's brilliant," I said. "Why don't you ask her? I would totally love to bake for her. Maybe we can drop off some samples for her next week?" All I could think of was coming back again.

"What's up with the Kleenex everywhere?" asked Katie.

"I noticed that too!" I said. "Mia said it's because brides make people cry."

Alexis grabbed a Kleenex and pretended to mop her eyes. "Oh, honey, you've never looked so lovely!" she said dramatically. Sometimes Alexis could be really funny.

The dress assistant came back with a cart laden with white dresses that hung in plastic protective covers.

Then Mona came out and smiled as she watched us ooh and aah over the dresses. "Why don't you each select two to try on, and then we can have a fashion show?" she suggested.

We didn't need to be told twice. Katie went first, then Alexis. It was like playing "Princess for a Day." Mona watched and laughed and clapped.

While Alexis and Katie tried on their dresses, I

tried to poke around on the rack to see if any had price tags on them, but none of them did. I started to worry again. Then I just chose the two plainest dresses I could find and sat down and waited my turn.

While I waited, I picked up one of the look books that Mona had laid out for us. Mia explained that a look book was like a catalog. This one looked like a photo album, but all the pictures were dresses. It was filled with one beautiful dress after the other. Alexis and Katie came to peer over my shoulders.

Suddenly I stopped flipping. In front of me was the prettiest dress I'd ever seen, excluding actual wedding dresses, of course. It was white and the top was a fitted, T-shirt kind of cut with short, puffy sleeves. It had pleats cascading down that were tulle. I knew it was tulle because it was the same material as the long tulle tutu Mom made me one year for a recital. It looked like a fairy princess dress.

"Wow," I said. "This is beautiful." My heart actually fluttered; it was that great.

"I love it!" declared Katie.

"Love what?" asked Mia, coming out from her mom's changing room.

Alexis smiled. "Emma has found our dress," said Alexis.

357

"Let's see!" said Mia eagerly. She rushed over. "No way," she said solemnly. "I don't believe it."

She stood up and flung her arm out toward her mom's door.

"What?" I asked.

"Here comes the bride!" sang Mia's mom, emerging from the changing room.

I gasped. Ms. Vélaz's dress was a nearly identical but grown-up version of the dress I had just found. It was like they were meant to be together. For a second I forgot about our dresses, though, because Ms. Vélaz looked so beautiful. Her dress was strapless, and her hair was pulled back. She looked really glamorous and not like a mom at all.

"Wow!" was really all I could say.

"Oh, Ms. Vélaz! You look like a . . . a . . . ," cried Katie, suddenly speechless. Alexis nodded in mute agreement.

"A princess!" I said. And it was true.

Ms. Vélaz laughed. "I do just love it. It's the prettiest dress I've ever worn."

"And it looks just like the dress Emma found in the book for us!" declared Mia.

"Oh . . ." I was embarrassed. I didn't mean to pick out everyone's dress for them. Plus, if it was like Ms. Vélaz's dress, then it was probably really expensive.

"Great!" said Ms. Vélaz. "I can't wait to see it! Let me just get this pinned and I'll come look."

Mona swooped over, her mouth filled with straight pins, and while Ms. Vélaz stood on a carpet-covered box, Mona began nipping and shortening, muttering, "Divine, just divine."

"It's divine," whispered Alexis, in a high voice. I tried not to laugh.

"Mona, I think the girls found another dress to try on," said Ms. Vélaz, watching in the mirror as Mona worked.

"Patricia, please go look," said Mona around a mouthful of pins. I wondered how she could talk like that. Patricia came over, and I pointed to the dress. Suddenly I hoped they didn't have it. Or that at least it was very cheap. Or on sale. Oh no! What if it was a fortune?

"Oh yes, the Jumandra. So pretty. That might be in the shipment that came in this morning," said Patricia. "Let me go look."

My heart sank. *Please let it be cheap. Please let it be cheap,* I repeated like a mantra in my head as Patricia flipped through the rack of dresses.

"Here it is!" said Patricia. She plucked it from the rack and whipped the clear plastic cover off of it.

My heart fluttered again when I saw the dress. It

was even prettier in real life! But I didn't want to get my hopes up. And the decision wasn't up to me anyway. But Katie, Mia, and Alexis all started yelling, "That's it! That's it!"

"You go try it on first since you found it!" said Mia generously.

"No, no," I waved my hand. "You go first. Or maybe you don't even want to try it . . . that's fine!" I felt like a dork.

"Honey, Mia has tried on dozens of dresses already between her two visits here. You run and put it on. I know it will look lovely on you," said Mia's mom. "Go on . . . Patricia will help you."

"Well . . ."

"Go!" commanded Alexis, and I was up off the couch like a shot, and into the changing room, practically ripping my skirt and sweater off in excitement. Patricia came in with me, which was a little embarrassing, but I just pretended that she was Mom.

As I was standing in my undies, Patricia carefully removed the delicate dress from its padded satin hanger, then cautiously she lowered it over my head. I poked my arms through, and Patricia buttoned me up. Then she gave me a pair of fancy satin shoes to slip on.

"Oh my gosh," I whispered as I saw myself in the mirror.

"Your hair might look pretty down," said Patricia. I pulled out my ponytail and shook my head. She was right. I felt like a fairy. Or a princess. Or a ballerina. Or all of them. It was a dreamy dress. A dream dress.

"Come out!" called Mia.

"How does it look?" called Alexis.

I almost didn't want to go out there. *Maybe,* I thought, *just maybe it wasn't too much. But it had to be expensive.*

"It looks terrible!" I joked through the door.

"What?" cried Katie in alarm.

"Kidding!" I said. I spun around again.

"Ready?" Patricia grinned at me.

And then, oh, what the heck, I nodded yes, and Patricia flung open the door.

"Oh my God!" said the Cupcake Club in unison.

"Oh my God!" said Mia's mom.

CHAPTER 6

The Dream Dress

$\mathcal{I}$ felt like everyone came at me at once. Mia's mom came bounding down from her pedestal, Mona and pins in tow. Patricia and the other assistant clustered around me, and they were all chattering at once.

"Oh, Mommy, this is it! Isn't it?" cried Mia ecstatically.

"It's glorious, and it looks spectacular on you, darling," said Ms. Vélaz.

"Divine, just divine," uttered Mona. (*Did she know any other adjectives?* I wondered.) Alexis giggled again.

"Come here, sweetie," said Mona. I climbed up on the box in front of the mirror, and Mona started pinning the dress on me. She fluffed my hair, fluffed the dress, and then stood back.

"Perfect," said Ms. Vélaz.

I could not stop smiling. I was so happy. It was the most beautiful dress I had ever seen, and it was the most beautiful I had ever felt. "It's pretty great," I said quietly. Then I remembered it was really more Mia's day than mine. After all, it was her mom who was getting married. "Mia, why don't you try it on?"

"Okay, but take one more minute. It looks so incredible on you," said Mia generously.

Ms. Vélaz had disappeared and returned with her phone. "Let me take a photo and send it to your mom," she said happily. "You look so fabulous."

I didn't think fast enough and the picture was snapped. Mia's mom's fingers flew over her keyboard writing the message to Mom. "What's her e-mail address again?" asked Ms. Vélaz. I panicked. Now Mom would see the dress and know we'd found something for sure. She would ask Ms. Vélaz how much it cost. I had to think.

"Umm . . . I don't know what her new one is since she switched jobs," I said in relief, realizing it was true. "Why don't you just send it to me, and I'll show it to her when I get home?"

Ms. Vélaz glanced at me, then took down my

e-mail address and pushed send as Mona returned to the room. The two of them stepped off to chat quietly, and Patricia led me back to the dressing room.

As I passed Mona and Ms. Vélaz, I heard the words "two hundred and fifty dollars." I felt sick.

Two hundred and fifty dollars!

This was way, way worse than I had imagined. *Okay,* I thought. *If they pick this dress for sure, I'll just excuse myself from being a junior bridesmaid.* It was crazy beautiful, but whole families (mine!) could be fed for weeks for that kind of money. Dream dress indeed. I could dream about it, but I would never be able to afford it. "Good-bye, beautiful," I whispered to the dress on its satin hanger.

I sat on the couch in a daze as one by one, all the girls tried it on and fell in love. It looked slightly different but equally amazing on all of us, just like the jeans in *The Sisterhood of the Traveling Pants*, I thought distractedly. By the time everyone had it on, the decision had been made. This was the dress. *Oh no,* I thought. *What have I done?*

Ms. Vélaz whispered to Mona about the dresses a little more. She turned to us. "Girls, is this okay with all of you? Are you sure your parents will be okay with this dress?"

Katie and Alexis nodded. "My mom is just happy I'll be in a dress," said Alexis, who almost always wore pants. For a second I was jealous of my friends. None of them seemed worried about spending $250 on a dress. They were acting like it was no big deal. I noticed Mia's mom looking at me with a worried look. I started to sweat a little. I smiled, as if I was agreeing.

"Well, that's the dress then!" said Ms. Vélaz. Then it was decided that the four of us ought to go put the dresses on hold up at the front desk, and we'd each come back with our parents to buy it. "If there's a problem, just let me know," said Ms. Vélaz. Mona nodded. I sighed with relief. On hold was different than sold. I might be able to figure something out.

The Cupcake Club followed Patricia the assistant out of the room and cruised soundlessly across the plush carpet to the front counter to fill out the paperwork. The store had filled up quite a bit, and there were groups of women and girls arranged all around in little seating clusters. Suddenly I spied a familiar shock of long blond Barbie hair. Sydney Whitman!

"Guys," I said quietly to warn them, but it was too late. Sydney had seen us.

"Oh my God! Mia!" she squealed, and she jumped up and pranced over to Mia, as if they were the best of friends. "What are you doing here?" she asked excitedly, completely ignoring the three of us.

Katie and Alexis stood frozen, like deer in headlights. Sydney ignored me so I tried to ignore her. Mia did the talking.

"My mom's getting married and we're all in the wedding, so we're getting our dresses. What are you doing here?" Mia was pleasant but cool.

"My cousin Brandi is getting married, and I'm the maid of honor," bragged Sydney.

"Wow," said Mia nicely. She had a hard time being mean.

"So what are you wearing?" asked Sydney, looking Mia over from head to toe.

Mia fielded the question again. "Oh, we found a gorgeous dress. It looks great on everyone. Especially Emma. Actually, she was the one who found it."

Sydney looked at me as if she had just realized I was there. Then she looked back at Mia. "Can I see it?"

"Oh, uh . . ." Mia hesitated.

Sydney looked at the counter, where Patricia was

calmly laying out four sets of paperwork and four pens, for us to order three more dresses. The dress was on a hanger, hanging behind the counter.

"Is that it?" cried Sydney. "It is too cute!"

Patricia looked up and smiled. "It looks wonderful on the girls," she said kindly.

Sydney squinted sideways at it, then tilted her head.

"Brandi?" she called over her shoulder. "Brandi? Can you come here for a minute?"

Another very blond, older girl, with lots of makeup and a pink sweat suit, came over to stand by Sydney.

"Cu-uuu-uuute," said Brandi, drawing the word out into three syllables. She snapped her gum. "Try it on, then come show me," she instructed, and she went back to her group on the couch.

"I'll try it too," said Sydney to Patricia.

Patricia looked dubious. "I'll check to see if there's another one in the back," she said diplomatically, then she disappeared.

Probably going to check with Mona on what to do, I thought. I knew it was bad luck for anyone out of the wedding party to know what the bride's dress looked like, but how about the bridesmaids' dresses? Was there a rule about that? *Please let Mona say yes, please let Mona say yes,* I thought fervently. I might not be able to afford it, but the idea of Sydney in my dress made me sick.

Patricia returned with a sympathetic look on her face. "I'm so sorry, miss, but we only have one of these in stock and we can only order a few in each size. We don't like too many of our weddings to look the same. As soon as we finish the paperwork here, I'll be happy to help your bridal consultant find something similar." She smiled and turned away, letting Sydney know the matter was closed. Then she started wrapping up the remaining dress for Mia.

"Wait!" said Sydney, never one to give up. "Mia, do you mind if I try this one? Then, if it looks good, maybe I can order it online or something."

I thought that was a pretty rude thing to say in front of Patricia and also pretty pushy. But Mia was so sweet.

"Uh, sure . . . I guess so." Mia shrugged.

"Great," said Sydney.

Patricia raised her eyebrows at Mia but passed the dress over the counter to Sydney. "Please be careful with it," she said.

"Of course," said Sydney. And she flew off, the dress flapping behind her from its hanger.

Seconds later Sydney returned, beaming, in the dress. Her whole group squealed and clapped as

Sydney twirled, and the Cupcake Club looked on in dismay. It did look amazing on her. It was just that kind of dress, and Sydney was beautiful after all.

"I love it!" Sydney called to Mia. Mia nodded, unsmiling.

Patricia shook her head and went and whispered in Brandi's bridal consultant's ear. The consultant nodded, and then went and spoke to Sydney. It was time for the dress to come off. With some difficulty, she persuaded Sydney to return to the changing room and remove the dress. Moments later it was back on its hanger, safely behind the register.

"Did that really just happen, or was it a nightmare?" asked Katie.

I felt the same way. I looked at her.

"It happened." Katie sighed.

"Sorry, guys," whispered Mia. "I didn't know what else to do."

"You are way too nice," said Alexis. "I would have charged her to try it on."

The Cupcake Club all laughed. "We know you would have!" I said.

Katie, Alexis, and I finished the paperwork and slid it across the counter to Patricia. She looked it over.

"Emma?"

Uh-oh. What now? I bit my lip.

"Can I have a daytime phone number for one of your parents, please?" She smiled encouragingly at me.

"Oh, um. My mom's just started a new job, and I don't know her number, so . . ."

"How about your dad?" asked Patricia.

I felt panicky. "Ugh, I hate to bother him with stuff like this at work. Why don't I . . . have my mom call you with her new number?"

Patricia nodded and handed me a business card. "That would be just fine. In the meantime we can order it for you so its here on time."

It would be fine, I said to myself. I would find the money somehow. It was a dream dress. And I could dream big. I wouldn't worry my parents. I would handle it.

CHAPTER 7

Between a Rock and a Dress

I spent the weekend counting money and adding numbers. I didn't even want to ask my parents for half the money for the dress, let alone all of it. I needed a plan to get to $250. I'd have to really scrimp on after-school treats, like getting candy for Jake or going to the movies. Then I'd have to up the dog walking and the cupcake making. The only problem was they kind of used the same time slot and the dog walking paid better. *I can do this,* I thought. *I can plan this out. But how?*

I was still thinking about it when I left school on Monday and walked to the bike rack. I was nearly next to Matt before I saw him waiting for me by my bike.

"Hey," he said.

"Hi, yourself," I said, eyeing him suspiciously. "What's up?"

"Well . . . I was wondering if we could trade days. If you could do today, I'll do tomorrow, I swear."

I sighed. I could barely figure out my plans, and they were already getting messed up. I was supposed to go to Katie's today to make cupcakes for Henry Garner's birthday party tomorrow. *I could bring Jake,* I thought. *He couldn't be that bad. Plus, tomorrow was a dog-walking day, so maybe it would be better if he were with Matt then.*

"Fine," I said.

The relief in Matt's face was obvious. "Thank you so much," he said, and he actually seemed to mean it.

"What do you have?" I asked. "Practice?"

"Uh . . ." Matt looked awkward for a second, and then looked a little embarrassed. "You know how I like to fool around on the computer?"

I nodded.

"Well, there's a three-hour intensive workshop for graphic design down at the computer center at the library, and I didn't realize it was today. Don't tell Mom and Dad, though, okay? I'm paying for it with my birthday money from Grandma."

"Cool," I said. I was surprised, though. Not that I really cared what Matt did, but I thought it would be something dumb, like pizza with the guys. I guess he didn't want to ask Mom and Dad for money either. We looked at each other for a second, understanding. "Well, good luck," I said.

"Thanks," said Matt, and he took off.

That was probably the most civilized conversation I've had with him in months, I thought as I pedaled home. I wasn't due to be at Katie's until four thirty so I'd go home, change, get Jake, and head over.

Poor Jake was not psyched about going to Katie's until I reminded him that he could lick the bowl (and the beaters, he insisted), and he could watch Katie's TV.

"What's up, Cupcakers?" I asked, trying to smile brightly as we arrived. "I've brought my apprentice, Officer Jake Taylor, along with me today." Then over his head I mouthed, *Sorry*.

Jake saluted the girls, and while Katie and Alexis giggled, Mia solemnly saluted him back. She was his favorite, and I could see why. Nobody seemed mad at me, so that was good.

Henry Garner was having a circus-themed birthday with a clown, so we'd decided to do clown cupcakes for the party. This meant yellow cake with red-and-white-striped cupcake papers, Froot Loops eyes, a licorice whip smile, red frosting hair, and frosted ice-cream cones as pointy clown hats. I put Jake in charge of sorting Froot Loops by color, and I said he could eat some but not all of them.

Alexis was also making some mini cupcakes that she was bringing over for Mona to sample that evening since we kind of burned the ones from the last Jake episode. Alexis thought Mona might buy them for the store, and I was really excited about that. Maybe it would mean I could go back there again. Plus, it meant more business, and that meant more money.

As usual, we paid for the cost of the supplies out of our treasury; all money received went into it too. It was tricky to price fancier cupcakes, like the clowns, because we had a hard time valuing our labor and time and, after all, we weren't professionals with degrees from culinary schools. But if we covered our costs and made at least a 20 percent profit—what Alexis had determined—for each sale, we were pleased. Actually we were all pretty happy to come out even, but everyone was afraid to tell that to Alexis. Once a month Alexis divided the extra money we had, and we used it to go out for ice cream or pizza to celebrate. After that we each kept what little we had left. I hoped we'd have a little extra this month.

We got right to work measuring, pouring, mixing, and pouring again. The first four trays of cupcakes went into the ovens (Katie's mom had two side by side), and while we waited, I began coloring some of the buttercream frosting a deep red for the Bozo hair.

We were quiet, which seemed a little weird. I looked over at Jake, who was also quiet, and realized why: He had cake batter dripping all down the front of him from licking the spoon and the bowl.

"Oh, Jakey, you need an apron!" I lunged across the kitchen for paper towels and an apron, but all I could find in the apron drawer were large, ruffled, flowery aprons.

"I'm not wearing that stinky girl apron!" Jake was immovable on the subject. "No, sir!" He also refused to take off his shirt.

"Jake, this is gross. And you can't go sit on Katie's mom's couch like that to watch TV."

Mia took over and, while pretending to arrest him and frisk him for weapons, she carefully wiped him clean. I watched in wonder and shook my head. He was like putty in her hands.

We started talking about the wedding. I thought Jake was watching TV but suddenly there was chaos. Jake had gone to remove the electric beaters that I had been using to make the red frosting so he could lick them, and had accidentally turned them on, sending red frosting spattering everywhere, including all over Mia and all over the kitchen.

At first I panicked that he lost a finger or something. When I realized it was all just frosting, I looked at the mess, and I just lost it. "I can't take you anywhere!" I shouted at Jake. "And it's not fair that I have to watch you all the time!" Everyone stopped working and stared at me.

"Shh, Emma, it's okay. We can clean it up," said Katie soothingly.

"I'll take Jake," said Mia, and she and Jake went off to borrow an old T-shirt of Katie's.

Once the tears started, I had a hard time stopping them. I was upset about the mess, upset about having to be in charge of Jake so much, upset that he always ruined everything, and most of all, upset about the dress. It just didn't seem fair. I cried and cried and cried.

"Okay," said Katie, after Mia had returned without Jake, who was now watching *SpongeBob* in the other room. "Emma, we need to talk."

Katie patted a seat at the table next to her, and I sat down, still teary. Alexis and Mia sat across from me. Everyone looked concerned.

"You seem really stressed out," said Katie. Her head was tilted to the side as she looked at me. I don't know why that made me cry more.

"Are you getting enough sleep?" asked Alexis directly. Alexis was a big believer in the basics of life. If you slept well, ate well, and exercised, pretty much everything else would fall into place.

"Not really," I admitted. "I'm pretty busy."

Alexis sat back and folded her arms in satisfaction. "A good night's sleep is so important," she said. She sounded like Mom.

"It seems like you have a lot on your plate," said Mia.

I nodded.

"You have the Cupcake Club. And babysitting. And dog walking. And orchestra. Plus homework. Can we help you?" Alexis asked kindly.

Not to mention saving money, I thought. Then I felt badly. I didn't really want to talk about this with them. What could they do? They would just feel sorry for me, and I didn't want that at all.

"Do you want a break from your responsibilities

with the club?" asked Alexis. "Like a leave of absence?"

I noticed Mia watching me carefully for my response. It gave me a little chill. Did Mia want me out of the club? I thought for a second. I could use the extra time for dog walking and make some money. But if I took a break, it would be like quitting my friends. Plus, I love the club. But if I stayed with it, I'd have to really be present and do a good job—an even better job than in the past because I'd have to prove how committed I really was. I'd have to figure it out. Gee, that seemed to be a theme these days.

Finally I said, "No, but thanks. The Cupcake Club is the best part of my busyness. I'd rather be baking and working and hanging out with you guys than anything else." It was true, after all.

I saw Mia and Katie exchange a glance.

"Well, if it starts to feel like it's too much, just, um, let us know. We won't cut you out of the earnings if you miss a baking session here and there," said Alexis, but I watched her look uneasily at Mia and Katie.

"Thanks, you guys," I said. "You're awesome." But I was really thanking Alexis. There was something going on that I couldn't put my finger on.

Mia and Katie seemed like they didn't believe me, and I wasn't sure they were exactly on board with Alexis. Good old Alexis.

And then, "The cupcakes!" cried Katie.

She leaped to the oven just in the nick of time. They were golden brown and perfect.

The tension was cut for now by our successful batch.

"Phew!" I said, but I wasn't only talking about the cupcakes.

CHAPTER 8

Dog Days

*T*he next day Alexis caught up with me as I was heading to the Andersons' to walk Jenner.

"Hey! I just checked my e-mail, and we have good news!" called Alexis as she came jogging up.

I was running late, but I stopped. "What's up?" I asked.

Alexis grinned. "Mona loved the sample minis!"

"She did?" I cried. I was so excited.

Alexis nodded. "Yup, and she wants to place an order for five dozen every Saturday for the next two months!"

"Oh my God! That is amazing," I said, thinking about the profits. Then I thought about dropping them off at the beautiful store. "What will we charge her?" I asked. "And how will we get them to her?"

Alexis nodded again. "Already thought of all that. The minis are fifty cents each, so that's thirty dollars a week. For eight weeks it's two hundred and forty dollars. My mom said she'll take me to drop them off on the way to soccer every week."

"That is so great! Thanks, Alexis! So we'll bake every Friday night?"

"We kind of already do, anyway," said Alexis. "But yeah. Where are you going? Jenner?"

I nodded. "Yup. I love him and the cool part is, he seems to love me back! He behaves so well for me. Unlike Jake," I added.

Alexis pursed her lips thoughtfully. "You know, you could really make it worth your while if you had more than one dog at a time."

I had already thought of that as part of the dream dress plan. "I know. I just haven't had the time to try to drum up more business."

"Well . . . you just need to maximize your time while you're doing it. So, like, wear a T-shirt that says 'Dog walking, five dollars a walk' with your e-mail address or whatever on it," Alexis said.

"That's a cute idea. I can do that with some fabric markers."

"And you could make a flyer on the computer

and hand it out or put it in mailboxes while you're out walking."

"Oooh! Good one!"

Alexis laughed. "And . . . you could, like, spray liver perfume on you or carry a lot of doggy treats in your pockets, so when you pass a dog on the street it goes crazy for you!"

I laughed too. "I think I'll skip the liver perfume, but thanks. Treats in my pocket is a good idea. I've been meaning to do that. Thanks!"

"Anytime. You know I love brainstorming about marketing," said Alexis with a smile. But then she turned suddenly serious. "Hey, maybe you should put cupcake flyers in the mailboxes too!"

"I could do that," I said. But something about her voice made me nervous.

"Just to, you know, help out a little," said Alexis casually.

I felt a pit in my stomach. "Oh. Am I . . . not helping out enough?"

Alexis looked away uneasily. "No, I mean, I think you are. . . ."

"Do the others think I'm not?" I asked anxiously. Was this what was going on at that last baking session? I missed some meetings, sure. And I brought Jake a few times. But I was trying, I really was.

"No, no, not at all. I think . . . Maybe they're just nervous about all the work we have these days, and they just want to make sure you're committed. You've missed a few baking sessions. And you seem a little preoccupied." Alexis shrugged. "That's all. But don't tell them I told you, okay?"

"Okay," I agreed hesitantly. "Thanks, I guess. . . ."

"Listen, Emma," said Alexis. "I know they might think you're flaking out a little on things. And you don't seem into the dress at all. . . ."

"What?" I cried. I hadn't thought about anything besides that dress!

Alexis cleared her throat. "Your mom told my mom about her job and that it's been a little . . . well . . . a little crazy at your house lately with all the babysitting."

I wondered how much Mom told Mrs. Becker and how much Alexis knew.

"I can help you," Alexis said. "Anytime. Just ask, okay? My mom's never home after school either." Alexis smiled. It was true, Mrs. and Mr. Becker got home really late, and a lot of times Alexis just ate dinner with her sister. My mom used to invite them over a lot for dinner, but I realized she hadn't done that since she started the new job.

I was glad Alexis knew something was up, but

I really didn't want to talk about it. And I knew she must be sticking up for me with Katie and Mia, which made me mad to think about, but still thankful.

"I don't think there's anything you can do," I said honestly. "But thank you."

Alexis saluted me. "You're welcome, sarge," she said, trying to lighten things up a little.

"Alexis?" I said. "Can you . . . um . . . can you not mention anything that's going on at home to Katie and Mia?"

Alexis looked like she was going to say something, but she didn't. She nodded yes. "Wouldn't disobey a sergeant!" she said.

And though we both laughed as we went our separate ways, I was left wondering what else the club was discussing without me.

That night, right before dinner, I tapped on Matt and Sam's door. "Matt?"

"Come in," said Matt.

I poked my head in. He was sitting at his desk and Sam was out. "Can you help me with something?" I asked. "I'll pay you," I added before he could say no.

Matt looked at me suspiciously. "Is it something heinous?" he asked.

I came into the room, which was all blue corduroy, sports posters, and team logos. I laid down a piece of paper I had been working on on Matt's desk. "I need to make flyers for my dog-walking business, and I was wondering if you could help me. Because you took that class and all." I held my breath hopefully as Matt studied the information.

He looked up at me.

"Well?" I asked, thinking he was going to make me trade extra Jake days for this.

"Do you really need more responsibilities in your life?" he asked.

I sighed. He kind of sounded like Dad. "I need more money. . . ."

He looked at me for an extra minute, and then he shrugged. "Okay. I'll do it."

"Oh my gosh, you will? Thanks, Matt! I take back every bad thing I ever said about you! Almost."

"No prob," said Matt. "I can probably put something together tonight, okay?"

"Thanks. That would be great. And also"—I laid another piece of paper down on his desk—"will you do some for the Cupcake Club, too?"

Matt took the second sheet of paper. "Sure," he agreed. "Anything that will get me extra cupcakes."

I thanked him again and left the room before he

changed back into the Matt I knew. *Huh,* I thought to myself. *Maybe Matt wasn't all bad.*

By nine that night Matt had two drafts for me to review. He had done a really good job, using cute art and eye-catching fonts. I was psyched, and I could tell Matt was pleased too. I almost wanted to hug him. I offered to watch Jake the next day.

By ten we had printed two stacks of fifty flyers, and then our parents insisted we go to sleep. *That was okay,* I thought, *since fifty new clients would be crazy. For dog walking or cupcakes.*

The next day Jake and I took Jenner on an extra-long walk around the neighborhood and handed out flyers and stuffed them in mailboxes. We stopped at the grocery store and bought a big bag of liver snaps to hand out to any dogs we saw, and Jake proudly wore a T-shirt that I had quickly created for him. It was just like mine, with all the dog-walking info, but his said OFFICER TAYLOR on the back. He loved it.

That night Alexis e-mailed to report they had two new inquiries from the cupcake flyers. "Good work," she said in her sign-off. Katie chimed in with a "Way to go, Emma!" e-mail, which made me feel good.

Phew! I thought, reading the e-mails. Later, four

calls came in for my dog-walking business, and using a chart I made, I scheduled the pickups and drop-offs for all the new dogs for the next day. It would be a lot of work, but I could handle it.

Or maybe I couldn't.

At 4:40 the next afternoon Jake and I were sweating. I had four leashes in my hands, and I could hardly walk down the street as the dogs kept wandering around and twining their leads around one another or around a tree or, worst of all, around my ankles. I'd already had to pick up two poops and leave one behind because it was disgustingly un-pick-up-able. Luckily, the dogs were all family dogs, so they got along pretty well with one another. It hadn't occurred to me that they might fight until we passed a neighbor's house and their dog had run to the property line, barking like mad and baring his teeth at the pack. Two of my dogs strained at their leashes, growling and baring their teeth, and it had taken all my strength to hold on to them. Jake was rattled and teary after the experience, and I was pretty fried. I had to face it: Four dogs was too many to walk at a time. Plus, I still had one more dog to go. Still, at five dollars a walk, I needed all five dogs. I was going to have to figure out a new walking plan.

We reached the corner of Pond Lane, and Jenner stopped to do his business. I sighed and waited patiently, glad for the brief break. Suddenly I heard a bike bell jingling, and I turned around, hoping maybe it was Alexis. It was Sydney and Mags, Sydney's best friend.

"Hey!" called Mags.

I nodded in greeting. I had nothing to say to these girls, and honestly I was so mad that I kept running into them. For some reason they stopped and stood with their bikes between their legs.

"Wow. Are these all yours?" asked Mags incredulously.

"No, I walk them for the neighbors." I was trying to be casual. I didn't need to get into a long chat with Mags right now.

"Good thing," said Sydney. "Your house would stink!" She wrinkled her button nose in distaste.

"I imagine so," I said, in what I hope came off as a "duh." Jenner was done, but I didn't want to bend down and scoop it up while the other girls were there.

"So I think I'm getting the dress from The Special Day," said Sydney casually. It was odd that she mentioned it because she had hardly acknowl-

edged me when they were there on Saturday. Why
wasn't she telling Mia this? Wait, did she say "the"
dress? As in my dress?

"Oh?" I said fake casually back. "Did they find
you another one?"

"No, but there's one still on hold that they
ordered and the lady said if it wasn't paid for by
next week, then I could have it," said Sydney,
shrugging innocently.

My heart lurched. What? That was my dress! And
I thought I had two weeks, not one. But if there
was only one left . . . So Katie, Alexis, and Mia had
already paid for their dresses and mine was still
hanging there, alone? When did they go back? And
how would I ever make enough money to pay for
the dress in one week?

My worry must have shown on my face again
because Mags asked, "Are you okay?"

Sydney looked smug. She was so awful.

"No, I'm fine," I said, recovering. "It's just . . ." I
looked down at Jenner's work. "I hate this part."

Sydney was still looking at me coolly. "We'll
leave you to it," she said. "Tell your friend she only
has a week to get her dress!"

I felt sick.

"Or actually . . . What am I saying? Don't tell her!

Then I can have it!" Sydney laughed and pedaled away with Mags.

I stooped to clean up after Jenner, and he licked my hand. I patted him on the head. He really was a good dog. *If only I were a dog,* I thought. *It would be so much easier.*

CHAPTER 9

Mix, Stir ... Mixed-up

On Friday I more or less sorted out the dog walking. I took the dogs out in pairs and Jenner alone, because he was my original customer and my favorite. It made for a long afternoon, but I was kind of enjoying it, especially since the weather was getting warmer. It wasn't too fun in the rain. But I got to visit all these nice houses and play with friendly dogs.

I really liked the Mellgards' house. They had Marley, a black standard poodle, who wore his fur long and curly rather than cut in any froufrou way. He was a cutie and really sweet. Also Mrs. Mellgard baked as a hobby, and her kitchen had racks of baking sheets and pans in every shape and size, and shiny copper saucepans hung from a rack overhead.

Mrs. Mellgard also had every kind of baking appliance, including a massive cherry red stand mixer. I felt sad every time I saw it. I still dreamed about my pink mixer.

After leaving Marley at the Mellgards', I hustled home. We were baking at Alexis's house tonight, and I absolutely had to be on time. Besides, I was excited to go because we were trying out my new bacon cupcake recipe. I'd have to stop at the Quickie Mart and pick up some ingredients on the way over.

Alexis's house was quiet, so there weren't a lot of distractions. Her sister was at after-school extracurriculars and her parents were at work. The Cupcake Club worked well there. Tonight we were also baking the first official batch of minis for Mona, so I was excited about that, too.

I was determined to try harder. And I did. I was on time, and I took charge with the bacon recipe. I creamed the butter and sugar for the caramel cupcakes in Alexis's mom's mixer. Meanwhile Alexis was making the fondant for Mona's bridal cupcakes, Katie was making the white frosting, and Mia was already filling the mini cupcake tins with little dollops of batter. We weren't as chatty as usual, but I tried to convince myself that it was because we were busy and not because anyone was annoyed with anyone else.

I was wondering what we were going to do over the weekend. We usually did something together. I didn't have any dog-walking jobs over the weekend, unfortunately, because all the owners were home and so didn't need me. So that was two days without income. I was hoping the order from Mona would help make up for some of that loss. I was also dying to talk with the others about Sydney and the dress—in fact, I had been since yesterday—but I couldn't think of any way that didn't mention not being able to pay for it in the first place.

"So what's up for the weekend?" I asked.

I looked up just in time to see Mia and Katie exchange a funny glance, and it gave me a prickly feeling in my chest. What was that all about? I looked at Alexis, whose head was down as she apparently concentrated on the frosting. I wasn't sure if she'd just witnessed something or not. Were Mia and Katie keeping a secret?

"Alexis?" I asked again.

Alexis looked up very innocently, as if she'd been daydreaming before. "Hmm? What?" she asked. She was not a spacey person, so this act did not hold up well.

I was now very suspicious. "What are you doing this weekend?' I asked, enunciating each word distinctly.

"Oh, not much," said Alexis, waving her hand.

This was weird. There was always something going on during the weekends.

"Do you have a soccer game?" I asked as I flipped the bacon out onto a paper towel to drain. I looked back at Alexis again.

"Oh, yeah. Soccer. For sure. And then dinner with my family tomorrow night. Oh, and we'll need a meeting on Sunday. We have to try out a new recipe of Mia's."

Well, this was the first I'd heard of a Sunday meeting, but I would definitely attend. "Hmm. What about you guys this weekend?" I asked the other two again.

They gave similar vague answers—family, chores, homework. They were definitely acting shifty. They all seemed to have a secret, and I wasn't in on it. I wasn't sure whether I should get mad or cry. But then again I had a secret too.

"Hey, let's play a game," suggested Mia in a bright tone of voice, like a nursery school teacher.

"Which one?" I asked, glad for the distraction. "Celebrity Cupcake? Wildest Cupcakes? Name

That Cupcake?"We had lots of cupcake games.

"Name That Cupcake," said Mia. "Definitely."

"You go first," said Alexis as she began molding the fondant into tiny edible flowers.

"Okay. Hmm." Mia thought for a minute. Then she said, "Aha! I've got it! A mocha cake ... with ... butterscotch mini chips throughout and . . . fudge frosting . . . with . . . tiny marshmallows sprinkled across the top! What would you call it? Um, Katie?"

Katie smiled. "Mocha, butterscotch, fudge, and marshmallow? How about 'The Winter Storm'?"

"Lame!" declared Mia. "Alexis?" she prompted.

Alexis tipped her head to the side in a thoughtful pose. Then she said, "Well, if you made it Godiva mocha powder and Ghirardelli chips, with Valrhona fudge frosting, you could call them 'Millionaires' because the ingredients are so fancy!"

"That is so good," I said. "We should do those."

"What's your name suggestion?" Mia asked me.

"Oh. Um." I thought for a second. Alexis's idea was hard to top. "Swampcakes?" I offered, shrugging. "Like really gross-looking, gooey cupcakes that sink in the middle?"

Everyone laughed again.

"I love 'Swampcakes'!" declared Mia. "But actually you could put shredded coconut on top and maybe another kind of mini chip inside to really swamp them. Too bad we can't use nuts. . . ."

The Cupcake Club had a vigilant no-nut policy because so many kids we knew were allergic to nuts. There was simply no point in working with nuts at all.

"I think 'Millionaires' is brilliant, anyway," I said. "Maybe we'll all be cupcake millionaires someday!"

Mia pulled Mona's order of mini cupcakes from the oven. They were perfectly white angel food cake with lightly browned edges. She turned the tin upside down over a cooling rack and tapped it to make all the cupcakes pop out. "Yum," said Mia, reaching for the next tray. "These things are so cute. Such a great size. You could eat ten and not realize it."

"That's the point," said Alexis. "That's why Mona liked them so much. She said brides are so careful about their figures that they're always hungry and therefore often cranky when they come into her store. She liked the minis because they're so irresistible, she figured the brides would eat at least one and it would perk them up."

We all giggled.

"I'm glad my mom's not like that!" said Mia.

"We'll see tomorrow . . . ," started Katie. Then

she stopped abruptly and glanced at me, then Mia.

I was confused. I looked at Mia just in time to see Mia shake her head a tiny, tiny bit at Katie. What was going on? And should I call them on it?

No. Instead I crossed the room and went to crumble the bacon for the bacon cupcake frosting. It might be best to frost the cupcakes and keep the crumbled bacon in a Ziploc bag until it was time to serve the cupcakes; then you could just sprinkle the bacon bits over the tops of the 'cakes and the bacon would still be crispy. I turned to suggest that to the others and discovered them in the midst of a silent conversation made up of wild gestures and gesticulations, as well as mouthed words. It was like they were playing charades.

Everyone froze. Even me, for a second. Then I said, "Guys. What is going on?" I was nervous.

Everyone looked at me. Alexis was the first to speak.

"Emma, um, we feel really funny about this, so we didn't want to tell you. But . . . we bought our dresses for the wedding already, and we're going to go get them fitted tomorrow. We know you haven't bought yours yet, so we didn't say anything."

My face turned hot. I felt humiliated. "Oh," I said. "But if I'd known everyone else had bought theirs . . . I . . . I . . . I would have already bought mine, too!"

Katie and Mia exchanged a look. "Really?" said Mia. She didn't look like she believed me.

"Yeah . . . totally. I just . . . You know, my parents' schedules are pretty off the wall these days, so I just haven't scheduled a time to go down there with one of them."

"Oh . . . ," said Mia skeptically. "Because actually, if you still want to be a junior bridesmaid, um, my mom offered to buy it for you, just so it didn't get sold to someone else. . . ."

I noticed Alexis was looking at me.

"Oh no! I don't need help!" I cried. I must have said it really loudly because Mia flinched. I felt so bad. For me and for Mia. Mostly for me. What was I saying? What was I getting myself into?

"You could pay her back, if you wanted," said Alexis. "So it wouldn't be like she was buying it for you. Just like a loan."

"No. Sorry, thank you, but . . . ," I said. I didn't know what to say. Did they know I couldn't afford it? Alexis may have pieced it together, but I wondered how much she really knew.

"I mean, that is such a nice offer but . . . I mean, no need. And I do still want to be a junior brides-

maid! Of course I do! I . . . I'll go in on . . ." I did
a rapid calculation in my head. I figured I'd earn
another seventy-five dollars for dog walking by
next Wednesday. I might be able to borrow a little
from Sam.

I felt like everyone was staring at me. I could
do it. I could figure it out for sure. "I'll go in on
Wednesday and get it. You can tell Mona."

Mia looked skeptical, but Katie butted in. "Great!
Then maybe you should just come to the fitting
with us tomorrow!"

"I don't think they will do that until you buy it,"
said Mia.

I knew Mia was right, but I wished I'd been the
one to refuse. It was kind of mean of Mia to say no.

"Yeah," I agreed, shrugging. "I have a lot to do
tomorrow anyway, so . . ." That was, of course, not
true. But at least I now knew what the other girls
were up to tomorrow and why they had been acting so weird and shifty this evening. "So I'll see you
on Sunday, and you can tell me all about it."

I thought I was going to cry, so I turned back to
the bacon frosting and pretended to be really busy.

Okay! Be organized! Be efficient! I told myself. *I'll
figure it out.*

I dipped a finger in the frosting, then tasted it.

It was insanely good. I sighed heavily. At least one thing was going right. Bacon cupcakes. *Oh, and also the dog walking,* I thought. The dog walking was good. Bacon and dogs. Well, at least they go together.

CHAPTER 10

On Thin Icing

The next morning the phone rang and it was Mrs. Mellgard. She had a change of plans and wondered if I was free to take Marley out for a long walk and playdate. She'd be willing to pay me double. Ten dollars! I jumped at the chance and said I'd be right over.

On my way out the door I loaded my pocket with liver snaps for Marley, then grabbed two of the remaining four bacon cupcakes from the night before for Mrs. Mellgard. The cupcakes were, if I do say so myself, delicious. The ribbons of salty caramel burst in your mouth when you took a bite of the sweet yellow cake, and the bacon gave a satisfying crunch as the frosting swirled across the roof of your mouth. Everyone had adored them; Sam had had four when he got home from work. One for each movie pass, he joked.

At the Mellgards', I left the cupcakes on the counter with a note for Mrs. Mellgard, then took Marley out for a good time. It was a nice day, and I tried not to think about everyone trying on the dress. The fresh air felt good and so did running around with Marley. When I got back after more than two hours of Frisbee and running with Marley, Mrs. Mellgard was back and standing in the kitchen.

"Emma!" she cried. "Oh my God!"

I was alarmed. "What?" I cried. Had I been gone too long? Was Mrs. Mellgard worried about Marley? I really should have checked my watch.

Mrs. Mellgard grasped at her chest. "The bacon cupcakes. Oh my God!"

"What?" I was panicked now. Had I accidentally baked something into a cupcake? For a second I thought maybe I poisoned Mrs. Mellgard. Then I saw her smile.

"They are the *best* thing I have ever tasted! Wow! Thank you so much!"

I grinned, relieved. "I'm glad you liked them. I really like them too."

"Like them? I love them!" said Mrs. Mellgard

giddily. "I wonder . . . is there any chance you might have time to make me some for my book club meeting on Wednesday?"

"Sure!" I said, without even really thinking about it. "I'd love to. How many do you need?"

"About two dozen, considering my husband will probably have four." Mrs. Mellgard laughed.

"Done. I'll deliver them on Wednesday around six, okay?"

"Great. What do I owe you?" asked Mrs. Mellgard.

"Oh, we usually charge thirty dollars for two dozen." I wasn't supposed to do this. I was supposed to run all orders by the club so we could agree and prioritize and price them. But . . . well . . . I needed the thirty dollars. I knew it was wrong. But Operation Dream Dress was about to be a bust. I had to do something.

"Who's we?" asked Mrs. Mellgard with interest.

"Well, three of my friends are in a Cupcake Club with me. We bake for parties and events. We're actually baking cupcakes for a wedding!"

"Well!" said Mrs. Mellgard. "Sign me up!"

It wasn't until I skipped down the driveway that I realized I should be heading back to Mona at The Special Day on Wednesday to purchase the dress.

I felt nervous again. Well, I'd just have to make it work.

On Sunday I had another dog emergency. The Jensens' daughter's swim team had made it into the finals at a tournament out of state, and their labradoodle, Wendy, needed walking while they were gone, in the morning and afternoon. Since it was a weekend I had the whole day to fit the walks in, so it was okay. I just had to do it before the Cupcake Club meeting. But part of me wanted to miss the Cupcake Club meeting. I was tired of Mia's looks and people talking behind my back. And in all honesty, I wasn't sure I could bear sitting through a reenactment of the magical hours spent at The Special Day. So like a coward, instead of calling, I sent off an e-mail to the group saying something had come up and I couldn't make the meeting. I knew it was lame. But when I pressed send, part of me was proud for doing it. After all, I didn't need those girls if they were going to be so mean. And I could do my own cupcake orders. I already did, with Mrs. Mellgard.

Katie and Mia didn't reply. Alexis e-mailed right back with "Are you okay?" *No,* I thought miserably. I hit delete without responding.

On Monday at school Mia and Katie were okay

but distant. Nobody asked what my emergency was yesterday, and I didn't ask how Mia's special recipe turned out. Alexis kept trying to talk to me, but I brushed her off. At lunch I managed to squeeze in a flute session in one of the music department's practice rooms, so I avoided the lunch table. I told myself I was just being organized and making the most of my time. But I knew I just didn't want to deal.

On Monday night I thought about telling Mom about the dress. But Mom seemed to have forgotten about it and, anyway, I just didn't know how to bring it up. As the days went on, Mom looked more and more tired, and she and Dad seemed worried.

I went to my room and laid all my money out to count, including today's dog-walking receipts. I calculated the thirty dollars I'd get from Mrs. Mellgard on Wednesday. The cupcake expenses were probably around fifteen dollars, so that was really only fifteen dollars profit. *Wow,* I thought coldly, *I can make a lot more money if I don't have to split it four ways.* Then I thought of my friends. I missed them.

Later that night there was an e-mail from Alexis requesting an emergency meeting of the Cupcake Club on Wednesday to discuss three impending new orders that needed to be addressed. Wednesday. Alexis didn't do her usual "Hi, Cupcakers" or sign off with "XOXO." Something was up. Plus, it was on Wednesday. Right in the middle of baking, walking the dogs, and buying the dress (if that could even happen). How was I going to do it all? And what's more, was it really to discuss new orders or were they calling the meeting to vote me out? I stared at the e-mail, trying to read between the lines. Alexis had sent another e-mail: "Call me." Nobody else replied.

Just then there was a knock on the door.

"Who is it?" I demanded crankily, hustling to gather up the money.

"It's me," said Matt.

"Come in," I barked. Great, now I probably had to watch Jake on top of everything else. I began folding the money to put back into the cosmetic bag I kept it in.

Matt opened the door. "Wow. That's a lot of money," he said first. Then, when I didn't comment, he shrugged. "Hey, is the favor department open?" he asked.

I sighed. After Matt had been so nice about the flyers, I felt I had to say yes. "Sure. What do you need?" I asked.

"Uh, do you think you could bake some bacon cupcakes for my team dinner? It's Wednesday."

Of course it is, I thought. "But Wednesday is a Jake day for you," I said with my voice shaking.

"Well, that's the other thing. I can do Jake from pickup till five thirty if you can take over after that. Then I'll owe you two hours."

Wednesday was starting to look like it would be the worst day of my life: I had to bake cupcakes for Mrs. Mellgard, walk three dogs, babysit Jake, make it to a Cupcake Club meeting to get kicked out, and somehow find time to buy the bridesmaid dress before Sydney. How was this all going to happen? But I did owe Matt. *I can do it,* I tried to cheer myself on. *If I just say it, it always gets done.*

"I'll pay you . . . ," Matt offered, eyeing my pile of money again.

"No, you don't need to pay me," I said. "I'll do it. And I'll take Jake." I should be all done by six thirty anyway. It would be okay as long as I was organized.

Matt smiled a huge smile. "That's awesome. People are going to freak out over those cupcakes. Thanks."

"Sure," I said, returning the smile. That was as much of a compliment as I would ever get from Matt.

"So what's all that money for, anyway?" asked Matt.

I shrugged. "Well, it's not enough for anything, right now. I need to buy a two-hundred-and-fifty-dollar bridesmaid's dress on Wednesday, or my enemy will get it and my so-called friends will officially also become my enemies. And I don't want to ask Mom and Dad to help me. I'll probably get kicked out of the wedding party and kicked out of the Cupcake Club. So actually, I don't know what this money is for." I zipped the cosmetic bag closed.

"Wow. It's expensive being a girl," said Matt, half teasing.

"It sure is," I said angrily.

Matt hesitated, as if he was going to say something but then didn't. He left, closing the door gently behind him and leaving me feeling sadder and lonelier than I had all day.

But on Tuesday I was feeling in control. It was a Jake day, but I only had two dogs to walk. I decided I'd get the dogs, then meet Jake's bus, then take them all to Quickie Mart to pick up the baking supplies for the bacon cupcake bakeathon the next day. It should be no problem. I had a plan. I felt good.

But what I hadn't banked on was Franco the

dachshund having diarrhea. Yes, it was a total mess and a total bummer. He must've eaten something in his house that made him sick because when I showed up, he had pooped all over the kitchen. Though it technically was not my job to clean it up, I didn't feel right leaving it. So I went around with cleaning spray and paper towels, then pocketed a wad of emergency paper towels and headed out to get the other dog. But now I was behind schedule. I knew I should just go home and wait for Jake's bus, but I also didn't want to just sit and wait, and I was better off having both dogs ready to go when Jake got home so we could then head in the other direction to the Quickie Mart.

Unfortunately, I didn't realize how long it would take me to get home. Again. By the time I got home, the bus had passed our house. I could see it a block up ahead. I set out chasing it, but Franco was butt-scootching across the pavement and couldn't be rushed. I tied the dogs to a pole and set out at a dead sprint to get to the bus, nearly getting hit by a car in the process. I had to catch it. They wouldn't let Jake off unless there was someone there. I ran faster than I ever ran before and caught up to the bus on the next stop as the door was closing, and waved at Sal the driver. Sal opened the door and called to Jake, but he had a concerned look on his face.

"Hey, Emma, I'm sorry, but I have to write you up for missing the bus today," Sal said. "I hate to do it, but it puts my job in jeopardy if I don't follow the protocol." He shrugged. "Sorry."

I sighed heavily in defeat. I understood. I had messed up and Sal was just doing his job, but the timing was terrible. If you got more than one write-up, you couldn't take the bus anymore. Dad was going to freak out. "Okay," I said, then nodded and tried to look as bad as I felt, hoping Sal would take pity on me. "I'm really sorry."

Jake came wearily down the stairs. He had fallen asleep on the bus again; I could tell by the way his hair was sticking up. "You forgot me!" he yelled.

"No, I didn't, Jakey." I sighed. "I was just late."

Here we go again, I thought. There would be no trip to the Quickie Mart. Not with Jake in one of his moods. We trudged down the block to the waiting dogs. I decided I'd be better off just taking them to our yard. That way I could get Jake home.

I sent Jake in to watch TV, and then I played with the dogs for half an hour. Franco had diarrhea two more times, and I had to get out the hose to spray it away, but the yard still smelled like dog poop. Eventually I had to get Jake to come with me to take the dogs home. Jake complained the whole way, but I managed to drop them off without Franco having another mess. "Let's go to the Quickie Mart now," I said cheerily. "I need a few things."

"I don't wanna," said Jake. I hoped he would just keep walking anyway. But as we passed our house on the way, Dad was standing in the doorway, his mouth set in a grim line and his hands on his hips.

"Hey, Dad's home!" Jake cried, running up the driveway.

"Jake, run up to your room to play for a minute. Emma and I need to have a little discussion," said Dad in his most steely, no-nonsense soccer-coach voice. I felt scared. This would not be good.

"Let's go sit in the kitchen," said Dad. He spoke firmly and decisively, but he did not seem angry as much as disappointed. That was worse.

"Emma, Sal told me you actually missed the bus once before," he said. "This is the third strike. You know what that means."

I wiggled nervously in my seat. I had learned never to offer up a punishment, but rather to wait until it was doled out. In the past I had made the mistake of suggesting something that turned out to be worse than what was coming.

"No more dogs. No more cupcakes. Just school, flute, and Jake."

"But . . . ," I began. What on Earth was I going to do about tomorrow? The most-booked day ever?

"No buts. You were fairly warned. Tomorrow you will come straight home from school and get right to work. That's all."

"But I have commitments," I protested.

"Call them and explain that you are no longer free. It won't be the end of the world," said Dad. "You haven't been employed by any of these people for very long. Though I'm sure they adore you, and rightly so, they did manage to get along just a week or two ago, before you started with them."

"But the cupcakes . . ."

Dad nodded. "We will revisit that issue next week. I think a week off is a very wise idea. Your friends will understand," he said.

"No they won't!" I wailed. "And the dress!" I cried, but instantly regretted it.

"What dress?" asked Dad, a look of confusion on his face.

Just then Matt walked in. He took quick stock of

the scene and put his hands in the air in a gesture of surrender. "Just passing through," he said, and he dashed up the stairs.

Dad looked at me. "What dress?"

"Oh, never mind!" I sobbed, and stood up from the table to leave.

"Do we understand each other?" asked Dad.

I nodded miserably.

"Okay, then," he said.

No, it was not. It was not okay at all.

CHAPTER 11

Add One Sweet Brother

There was a knock on my door later. It was Mom, home from work. I had eaten the hamburger Dad made for dinner in stony silence, finished my homework (the best job I'd done in weeks, even I had to admit), and I was practicing my flute. I was trying hard to not think about cupcakes or dogs or dresses.

"Come in," I said, pausing with the flute at my chin.

Mom opened the door. "It sounded lovely from outside," she said.

I rolled my eyes. "I was only doing scales." I was cranky and even a little mad at Mom, even though I knew none of this was really her fault. I got myself into this mess.

"Honey, we need to talk," said Mom.

First Dad, now Mom. I sighed and put down the flute.

"I heard about what happened with the school bus. Again, I am so sorry that I have put this on you, with my new work schedule and all. I don't think it will be for too much longer, though. It's looking like they might be able to end my work suspension soon. A foundation has kicked in some money for staffing the library so that could be great news for us." Mom smiled brightly.

"Great," I said softly. It was great. It was just probably a little too late.

"Dad told me you had a lot on your plate. I was wondering if there's anything I can help you with?" Mom asked.

Well, I thought, *how about: a trip to the Quickie Mart, baking four dozen bacon cupcakes going to two locations, calling the dog-walking clients to let them know I had to cancel, attending an emergency Cupcake Club meeting, taking care of Jake, and oh, yes, buying the dress.* I really thought I could handle everything. And tonight was the first time I realized maybe I couldn't.

"Honey?" prodded Mom.

"No, thanks," I said finally. I couldn't handle it,

but that didn't mean Mom had to.

Mom looked like she didn't believe me. She paused for a minute, watching me carefully. Then she said, "Well, how are the wedding plans coming along? Did they settle on a dress?"

I knew I should tell her. This was the perfect opportunity. And I don't know why I didn't. "Almost, I think," I said. "Pretty close."

Mom smiled. "Well, at least that's something to look forward to. When's the wedding? A month from now?"

"Three weeks," I said. Three very short weeks in which to buy a dress and have it altered. Three very long weeks in which your best friends are not talking to you.

"Wow, they'd better get going on those dresses," said Mom. She put her hands on her knees. "Well, I have to go to the grocery store really quickly to pick up some milk. Is there anything I can get for you?" She stood up.

Well . . .

"Honey?"

Okay, I thought. *I need help.* Mom has always said she would always help me and all I had to do was ask. I thought about it for a while. Then I said, "Yes. I promised Matt I'd make cupcakes for his team dinner tomorrow." I didn't tell her about Mrs. Mellgard. I was still trying to figure out if I could make four dozen cupcakes and deliver them without anyone noticing.

I got a piece of paper and wrote a list of ingredients for the bacon cupcakes.

"No problem," said Mom. "And I think it's very nice that you're doing this for Matt. I'm so happy to see the family pulling together." Then she gave me a kiss. I felt guilty. We might be pulling together, but I was falling apart inside.

Late that night I went online and e-mailed my dog-walking clients to say that due to an unforeseen workload, I would have to put them on a waiting list for the time being. I didn't want to admit I'd been grounded. In my e-mail to Mrs. Mellgard, I made it clear that the cupcakes would still be delivered on time tomorrow (how, I was not sure), and I let Mrs. Anderson know that Jenner would be the first dog off the waiting list when my normal workload resumed.

Next I e-mailed the Cupcake Club to say that I was so sorry, but I would have to miss the meeting the next day. I kept it brief. I was fully prepared to be kicked out. And I knew I wouldn't be a bridesmaid.

Alexis wrote back right away: "Please tell me what's going on."

But I couldn't. I didn't think she would understand and, besides, I didn't want to. My real friends should want to be my friends even if I couldn't be a bridesmaid. I shouldn't have to prove that I was pulling my weight. I was pulling plenty.

Still, I couldn't sleep that night, and I checked my e-mail again first thing the next morning, but there still wasn't any response from Katie or Mia. I was nervous to get to lunch, and I wondered if they would even let me sit with them. Or if I wanted to.

But when I got to the cafeteria, it was Sydney I ran into first.

"Hey! I'm going to get the dress today!" said Sydney, all dressed up in a tight, sleeveless turtleneck and a miniskirt. "I guess your friend never coughed up the dough."

"How do you know . . . I mean, how did you hear?" I asked, my face getting hot.

"I called the store to check, silly!" said Sydney brightly. "I'm going tonight with my mom and Brandi, right after cheerleading. I can't wait!" She flounced away, leaving me standing alone, breathless in the middle of the cafeteria.

I saw Mia, Alexis, and Katie staring at me, already

eating. They hadn't waited for me in our usual meeting spot, which wasn't a total surprise, but it was a pretty strong move on their part. I took a long look at them, gulped, then turned and fled. "Emma!" I heard Alexis calling. But I didn't turn around. I just kept going. I'd eat my lunch alone, in the gym, with all the weirdos. *I'd better get used to it,* I thought bitterly.

I managed to avoid everyone all day, even Alexis, who almost tried to chase me down the hall. After school I ran out the door to the bike rack and pedaled home furiously. I had decided to ask Sam to drop off the cupcakes for Mrs. Mellgard on his way to work. I thought I could hear Alexis calling me again, but I didn't turn around. I hated everyone right now. If they couldn't understand, then I didn't want to be friends with them anyway.

At home I went into a baking frenzy, relieved that Mom had bought the baking supplies the previous night. Matt had met Jake at the bus and taken him to the park for a while to get him out of my hair while I got the cupcakes ready, and I was grateful for that. Jake was the last thing I could handle right now. The cupcakes were cooling on a rack and the frosting and bacon was sitting mixed and crumbled and ready, when the phone rang.

I went to answer it and saw that it was The Special Day bridal salon! What should I say? I couldn't let it go to voice mail because then Mom or Dad would get the message. I picked up the phone, cold with fear and dread.

"Hello?"

"Hello, is Emma there please? This is Patricia from The Special Day bridal salon."

"This is Emma," I said, gulping.

"Oh, hello, dear. I was just calling to see if you could come into the store today. We had set aside the dress for you for Ms. Vélaz's wedding, and Mona is getting nervous about the alterations as the time draws near."

I realized that Patricia was being nice. Instead of saying that I couldn't pay for it, Patricia merely suggested that I was late.

"Oh," I said. "I'm . . . I'm not sure I can make it today."

There was a pause. "Well . . . I can ask Mona about extending the hold period for another day or so. I just have another customer who is eager for the dress. You are going to go ahead with it, are you not?"

"Uh . . ." I had to think.

"Let's do this," said Patricia. "If you can get in

here today, I can legitimately hold off the other customer for another couple of days, or I can put her in a different dress. I think once you see the dress again, you'll realize how marvelous it is on you and you'll be able to organize everything very quickly. Okay?"

I didn't know what to say. I should have said, "Oh, let Sydney have the dress. End my friendship with Mia, Katie, and Alexis. I'm going to quit the Cupcake Club." It was all done already anyway, pretty much. But what I said was, "Okay."

"Great. Then we'll see you soon," said Patricia. "Bye!"

I hung up. I went to frost the cupcakes and put them in their carriers. I was halfway through packing them up when Sam came in, banging the back door.

"Oh! Please tell me those are bacon cupcakes!" he cried happily.

I smiled, despite my gloom. I had made a few extra, partially in hopes of buttering up Sam.

"Yes, Sammy, these are for you." I handed him the plate. "And now I have a favor to ask."

"Uh-oh," he said, through a mouthful of cupcake.

"I need you to drop these off for me in half an

hour. Two dozen go to the Mellgards' on Race Lane. And two dozen go to the gym with Matt, for his team party."

"Ugh," said Sam with a sigh. He thought for a second. "I guess I can do it," he said. And he grabbed another cupcake.

Just then his cell phone rang. "Hello?" he said.

I was so happy I could kiss him. I packed up the rest of Matt's cupcakes. All set.

"Where? What? Dude, slow down," said Sam in annoyance.

I glanced at him and saw that he was looking at me, his eyebrows knit together in concern.

What? I mouthed at him, but he didn't react. What did I do now?

"Okay, let me just write down the address. Darn it all, I'm going to be late for work tonight," he huffed. "Bye."

"What was that all about?" I asked, a little worried. "Is everything all right?" I pressed the tops down on the carriers. Sam was looking at me strangely.

"Nothing," he said finally. "I'll be ready in twenty. But you're coming with me," he said. "You can run in with the cupcakes while I wait in the car. It'll be faster." And he left the kitchen in a hurry.

"What? But I have Jake! And Dad will kill me if we leave!" I called after him. "Sam!" but he didn't come back.

Ten minutes later, Jake and Matt walked in, and Matt ran to shower and change. He gave me a strange look, one that made me say, "What?" in annoyance, but he didn't answer.

Jake actually helped wash the baking dishes—sort of—and shortly after we finished, Sam came down, freshly showered, followed by Matt, also freshly showered, with a backpack. Something about Sam still looked fishy, but I wasn't going to press it, especially since I needed his help.

"Let's hit it, kids," Sam said, grabbing the keys to the minivan.

"What about Mom and Dad?" I asked. I couldn't deal with more punishment.

"I'll deal with them later," said Sam.

The novelty of going anywhere with Sam was enough to make Jake cooperate, even without a bribe. But he was curious. "Where are we going, Sammy?" asked Jake.

"Down to the station house," said Sam with a wink. "We're going to book her." And he jerked his thumb at me. I rolled my eyes and decided to go along with it all. If Sam was willing to deal with

Mom and Dad, then how much trouble could I get into? The four of us got into the minivan and set off to drop off the Mellgards' cupcakes, Matt and his cupcakes, and return home. Or so I thought.

CHAPTER 12

Brothers and Bridesmaids

Except that we didn't go straight home. After the cupcake delivery to the Mellgards', which went smoothly, and dropping off Matt, Sam turned his car in the opposite direction of home.

"Hey! Where are you going?" I asked in alarm. I was already treading on thin ice. I knew my parents would kill me for dragging Jake around this late and not doing my homework. Plus, no one had started dinner.

"Just downtown for a minute. Chill."

Now I was annoyed. This week was just getting worse by the day. I turned and glared out the window. Then I turned back to Sam.

"Are we going to the mall?" I asked. Maybe I could run into The Special Day after all and tie up the loose ends. Just tell Patricia thanks anyway, but it wasn't going to happen. I didn't want her to be mad at me. I looked over at Jake in the backseat, and I suddenly spied Matt's backpack.

"Sam! We have to go back! Matt left his bag!" I said urgently. I didn't want to open it because it was probably stinky, but I was pretty sure his practice clothes were in there.

"Oh," Sam waved his hand. "I'll . . . I'll deal with that," he said.

"But . . ." Then I sighed. Everyone was weird and getting weirder. The cupcakes were delivered. The dress was gone. I was done.

We parked in the mall lot and headed in. Sam carried Matt's backpack. "What are you doing with that?" I asked, but Sam kept walking fast and didn't answer. Sam was walking briskly right toward The Special Day. *What on Earth was going on*, I wondered. Poor Jake was jogging alongside to keep up with Sam's long strides.

"Sam! Slow down! What's the rush?" I asked breathlessly. "And where are we going?"

"I can't be too late for work," said Sam. "There's a six-thirty show, and they need me."

And then we were there: The Special Day.

Sam held the door and ushered us in.

"I . . . I . . ." I didn't know what to say. Did Sam know? Was he going to make me apologize to Patricia and Mona for telling them I was going to buy the dress?

Sam strode to the counter, and all I could do was follow him.

"May I help you?" asked Patricia, gliding to the counter. "Oh, hello there! You came in after all!" said Patricia to me.

I blushed furiously. Now I was going to have to explain it all in front of my brothers.

"Hey! It was you!" said an indignant voice behind me. I whirled around to find Sydney Whitman standing there with her mother and cousin, the tarty Brandi.

"Wh-wh-at?" I said.

"You were the one who hadn't bought the dress! But then why are you here now? I came to get it!" Sydney's eyes flashed angrily.

I felt mad all of a sudden. That was my dress. And Sydney was not going to take it from me. Sam and Patricia were in an intense conversation, their heads nearly touching. Then Patricia waved Sam to the back of the store to Mona's office.

I just stood there, not knowing what to do.

"I guess they're going to get the dress for me

after all," said Sydney smugly. "So who's that hottie?" she asked, flipping her hair.

"My brother," I said. "And he has a girlfriend." Sam did not have a girlfriend. Not one I knew about, at least. But it sure wasn't going to be Sydney.

Before Sydney could say anything else, I saw Alexis, Katie, and Mia walking from the back of the store. With Mona, Sam, and Patricia!

"What is going on?" I almost cried. I was so confused.

Mona had the dress on a hanger, and she crossed behind the counter, hung it on a pole, and waved me over to her.

I was so embarrassed. Now everyone was going to hear me turn down the dress, and they'd all witness Sydney's glory as she purchased it. I felt like I was walking off a cliff as I walked over to Mona.

"Honey," whispered Mona. "You have a lot of people who love you. You must be a very special person."

I didn't even hear her. I just started to cry. "I'm sorry, but . . . I can't buy the dress." I started crying really hard then, and I couldn't stop.

"Oh no, sweetheart. Please, don't cry. Everything is all right." She gestured at Patricia for a Kleenex, and Patricia scurried to grab one from one of the many nearby boxes.

"I have your dress all ready for you," Mona continued, as if she hadn't heard me at all. "We'll just have you try it on and then we can fit it."

"But you don't understand. . . . I can't afford it," I said. "I'm sorry I let it go on so long. I didn't know how to tell you. Any of you," I said, turning to look at the Cupcakers.

"Oh, Emma!" cried Mia, and she ran over and hugged me. Alexis and Katie piled on.

"I know you all hate me. I'm so sorry," I said. "I couldn't go to the meetings because I was trying to make extra money dog walking. And I had to babysit. And . . . and . . . well, I guess I just couldn't do it all." I didn't even mention the order for Mrs. Mellgard.

"We don't hate you!" said Mia.

"Why didn't you tell us?" said Katie. "We could have helped you."

"They did help you!" interjected Mona. "These girls came down here today to negotiate a reduced rate for your dress. And we've struck a deal!"

Alexis smiled. "Mona is knocking ninety-nine dollars off of the dress in exchange for four weeks of mini cupcakes!" said Alexis.

"This one drives a hard bargain," said Mona, gesturing at Alexis. "She's coming to work for me one day."

Alexis beamed.

"But how did you know I was . . . that I couldn't afford it?" I asked.

"I e-mailed your brother last night," said Alexis. "When I didn't hear back from you, I knew something was really wrong, and well, I knew about your mom's job. I asked Matt if he knew about the dress, and he put two and two together."

I remembered Sam was there, and I turned around to look at him. He smiled and shrugged.

"Matt e-mailed me and told me that he and Sam wanted to chip in for the dress for you, but we still didn't have enough," said Alexis. "So I decided to see if we could work out a deal for you. And, well, I told Katie and Mia. Please don't be mad. I just wanted them to know the real reason you hadn't been around."

"You should have told us!" said Mia. "I just thought you didn't care about the wedding and didn't want to be in the club! We could have helped you figure it out. Or I wouldn't have cared if you wore an old dress!"

"I don't know what to say," I said. I really didn't.

So many people helped me: Alexis, Mia, Katie, Sam, even Matt.

"Well, instead of saying anything, let's go get that dress on," said Mona. "We need to make sure it fits you perfectly."

"Wait! That's my dress!" shrieked Sydney.

We turned to look—we had completely forgotten about her.

"Now, dear, we have a lot to discuss," said Mona smoothly, and she steered Sydney away from us as she cast a strong look at Patricia to manage the rest of the situation.

I was on cloud nine as I stumbled into the dressing room, and once the dress was on, I felt even better. I still couldn't believe my brothers had done this. I mean, Matt? And my friends. It was amazing. I thought for a second about how much heartache I would have saved myself if I had just told them from the start. Live and learn, as Dad always says.

I smiled in the mirror. The dress really was gorgeous.

There was a knock on the door.

"Come in," I said.

Jake stuck his head around the corner. "Wow, Emmy! You look like a princess fairy!" he said breathlessly.

I laughed. "Thanks, Jakey."

The door opened wider. And there was Mom. "Oh, honey," she said, and she burst into tears. "I saw Sam when I was leaving work, and I was so confused. . . . You look beautiful!"

I laughed as Alexis handed Mom a Kleenex from one of three nearby boxes.

"Doesn't she look divine?" asked Alexis, and all of us started giggling.

CHAPTER 13

Sweet Endings

That night all of us (minus Jake, who was asleep in his bed) sat in the kitchen, a plate of bacon cupcakes on the table. It was late and everyone was tired but very, very happy.

Mom was happy because the director of the library had called to say that the new grant funding would cover reinstating her job, and that she'd be back on board as of the first of the month, which was in only eight days.

Matt was happy because the bacon cupcakes had been a huge hit at his team dinner; his coach had even implied that someone with the great idea of bringing such delicious cupcakes to a team dinner ought to be captain next year. Matt was thrilled.

Sam was happy because he could have his Friday

nights back once Mom went back to work at the library. He had been missing out on the best shift at the movie theater and hanging out with his friends afterward.

Dad was happy because Mom was going back to work and because his kids were happy.

And I was happiest of all. I had amazing friends, generous brothers, a dad who had revoked my punishment once he heard the reasons why I was so overworked, and a mom who was going back to a normal work schedule. I also had a gorgeous dress that was being altered to fit me and permission to run the dog-walking business one weekday and one weekend day each week for two hours. Plus, Mrs. Mellgard had just called to place a very large order and was referring the Cupcake Club to all her friends. I had come clean about that order earlier. No one was angry, and Alexis was really happy we had another client.

"This has been a crazy few weeks," said Mom.

"Tell me about it," I said.

"Honey, I'm so sorry that Dad and I were so out of touch with what was going on in your life. I just feel awful about it," Mom said.

"That's okay," I said. "After all, I can always handle . . ." And I trailed off.

Dad looked at me.

"Emma, you know we're always here for you. Please don't let things get that out of control again without asking one of us for help or at least filling us in on what's going on, okay? You're lucky you have such great brothers, kiddo." He nodded toward Matt and Sam.

"The greatest," I said.

"Just don't stop baking, even if all else fails," said Matt, laughing as he peeled the wrapper from a cupcake he'd just snagged.

"Yes, cupcakes should be the last thing to go, after schoolwork and flute," agreed Sam through a mouthful of cupcake.

"I just can't wait until the wedding," I said dreamily.

"Speaking of weddings, who was that cute girl in the bridal salon? The blonde?" asked Sam.

"Aaargh!" I groaned. Maybe Sam wasn't the greatest brother ever!

On the day of Mia's mom's wedding the Cupcake Club, minus Mia, was meeting at my house to put the final touches on the bridal cupcakes and the groom's cake, which was the bacon cupcakes, of course. I now thought of them as my lucky recipe.

Mia's mom had decided to go with the sheet of minis in the shape of a heart for her wedding dessert. She had sampled some at Mona's during her final fitting and found them irresistible. The club decided to do them just like Mona's: angel food cake, white fondant frosting, and white sugar flowers as decoration. There would be a heart made of raspberry cupcakes with pink frosting in the center of the sheet of cupcakes on the buffet.

At eight thirty that Saturday morning, I heard a quiet knock on the back door. It was Alexis. She had already been to The Special Day and dropped off Mona's cupcakes that we'd made the night before. Now she was ready to work some more.

"Hi," she whispered.

"Hi," I whispered back. "We don't have to whisper. There's no one here."

"Where is everyone?" whispered Alexis.

"Practice," I said in a normal voice. We both laughed.

There was another knock on the door. It was Katie.

"Hey," she whispered.

"No whispering," whispered Alexis. We started laughing really hard. Katie gave us a look that said she thought we were cuckoo, and she came in.

We each ate a big bowl of cereal and then got down to business. I was making the bacon, and Katie was making the fondant frosting for the white minis; she would set aside a bit of my buttercream frosting and tint it pink with raspberry jam for the pink cupcakes. Alexis was working on the edible sugar flower decorations, which were kind of hard, but Alexis did them perfectly, of course.

"Anyone talked to Mia yet?" I asked.

"I e-mailed her this morning to say good luck," said Katie.

"I think they were going to a spa this morning with her aunts and cousins," said Alexis. "Group rate, I bet. Probably a wedding package."

I rolled my eyes at Katie, and we both giggled. *Oh, Alexis.*

The bacon was done, nice and crispy. I set it on paper towels to dry and turned to make the buttercream. We were tripling the recipe, which meant three boxes of confectioners' sugar, six sticks of softened butter, three teaspoons of vanilla, and almost a half a cup of milk. The hand mixer groaned and strained against the ingredients and gave off a light smell of burning plastic. This was nothing new, but it was all part of the reason I still wanted that new pink mixer.

It felt so good to be with my friends again. But I guess we were talking so much that we kind of lost track of time.

"Oh no!" cried Alexis as she looked at the clock. "How will we get this done?"

I started to panic. "I can . . . I will . . ." Then I stopped.

Mom, Jake, Sam, Dad, and Matt came in.

I took a deep breath. "Mom!" I cried. "Mom, we need help!"

Mom smiled. "Okay, whatever it is, we can handle it. Come on, guys," she said, gesturing to the boys. "Everybody's in on this one."

"We can do this!" said Alexis, and she smiled at me. "Emma and I can figure out a plan."

And we did. Mom whipped up the buttercream, Dad began packing frosted minis, Jake crumbled the bacon ("Yes, you can taste it. But only once, or I'll arrest you!" I said), Matt helped Katie frost the bacon cupcakes as soon as they were ready, and Sam started carrying boxes out to Dad's station wagon. Alexis and Katie rushed to help him.

With everyone else running around I suddenly realized I didn't have much to do. The kitchen was a hive of busy activity, and everyone was doing his or her job well. I went to check my e-mail. Mia had sent all the club members an e-mail asking us to be at her house a shade earlier. I also had an e-mail from Williams-Sonoma, announcing a new version of the stand mixer. It cost $199! A price reduction! I smiled. The day just kept getting better and better. *Someday,* I thought, *you really will be mine!*

CHAPTER 14

The Special Day

I couldn't wait to put on the dress. Mom buttoned me up and helped brush out my hair. She got a little teary again. Then I went downstairs, where Dad, Sam, Matt, and Jake were all waiting.

"Wow!" said Dad.

"You look so pretty," said Jake.

I blushed a little bit. I wasn't used to everyone looking at me.

"You do look good," said Sam.

Matt nodded.

Dad snapped a few pictures, then we picked up Alexis and Katie and got to Mia's house right on time. Mia opened the door in her matching dress.

Behind her, Ms. Vélaz came floating down the

stairs, and we all just stared at her. I'd never seen anyone look more beautiful.

"Come on, my beautiful bridesmaids," she said. "We're off to get married!" We all giggled and followed her outside to the limousine, which would take us to the ceremony. We had never been in one before, and we were all excited.

I tried to take in everything, but it all went so fast. First we posed for pictures, and then we lined up to go down the aisle. I was a little nervous, but I did it slowly like Mom had practiced with me and I smiled, just like Mia's mom told us. We stood under the canopy and I was looking around and then—bam—it was over and we had to walk back up the aisle.

The party got underway, and we all sat together at a table with lots of pink roses. We were having such a good time. I had never been to a fancy party like this before. Then the band started playing, and we all jumped up to dance.

The cupcakes were a big hit. Everyone loved them, and everyone really chowed down on the bacon cupcakes. "Oh," a woman said, stuffing a few in her purse, "these are divine."

"Did she say 'divine'?" Alexis shrieked, and we all burst into giggles.

"What can I say," said Alexis. "You were right about the bacon!"

"Hey, in a house with three brothers, I know bacon!" I said.

"Emma," said Mia. "You have to promise us something."

I looked up, a little worried by her tone. Katie and Alexis were looking at me too.

"You have to promise us that whatever it is, good or bad, you won't keep secrets from us. Friends tell one another everything, and they help out. I want you to promise that you won't be embarrassed about anything and feel like you can't talk to us."

"I know," I said, hanging my head. I still couldn't believe all that they did for me. I looked down at my beautiful dress. "I'm really sorry. I won't keep anything from you again."

"Honey, this is for you." Mia's mom was at my side. She handed me a white envelope. "It's just a little something I'm giving to each of you as a traditional bridesmaid gift. Thank you for helping to make this such a special day."

"Oh, Ms. Vélaz . . . I mean Mrs. Valdes!"

"I know!" said Mia's mom, rolling her eyes. "I went from Vélaz to Valdes! It's going to confuse everyone."

"I don't know what to say!" I blushed. I hadn't expected a gift.

Mia's mom planted a kiss on top of my head. "Don't say a word," she said. "Just get yourself something you've really wanted." Then she winked at me. She handed a box to Alexis and one to Katie before gliding off.

I looked down at the envelope. I put it on my lap, not wanting to appear greedy, but I was really curious.

"Open them!" said Mia.

Alexis opened a beautiful set of stationery, a journal, and notepads. "So good for making lists!" she said.

Katie opened three new cookbooks.

I slid open the envelope with my finger. Inside was a gift card.

The gift card was for Williams-Sonoma. And it was for fifty dollars!

I looked up and caught Alexis's eye, then Katie's, then Mia's. They all grinned. "But . . . ," I asked, confused. "How did she know . . . ?"

Alexis blushed. "Well, some secrets you do keep from friends. But just for a little while!" And we all laughed. I tucked the envelope into the purse Mom had let me borrow, and I smiled.

The wedding was going by so fast but so had the past few weeks. A lot of things had been burned, rushed, worried over, and hidden. All bad. I looked around at Mia's beautiful mom, all the pretty pink flowers, and saw how happy everyone was. Now everything was pretty good. I had my friends. I had people who loved me. I had brothers who weren't half bad most of the time.

"A toast!" I cried, lifting up my glass of lemonade.

Alexis, Katie, and Mia held up their glasses too.

"To friends!" I said.

"Here, here!" cried Mia.

"To no more secrets!" said Katie.

"To helping each other out always!" said Alexis.

"And," I said with a little bit of a giggle, "to the divine pink mixer that will soon be mine!"

Alexis

and the

perfect

recipe

CHAPTER 1

My Sister Takes the Cake

My name is Alexis Becker, and I'm the business mind (ha-ha) of the Cupcake Club. The club is a for-profit group that my best friends—Mia, Katie, and Emma—and I started, and we make money baking delicious cupcakes!

I love figuring out how to run a business and putting together the different building blocks—math, organization, planning—that's why the girls can *count* on me for this kind of stuff. Plus, as you can tell, I love math-related puns! My friends are more creative with the cupcakes, so they come up with the designs and other artistic stuff. My one specialty, though, is fondant. I am very good at making little flowers and designs out of that firm frosting. Otherwise, I'm mostly crunching numbers and wondering how to make money. Mmm . . . money!

If the Cupcake Club was an equation, it would look like this:

$$(4 \text{ girls} + \text{supplies}) \times \text{clients} = \$\$\$\$$$

Or really, more like this:

$$(\text{Profit} - \text{supplies}) / 4 = \$$$

We actually have lots of fun doing it. Most of our clients are really nice people, which is much more than I can say for our latest client: my sister, Dylan. I can practically still hear her fuming.

"It is *my* party, *I* am the one turning sixteen, and I have budgeted *everything* down to the last party favor. I know *exactly* what I'm doing!" She was talking to our mom behind closed doors, but I heard every word since I was right outside her bedroom!

Dylan never gets out-of-control mad; she's always in total control. Except that ever since she'd started planning her sweet sixteen party (which was now four and a half weeks away), she'd been cranky *a lot*. But she never raises her voice when she gets mad. She lowers it to a whisper, and you can hear the chill in it as if actual icicles were hanging from the words. I had to put my ear to her bedroom door to hear everything that was being said. Knowledge is power; that's one of my mottoes, and I need all the information I can get. About everything.

My mother was sounding kind of amused by the fight, which was about two things: the guest list for the party and the cake. I had an interest in the outcome of both, since I wanted to be able to invite my best friends, and *we* wanted to bake the dessert for the party. (It wasn't about the money as we wouldn't charge a lot; it's just that it would be great exposure for our business!)

I could picture Mom trying not to smile and to take Dylan seriously. "Darling, I know how careful you are, and I am impressed, as always, by your work," she said. "I admire your attention to detail on these spreadsheets. However, not everything will be according to *your* plan, as your father and I also have a say in what works best for this family. Now let's take a look at this guest list again."

I grinned. Mom was on *my* side.

There were some muffled comments and I strained to hear them. Maybe I'd hear better if I put a glass against the wall like I'd seen people do on TV. Or maybe I should lie down and listen through the crack under the door. I pulled my hair into a ponytail, and then lay on the hall rug outside the door.

"The Taylors! *Mom!* The whole family? That wasn't in my head count!" The Ice Princess was losing her cool, but I didn't focus on that. All I could think of was that Emma's whole family might come. And *that* was very interesting.

Emma has three brothers. They've always all been in the background of things—rummaging around their mudroom looking for a lost cleat or watching TV in the living room. They're kind of like furniture. When we talk to them at all, it's just stuff like "Please pass the ketchup" or "Hey! We were watching that!"

Jake is much younger, so he's cute but not exactly a pal of mine, and Matt and Sam are older, so we don't really pay attention to them, and they don't pay much attention to us.

Until recently, that is.

What changed everything was that I had a little direct contact with Matt. He's eighteen months older, but only one school year ahead (he's in eighth grade at Park Street Middle School). Usually I am with Emma when her brothers are around, so I guess I see them from her point of view.

But this time I had to call Matt for help with something for Emma, and it wasn't until he said "Hello" on the phone that in one strange, sudden moment, *everything* changed.

So what happened? First off, I am very efficient. When something needs doing, I just do it. When someone needs calling, I just pick up the phone and dial. And that was what I had done, without even thinking about it.

But Matt's voice sounds much deeper on the phone than it does in person, and when I heard it, it threw me off and I panicked, like, *Who is this person I am talking to?* and *Why did I call him, exactly?* I kind of had an out-of-body experience. I suddenly realized I'd called a boy, and I almost dropped the phone!

But thanks to caller ID he already knew who was calling, so I couldn't exactly hang up. Then, just to confuse me further, in the course of our (very brief) conversation, Matt told me how worried he'd been about Emma, and that he felt bad for some things she was going through at the time.

I was shocked!

I didn't think boys *worried* about anyone! And feeling bad for someone? That is just unheard of! Suddenly Matt seemed like . . . a real *person*. With feelings! In the end, it was I who rushed us off the phone. I suddenly got really, really nervous and couldn't believe I'd had the guts to call Matt in the first place. You know in the old cartoons when the coyote runs off a cliff and his feet are still spinning, but he's in midair and he only falls when he realizes it? That's what happened to me.

And now, when I heard Dylan talking about the Taylors, all I could think of was Matt. And that gave me a funny feeling, like fish were swimming in my stomach.

I hope he comes to Dylan's party, I thought. *Or maybe I don't. Ugh! I don't know what I want!*

Suddenly the door flew open, and Dylan shrieked when she saw me lying on the floor. I blinked as the bright light from her room hit me.

"I hate this family!" Dylan wailed, stepping over me. She stomped down the hall to the bathroom and shut the door as hard as possible without actually slamming it.

"Alexis, honey, what are you doing there?" my mother asked in her "patient" voice.

I rolled up on one side and propped my head on

my fist. "Just interested in the outcome of every-thing," I replied.

My mother smiled at me and shook her head.

"What?" I said in my most innocent voice. "I just want to make sure that we get the job."

"You'll get the job, all right, but these better turn out to be the prettiest and tastiest cupcakes you've ever baked," Mom said. She's pretty tough. She's not a CPA and a CFO for nothing.

"Mom, please. We run a very professional outfit."

Dylan came stomping out of the bathroom and glared at my mother. "This is the person you'd like to entrust my dessert to? This . . . worm, lying on the floor like a two-year-old?"

"That's enough, Dylan. Don't speak like that about your sister," Mom warned. (She went to parent training when we were little, and she has all these certain voices and techniques she uses on us.)

"Yeah," I added. "I'm not two. Or a worm!"

Dylan drew back her leg like she was going to kick me, and I rolled away and sprang to my feet.

"Girls! Counting to three!" Mom yelled.

Dylan shook her head in disgust and stormed into her room, where she collapsed dramatically onto her bed. "The Cake Specialist said they'd even give me a discount," she muttered. "I would be the first discount they've ever given. They said I drive a hard bargain."

Mom patted Dylan. "I would expect nothing less, darling. But we need to support a business that is in our family. And I know the Cupcake Club will do a wonderful job for you."

"Wonderful!" I repeated, raising my arms in victory.

"Argh!" cried Dylan as she pulled a pillow over her head. "Just leave me alone!" After a moment she added, "And just make sure whatever you Cupcakers propose is in my party's color scheme of—"

My mother and I answered together, "We know, we know, black and gold!"

I put up my hand and my mother gave me a stiff-handed, silent high five. (She's not the high-fiving type).

"I saw that!" accused Dylan from under her pillow.

My mother and I exchanged a guilty smile.

"They'd better be the best black-and-gold cupcakes you've ever made!" said Dylan. "Or else!"

I rolled my eyes, and we left Dylan to her moping.

"Thanks, Mom," I whispered once we were out

in the hall with Dylan's door safely closed.

"You're welcome, dear," she whispered back. "But you owe me some pretty spectacular cupcakes!"

"Black-and-gold ones! Coming right up!" I said, and we laughed.

We started down the hall. I did a little cha-cha-cha step. I'm obsessed with all the TV dancing shows and like to practice dance moves whenever I can. Music and dance is kind of mathematical, which is why I love it. There's a logical and organized pattern to everything—the chords, notes, and dance steps.

"Is Dylan really mad, do you think?" I asked. All joking aside, I did not want Dylan as my enemy. She is my only sibling, and we are usually pretty good friends.

My mother thought for a moment. "She is getting everything she wants. The place, the music, the food, the date, the decor, the favors. Everything. Now, she is contributing quite a lot of her own money to it, so she does get her say. But I think she can accommodate me on a few extra faces and a special dessert."

"Sounds fair to me," I agreed, and I went to e-mail the Cupcakers with the good news. All we needed was a great idea, one that would keep Dylan from killing me. Oh yeah, and it had to be black and gold!

I just wished I could e-mail them about Matt Taylor being invited to the party. But what would I say?

CHAPTER 2

Earth to Alexis

A couple days later we met at Emma's house. I have always liked baking there because her parents don't mind if things get messy. Mom kind of freaks out when we're baking in her sparkling clean kitchen. (Needless to say, I am not messy, but *some* people can be!) We were just brainstorming that day, but I was still glad to be at the Taylors'. I felt a buzz of nervous happiness and had taken a little extra time laying out my outfit the night before. I told myself it was just because it was a Monday and I wanted to start the week off looking good, but deep down inside I knew the real reason: I might see Matt! Was that weird or what?

Thinking about Matt in this new way was weird too. I wished I could tell someone, but even if I could, I wouldn't know what to say. Was this what a crush felt like? Or was I just being silly? I'm *never* silly!

Meanwhile, Emma and I were in a debate.

"*Please*, Alexis!" Emma was begging, and her big blue eyes widened as she looked at me.

"No," I said firmly, and drew myself up as tall as possible to look like I was in charge.

Mia and Katie were laughing at us as Emma and I argued about whether or not we could use real gold flakes in our proposed cupcake design for Dylan's party. It was true that they would look spectacular, but they were so expensive and, to be honest, I didn't want perfect Dylan to have *real* gold cupcakes! She was being such a brat about everything these days, it would feel like we were rewarding her for her bad behavior.

But of course Emma didn't see it that way as she huffed and crossed her arms. I could see the glimmer of a smile underneath, though, and I smiled at her, narrowed my eyes, and dared her to smile back. Finally she smiled back—victory!

Just then a voice asked, "Hey, what's the deal?" *Matt!*

We hadn't heard him come in and now we all whipped around in surprise. My heart leaped as my stomach got all fluttery again. Matt has light, curly hair and blue eyes, and seemed to look especially cute today.

"Oh, Alexis is just being a tough CFO," said Mia.

"Well, someone has to be, or you'd all just be *giving* these cupcakes away," I said huffily. I wasn't really annoyed, but it made me feel less nervous to act like I was in front of Matt.

"You tell 'em, Alexis!" he said, smiling at me as he went into the kitchen. Was I imagining things or did his eyes twinkle? I was definitely feeling a little light-headed.

Emma grinned. "Huh! Look who's best friends now that you saved my life together," she said, reminding us about the time a few weeks ago when Matt and I worked together to help her out. "Usually he acts like he doesn't even know any of your names!"

Best friends! Hardly, but the idea of Matt and me linked in any way, shape, or form (plus, he'd smiled at me!) caused a warm feeling in my chest that quickly spread up into a blush.

Noticing how red I'd turned, Emma's grin quickly faded, and she gave me a strange look. Uh-oh. I ducked my head down and looked back at my leather-bound account ledger.

"Okay," I said, quickly trying to think of something else. "We have about twenty-five cents per cupcake to work with. Batter is ten cents per cupcake and frosting is five cents, so that leaves us with ten cents for any kind of decoration. By my calculations, the gold costs twenty cents per cupcake and that is just too much!"

"How does she figure this stuff out?" Katie asked the others.

"And why does she *want* to? That's the real question!" said Mia with a laugh.

"Ha-ha. Very funny. *Not*," I protested.

Even though I was talking to my friends, my mind was still on Matt. I heard his footsteps cross the floor above us, and I wondered what he had for homework and what subjects he liked. I also wondered what I would say to make conversation if he came back down. I chewed on my pen cap as I thought.

Suddenly I heard Katie saying, "Earth to Alexis!" and looked up to see everyone staring at me. Apparently Katie had been asking me a question.

I shook my head to clear my thoughts. "Oh, sorry. What?"

"Alexis, did you take your omega-threes today?"

Mia teased. "You seem really spacey!" She always makes fun of me and my vitamins, but I know they work. My whole family is about "optimizing our engines," so we eat superhealthy meals and exercise together, and we like to take supplements.

"Yes, I did," I replied, making a face at her. Usually I don't mind if my friends tease me, but I get annoyed when they make fun of me in front of other people—like Matt. I hoped he couldn't overhear any of this.

"Someone's a little testy!" said Katie as Emma frowned.

"What?" I asked, looking at Emma, and it came out a little harsher than I meant it to.

"Oh, nothing," Emma said, but I knew that wasn't true. Maybe she could tell that her brother was the cause of my freak-out.

Luckily Mia started talking about something else. "Hey, what are you going to wear to Dylan's party?" she asked. Mia is really into fashion, and her mom is a stylist, so clothes are always on her mind.

I was glad for the change of subject, even though it meant we hadn't yet figured out our budget. I told Mia that Dylan was going to set some things aside for me at Icon (Mia and Dylan's favorite store, but not mine), and I could bring the Cupcake Club with me this weekend to go try them on. As long as there wasn't anything too racy, that was good for me. Showing a lot of skin made me nervous. I wished I could get something at Big Blue, which was my favorite store since it was kind of preppy-casual, but they didn't have anything "special" enough for Dylan there. Or anything black and gold enough.

"So we'll go with you before we bake on Saturday, then," offered Katie. "Where are we baking again?"

It should really be my turn, but I didn't say anything for a minute, hoping Emma would offer. I looked down at the ledger.

Mia thought out loud. "Well, today is Emma's, tomorrow is my house, and Friday is Katie's, so . . ."

Everyone was looking at me, so I had to answer. "We could do my place, I guess. It's just that Emma is way closer to the mall . . . if we need to walk."

"Your dad would totally drive us! He's so nice about it!" Katie said. It was true. My dad was willing to drive us anywhere ever since he got his new car.

"I'd much rather be at your house," Emma added. "It's so peaceful and organized and clean! And there aren't any boys. . . ."

Yeah, that's not good news, I said to myself. Inside

I felt bummed that we weren't going to be at the Taylors', but I knew it wouldn't be fair not to offer, so I said, "Okay, my house it is."

Then we kept brainstorming and came up with three pretty good ideas for Dylan's party. Well, the other girls did most of the thinking. My mind was upstairs where Matt was the whole time. I kept wondering if and when he was going to appear again. And what I would say to him if he did.

If that afternoon was an equation, it would have looked like this:

$$\text{(Friends + business) / cute boy = brain dead}$$

Here's what we finally came up with:

Option A. Disco cupcakes: white cake with black vanilla frosting and Emma's coveted gold flakes strewn across the top.

Option B. S'mores cupcakes: angel food cake injected with liquid marshmallow and frosted with dark (black-looking) chocolate. They would have a sprinkling of graham crackers on top. They would probably be the best-tasting but not the coolest-looking.

Option C. Gift cupcakes: small yellow cupcakes peeled out of their wrappers and coated with raspberry jam, and then wrapped in a round sheet of black fondant tucked under at the bottom so they looked like a smooth hill. They would be individually wrapped like a gift with gold ribbon tied in a big bow on top. They would definitely be the prettiest ones.

It was a good day's work, though I hardly remember what was said after Matt showed up. Thank goodness I take good notes!

Unfortunately, Matt never came back down before we had to leave. I was tempted to call up the stairs to say bye to him, but that would have been truly weird. I did whisper it as I walked down their driveway, though. No one heard me, so why not?

CHAPTER 3

Project M. T.

My desk is my command center, and I take pride in keeping it superorganized. There are little drawers with all my supplies in tidy little boxes and packages. My pencil cup holds only Ticonderoga #2 pencils, all sharpened, points up, and my pen cup holds only blue erasable FriXion pens. I have a small container of white erasers (the best kind), and then there are my tools: very sharp Fiskars scissors for projects, a flat tin of rainbow-hued watercolor pencils (for graphs and pie charts), an electric pencil sharpener, a three-ring hole punch, a heavy Swingline stapler, and an old-fashioned Scotch tape dispenser.

My family shops the Staples sales religiously, and we are good with coupons and points and our club card. My parents figure that homework time spent looking for supplies is homework time wasted, so they like us to be well-stocked. When we run low on something, we just leave it on the kitchen island and our mom has her assistant reorder it immediately, putting it on her personal account. It's that easy, as they say on TV.

That night, though, despite my desk being fully stocked with supplies, my mind kept drifting away from my homework. It was really infuriating because I hate being unproductive. I had to admit that it was Matt who was distracting me. I was wondering if this was a crush. And if it was, what did I want to come of it?

Did I want him to be my *boyfriend*?

I wasn't sure, but I had to say *not really*. And to be absolutely honest, the idea of having a boyfriend kind of terrified me.

Well, then, did I want him just as a friend?

I was thinking definitely not just as a friend. Maybe something in between? It was hard to quantify it! My feelings about Matt would not organize themselves, and that was superfrustrating. I had no control whatsoever over anything—whether I'd see him, whether he'd speak to me if I saw him, and what we'd say. I played out all kinds of scenarios in my mind as I sat at my desk, watching my timer tick away the half hour I'd allotted to writing flash cards for my vocab test next Tuesday.

Now I was really frustrated. I sighed loudly, slapped the timer off, shuffled the flash cards into a neat stack, clipped them tightly together with a binder clip, and put them in my English bin on top of the desk. I was at a total loss. I grabbed a fresh sheet of white paper from the stack, and then reached for the calculator. Then I started fooling around with numbers, which *always* relaxes me.

I began scratching figures on the page as I thought. First, if I spend twenty minutes a day thinking about Matt, then that's one hundred and forty minutes a week, or two hours and twenty minutes. If I were working, say, at Big Blue for that long, I'd make twenty-five dollars, before taxes. If I were studying, I'd probably get an A on whatever it was. If I were exercising for those twenty minutes a day, and figured on a five minute warm-up and a five minute cool-down, then that was still ten minutes at my optimum heart rate, which was pretty good.

I rested my cheek on my hand and stared into space. Part of my brain was flashing a warning: "This is not scheduled into your planner for today! You are wasting time!" It was true, but I felt sluggish, like I had no control over myself. I certainly had no control over the object of my interest.

Or did I?

I sat up straight in my chair. That's it! What if I took a mathematical approach to my crush? What if I turned my mini obsession into a mathematically quantifiable experiment? I began brainstorming and scribbling onto my sheet in excitement.

My hypothesis was this: Could a crush be manipulated with results that can be replicated every time? Was there a predictable pattern of stimulus and response that I could plan and follow and chart, perhaps ending up with actual mathematical equations to predict Matt's behavior? In other words, could I come up with the perfect formula (or recipe, ha!) for getting Matt to fall for me?

This would be brilliant, I thought, as the neurons in my brain started firing up. It would also kind of justify any lazy daydreaming about Matt by turning those spacey moments into strategy sessions for my experiment. Let's see, what could I hypothesize and test?

What about wardrobe? I usually wear pants. It's kind of one of my trademarks. They are functional, comfortable, and easy to mix and match. But Dylan always wears skirts, and the boys flock to her. So, I wondered, what if I were to wear a skirt or a dress when I saw Matt? Would he react differently to me? Hmm. I wrote:

Project Matt Taylor

M. T., I thought. *More secretive.*
Then I scribbled:

Clothing experiment: Does he pay more attention to me if I am wearing pants or a skirt/dress?

I would need to conduct an experiment with each, where I timed the length of our interaction and compared the two figures. That would be easy. I could do it at school.

I chewed on my pen cap. What else could I test? Hair up or down? I almost always wore my hair in a ponytail or headband, but Sydney, the head of the Popular Girls Club in my class, always wore her hair down and boys paid lots of attention to her. Granted, her hair was long and blond and mine was long, frizzy, and red, but I could still do a hairstyle test. That sounded good, so I wrote it down.

Ooh! Another idea: comparing the frequency of who initiated our greeting, like in the hall at school. Sydney was giggly with boys, always starting conversations with them, while I only spoke to them if they spoke to me first. Maybe I could try to switch that up a little.

I decided to track my interactions with Matt (in the hall at school? At Emma's?) and collect the data and assess it. That was good.

This experiment called for a dedicated graph paper notebook, so I pulled one out of a cubbyhole in my desk and smoothed the cover with my hand. I could also write conversation starters in it (I had no idea what to say to him if I did see him), and maybe track things I could research that I know he's interested in, like sports and computer graphics. I was excited. At least now if nothing ever came of my interest in Matt, I wasn't *totally* wasting my time. I was practicing math skills!

Just then there was a knock on the door.

"Come in!" I trilled happily. I am always happiest when I am feeling busy and productive.

Dylan opened the door. "Dinner is in five minutes."

I looked at the clock, which read 6:55. We always eat exactly at seven. "Okay!" I said, still writing in my notebook.

My sister narrowed her eyes and folded her arms. "What are you working on?" she asked suspiciously. I guess it looked like too much fun to be homework. But I suddenly realized I did not want this notebook falling into the wrong hands, so I slammed it shut.

"Oh, just some cupcake ideas," I said casually.

"Stuff for my party?" Dylan asked.

"Not quite. Mostly budget stuff right now." *Please don't let her ask to see it.*

There was a pause before she asked, "When are we having the taste test?"

Okay, good, she didn't ask to see the notebook. "Oh, this Saturday. We're baking here, and then you can try all three of the options in the afternoon."

"But I have cheerleading practice on Saturday!" she said with a pout.

"Well, what time?" I asked patiently, ignoring her whiny voice. Sometimes I wondered who was the older sister!

"Four o'clock!"

"Oh, no prob," I assured her. "We'll be done making the samples by three for sure."

"Yeah, but I can't eat all that sugar and then go out and exercise. That will not work! I'm going to talk to Mom." Dylan immediately turned and walked away, not bothering to close the door. She was determined to make this hard for me.

"Whatever, Dyl pill," I said, annoyed.

"I heard that!" she called from the hallway.

"Good!" I whispered, and turned back to my desk, eager to get back to planning my experiment.

Tomorrow was the first day of Project M. T., and I decided that I would wear a skirt and see what happened. I was already dreading wearing the skirt—and what's more, I dreaded seeing Matt almost as much as I looked forward to it!

Who knew superorganized me could be *so* confused?

CHAPTER 4

Can He See Me Now?

*B*rrring!

The bell rang, and Eddie Rossi slammed his book shut and whipped it into his backpack. I thought this was pretty rude to Mr. Nichols, who was kind of old but not totally boring. *I mean, how badly do you want to get out of here, mister?* I thought.

I stared at Eddie with my most disapproving glare, but he didn't look around. Just sat with his backpack on his back, his hands gripping the edge of his desk, poised to launch out of his seat and out the door. I'm usually not that devious, but for some reason, his attitude really bugged me today. So I raised my hand.

"Yes, Alexis?" asked Mr. Nichols.

"Oh, you forgot to assign the homework," I said,

and it didn't take long for Eddie to react. His head snapped around and he glared at me. I gave him a closed-mouth smile and shrugged. *That's what you get, Mr. Rude,* I thought. *Teachers are people too!*

"Ah, thank you, Alexis," said Mr. Nichols distractedly. "I almost forgot . . ."

On autopilot, I copied down the homework and then packed up my bag. Eddie had already sprung out of the room and down the hall. From the back row I could hear Sydney Whitman and Callie Wilson restart their almost incessant chatter. The day was one long gossipfest for them, about movie stars, kids they went to camp with, kids from school, boys—anyone and anything. And it all sounded so utterly mindless and unproductive.

"Good catch on the homework, Alexis!" said Callie brightly. I looked up at her to see if she was making fun of me. She didn't seem to be.

"Yeah," sneered Sydney. "I'd hate to get out of here without something to keep our skills sharp at home."

Well, Sydney's response wasn't surprising. I ignored her and kept stuffing my books into my bag. My cheeks felt hot, but I willed myself not to blush.

Then she started laughing hysterically as she

sauntered out of the classroom with Callie. The next class shuffled in, and I was going to be late. I had no choice but to fall into step right behind Callie and Sydney. I had worn a skirt today as part of Project M. T., and its unfamiliar swish against my legs made me feel insecure. I had worn my hair up, as usual, as a control, so I could isolate the effect of the skirt.

I wondered if I'd even see Matt, after all this strategizing.

Just ahead of me Sydney said to Callie teasingly, "I wonder if we'll see Mr. Hottie today?"

"Oh, I almost hope not! I look terrible!" moaned Callie, who couldn't have looked more perfect.

"When was the last time you saw him?" asked Sydney.

Callie made a sad face. "Last week. And I used to see him every day at camp! It's so unfair!" she wailed.

"Well, maybe you need to get your hands on a copy of his schedule and just make sure you're putting yourself in the right place at the right time!" said Sydney. "I mean, what are we here for, right?"

Wow, scary! I thought. *Is that what we're here for? To get boys to notice us?* But then I realized Sydney had a point. And if so, maybe I should be listening to these two. They did certainly know how to attract boys' attention.

Suddenly Sydney squealed. "Oh my God! Two o'clock! Two o'clock!"

What? What was happening at two o'clock?

Callie flipped her hair and I could see her straighten her clothes. She grabbed Sydney's arm and linked her hand through it, squeezing tightly. I hate when girls walk together like that—it's so annoying! Anyway, I watched to see what was happening.

And just then, I spotted Matt! My stomach felt like it dropped to the floor, and I was hot and cold all over. I'm pretty sure I had an insta-blush. I looked down at the linoleum tiles, then at the lockers on either side of me, the ceiling, anywhere but toward Matt, who was ahead and to my right, walking with a friend toward me. Should I say hi? What was my plan? Suddenly I couldn't remember what I had planned to do! Why didn't I have my strategy book with me? I stared—past my skirt—at my toes.

"Hey, guys!" Sydney called in a loud, high-pitched voice that was sickeningly sweet in a very fake way.

I looked up to see who she was talking to, and it was Matt and his friend!

Callie was pink and she was grinning from ear to ear. What was going on? In confusion, I looked back and forth between the two pairs of friends.

Matt and his friend smiled at Callie and Sydney and nodded in greeting. Matt's friend said something quietly to Matt and Matt nodded again, laughing.

I opened my mouth to say hi to Matt, but thought better of it. I snapped it shut and put my head back down. I couldn't tell if he had seen me. I wondered if either of the boys was the one that Callie liked from camp, and crossed my fingers that it wasn't Matt. Talk about variables! I definitely didn't factor *that* into my experiment!

Okay, calm down, I told myself. *Deep breaths, Alexis.* This was excellent data to collect. I didn't say hi first and he didn't say hi either. But if I said hi first, he certainly would have said hi back. And, maybe next time, he would say hi first. I mean, maybe he didn't even see me, right? And if he didn't see me, how would he know I was wearing a skirt?

How utterly humiliating.

Later, at lunch, I tried to casually grill Emma for information on Matt. I wanted to see if I could piece together whether Callie liked him, or the friend he was with in the hall. But I had to do all this without making Emma suspicious—and that was not easy.

I peeled off the top of my yogurt container and as casually as I could, I asked, "What are you guys thinking of for next summer?"

Mia sighed. "I'd really like to do a fashion design camp in the city," she said. "It's almost like summer school. The only problem is that it's expensive and my mom's also not wild about me sitting indoors under fluorescent lights all summer. I think I have Eddie on my side though, so we'll see." Eddie is her stepfather, and he is awesome.

"I think I might go to the camp that my mom went to when she was a girl," Katie said. "You know, the one she went to with Callie's mom?"

Bingo! "Oh," I said. "Is that the camp where Callie went last summer?"

Katie nodded as she unwrapped her sandwich. "It's supposed to be really fun."

"Right, I was at the same camp," I reminded her. "It was fun. You got to try all different kinds of sports and activities."

Emma nodded, swallowing a gulp of chocolate milk. "Matt went last year too, and he loved it. He was a lifeguard so it was, like, half-price."

What? Matt was at the same camp as me last

summer? Why didn't I remember this? I sputtered and almost choked.

"Whoa! Hands up in the air!" said Mia, patting my back.

Mortified, I looked around the lunchroom to make sure no one else had seen me. I coughed and cleared my throat.

"That's cool," I said in a froggy voice. "Did he ... *ahem!*" I cleared my throat again. "Did he go with friends?" I asked as innocently as possible.

Emma looked quizzically at me, then slowly said, "Why, yes. He went with Joe Fraser."

"Oh!" I nodded and quickly looked down, pretending to scrape the bottom of my yogurt cup. So there was hope! Maybe that guy today was Joe Fraser! "Anyway, maybe you'll be in my bunk," I suggested to Katie.

"That would be great!" said Katie enthusiastically.

Emma was still looking at me, so I shrugged and added, "Or maybe I'll go to math camp ... or this cool business camp I read about."

Katie looked puzzled, but didn't say anything.

"Oh, Alexis!" said Mia playfully. "Leave it to you to find a business camp for kids!"

"Speaking of which, are we meeting today?"

Emma asked, finally turning her attention away from me. Whew! There would be no more fishing for information about Matt today. Emma was definitely suspicious, and I knew in my heart of hearts that it would not be a good thing for Emma to find out that I had—yes, I had to admit it to myself after today's noninteraction in the hall—a *major* crush on her brother.

"Oh! It's supposed to be at my house, but my mom asked if we could move it because she's having a dinner party tonight," said Mia. "She doesn't want the kitchen all messed up. I'm so sorry!"

Katie spoke up. "We can't do it at my house either because my grandma is visiting and she will, like, take over if we have it there. I love her, but it's just a little annoying."

Here was an opportunity! I had to think fast. "Oh, bummer! I think Dylan has her study group at our house on Tuesdays . . ." I started to say. Didn't she? Yikes. I'd better check or risk getting caught in a lie. We all looked hopefully at Emma.

Emma sighed. "Fine, we can do it at my house again," she said. "I just think it's so boring and gross. I'd so much rather be at someone else's house where it's quiet and clean and private! Anyway, Jake might be there."

Jake was Emma's little brother, and he could be a bit of a bother.

"Thanks, Emma!" I said. I think I sounded a little too gushing, because she gave me another funny look.

"Okay, *not* a big deal," she said.

"Right!" I agreed, trying to stop myself from smiling too broadly. Tonight I might have another Matt encounter.

And then my heart stopped as I spotted Matt walk into the cafeteria with a group of guys. I could feel my face growing warm, so I quickly looked down at my lunch tray, hoping no one noticed. There was no way he'd come over here, I told myself. But if he did . . .

I reached up and pulled the elastic band out of my hair, casually fluffing my hair and rolling the elastic band onto my wrist. If Matt stopped by, he wouldn't see the skirt, but the hair might be quantifiable.

I watched as he went through the line, and half listened to Emma's summer plans. Suddenly Matt gestured to his friends and began making a beeline toward our table! My mind said "Oh no!" and "Oh yes!" at the same time I quickly sat up and tucked a piece of hair behind my ear. My stomach started doing flip-flops—and then he was next to me!

"Hey, guys," he said.

"Hi," I squeaked. He looked down and smiled!

"Emma," he continued, "Mom asked me to watch Jake on Thursday night, but I just got assigned a group project due Friday. Any chance you can watch Jake and I'll owe you?"

Emma frowned. "I guess so. But it has to be a date of my choice!"

"Fine. Thanks!" he said, and ruffled her hair before taking off.

Emma rolled her eyes. "Brothers," she muttered.

I was thrilled! He had acknowledged me! He had said hi first (sort of!). I couldn't wait to get home and log all this info into my notebook: Score one for "hair down," and none for "skirts." (Whew!)

Now I just had to wait and see if Matt would be at home later today.

CHAPTER 5

Collecting Data

We all arrived at Emma's after school only to find that it was definitely not an option to hold a club meeting there. Emma's mom was having coffee with a friend, and Jake had three little friends over. They had turned the kitchen into a "goo factory," where they were experimenting with every kind of oobleck and gunk that could be created from basic household ingredients.

4 little boys + gooey gunk = total mess

What was amazing was that Emma's mom didn't seem bothered by the mess. My mother would have needed serious CPR if that was going on in her kitchen!

But Emma wasn't pleased.

After I said a quick hi to Emma's mom, I casually (as casually as I could) walked out to the TV room, but no one was there. I went back to the mudroom to Matt's locker (the Taylors all had lockers to hold their gear), and I saw that it was empty. I sighed heavily.

Emma narrowed her eyes at me when I returned. "Did you lose something?" she asked, almost in an accusing tone.

"What? Oh. No . . . no. What?" I stammered awkwardly. "Hey, uh, we can go to my house instead. It's okay," I offered.

Emma was still staring at me.

"I thought Dylan had her study group there?" asked Mia. Mia kind of worshipped Dylan so she filed away every tidbit I said about her.

I shrugged. "Well, maybe they can sit in the den," I said, then heard Emma mutter something under her breath.

"What?" I asked. "Is something the matter?"

Emma looked annoyed. "I don't know why we didn't just go there in the first place," she said.

Now I felt a little annoyed. "It's not exactly ideal

if Dylan's there," I countered. "You know how irritating it is when your siblings are around. It can be really distracting."

"My point exactly," said Emma, looking right at me.

Wait, did she know? But she couldn't. I hadn't done anything to give it away, had I? I shifted uncomfortably and said, "Let's go."

We trudged over to my house. And thankfully (for not making a liar of me) but annoyingly, Dylan was there with her two best friends, Meredith and Skylar.

"Hey, kids," Dylan called out, acting superfriendly for the sake of my friends, I supposed.

"Hi. Are you having your study group here?" I asked.

"Yes," she replied. "We're also working on some new cheer routines."

Have I mentioned that Dylan is maniacal about cheerleading? Maybe more manic about it than about anything else! When she decided she wanted to try out for cheerleading, she was still in eighth grade, but she went to all the practices over at the high school *a year in advance* and videoed them on her Flip. Then she uploaded the videos and studied the routines on her computer and learned them all.

She practiced and stretched and ran and did their whole warm-up routine. And when tryouts started freshman year, they signed her right on. It was like she'd already been doing it for a year anyway. Now she's assistant cheer captain and she's only in tenth grade! Talk about an overachiever. Rah-rah!

"Can we use the kitchen to bake?" I asked. "We have one more test recipe to run through for your party proposal." I knew that if I made it about her, I'd have a better chance at taking over the space.

"Yay! Do we get free samples?" squealed Meredith, who had a major sweet tooth.

I smiled and nodded. You had to love a fan.

Dylan looked at me. I hoped she wasn't going to get all power-trippy on me and say no just for the sake of saying no. Luckily, she simply said, "Just let us finish our drinks, and then we'll move." In our house we aren't allowed to have food or drinks anywhere but the kitchen.

I nodded. That was fair. Maybe the old Dylan was back. She turned back to her friends, and we began dumping our stuff on the couch near the back door.

My ears pricked up when I heard Dylan ask, "So what did he say next?" I glanced back at them. Were they talking about boys?

Meredith smiled shyly in response. "He said he'd like to see me again!"

It sounded like I might get useful info from listening in. Just as I was turning my head to hear their conversation better, Katie asked, "Want to go watch TV? Maybe I can find a *Dancing with the Stars* rerun."

Besides the fact that I live for TV dancing shows, I normally would have said yes just to get away from Dylan and her posse. But today I really wanted to hear what they were discussing.

"Um, you guys go ahead," I said. "I'll just get some stuff set up in here first so we're all ready to go when they're done." I was determined to get as much info as I could from these veterans of the romance trenches.

"Do you need help?" Mia asked sweetly. But that was the last thing I wanted right now! Even though it was Mia, I didn't want to have to make conversation and not be able to pay attention to what Dylan and her friends were saying.

"No," I said more forcefully than I meant to. "Thanks," I corrected myself. "I'm good."

I watched as Mia and the others exchanged looks, then shrugged their shoulders before heading to the den.

I turned back to hear what Dylan and her friends were discussing, only to hear Emma ask me, "Do you have a copy of *Jane Eyre* here? I'm supposed to read two chapters for homework, but I left my copy at home."

Sigh. I love my friends, but they were really bothersome right now! "Sure," I said without even looking at Emma. "Upstairs on my desk."

With my ears tuned to my sister and her friends, I quickly busied myself with measuring out ingredients. The Cupcake Club buys in bulk at a warehouse club and then we divvy up the supplies between our houses. My house, though, holds the bulk of the stuff since I'm in charge of purchasing. I also set out our supplies and preheated the oven.

> Room-temperature
> ingredients x 5 minutes
> of mixing with paddle
> attachment = light cupcakes

I made sure everything was neatly aligned on the counter: mixing bowls, measuring spoons and cups, rubber scraper, stand mixer, and timer. I adore the order and mathematics of baking: Add this amount of something plus this amount of something else, cook at this temperature, and you will get this—every time! Now if I could just get the right recipe for Matt + Alexis! I laughed at the thought.

As I took stuff out of the cupboards, I tried to figure out what Dylan and her friends were talking about. Apparently there was an upperclassman Meredith had met at the library where she worked after school, and things were "getting hot" between them. Usually I would have found this kind of talk really boring and a waste of time, but today I felt differently. It looked like I could get a lot of useful info from them.

I quietly moved closer to the table, trying not to miss a word.

"So I wore the sweater you suggested," Meredith told Skylar.

Skylar nodded. "Good," she said. "And?"

"Well, it looked good, and like you said, it's very . . . soft and fluffy, and it's a girlie color. I guess guys really do like that stuff because he did touch my arm when we were talking, like he wanted to feel the material."

"And the perfume?" asked Dylan.

"Yes," said Meredith. "I did just what you said. I wore that vanilla spice from Bath and Body Works. I felt like a doughnut! But I noticed him kind of sniffing the air—in a good way!—when I bent over to stack some books on the cart."

"Well, I told you about the study! Men love vanilla and pumpkin pie above all other scents! It has been tested!" Dylan said, laughing. I was surprised. Boys love Dylan, but I never thought it was something she put any thought or effort into!

"They're all just little boys at heart. They want baked goods and fuzzy things!" Dylan added. She sounded so mature saying that, like she had done it all. She did have a lot of boy friends, but Mom and Dad had just started letting her go out on dates this year. I knew Skylar had a boyfriend over the summer, but I didn't think he was still in the picture. I remembered hearing about some breakup story, but that was way before I was interested in that kind of thing. Like, more than a week ago.

Okay, I thought, the baked goods part sounded easy, especially for me: smelling like them, providing them, describing them in tantalizing detail. No problem! Next I mentally raked through my closet. I didn't really own anything that could be described as fuzzy. I definitely had to do something about that.

My data collecting was going so well that I grew a little bolder. I jumped up to sit on the kitchen island to make sure I didn't miss a word they were saying. I couldn't tell if they noticed me and were ignoring me, or noticed me and were kind of putting on a show for me, or if they just didn't notice me at all (most likely). I waited for Dylan to order me to leave while they finished their drinks. But she didn't.

"And how about your hair?" Skylar asked Meredith. "Was it 'touchable'?" She made quotation marks in the air with her fingers.

Meredith nodded. "I didn't blow it out that day. I set it in rollers, just like we discussed, so it was all springy and curly. He said that it looked different and he actually told me he liked it!" She blushed. "So getting up extra early was worth it!"

"Good." Dylan nodded. "The *Seventeen* survey said that men prefer wavy or loosely curly hair above all else." Boy, I had no idea my sister knew so much about this stuff!

I started thinking about curls. I have a little pack of rag curlers my grandma gave me one Christmas when I was in a *Little House on the Prairie* phase. I had wanted to create curls the way the Ingalls girls did. I could find those and see if they still worked!

I wished I had my notebook so I could write all this stuff down. I tried to visualize equations in my mind to help me remember what the older girls were saying:

Fuzzy texture + girlie color = boy touching your arm

Loopy curls - straight hair = compliment

Food scents / vanilla + pumpkin = boys sniffing

I was intrigued by the studies the girls were saying they had read about boys and what they liked. I had no idea that actual research dollars were being spent on this kind of thing! But now that I thought about it, it made sense. For instance, perfume companies spend a fortune developing perfumes that are supposed to make men fall all over the women who wear them (if you believe the ads). So why wouldn't they put lots of dollars into researching which smells men like best? And shampoo companies of course research what kind of hair men like best. Then they release that information right at the same time they're releasing the new products that make women's hair do just that! I liked figuring out businessy things like this. When things fit neatly into place, it makes me very, very happy. But I also liked the fact that people—scientists, even!— were spending valuable time and money on just the kinds of experiments I was conducting myself. It made what I was doing seem worthwhile.

But more important, I couldn't believe that I'd never paid any attention to the magazines and websites that Dylan and her friends liked to read. It was crazy to think that they were chock-full of all this scientific information about attracting boys, and I'd never known it! Well, I made a mental note to borrow some magazines from Dylan and go online as soon as I could.

Just then Emma came back into the kitchen holding my copy of *Jane Eyre*. She also had a funny look on her face. But I didn't want her interrupting my fascinating information session, so I kind of ignored her. But she just kept standing there, like she wanted to say something to me.

"What?" I finally whispered.

Emma looked at Dylan and her friends, then she shrugged and turned to go back to the TV room. *Whatever,* I thought, and sighed loudly.

Dylan turned to me. "Is that really a hint?" she snapped.

"What?" I was alarmed. I wasn't trying to get rid of them! "Oh, no, not at all!" I said quickly. "Take your time. I wasn't rushing you. . . ." My fear must've been obviously genuine, because Dylan's face softened.

"We're ready, actually," she said. "Come on, girls. Let's go outside for a few minutes to work on cheering before we start the chem review."

Meredith and Skylar gathered their mugs and things and, still chatting, went out to the yard. I wish I could have gone with them. I had really gotten some good intel, but it only left me hungry for more.

Then Emma and Katie wandered in. "Ready?" they asked.

"I guess," I said, then realized how I sounded. What was I thinking? We were here to work on our business! We were here to make money! Why was I moping about some boy and filling my head with silly tricks and tips? This was so not me at all! "I mean, yes, I'm ready!" I said brightly. "Let's make some money!"

"Well, all righty then!" said Katie. And we eagerly set to work.

It wasn't until I got upstairs after everyone left that I found my Project M. T. notebook on top of my desk. I had forgotten to put it away last night, not thinking anyone would see it. My heart raced as I thought about Emma. She must have seen it; that's why she gave me that look.

I flipped through it. Luckily, I never mentioned Matt's name. I only called him "The Crush." I actually shivered in relief, but that was a close call. And now I'd have some sort of explaining to do with Emma if it came up (I certainly wasn't going to bring it up myself). I picked up the notebook and looked around the room. Everything in my room was as neat as a pin. All except one place.

I lifted a key out of my desk drawer and used it to open the top drawer in my antique wood dresser. It is a wide and deep drawer, and inside is total chaos. It's the only place in my world that's not organized . . . well, until now with this Matt thing. My messy drawer is where I stash makeup, cheap trinkets, sunglasses, and old candy. I dropped the notebook in and shoved the drawer closed, then relocked it. I was probably too late, but better late than never (which is definitely *not* one of my mottoes).

CHAPTER 6

Mall Madness

$\mathcal{T}$he music they play at Icon is so, so loud, and the air freshener or incense or whatever they use to scent the store makes me gasp for clean air. Plus, it's dark. I mean almost pitch-dark. It is not a place I like to spend any time. But there I was on Saturday, with all the Cupcakers (including Emma, who was being a little weird), looking at the dresses that Dylan had placed on hold for me as "pre-approved" attire for her party.

I couldn't believe it. All three of the dresses she chose matched her party decor: black and gold. Was she trying to tell me that I was simply part of the decor? Whatever it was, I was annoyed. Black is really not my color. I don't think it makes me stand out, and I would like to stand out a little—especially if Matt might be there.

Most of all it just got on my nerves that Dylan felt she could pick what I wore. As if otherwise I would wear something that would embarrass her.

Katie scrunched into the corner of the dressing room. "Can you make some room, please?" she shouted over the music. I don't think Mia could hear her, even though she was wedged right up against her. The attendant had warned us we wouldn't all fit, but we had insisted. I didn't want to do this alone.

The room was so tight that Emma was basically sitting on Mia's lap. I was in a corner, trying to pull the first dress over my head.

"What do you think?" I asked after I finally— after struggling for five minutes—got the dress on.

"What?" shouted Mia.

I sighed. Talking was pointless. I jerked my thumb at the door and then went out into the communal viewing area, which was packed with other girls. We waited our turn in front of the only mirror. Finally we got a spot with a spotlight right above it. At least I could now see myself!

I tipped my head to the side and looked at the dress. It was horrible, all black and droopy. Not my style at all.

"It's fine," I said with a shrug, "if lumpy is the look I'm going for."

"What?" yelled Emma.

"Never mind!" I shouted, then looked at the price tag. "Really never mind!" I added, though no one could hear me.

Katie, Emma, and I went back into the dressing room, but Mia decided to wait outside for my "reveal." I looked at the other two dresses. One was short and flouncy. It had a black tulle skirt and a gold bodice. It was kind of prom dressish. The other one was strapless (nightmare!) and long, with a slit up one whole leg. I couldn't imagine my mother approving that one, but it was the kind of dress that a guy might like to see a girl in. Hmm. That would be my next choice. I grunted my way out of the first dress and slid the leg-slit dress over my head. It was no more than a thin piece of satin, with some gold details at the top in a kind of bandeau bathing suit style. Luckily, because it was so slinky, it slid down easily.

I went back out to look at the dress, then gasped when I saw myself in the mirror. Mia, Katie, and

Emma gasped too. I looked like I was twenty-five years old!

"Wow! You're a hottie!" yelled Katie.

"Yeah, you just need to take off the socks!" Emma said in my ear. I looked down. I had on fuzzy pink crew socks. That part did not look so good, but the rest of me screamed *Dancing with the Stars*!

Mia was nodding, but she had her head tipped to the side. "You look amazing, but you do not look like Alexis Becker." She reached over to a dress hanging on a hook. "Here, I grabbed this from a girl who was going to put it back. Try it."

I looked at the dress in her hand. It was not black. It was not gold. It was not too mature. It was a deep raspberry pink V-neck sweater dress—fuzzy and touchable!

"Look," said Mia. "It has slits up each side to make it dressier, and you'd wear it with pale or gold heels, a gold belt—maybe a chain, even— and a great-looking chunky necklace. Go on! Try it!"

I took the dress from her and went back in alone. Seconds later I was out again and staring in the mirror. The color looked amazing on me. The fabric felt amazing. I really, really loved it!

Suddenly someone tapped me on my shoulder.

I turned around and it was Meredith, with Skylar.

"Hi, Alexis!" they yelled, waving.

"You look awesome!" said Meredith.

Skylar nodded. "If you don't get that, I'd love to try it on!" she said in my ear.

I smiled. "Sorry, but I am getting it!" I replied. "Even though it's not black and gold!"

"I can't hear you!" Skylar shouted, giving me two thumbs-up. "But you look great!" she yelled.

I suddenly felt warm and happy, even though I was a little nervous about what Dylan would say. But I decided that she couldn't control everything!

On my way to pay with the money Mom had given me, I looked around—and spotted the only other nonblack clothing in the store. It was a really nice ice-blue long-sleeved V-neck shirt. And it was marked down from $40 to $19.99! I held the shirt up in front of me. It was my size. And I did have enough cupcake money saved up. I decided I couldn't pass up this great bargain, so I looped it over my arm and walked toward the long line at the cash registers.

"We'll wait for you outside!" called Katie.

I nodded and waved to her. As the line snaked around, I looked at what other people were buying. I couldn't believe how many people liked dressing all in black, and they weren't all Goth girls! Icon clearly knew what they were doing and how much people like buying cheap black clothes in a dark, loud, and stinky store.

I stood in line and found myself right behind Sydney and Callie. Before I could decide what to do, Callie said hi. She's kind of nice. I think if Sydney wasn't around to boss her, and Katie was okay with it, she might even be good in the Cupcake Club, but that just won't happen. I just hoped she liked Joe Fraser and not Matt Taylor. I didn't think I could compete with her.

I looked at Sydney, but she ignored me and talked away on her phone.

Callie pointed at my clothes and said, "Those look nice."

I wasn't sure if she was being serious or ragging on me, so I simply shrugged. But it seemed like she was really interested in talking to me, so I asked, "What are you getting?"

She held up a silky black dress with gold detailing—it was my *Dancing with the Stars* dress!

I smiled. "Wow! That is some dress!" *For a grown-up,* I wanted to add.

Callie giggled. "I don't even have anywhere to wear it, but the price is good and when I tried it on, it looked"—her voice dropped to a whisper—"amazing, if I do say so myself!"

"Yes, it would look great on you," I said, trying to be nice. *Just don't wear it in front of Matt Taylor,* I added silently.

Just then the line began to move, and Sydney hung up her phone.

"See you later!" said Callie.

I waved and turned away, then looked back to see Sydney grab Callie's elbow and whisper something in her ear. Callie looked at me guiltily and then at Sydney. She shrugged but her smile faded. Sydney probably yelled at her for talking to me. *Whatever,* I told myself. But I did feel bad for Callie.

After I paid I caught up with the others outside the store.

"Do we need to go meet your dad now or do we have time to go look at stuff at Claire's?" asked Mia. "They have some chunky necklaces that would look pretty with your dress. Then we still need to find a gold belt and some gold shoes." She thought for a moment, then added, "Kitten heels, I think."

"Let's go meet my dad," I replied. "I can't spend any more money! I'd rather be making money!"

"We know!" said Emma, and we all laughed.

I was just about to tell them about Sydney and Callie when who should come around the corner in front of us but Matt and his friend (was that Joe?)! I froze. How did I look? Was I wearing anything touchable? Pink? How was my hair? Did I smell good? What would I say?

"Hey," said Matt. "What's so funny?" (Ooh, score one for Matt saying hi first! Even though it was to all of us, it still counted! I would need to write that down in my notebook.)

"Hey," Emma replied. "Oh, we were just laughing about Alexis."

"Tsk, tsk, tsk, Alexis! Always making the crowd laugh," Matt said with a wink at me. I almost died! But I wished Emma hadn't said that they were laughing at me. What was I? Some kind of clown? Hmm. Okay, maybe it was all right if he thought I was funny. I mean, funny isn't bad, is it? Anyway, I was happy just to hear him say my name. I giggled and nervously looked around.

Then I caught Emma's eye. And I could tell that she knew. Cripes. What was I going to do now? I looked down at my shoes, which were my dorky-looking Merrells. I would absolutely have to ditch them forever when I got home. I looked up again and willed myself to say something, anything, when suddenly someone called out, "Hey, boys!"

Ugh! Sydney! She and Callie walked up to our group, but their eyes were only on the boys.

Matt turned around. "Oh, hey," he said very casually. I caught his friend looking over at Mia (what is that all about?) and then at Callie and Sydney. Ignoring the rest of us, Sydney linked her arm through Matt's and gave it a squeeze. I started to tense up.

"What are you boys up to?" Sydney asked in a very flirty way, flipping her hair from one side to the other. "Have you eaten lunch yet?"

"What? Oh." Matt looked unsure. "Not yet. Have you guys?" he asked us.

Opportunity knocking! I started to shake my head no, but Emma spoke up. "No. We were just leaving. See ya!"

And she started walking away! Mia and Katie followed her, but I was stuck in my spot. *Wait!* I wanted to yell. *Let's stay! Let's have lunch with them!* Joe seemed to feel the same way because he looked disappointed as Mia walked away.

Sydney was now sort of pushing Callie at Matt, and they were both looking embarrassed.

"Bye!" Matt called to us.

"Later," I said in as casual a tone as possible. I

turned to go with my friends, and I was trying my best to look like I didn't care at all that I just lost out on a chance to have lunch with Matt.

We rode the escalator down in silence to meet my dad in the parking area. I hated Sydney, but that was nothing new. I also kind of hated Matt now. And Emma. Why couldn't she have said, "Oh, sorry, Sydney Horrible Whitman, but we are all going back to my house with my cute brother and his cute friend and we are going to hang out all day and play Wii and you are so not invited." *Why couldn't she have done that?*

Outside my dad waved from his spot in the pickup area. He looked so happy to see us that I felt a tiny bit better.

What cheered me up more was when he said, "Want to go to Harrison's for lunch?"

Harrison's Roast Beef is my absolute favorite lunch place in the whole world. It would be hard to stay upset if I was going there. Plus, if we all went to lunch together, it meant Emma would not catch me alone and have a chance to grill me about what she found out today.

So I called back, "You betcha!" to my dad, and we all hurried to the car.

I'll have another chance to say hi to Matt again soon,

I told myself. *And maybe I'll be dressed better then, anyway,* I thought, looking at my boring outfit. Maybe it was a good thing this happened. This way I could keep up a mysterious air and let Matt think I'm really funny without me having to actually prove it. ("Better to remain silent and be thought a fool than to open your mouth and remove all doubt." That quote is one of my mottoes.)

CHAPTER 7

My Sister Really Takes the Cake!

During lunch at Harrison's my father and I told the Cupcakers about the dance we were planning for Dylan's party. We had been practicing most nights after I finished my homework.

"You have to see how graceful Alexis is!" my father bragged. "She can really cut a rug." He nodded proudly. Some people might say he is a total nerd, but I love him.

"Oh, *Dad*!" I said, like I was embarrassed, but I wasn't really. Our dance was the one thing that I was feeling really good about, as it took me away from all the crazy feelings that were going through my head: my dislike of Sydney, my crush on Matt, my frustration with Emma, the nervousness I was feeling about Dylan and the cupcakes we were about to present to her.

We had a great time at Harrison's. Dad kept us laughing with his corny jokes.

When we got home, Dylan and Mom were at the kitchen table, addressing the last of the party invitations on black envelopes with gold gel pens.

"Hello, Mom! Hello, Dylan!" I called as we walked in.

Dylan nodded at us without saying a word before going back to writing. The scent of the pens was so strong that I could feel it going to my head and making me a little light-headed. I was dying to see if Dylan had addressed the invitation for the Taylors yet; I wouldn't believe Matt was actually invited until I saw it in black and . . . gold. I craned my neck to see where she was on her list (created as an Excel spreadsheet on the computer, of course).

Dylan looked at me. "What?" she demanded.

"Oh, nothing!" I replied, waving my hand, and got ready to start baking.

"Just get going on the cupcakes, because I have to leave for practice at three thirty, and an athlete can't practice on a system filled with sugar."

"Ah, don't worry, we'll be done in plenty of time," I said, smiling at my friends.

Just then Mom asked, "So how did the dress turn out, Alexis?"

I could feel my face grow instantly hot. Should I make up a fib?

"Oh, you know . . ." I was stalling for time, but Katie cut in.

"Oh, Mrs. Becker, you have to see the dress that Alexis bought! It looks so beautiful on her!"

I glared at Katie and elbowed her. Poor Katie looked at me in pain and surprise. Luckily my mother was looking down, so she didn't see this exchange.

What? Katie mouthed at me. I shook my head vigorously, but they had already heard Katie.

"Are you going to show us the dress?" asked Dylan.

"Not right now," I said briskly. "Let's get the cupcake samples ready, and then I'll model it if you have time before practice." This made sense to Mom and Dylan, so they both nodded and went back to what they were doing. Now I could focus on the cupcakes! I would deal with what was sure to be a dress crisis later.

Without any more interruptions, my friends and I were able to work quickly to turn out samples for three different cupcakes: the disco, s'mores, and the gift one. Much as I hated to admit it, Emma had been right about the gold flakes. They looked magical and I knew Dylan would totally go for them. The s'mores were tasty but not elegant, just as we had suspected, and my little gift idea looked great, but not very appealing.

We stood holding our breath as Dylan and my parents inspected our treats.

"Oh, girls, these are lovely!" Mom said.

"I'll take them all," said Dad as he playfully lifted the platter, pretending that he was going to run off with it.

"Dad!" I called out just as Dylan took the plate away from him. Suddenly everyone was really quiet and serious as Dylan examined the cupcakes from all angles, tilting her head this way and that like a judge on a cooking show.

"Oh, Dylan, come on!" I said. My sister could be so exasperating!

But Mia grabbed my arm and whispered, "The customer is always right." Since that is one of my own mottoes, I didn't say anything else. I set my mouth in a firm line to keep it shut and crossed my arms in front of me.

Then Dylan leaned over the platter and smelled the cupcakes. I was about to have another outburst, but my mom shot me a look. What was wrong with Dylan? Why couldn't she say "Wow" or "Hmm . . . not what I want," like normal people would?

After what felt like several long minutes of sniffing, Dylan asked, "Do you have a knife?"

I groaned. I couldn't believe she asked for a knife! We were at home, and Dylan knew very well where the knives were. I was just about to say something when Mia replied cheerily, "Yes, we do!"

She picked one from the butcher block and handed it to Dylan with a flourish. Dylan cut each cupcake in half, and then in quarters. They looked really awful all splayed out like that.

"Dylan, honey, what are you doing?" Mom asked.

"I want to see what they look like inside," Dylan answered. "Then I'm going to taste them, but it's not like I'm going to eat an entire cupcake of each!"

"Well, I'd love to try one—a whole one," Dad said. "I've been waiting long enough. Do I have your permission, your highness?" He looked at me and the other Cupcakers and wiggled his eyebrows.

Dylan rolled her eyes. "Okay, let's sample."

My father took a s'mores cupcake, which he'd been eyeing the entire time, and took a huge bite.

"I'm not usually a fan of marshmallows, but this is dynamite!" he said. "I vote for this one."

My mother also picked the s'mores cupcake, and agreed with him. "Oh, the cake alone is so wonderful, but the marshmallows and the cracker crumbs make this absolutely delicious!"

I smiled. I knew those would be the tastiest.

Dylan took a bite of a sliver of the gold flake cake. She chewed it thoughtfully as we waited for her comment. When she put down the rest of her sliver, Emma asked anxiously, "Is it not good?"

"Oh, no, it's fine. I'm just not a big dessert person," said Dylan with a shrug. Argh! I wanted to scream. Poor Emma looked disappointed.

Next Dylan tried the gift cake. She pinched off a bit of the fondant and nibbled on it. Then she took a tiny bite. She bobbed her head from side to side as she chewed, as if she was weighing it against the previous cupcake. Finally she swallowed and turned toward the cabinet.

"Well?" I asked.

Without answering me, Dylan took her time getting a glass and filling it with water. Then she held one finger up while she drank and we all waited.

"Fine," she said finally.

"Fine?" I asked, annoyed. "What does 'fine' mean? Do you like it or not?"

"Dylan, try the s'mores one. You will love it," said my father.

"Okay, okay," she said, like she was doing us a huge favor. As with the other samples, Dylan took a small bite, and we all watched as she chewed. Now, I spend a lot of time around people eating cupcakes, and I know what I see. I could tell that Dylan *loved* that cupcake! Her features softened, her eyes lit up, and her mouth lingered over the bite before swallowing it. I'm sure I even saw a slight smile on her face when she was done.

"So?" My mom asked, as sure as we were that Dylan's choice would be the same as hers and Dad's.

Somehow the Dylan who enjoyed that very delicious s'mores cupcake two seconds ago was able shake her head and look sympathetic. "I am so sorry, kids, but none of these is right for my party," she said.

There was silence for a moment. We were all stunned, even my parents.

"Wh-wh-what?" I stammered. "What do you mean? You loved that last one! I saw it on your face!"

Dylan shook her head again with a look of

pity. "No, Alexis, the problem is that the tasty one is ugly and the pretty ones aren't very tasty." She shrugged. "Back to the drawing board?"

"Argh!" I screamed.

"Girls, girls, you all did a wonderful job. Dylan, how about a thank-you, first of all, to the Cupcake Club," instructed my mother. I could tell she was mad.

"Thank you," Dylan muttered without looking at us.

My friends were all standing there, not sure what to say. I was mortified. Who was this mean girl and what had she done with my sister, Dylan?

My mom took Dylan by the arm and led her out of the kitchen, which was a good thing, for Dylan's own safety.

"Well, I loved them!" Dad said enthusiastically. "How could anyone possibly choose? Now, let's see, if I was having a birthday . . ." He was clearly trying to make us feel better, but it was not helping.

"It's okay, Dad. We'll just clean up," I said, gently shooing him out.

Later, as I was washing off the frosting bowl, thinking about how mean and ungrateful Dylan was, my party dress popped back into my mind. *Ha!* I thought. *I'm glad I got a pink dress! Why should I have to go along with everything Dylan says and wants, anyway? I'm sick of having to do everything she says.* Now, instead of dreading what she would say about my dress, I couldn't wait to see her face when I put it on!

CHAPTER 8

Hello, New Me!

$\mathcal{R}$ight before Dylan left for cheerleading practice, she sent out an e-mail my mother made her write. It was to everyone in the Cupcake Club:

> Dear Cupcake Club,
> Thank u 4 the cupcakes u baked 4 me.
> I'm sorry if I was a difficult customer, LOL.
> I'm sure we will reach an agreement at
> some point.
> Dylan

It felt a little halfhearted, if you ask me. Note that she said "*if* I was a difficult customer" not "*that* I was a difficult customer." That is pure Dylan. Anyway, I figured that my parents are the real clients and

I knew we could find something that would work for everyone. I just felt bad about Emma and her gold flakes, not to mention embarrassed in front of my friends that I had such a jerky sister.

The others were nice about it, though, and in the end we were all laughing. Plus, they got me excited about my dress, and I actually tried it on and modeled it for my parents a few minutes after Dylan had left for practice. My parents loved it, and my mother said, "eh," when I told her that Dylan would probably be really mad. My father twirled me around, and we both decided it was perfect for our dance. I only hoped Matt would like it as much as everyone else did.

My father and I were still twirling, and my friends and mother were talking in the living room, when Dylan suddenly rushed in, breathless. I froze.

"Has anyone seen my other sneaker?" she cried in despair.

Then she saw me and narrowed her eyes. "*What* are you wearing?" she asked.

All the courage I felt before about standing up to her left me. "Um . . . ," I said.

"It's her dress for your party!" Mia sweetly answered.

"Yes, doesn't she look amazing?" Katie added.

Oh, great. I braced myself for a big speech from Dylan.

"What?" she shrieked before stamping her foot. "It's pink! This is not one of the dresses that I picked out! You know what the party colors are—"

Before Dylan could launch any more ugly words at me, Mom grabbed her and pulled her out of the room. Again! My friends and Dad and I were all speechless for a minute.

"Whoops," Emma finally said.

"I should not have said anything!" Mia said, looking really upset.

"Don't worry, girls," Dad said, "I apologize for Dylan's rude behavior . . . again. Don't ever turn sixteen!" He left the room to look for Mom and Dylan.

"Wow," I said. "Sorry about that. I guess I knew it would come, sooner or later."

No one knew what else to say, so we stood around awkwardly until Emma suggested that they leave. I hated for my friends to leave on such a sour note, but it was probably a good idea.

As the girls headed out the door, Emma turned to say, "Thank you for a lovely afternoon." And we all started laughing, hard.

"Oh! Don't forget these!" I said, handing each

of them their black-and-gold party invitations. "Dylan can't wait to see you all at her party next month! Just don't forget to wear pink!" This got us all howling again.

"What are we doing tomorrow?" asked Katie once she stopped giggling.

"Is Dylan free?" Mia asked with a straight face, and we all fell down laughing.

When we finally stopped laughing, my friends left, promising to talk again later. I cringed at the thought of them discussing Dylan. Ugh. Emma was lucky she had brothers.

Mean sister + friends
witnessing = total
embarrassment

As mad as I was about Dylan's behavior, I didn't feel like asking Mom what happened when she talked to Dylan. I needed a break from thinking about her. All I could think about was working on Project M. T. But first I had to throw my Merrells to the back of my closet. "Buh-bye," I whispered. "See you guys some time after never."

Then I opened my locked drawer and took out my notebook, grabbing some forbidden SweeTarts along with it. I sat at my desk and first logged in my most recent encounters with Matt, noting who said hi first and (possibly) why. Then I turned on my computer and googled some studies about how to attract boys.

I found out some crazy stuff! Like girls care more about boy's looks than boys care about girl's. And that boys like faces that are symmetrical. That is their main thing, not that they actually realize it. Just the researchers did.

Hmm. I wondered about my face. Do I have a symmetrical face? Doesn't everyone? I mean, I have two eyes, two eyebrows, two nostrils. I stood up and looked at myself in the mirror. I looked pretty sym-metrical. But was I really?

I clicked on the lamp and propped my chin on my fists. I wanted to examine myself scientifically. Here's the data I collected: My left eye was a little bigger than my right eye if you looked really closely. Also, my left eyebrow kind of had a pointed arch while my right one was more of a smooth arch. Eek! Was that bad? My nose looked the same on both sides, and my cheeks, ears, whatever. I couldn't tell if one was off.

I went back to the computer. How symmetrical did you have to be? I googled again and learned that on a scale of one to ten, Angelina Jolie is only a 7.67 in symmetry. The researcher said she lost points because of those lips. Gosh. If Angelina wasn't a perfect ten, that was not good news for me. I am no Angelina Jolie, that's for sure.

I read on. Another article said boys liked makeup on girls, but only two kinds: foundation to even out skin tone, and eye makeup, to darken the eyes. My skin is pretty even, but eye makeup was something I could try.

I reached into my top drawer and took out an eye makeup kit that Mia had given me at a sleepover. It had dark shadow, light shadow, medium shadow, eyeliner, and mascara. I had no idea how to use any of them, but how hard could it be? If I needed help, there was a little map in the box that showed how to put it all on.

I suddenly decided I needed a total makeover.

Makeup + hairdo + new outfit = gorgeous and noticeable Alexis!

I grabbed the eye makeup kit, along with the curlers from my grandmother, the new ice-blue shirt, and purple beads I already had, and hustled down the hall into the bathroom. I ran a shower, shampooed my hair, and then, following the directions on the package, I rolled my hair up in the curlers and used a blow-dryer. Next, I put on the blue shirt and beads, and began applying the eye makeup.

I used eyeliner to draw a thick line along my upper and lower lashes, just as I'd seen my old babysitter do when I was younger. I stood back to look at what I'd done. Wow, I looked a lot older! Then I leaned back in and brushed light shadow just below my (asymmetrical) eyebrows and then, following the diagram in the kit, medium shadow in the creases of my eyes, and finally, the darkest shadow along the rim of my lid. Finally, I opened the mascara and brushed my eyelashes to a staggeringly long length.

I stood back again. OMG.

I either looked like a raccoon or a supermodel. I couldn't decide which. I turned my head all the way to the left and looked back at the right side of my face; then I looked back at my left side. I liked the left better. Next, I looked straight at the mirror and sucked in my cheeks, trying to look vampire-ish. Then I tucked my chin under and looked up through my eyelashes. That was the best look, I thought. The only thing ruining it was the curlers. I put my hand to my head and touched them. They were dry. Time for the big reveal!

I loosened the curlers without looking, then I flipped my head down and ruffled my hair with my hands, finally flipping my hair back as I stood up and looked in the mirror.

Uh, wow? I had a huge head full of curls—and it looked ridiculous! Or maybe it looked great? I didn't know! I knew I looked different, that was for sure.

Just then there was a knock at the door. "Alexis, dinner," Dylan called.

Yikes! I had been so busy making myself over that I forgot what time it was.

What do I do now? Wash it all off and pull my hair back into some kooky kind of ponytail? Or go down there as if nothing was different? I didn't want to spill anything on my new shirt, though.

"What's for dinner?" I called back.

"Grilled trout, broccoli rabe, and quinoa," replied Dylan.

It sounded pretty stain-free. And it was only my family. They've seen me at my worst.

So I smiled and winked at myself as I took one

last look in the mirror. Then I gave myself a big spritz of the cinnamon bun perfume that Dylan had on her side of the vanity. Yum! I smelled like . . . the food court at the mall. Oh well.

"Ta-da!" I cried as I flung open the door, but no one was there.

Just then the phone rang. I looked at the caller ID. It was Emma.

"Hey!" I called out, when I picked up the phone.

"Oh, hello, dear. Is that Alexis?"

It was Mrs. Taylor! "Oh, sorry, Mrs. Taylor. I thought you were Emma!" I said, laughing. "Are you calling for my mother?"

"Oh, no, don't bother her. I'm just calling to RSVP to the lovely invitation to Dylan's party! You were so kind to invite us all. We'd love to come."

"W-w-we?" I stammered.

"Yes, Mr. Taylor, Emma, and the boys and I. It sounds like great fun!"

I couldn't believe it! Matt was coming to Dylan's party! I had visions of seeing him at the party, of him seeing me in my new, fuzzy, touchable dress.

"Alexis . . . are you still there?" Mrs. Taylor asked. Oops!

"Oh, yes, I'm sorry," I said. "It's great that all of you can come!"

"Will you tell your mom for me, please?"

"Of course! She'll be so happy. Thank you! Thank you so much!" I gushed.

Mrs. Taylor laughed. "Actually, we thank you! We'll see you soon, dear."

I did a victory dance after we hung up, then ran down the stairs. "Mom!" I yelled. I couldn't wait to share the good news.

CHAPTER 9

The Beckers Try Harder

$\mathcal{M}$om!" I skidded in my sock feet into the kitchen, breathless. "The Taylors can come! All of them!"

"Oh, that's wonderful, honey. Write it down in the RSVP notebook by the phone, then grab a plate," Mom said without looking at me. She seemed extra focused on tossing the salad. "We have a lot to discuss."

I frowned at what she'd said. Her tone told me someone was in trouble, and I knew it was not me.

But Dad did look up and did a double take when he saw the new me. "Whoa, tiger!" he said, laughing.

I wrote the first RSVP on the list and turned to face him. "Hello, Father," I said casually—just as

Dylan walked in and immediately screamed.

"Alexis! What on Earth did you do to yourself?"

At that, Mom finally looked up. "Oh, Alexis!" she exclaimed.

Suddenly I wasn't so sure about my new look. "What? Don't you like it?" I asked (fake) confidently.

Mom came over and lifted a curl. She let it go, and it sprang back against my head. "I love the curls!" she said. "I'm not wild about the makeup, though."

"I'm trying to play up my eyes," I said.

"Well, sister, they are played up, that's for sure," Dylan said with a snicker. Then she peered over my shoulder to look at the RSVP book. "Who called? The Taylors? Already? And they're *all* coming? Ugh! What's that smell? Are we having apple crisp for dessert?"

"It's my perfume," I said stiffly.

"All right, before any of this goes any further, I'd like you to get your food and sit down at the table. We are having a family meeting." My mother was using her firm voice (parenting class), sounding the way she does when I talk to her on the phone while she's at work.

Dylan huffed, but didn't say another word as she

sat down. I had to admit I was looking forward to seeing her in the hot seat.

"Girls," my mother began, "we are not acting as a fully functioning family unit. There is discord, agitation, unhappiness, malice, greed, envy, you name it." She looked at both of us until we returned her level gaze. As I was pretty guilt-free, I just sat there, but Dylan did squirm a little.

"Your father and I are disappointed in the turn things have taken. In our family, we do not condone speaking rudely to one another, nor treating one another dismissively or high-handedly, nor do we humiliate one another in public. The Beckers are loyal, supportive, and kind. The Beckers . . ."

"Try harder," I finished. It was our family tagline. Ever since my mom had read *The Seven Secrets of Successful Families*, we had to have a motto as well as other "guiding principles." Never mind that our tagline was the same tagline as some international car rental company.

"Exactly right," Dad said, nodding.

"And there hasn't been enough trying lately," Mom added, looking at me.

I was surprised. Why me? "I have been trying!" I protested. "I made the cupcakes, I went to that smelly clothing store—"

"Okay, Alexis. We know." My mother raised her hand. "Dylan—"

"Oh, it's always me!" Dylan cried. "Why is she never in trouble?"

"Because I'm perfect!" I gloated.

"That's enough, Alexis," Mom warned. "You need to be more gracious. We have seen to your wishes, inviting your friends to the party and hiring you to create the cupcakes—"

"Wait! That's not a done deal!" Dylan yelled.

"Yes, it is," said my father sternly. "And you don't have to yell."

"But they haven't even presented a good option yet—"

"I am sure that they will," Dad replied as Mom nodded in agreement. "The Cupcake Club will be providing the dessert."

Yay!

"That is so unfair!" Dylan said, leaning back and crossing her arms. "It's *my* birthday party! I should—"

"Dylan, listen to me," Dad said. "What is unfair is how you humiliated Alexis in front of her friends today. Twice. You put them through the wringer on timing and color scheme. Then you treated them like peons when you sampled their hard work. You acted like a spoiled brat and were totally ungrateful. These girls all look up to you, and any one of those wonderful cupcakes is worthy of your party. Then you were absolutely horrid about Alexis in her pretty dress. This party-planning has made you high-handed and inconsiderate. We understand that you want it to be a wonderful event, but nothing is perfect. You must understand that people will still like you even if your cupcakes don't look like they were made on TV and your sister doesn't match the color scheme!"

Dylan was looking down. It looked like Dad's words were sinking in.

"The most important thing in life is how we treat people," he continued. "And you have not been treating any of us nicely. So before things get any worse, your mother and I say stop! Stop it right now! And bring back the wonderful daughter we had before all of this started."

I looked sideways at Dylan, but couldn't tell what she was thinking.

A heavy silence hung over the table. Then finally, Dylan said, "I'm sorry," in a very quiet voice. "It's just . . . oh, never mind. I'm just sorry."

My mother came around the table to give her

a hug. She kissed her on the top of her head and said, "We love you, honey. The real Dylan. Not this party-planning nightmare person, do you understand?"

Dylan nodded, tears filling her eyes. My father reached over and took her hand. "We know you want this party to be special, and it will be," he said. "We will all work hard to make it so. You just need to do your part and be gracious. Take a deep breath and know that everything will be fine. Okay?"

Dylan nodded again, then picked up her fork. I think she finally realized how mean she'd been lately. My parents and I chatted about random stuff as we ate, but we all finished quickly. I went upstairs to shower again and get rid of the makeup. Then I changed into my pj's and went back to my room. When I got there, I found Dylan sitting at my desk! My Project M. T. notebook was on the table in front of her and she was staring at me.

"Oh my God," I said.

CHAPTER 10

Is She Really My Sister?

Dylan had the notebook in her hand and started walking around me. "What is this?" she asked in a teasing voice.

I thought I might throw up. I studied Dylan's face to see if I could tell which way this was going to go. Was she going to mock me? Pity me? Blackmail me?

"Um . . . ," I said, stalling for time.

"Are you . . . Do you like someone?" she asked.

I decided to take a breezy, confident tone. "Well, what if I do?" I asked.

"So what is all this . . . math and stuff in here?"

"Oh, just data!" I waved my hand dismissively. The less she thought I cared, the less she would press me. Probably.

"Who is it?" she asked.

I didn't know if the talk at dinner made her turn over a new leaf or if it made her resent me. I wasn't sure I should tell her. What if she ended up using it against me?

"Um . . ."

"You can tell me," she said encouragingly. "I won't say anything." Dylan even looked sincere, so I decided to tell her.

"Um . . . it's Matt." Maybe if I didn't say his last name . . .

"Matt Taylor?" she guessed immediately.

I looked down at my feet and nodded, feeling my cheeks suddenly getting hot.

"He's cute," she said, and for some strange reason I was happy that she "approved" of my choice. "Does he know you like him?" she asked, flipping through the pages.

"No!" I said quickly, horrified by the idea.

"Do you want him to know?"

"What? No way!" I'd rather die.

"So where are you going with all this?"

"I just . . . I just want him to notice me. And like me, I guess." There. I'd said it.

Dylan was quiet for a moment. Then she asked, "Do you want my help?"

I eyed her suspiciously. "What do you mean?" I could just picture her telling Matt flat out that I liked him, and that would be a disaster.

"I know what it's like to have a crush who hardly knows you exist, that's for sure!" Dylan said, laughing.

I paused. Was this a trick?

Dylan continued, "I also know some stuff about boys and what they like. And about how to present yourself." She looked at me critically. "And I do think you're ready for a more mature look. The makeover you did wasn't a bad idea. You just went too far, too fast."

I kept looking at her, not sure if I could really trust my own sister.

"Come on," she said in an encouraging tone. "I owe it to you. Let me try."

"Okay . . . ," I finally agreed. "But in the morning. I can't do it again tonight. I have too much other stuff to do."

"Fine. We'll get up early and do it, okay?"

I nodded, still waiting for this to turn into some sort of prank.

Dylan got up and headed for the door, then turned around. "And Alexis?"

"Yes?"

"I'm sorry."

Wow. An apology from Dylan, and I didn't even have to ask for it!

"For which part?" I asked.

"Everything." And she closed the door.

I sat down and sighed loudly, part of me wondering if I had just imagined the past five minutes. Dylan had really turned around! I started to finish entering the new data and notes on some new techniques, like hair-flipping, arm-grabbing, and lunch-inviting—not that any of them were my style.

I chewed on my pen cap as I asked myself the question Dylan had just asked. What did I want? What was my goal with Matt? Was it that I wanted him to just notice me? He already had. But wanting him to like me back seemed major, and maybe too big of a goal. Like more than I really wanted. I think.

My parents always tell us, when we have a big project due, to break it into smaller, more manageable chunks or goals. So if my big project is for Matt to fall madly in like with me, what would a smaller chunk be?

Chew, chew, chew. I looked at my pen cap. It was totally mangled. I twirled it around, and it looked like it was dancing. And then the answer came to me.

A dance. One wonderful, dreamy dance with Matt. Then he'd see how graceful and talented I was, and I'd have the chance to really charm him.

I smiled just picturing it, like a scene out of a Disney movie: *Cinderella, Beauty and the Beast, Enchanted.* One dance with the prince, and the rest is history. That was my goal.

Relieved to now have an actual goal, I put the notebook away, then did a huge e-blast to all of the Cupcake Club's previous clients, advertising our new flavors (s'mores being one of them), wrote out forty vocabulary flash cards, did a math crossword puzzle, reorganized my planner, and cleaned up my room.

Later that night, when I went to brush my teeth, I nearly tripped over a pile of teen magazines that Dylan had left outside my door. "Get Him to Notice YOU!," "7 Days to a Brand-New You!," "Flirty Tips & Tricks to Wow Him!" the headlines screamed. Well, I certainly had my work cut out for me.

The next morning Dylan gave me a crash course in flirtation and a real makeover. I think even my parents were happy that we were doing something together and not bickering. It was like when we were little and we used to play Barbie dolls together for hours. My Barbie would run the clothing store and Dylan's Barbie would come in to shop. My Barbie would bargain and haggle and put stuff on sale, and her Barbie would try everything on and leave it in a pile on the dressing room floor.

First Dylan and I looked through the magazines together to find a good new look for me. She talked about what I had heard her discussing with Meredith and Skylar, about pretty colors (no black, gray, or brown), touchable fabrics (fuzzy, floaty, silky, smooth), and patterns (floral is good; plaid, not so much). She went through my closet and also brought out some of her own(!) clothes to put together five new school outfits for me—complete with shoes and accessories!

I have to say, she was really getting into it, and she was being a big help. I think she liked that I was agreeing with everything she said.

Next Dylan made me shave my legs, which was gross and hard and took forever (I cut myself twice), but the result was pretty dramatic. She gave me a mud mask for my face and a quick manicure/pedicure (just clear nail polish because, she said knowledgably, boys don't like colored or fussy nails). Then she had me wash my hair and deep condition it, and she set it in hot rollers we borrowed from our mother. They were heavy and felt like they were pulling out my hair, but when she took them out, my hair fell in soft waves, like a Disney princess!

Finally she taught me how to put on makeup. "The point," explained Dylan, "is that no one should notice you are wearing makeup. You should look like yourself, only better."

Dylan gave me a tiny hint of pink blush to perk up my face and make me look healthy. (According to Dylan, boys respond to healthy looks. It has to do with the evolution of the species.) Then she gave me a cinnamon-and-ginger-laced pale pink lipstick with what she called "blue undertones" to make my lips plump up and my teeth look even whiter. Finally, she drew the faintest lines with brown eyeliner at only the outer corners of my eyes, and then she curled my eyelashes and lengthened them with a little brown mascara. When she turned me around to face the mirror . . . I loved what I saw! I looked great!

"Wow! Thanks!" I exclaimed. It was me, just a better-looking me!

Dylan smiled proudly at me, her handiwork.

"Now let's talk flirtation," she said. "There are two ways to get guys," she said, holding up two fingers. "You can be a normal girl or a supergirlie girl. The supergirlie girl technique tends to work well on younger guys and dumber guys; guys who don't really understand girls and are too shy to pursue them. The normal girl technique attracts the better guys, but it takes longer. Like sometimes years longer. Do you follow me?"

"Um . . ." I wasn't sure what she was talking about. "Do you mind if we go in my room, so I can write all this down in my notebook?"

Dylan laughed. "Fine, whatever," she said.

I made her wait outside while I took the book out of the drawer. "Okay!" I called, and she came in and continued her lecture. I scribbled madly, happy to have specific directions to follow.

From what Dylan was telling me, it seemed that Sydney and Callie go with the supergirlie girl technique, and I prefer the normal girl way.

The supergirlie girl approach meant you had to be aggressive, giggly, loud, super touchy-feely, overdressed, made-up, and perfumed, and you always traveled in pairs, never alone. Super-girlie girls often act grossed out or incompetent to try to get help from boys, and this would in turn make the boys feel good about themselves. However, the supergirlie girl way could backfire because it makes girls appear so different from boys, and some boys could get scared off. But it often worked because boys are so shy and clueless, especially when they're younger, that the girls just go after them and grab them, and the boys never see it coming. They think girls are supposed to be like that, and they're just happy to not have to do the work of asking girls out and stuff. The supergirlie girl approach was based on the idea that boys and girls are totally different and foreign creatures to each other, and girls had to do a lot of planning to get what they wanted.

Whew! I was so glad that Dylan explained all this to me. I never would have known. And I was beginning to think that there might be a perfect recipe for finding love after all.

The normal girl technique was more subtle. You dressed pretty but not overly fancy (you could still ride a bike or play catch in whatever you're wearing), and you might wear a little makeup, but never so the boys could notice it or, God forbid, see you putting it on. You are chatty and fun but not silly or giggly, and you are friendly but not aggressive. You don't travel in big packs and you try to be friends with a boy first. Some boys might be too clueless to realize when a normal girl likes them—that's the bad part—but in the long run, Dylan assured me, you attract better boys with this approach. Most important, the normal girl approach reminded you that boys are not that different from girls. They are people with feelings who are often shy and they just need to be treated with the same consideration you'd give a friend.

"I think I'd rather be a normal girl," I told Dylan.

"Good," Dylan said. "Slow and steady wins the race."

My hand ached after copying all of this down. I couldn't wait to put everything I learned into practice. I only wished I could discuss it all with my best friends.

"Thank you, Dylan," I said. "This is so helpful."

Dylan smiled, looking a little weary after sharing everything she knew.

Just then the phone rang. Would you believe it was Emma, inviting me over? I couldn't get the words out of my mouth fast enough. "Be right over!" I said, and hung up before I made the mistake of asking if Matt was going to be there. I was dying to, but slow and steady wins the race, I reminded myself. I might have to add that to my list of mottoes.

Dylan winked at me. "Go get him, tiger," she said.

"So, I'll let you know how it goes, in case he's there?"

"Who?" Dylan asked.

What? "Dylan!" I cried.

"Kidding!" she said with a laugh.

"Thanks again," I yelled as I ran down the stairs, hopped on my bike, and flew to the Taylors in record time.

CHAPTER 11

Slam Dunk!

*H*ey," said Emma when I walked in. "You look nice." She circled me and took in my outfit and hair and everything.

My stomach was all butterflies, and I glanced uneasily around the kitchen. "What's up?" I asked. I wasn't going to tell her about the makeover. Not now, anyway.

And then Emma flatly said, "He's not here."

"Who?" I asked, a little taken aback.

Emma made a face. "Lover boy," she said, exasperated.

I blushed. "What?"

"I knew it!" shrieked Emma. "I was just testing you, but now I know for sure!"

"Know what?" I persisted.

Emma leaned in close. "I know you're in love with Matt," she whispered.

"Me? Matt? *What?*" I felt the heat rising in my cheeks.

Emma nodded, a look of satisfaction on her face. "I figured it out yesterday when we saw him at the mall. You got all blushy and nervous and then I saw that kooky notebook on your desk—"

"You did?" I interrupted.

"Ha!" said Emma. "So you are." It was a statement, not a question.

I sighed and looked down at my feet. "Yes. I'm sorry," I mumbled. It felt good to finally admit it, although it felt really weird. I looked at her. "I just can't help it!"

"It's a little awkward," she agreed. "And why Matt? I mean, Sam, maybe. He's cute and girls seem to really like him. But Matt? Smelly sock Matt? Computer geek Matt?"

"Cute, funny, nice Matt," I countered.

"Gross!" Emma exclaimed, playfully slapping me on the shoulder. After a moment she added, "Too bad Callie likes him too."

"Oh!" I said. "I wasn't sure if she liked him or Joe. I thought Sydney might like Matt."

"I can't believe you like my brother," Emma said as she shook her head.

"Well, it's not that surprising. I mean, you and I are good friends, and our moms are good friends. I guess the Taylors and the Beckers are just well-suited to each other!" Emma smiled. "I wonder if he likes you back?" Then she added in a mischievous tone, "Want me to find out?"

"No!" I screamed. "*Please* don't ask him, Emma." I was begging her, but part of me really did want to know.

"Well, at least he'll be at Dylan's party. Even if my mom has to drag him there," said Emma.

"You don't think he wants to go?" I asked, feeling a slight sting.

"No way! He and my mom had a big fight about it. Sam, of course, wants to go, because there'll be all those cute girls there. Jake will go anyplace where there's Mia or cupcakes, and both is even better. Matt is just . . . I don't know. I think he might be kind of shy about girls."

"Really?" I asked, surprised. From what I'd seen, he seemed pretty comfortable with the attention he got from girls. "He doesn't act that way."

Emma thought for a minute. "Hmm . . . I think what I mean is that I don't know if he's mature enough to like girls, you know. The thing he's really into is sports, especially basketball. So you could brush up on your dunking! That's something to put in your notebook."

The notebook! "Look, the notebook was just—"

"Pure Alexis," Emma said, laughing. "Always taking the business approach. Don't worry, I won't tell anyone about it. And I'm sorry for looking at it. I shouldn't have, but I thought it was a math notebook!"

"Yes, you shouldn't have," I replied. But I couldn't be mad at Emma. She was one of my best friends. Besides, I was happy we were talking about Matt!

"Let me see, what other 'data' can I give you?" Emma asked, looking upward and tapping her chin with one finger. "He loves cupcakes. And he's really into computer graphics. Maybe you could call him up and ask him to help on a project for the Cupcake Club? And then pay him in cupcakes?"

"Oooh! Good idea," I lied. As if I'd call him again.

Emma looked at me with a serious expression. "Can I ask you if you want him to be your boyfriend? I can't imagine Matt being anyone's boyfriend, but whatever."

I hesitated. Should I tell Emma my goal? She was my friend, but she was also Matt's sister. She looked at me expectantly. My goal was much easier to explain than any of my other feelings, so I took a deep breath and confessed, "I want to dance with him at Dylan's party."

Emma's eyes widened. "Wow. That's it? It seems like a small thing, but it actually may be impossible to accomplish. I don't think he dances."

I hadn't thought of that! "Well . . . ," I said, not knowing how to respond.

Suddenly the back door opened. "Hello!" hollered Matt.

"Eek!" I squealed. I was totally caught off guard, even though I had been hoping he would show up.

Matt was all sweaty from practice and had on a hideous pair of ripped sweatpants and a T-shirt. His hair was sticking up every which way. But he still looked gorgeous to me.

He seemed surprised to see me. "Oh, hey, Alexis," he said.

My heart leaped. He had said hi first! I couldn't wait to log *that* data in the notebook!

"Got any cupcakes?" he asked.

I laughed nervously. "No. Not yet." Should I ask him a question now? I didn't know what to do or say. Thinking of Sydney, I flipped my hair from one side to the other. "Huh," was all he said before heading for the fridge.

"Where's Mom?" he asked Emma.

"At Jake's practice," Emma replied, then she winked at me. "Hey, Alexis and I were just going out to shoot some hoops. Want to come give us some pointers?"

I stared at her. What was she doing? I couldn't believe what she had just suggested! I looked over at Matt, who was chugging a Gatorade. He turned and looked at us over the rim of the bottle. When he finished, he let out a really loud burp and grinned.

The burp was gross, and I wondered why he felt it was okay to do that in front of me. But then he said, "Sure," and shrugged, and the next thing I knew I was playing H-O-R-S-E in the driveway with Matt Taylor, man of my dreams! I silently forgave him for burping and quickly got caught up in the game.

I have to say that I am decent at basketball. Not sure why, but maybe because it's kind of like dancing to me. I don't know. Anyway, we were having a pretty good time. I think Matt was even impressed by my skills. This was definitely the normal girl approach, and it seemed to be working.

After about fifteen minutes, Joe Fraser showed up, and he joined the game too. I was so happy! Emma and I challenged the boys to a two-on-two, but they insisted we split the teams, so Matt and I played Joe and Emma. It was awesome. We were winning, 8 to 2, when suddenly somebody called out, "Yoo-hoo!"

Sydney and Callie!

Emma and I looked at each other and frowned. I couldn't tell if Matt and Joe were happy or annoyed. But the girls were definitely happy. They were super dressed up for a Sunday morning, in skin-tight jeans and tight sweaters with tiny down vests, and boots with high heels. Their hair was super-fluffy and they had on tons of makeup and perfume and dangly earrings. I wondered when Sydney had planned this little outing.

"Can we play?" asked Sydney in her high, flirty voice. Callie at least had the grace to look nervous.

Matt shrugged. "Okay." He didn't sound excited, but he didn't sound mad, either. I think he was just being polite. Emma, on the other hand, was really mad. Her face was set like stone.

"I think we need to play H-O-R-S-E again," said Matt.

"What's that?" Callie said, giggling.

Matt explained the game, and he went first, tossing the ball in high over his left shoulder, facing away from the basket. It was an impressive shot.

Sydney clapped and whistled, and Matt grinned. Why hadn't I thought to praise him like that? Then she stepped up to take the shot and threw it so badly that it just flew over her shoulder, landing nowhere near the basket.

"Whoops!" she said with a laugh, covering her mouth with a hand that showed off fresh scarlet nail polish. Sydney clearly didn't care that she had missed. In fact, she probably missed on purpose.

Callie took the ball. She bounced it once or twice, then flipped it over her shoulder, but her sweater was so tight it made her lose control as the ball left her hand; it fell weakly to the ground and rolled away. "Oh dear! I stink!" Callie said, but it was clear she didn't really care how badly she played either.

Now it was my turn. If ever I had wanted something in my life, this was it. I focused like a laser beam and took a deep breath, closing my eyes. Then I bent my knees like Matt had and lifted the ball in a gentle arc over my shoulder. *Slow and steady wins the race,* I told myself. I didn't dare to look, but when I heard the ball thump the backboard and

Matt yelling, my eyes flew open. Matt had both fists straight in the air. "Yes!" he cried. "You made it!" He stuck out his hand for a high five and I slapped it, laughing in giddy relief.

I stole a quick glance at Callie and Sydney and they were both standing there with their mouths open. Sydney started chewing on the end of a piece of her fluffy hair, probably wondering what she should do next. I had a new equation for my workbook:

Sports skills + comfortable clothes = boys impressed by YOU!

A few minutes later Mrs. Taylor pulled up to drop off Jake and pick up Matt and Joe to go to their friend's house for a school project. I didn't really get the chance to say good-bye to Matt, but it was all good. I was still on a high from my totally awesome shot.

"Let's hit it," Sydney said to Callie as soon as the boys left. Sydney didn't bother to say good-bye to Emma and me, but Callie turned to us with an awkward expression. "Well, thanks . . . ," she said.

"See ya," Emma muttered without bothering to look in their direction. We went inside, and Jake immediately went for the couch in the TV room. Emma started to make him a snack in the kitchen.

"Wow," I said.

"I can't believe you made that basket!" said Emma, laughing.

"Me neither!" I howled. "Talk about luck!"

"It was skill," said Emma. "And Matt was impressed."

"You think?" I asked, but I knew he was. My chest was bursting with pride and happiness.

As we headed to the TV room with drinks and Jake's snack, Emma said, "We still have to figure out Dylan's dessert. Let's get the others over here and bake."

"Yay! Cupcakes!" Jake yelled.

"Good idea," I agreed, thinking of the extra cupcakes we could leave behind for Matt!

"Oh, hey," Emma replied like she didn't care.

"We have a question. Someone said Matt is going to Dylan Becker's sweet sixteen on the twentieth. Is that true?" She was asking about my sister's party and she didn't even look at me! My blood began to boil.

Emma looked at me and raised her eyebrows. She turned to Sydney. "Yes. Our whole family is going."

"We're all going, actually," said Mia in a cold, snooty voice I'd never heard her use before.

I seemed to have lost my ability to speak.

Sydney and Callie exchanged a look. "Okay, thanks," said Sydney, before she and Callie walked away, their heads bent close as they whispered.

"What was that all about?" I burst out. "Wouldn't you think they would ask me? It's *my* sister they're talking about! And why do they want to know, anyway? It's not like they're invited!"

"They have some nerve," said Katie, shaking her head.

"I am so sick of those two. They just can't leave Matt alone. Someone keeps calling and hanging up, and I swear it's them!" Emma complained.

My stomach flip-flopped. They were calling Matt? That was pretty major!

CHAPTER 12

Confession

Of course, after that wonderful Sunday morning, I didn't see Matt for an entire week. I wore each of the outfits that Dylan had planned for me, and I took great care with my hair (down) and makeup, but no luck. My friends all noticed the change though, and Mia and Katie pestered me about my new look. I was happy that Emma did not let on about my crush, but it wasn't long before they figured it out.

It happened while we were sitting at lunch one day, when Sydney and Callie came over to our table.

"Hey, Emma," said Sydney. We all looked up in shock. Sydney usually just ignores us and rarely calls us by name.

"Has he actually *spoken* to them on the phone?" I asked, probably with a little too much feeling, because Mia and Katie turned to me with raised eyebrows.

Emma shrugged. "I'm not sure," she answered.

I could feel Mia still watching me. Then she asked with a shy smile, "Alexis, is there something you want to tell us?"

I was so bothered by Sydney that I simply admitted, "Yes, I have a crush on Matt." Then I added, "I'm sure you all already know."

"I didn't tell them!" Emma cried out defensively, even though I didn't look at her.

Katie immediately jumped on Emma. "Wait, you knew?" she asked.

Uh-oh. This had the makings of a cupcake war. I had to stop it before it went too far. "I'm sorry, guys," I told Katie and Mia. "I was going to tell you guys, but there just never seemed to be a right time."

"Well, there was clearly a right time to tell Emma, it seems!" Mia said, sounding a little offended, but I don't think she was actually mad.

"Oh, no, I guessed, actually," Emma said, "and made Alexis fess up. Then she swore me to secrecy. It is just too weird. I can't imagine anyone liking my brother, but now it seems he's getting all this attention from girls."

"Humph!" I said, and crossed my arms.

"So what are you doing about this crush?" Mia asked me.

"I've been doing some research," I said without thinking, and my friends all burst out laughing.

"Research!" Mia yelled. "Alexis, that is just so typical of you!"

"Wait, is that why you've had this sudden make-over and everything?" Katie asked.

I nodded shyly and muttered, "A lot of good it's doing. I've barely even seen him since."

"But it worked when you did see him!" said Emma.

"You think?" I asked, hoping that all my work wasn't going to waste.

Emma nodded. "Hello? He came out and played basketball with us!"

"You don't think he was just . . . bored or trying to be nice?" I pressed.

Emma shook her head. "Uh-uh. He would never be nice for no reason."

"Actually, I think he's really nice. Like when he helped you—"

"All right, all right! We know *you* think he's

nice," interrupted Emma. "I guess he is a little bit. I'm just not sure he's worth the time and effort, that's all."

"Yes, well, if he was a client, I think I would have stopped my aggressive marketing efforts by now," I said, and everyone laughed again.

"So when you say you have a crush on him, what does that mean?" asked Katie.

"Oh, I think he's cute. I want him to like me back. And . . ." I looked over at Emma, and she finished what I was too embarrassed to say.

"She wants to dance with him at Dylan's sweet sixteen."

I bit my lip nervously, unsure how my friends would react. But I didn't have to worry.

Mia clapped excitedly. "Ooh! Once he sees you dance he will fall head over heels in love with you!"

Katie grinned. "Are you going to ask *him*?"

"I haven't quite worked that part out yet," I admitted.

"Between the dancing and the cupcakes, I know he'll be wowed," said Katie loyally.

"Anything we can do to help?" asked Mia.

As much as I wanted to keep talking about Matt, I suddenly remembered there was something more important that we needed to do. "Yes! Let's figure out those cupcakes!" At least that was something that I could control. "Dylan has been on a rampage, so we need to sort it out before she goes nuts. The only thing is, she's also been really nice to me lately, with the makeover and stuff. I think she's just stressed. Let's give her the works!"

"The works?" Katie asked.

"I've been thinking," I said. "Let's forget about the budget for now. Instead, we should wrap up all of our great ideas into one slam dunk of a cupcake."

Emma smiled. "So what is it?"

"The s'mores disco gift cupcake. Chocolate cupcake filled with marshmallow, topped with chocolate frosting with graham cracker and gold flake crumble, and tied with a gold bow. She'll love it. And it will cheer her up."

The girls all agreed, so we made plans to start working on the cupcakes soon.

Dylan had, in fact, been even crankier than ever this week. As the RSVPs for her party rolled in, she became compulsive about checking voice mail and the list. I wondered if there was someone special she was waiting to hear from. Dylan is class president and assistant cheer captain, so I knew she wasn't exactly lacking for friends or popularity. But as I watched her flip through the RSVP notebook one afternoon, I kind of felt sorry for her.

"What's up?" I asked.

"Nothing," she replied. *Flip, flip, flip.*

I tried again. "Are you waiting to hear from someone?" I asked.

Dylan stopped flipping and sighed heavily. "*Don't* ever fall in love, Alexis."

"Too late, Dyl, I'm a goner," I said. "Who are you in love with?"

"Never mind," she said. "Nothing will come of it. He hasn't even RSVP'd."

"Sounds like a jerk," I said. The invitations had been out for days. Whoever she was talking about should have already received it.

But Dylan had bristled. "No, no, no, he's not a jerk," she replied defensively. "He's just very busy! I'm sure he'll . . . he'll let me know soon."

"Okay!" I said brightly, not wanting to upset her. But inside I thought, *Why do boys cause such heartache?*

That night, when my mother came in to say good night, I told her, "Mom, I think I know why Dylan's been such a jerk lately." I'd been puzzling over it all evening, and I was pretty sure I was right.

"Why? I'd love to know!"

"I think she's in love with someone and he might not love her back."

"Hmm . . . that *would* explain a lot."

"I think she wants everything to be perfect at the party so he'll fall in love with her."

"Oh! Is he coming?"

"Well, that's the other thing. He hasn't RSVP'd."

"Poor Dylly."

I nodded and sighed. At least the love of my life was coming. Granted his mother had RSVP'd for him, but it was a start!

"Well, I'll see if I can discuss it with her," Mom said before pulling the covers up tight under my chin. "I love you, sweetheart. Thanks for the tip."

"Of course, Mom. Love you, too."

CHAPTER 13
not
BF∧F :(

The day of Dylan's party was gorgeous: The sky was blue, the sun was shining, and birds were literally singing in the trees. It promised to be a beautiful night. But first there was lots of baking to be done!

The Cupcake Club met at Mia's that morning, which was a good thing, even though I was bummed not to have a chance to see Matt. It was better, because I could focus on making our cupcakes.

We ended up going with my idea of combining all three original cupcake ideas. Dylan had surprised us when she said she "loved" this idea. But these were going to take a lot longer to decorate, so we had to be really organized.

We had an assembly line going once the cupcakes were baked and cooled. I lifted them off the cooling rack in their gold foil papers and filled them with liquid marshmallow using a baker's syringe. Then Katie would frost the cupcakes with dark chocolate frosting, and Emma would add the crumbled graham crackers and gold sprinkles. Finally Mia would tie the base of each one with a big gold ribbon, and set it back on the cooling racks to pack later.

Even though I wasn't anywhere near Matt, I was glad to have him on my mind as Katie and Mia kept asking me questions.

"What position does he play on the basketball team?" Mia asked.

"Oh, point guard, I think," I said.

"Center," corrected Emma.

"Right. I always get those mixed up."

"Have you been to any of his games yet?" asked Katie.

"No, but I think I'm going to go this week. Anyone want to go with me?"

"I always go," said Emma, "if I can. We have a rule in our family that if you can possibly make it to a sibling's game, you have to go, to show support."

"Let me know if he ever needs any extra support!" I said, laughing. "I can always sub for you if you can't make it!"

Emma's response was to playfully stick her tongue out at me. I stuck mine right back at her.

"So what are his favorite cupcakes we've made so far?" Mia asked.

I didn't know the answers to any of their questions, but I wanted them to think I knew something about Matt.

"Oh, I think the . . ." I looked around.

"Bacon," said Emma. "He liked the caramel cupcakes with the bacon caramel frosting. He had me make them for his team dinner."

"Runs in the family!" Mia laughed. The recipe had been Emma's idea.

"He also liked the mini vanillas we made for Mona," I added.

Emma shook her head. "That boy would eat anything if you frosted it."

The vanilla minis were *my* recipe! "Well, he certainly wolfed them down," I retorted.

"Alexis, you don't live with him like I do," Emma insisted. "He even eats burnt cupcakes, as long as they're loaded with frosting."

"Wait a second," I protested, suddenly getting

mad. "Are you comparing my vanilla minis to burnt cupcakes?" I couldn't believe Emma was so rude! She was supposed to be on *my* side.

"Okay, you two," Katie said as she exchanged a look with Mia.

"I just don't know who made you the Matt expert all of a sudden," said Emma. "You barely know him!"

"That's not true!" I said. But it kind of was.

"The only times you ever interact with him, I'm there! So how could you suddenly have this great romance blooming?"

Now I was really mad. "There's no 'great romance blooming,' Emma. I just think he's really cute. And the time when I decided I liked him, you *weren't* there!"

"Well, it's annoying! I'm sick of hearing you talk about him like you own him! You're no better than Sydney Whitman!"

"It's Callie who likes him." I spat the words out furiously.

"Well, it's Sydney who's doing all the work!" said Emma. "Just like me for you!"

"What?"

"Stop, you guys!" cried Katie. "Come on!"

Emma and I glared at each other.

"Speaking of work, we have a whole lot of cupcakes to bake," said Mia, sounding like a parent. "And we need to get them all done today. Business first, Alexis. That's your motto."

"So let's just focus on what we need to do, okay?" Katie added.

I nodded without looking at Emma. I decided I would not speak to her. In fact, I would not speak at all.

Emma muttered something, but I didn't care to ask what she said. I was all business now. For the next few hours, I worked quickly to fill two hundred cupcakes, and by noon we were done. I only talked when Mia and Katie spoke to me. No one was happy that things were tense, but it wasn't *my* fault!

Mom came to pick up the cupcakes and take them to the restaurant. Mia, Katie, and Emma had plans to dress together for the party, and I wasn't happy about that. I didn't want them to all be having fun without me (or worse, talking about me), but I couldn't ditch my family, and it would just be too hectic to have my friends get ready at my house, what with Dylan's chaos going on.

Dylan's crush still had not RSVP'd, which made him uncrushworthy in my book. But I think she was still hoping. Every time the phone rang that afternoon, she dashed to check the caller ID (not that she'd answer the phone, because that would seem desperate).

Meredith and Skylar came over to get ready with Dylan, almost like bridesmaids before a wedding. They were all in black and gold, of course, and when they were ready, they offered to help me with my hair and makeup. Of course I said yes!

Meredith was working on my hair with rollers. "Is there anyone special coming tonight that you're looking forward to seeing?" she asked.

I narrowed my eyes at Dylan. "Did you tell her?" I snapped.

"No, Alexis," Dylan calmly replied. "I didn't say anything to anyone."

"Chill, Alexis, she didn't," Meredith said, a little taken aback. "I was just asking to make conversation, like they do at the hairdresser."

I felt bad. "Oh, sorry. Actually, there is one guy I like. He's . . . he's my friend's older brother. But she's mad at me right now for liking him."

"That's ridiculous! She doesn't own him!" said Meredith.

"I know!" I felt myself getting riled up all over again.

"And it's not like she could marry him, anyway!" she added, laughing.

"You're so right!"

"That happened with me at day camp one summer," Skylar joined in. "I lost a friend that way. I totally regret it."

"What do you mean?" I asked.

"Well, I was about your age, and there was this really cute junior counselor named Tom. And his sister Madison was my best friend at camp. But I became so obsessed with Tom that every time I called Madison, every time I went to their house, it was like it was really to catch a glimpse of Tom. Madison ended up feeling like I was using her just to get to Tom."

"Were you?"

"No! I really liked Madison! It was just inconvenient that the guy I liked happened to be her brother!"

"Well, it was also probably convenient, too," I said knowingly.

Skylar nodded. "Sure, because I got the insider's perspective, and I got to see him casually, without having to go on a date or anything. I could see him in his normal environment."

"But you lost a friend," said Meredith.

"Yes, a good friend," Skylar replied. "And I was so over him by the end of the summer."

"How did you get over him?" I asked.

"We finally went on a date, and I realized we had nothing to talk about when Madison wasn't there."

Just then the phone rang. I was holding the cordless in my lap, and I flipped it over to see what the caller ID said.

"Hanson?" I said aloud.

Dylan screamed, "It's him! Get it! No wait, don't!" But it was too late.

"Hello?" I said.

A deep voice kind of stammered, "Uh ... hi ... is Dylan there, please?"

I looked at Dylan and she was shaking her head no.

"Um, no, I'm sorry, she's out right now," I lied. "May I take a message?"

"Yes. This is Noah Hanson. I'm so embarrassed. Dylan invited me to her party, and the invitation got mixed up with my mother's bills, and I only just opened it. I know it's too late to say yes, so I was just calling to apologize. Will you tell her, please?"

I froze for a second.

"Hello?" he said again.

"No! Come! It's not too late! It's . . . a buffet. One more person won't make a difference. Don't worry. Just come! I'm sure she'd be happy to see you." I said, crossing my fingers. *Please say yes, please say yes.* I hoped for Dylan's sake.

He paused. "Well, if you think it's okay . . . Um, who is this?"

"I'm Alexis, her sister, and my mom is here, and she's nodding, so it's totally fine for you to come," I lied again, holding my crossed fingers up in the air. I looked over at Dylan. Her face was hidden in her hands as she waited for the final verdict.

"Oh, okay, that's really nice," Noah said, sounding very relieved. "Thanks! So, I'll be there at seven, right?"

"Yup, seven it is. See you there!" I sang out and uncrossed my fingers to switch to a thumbs-up sign before hanging up.

"Yessss!" Dylan screamed as soon as I put the phone back on its base. "Oh, Alexis, you are the best! Thank you, thank you so much!" She jumped up and grabbed me in a big hug.

She and Meredith and Skylar started yelling and dancing around together in a circle. "Yay! Noah's coming!"

At that moment Mom poked her head in to see what the noise was all about. "He's coming," I whispered. She didn't need to ask who.

"Phew," she said, and with a wink, she closed the door.

This was going to be a great night.

CHAPTER 14

Nothing > Friends!

Girls, you look spectacular!" my father said proudly as he wrapped his arms around Dylan and me for the photographer.

"Gorgeous," my mother agreed.

"You two look pretty great, yourselves," I said. And they did.

We had arrived early, along with Meredith and Skylar, to make sure everything was set up just right. I checked the cupcakes first, of course, but the restaurant had arranged them beautifully on three tiers of a gold cake stand. They looked really pretty and I knew they'd taste even better!

Dylan looked really happy about the cupcakes and gave me a hug as we stood in front of the display. "Thank you," she whispered. She looked really beautiful in her gown, and I even started to tear up a little. I think I was just relieved that we were done with all those weeks of arguing, the cupcakes were done, and this day was finally here!

I watched as Dylan glanced nervously at the front doors. I knew how she felt. I kept waiting to see handsome Matt walk through the door myself (never mind that he'd be with Emma!) and had gone to the ladies' room twice to check my appearance in the mirror.

I had worn my hair down and in loopy curls (thanks to Meredith). I had on a little bit of Mom-approved makeup and a tiny bit of vanilla spice perfume (thanks to Dylan). I was wearing the fuzzy pink dress (thanks to Mia) with a gold chain belt of my mother's and some gold sandals of Dylan's. I had a chunky ice-cube necklace from Mia, and it looked fantastic. I had to admit, I was looking pretty good.

The band was warming up, and my father asked them to play a little bit of "The Way You Look Tonight," so we could practice our dance. They played the whole thing and when we finished our dance, the whole band applauded!

Just before seven, people started to arrive. That's when I got really, really nervous. Luckily,

Mia and Katie arrived together right at the start. Emma had gone home after getting ready, so she could come with her family. I wasn't sure what I would say to her when she came. Still, I watched the door eagerly for the arrival of the Taylors—and for Noah!

Mia and Katie were getting a soda by the bar and I was saying hi to Dylan's godmother when Sydney and Callie walked in! And would you believe Callie was wearing that black *Dancing with the Stars*-type dress from Icon!

I rushed over to Dylan. "Look who's here!" I said angrily, grabbing her arm.

She looked at the door, just as a gorgeous, tall, blond guy walked in.

"Noah!" she screamed.

"Noah? No, no, not him!" I said. "He's cute though! No, Sydney and Callie are here! There they are!" I pointed across the room to where they were standing.

"Did you invite them?" Dylan asked as she hurried to the door to meet Noah. She didn't seem concerned at all that the devilish duo had crashed her party!

"Of course not!" I said, trying to keep up with her.

"Callie is Jenna Wilson's little sister, right? Jenna's here," said Dylan. Of course! Callie's older sister was on cheerleading with Dylan. So of course she'd be invited, but that didn't explain Callie and Sydney.

"Why don't you go find out why they're here?" Dylan said just as we got to the door. "I'm going to say hi to Noah."

I watched as Noah kissed Dylan on the cheek, and then Dylan took his hand, guiding him toward the drinks. I was happy for Dylan that Noah showed up, but superannoyed that she wasn't mad that Sydney and Callie had shown up at her party uninvited! (And after the hard time she'd given me about inviting my friends!)

I stared at Sydney and Callie for a minute, trying to figure out what I wanted to do. Just then Callie pulled Sydney with her across the room, toward an older girl who I now recognized as Callie's sister. Jenna had been talking with her friends, and turned around when Callie tapped her on the shoulder. Jenna seemed genuinely shocked to see Callie and Sydney and looked really annoyed.

Mia and Katie came over. "Did you invite them?" Mia asked, nodding her head toward Sydney and Callie.

"As if!" I said.

"Then why are they here?" Katie asked.

"I . . . ," I started to say, but then something—or rather, some*one*—caught my eye. It was Emma, with the rest of the Taylors. I wanted to run across the room to greet them, but then I remembered my fight with Emma, and I held back.

I checked my dress and my hair, patting everything nervously as the Taylors walked toward me. Jake looked really cute in a little jacket and tie, and Matt and even Sam looked, frankly, gorgeous in their suits.

"Hi, Alexis, darling! Don't you look beautiful!" Mrs. Taylor said, greeting me with a kiss. Mr. Taylor did the same as Mrs. Taylor looked around the room. "Now, where's your mom? Wow, it looks wonderful in here! What a lot of planning you've all done! Oh, there she is. I'll go say hello. Come on, sweetie." And Emma's parents took off, leaving their kids standing with me.

Jake went up to Mia and tugged on her dress to say hi, and they and Katie began chatting about law enforcement, Jake's favorite subject.

Sam said, "Great party. Oh, wow, there's Dylan!" and he walked over to her.

Then it was just me, Matt, and Emma. It felt

really awkward. I hadn't made eye contact with Emma yet.

"Hey, would you guys like a soda?" I finally said, looking somewhere between the two of them.

"Sure," Matt answered. "Why don't I get something for you two?"

Emma and I looked at each other, and suddenly we both burst out laughing. Hard! We couldn't stay mad at each other, especially not on such a big night.

Emma put her arm through mine. "Sure," she told Matt. "I'll have a Sprite."

"Me too, thanks," I said, giving him my best smile.

Matt grinned, and as he walked away I pretended to swoon. "He is too cute!" I whispered. "Sorry!"

"It's okay," said Emma. "I'm sorry I was so mean earlier. I guess it was just a little hard to take."

"I know I've been kind of annoying about it," I said, thinking about the story Skylar told earlier. "Anyway, I would never sacrifice our friendship for love. If it came down to Matt being my boyfriend or you being my friend, I'd pick you. I swear."

Emma looked like she didn't believe me, but she hugged me and said, "Thanks, but I don't think you need to make a choice. I love my brother too, you know." She swatted my arm playfully, then gasped.

I looked over to see what she was looking at and rolled my eyes. I had, for five minutes, forgotten about Sydney and Callie, but there they were, still standing around. "Yeah, can you believe they had the nerve to show up?"

"Unbelievable!" Emma said in a disgusted tone. When Katie and Mia came back (without Jake, who was now with his mother), we started trying to figure out what we should do. We decided that Emma would say something to Sydney, since Sydney had approached her about the party in the first place. I wondered if we should kick them out, but Mia thought that wouldn't be very ladylike and suggested we tell the manager that there were crashers.

Emma took a deep breath before crossing the dance floor toward Sydney and Callie, who had just spotted Matt. I watched in horror as they surrounded him, and Sydney snaked her arm through his. It made me wonder about Emma's comment about Sydney doing all the work for Callie. Maybe Sydney secretly liked Matt herself.

When Emma joined them, she began talking, and they were all listening to what she was saying. Then Sydney began gesturing and telling some sort of story. Matt watched the whole thing in silence, I was glad to see, and when the bartender handed him the sodas, he took them in his hands and took a few steps away from the group.

Emma must have made Sydney and Callie feel bad enough to leave, because Callie suddenly grabbed Sydney's arm and was pulling her toward the door. I hoped they would leave!

When Emma and Matt came back with the drinks, Emma looked really mad, but Matt was laughing.

"I hate those two. They are so evil!" Emma exclaimed. "They said Callie's sister, Jenna, had 'lost' her precious cell phone, so they had to deliver it to her. They didn't want to look out of place, so they dressed up."

I looked at Sydney and Callie, slowly making their way to the door. "I wonder how it got 'lost' in the first place if it was so precious?"

"Exactly! So I told them to go," said Emma.

Matt was still laughing. "The drama with all you girls!" he said. "I can't believe it. It's so dumb!"

"Believe it, mister," said Emma as she took our drinks from him.

"Thank you," I said to Matt. But as I took a sip, I saw my mother talking to Sydney and Callie at the door. She seemed to be guiding them toward the refreshments instead of the door! What was she doing?

Now Sydney and Callie headed toward us. That made me madder than ever, and when I am mad, I think the adrenaline makes me do things I would normally be too afraid to do! I looked over at Matt, and he was looking at them, then at Emma, then at me. And right then he and I both said at the same time, "Wanna dance?"

I couldn't believe it! I know where my courage came from (the adrenaline from being mad!), but I will never know what made Matt ask me to dance. I don't know if Emma said something to him before the party, or his mom, or if he decided it himself, but whatever it was, the timing was great.

Matt and I laughed and hit the dance floor just as Sydney and Callie arrived where we'd been standing. Emma winked at me and went off with Mia and Katie to get some hors d'oeuvres.

The truth is, Matt and I didn't have anything to say to each other. We smiled a lot, and since I am a good dancer, I think I impressed him. He is an okay dancer, but for someone so athletic, he's not that great. I don't want to say I fell a little out of love with him right then, but between Emma's and my friendship being on the line, us having nothing to say to each other, and him being only a so-so dancer, my crush kind of lost a little fizzle that night. And I was okay with that. I was proud to have set a goal, and to have reached it!

As Matt and I danced, I thought about all of my equations and my research. Oh, I was superhappy the whole time I was with Matt, but I decided that when it comes to love, there is no perfect recipe. There are so many ingredients, and things just have to happen naturally. If you need to force them or manipulate them, then they just aren't meant to be.

There was a lot of crushing going on that night at Dylan's party: I liked Matt, Callie liked Matt, maybe even Sydney liked Matt, Dylan liked Noah, Sam liked Dylan . . . and I'm sure there were a lot more equations that may not have a solution. All I know is this:

$Nothing > friends$

I repeat: Nothing is greater than friends!

CHAPTER 15

Later that Night . . .

Dylan's friends freaked out over the cupcakes. People came up to her all night to rave about them, and in the end, Dylan declared that the s'mores disco gift cupcakes made the party. That and Noah coming. They had a plan to go to the movies the very next night, which just goes to show you that if something is meant to happen, it just does.

For me, what made the party were the dance with Matt, the look on Callie's and Sydney's faces when he and I danced, making up with Emma, Dylan loving the cupcakes, and my big moment on the dance floor with Dad. Everyone gathered around and cheered. We were so good! We would have won if it was a contest! At the end he gave me a big hug and said, "Alexis, you are wonderful.

Just the way you are!" I looked over and saw Matt smiling at us, and I smiled back.

When we got home that night (along with Meredith and Skylar, who were sleeping over), I opened my locked drawer and took out the Matt notebook. It had been fun doing the research online and reading all the studies and their results, but it had been hard to quantify the results in a real-life setting. I needed data that was more concrete. And real feedback. Like tonight. I had reached my goal, and I could cross it off in my planner. Matt and I had danced together.

I read a quote somewhere that said, "The essence of mathematics is not to make simple things complicated, but to make complicated things simple." Someone named Gudder said it. I think he or she was right. The whole math thing complicated a simple crush. But on the bright side, I got a great makeover, some good love advice, and a dance with a cute boy. It was all good.

I wasn't sure what would happen next with Matt, if anything, or if I even wanted anything to. I needed a new goal, whether it was love-related or not, because when it comes down to it, I am all about setting and reaching my goals. Failing to plan is planning to fail. That's one of my mottoes.

So maybe it was time to focus on business again, instead of love. One thing is for sure: If I'd spent as much time on the Cupcake Club this month as I did on Matt, my friends and I would all be a lot richer!

I ripped the pages out of the Matt notebook. Then I dumped them into the shredder under my desk. It was time for a new goal. I picked up my planner again and on a new goal page I wrote:

SELL MORE CUPCAKES!

I sent an e-mail to the Cupcake Club:

> Great work! Thanks for putting up with Dylan. And me. Now on to the next assignment!
> xoxo,
> Alexis

Then I grabbed some SweeTarts and went to see if anyone wanted to watch *Dancing with the Stars* with me.

Want another sweet cupcake?
Here's a sneak peek
of the next book in the

CUPCAKE DIARIES

series:

Katie, batter up!

Katie,
batter
up!

My Cupcake Obsession

My name is Katie Brown, and I am crazy about cupcakes. I'm not kidding. I think about cupcakes every day. I even dream about them when I sleep. The other night I was dreaming that I was eating a giant cupcake, and when I woke up I was chewing on my pillow!

Okay, now I *am* kidding. But I do dream about cupcakes, I swear. There must be a name for this condition. Cupcake-itis? That's got to be it. I am stricken with cupcake-itis, and there isn't any cure.

My three best friends and I formed the Cupcake Club, and we bake cupcakes for parties and events and things, and sell them. We're all different in our own way. Mia has long black hair and loves fashion. Emma has blond hair and blue eyes and lots of brothers. Alexis has wavy red hair and loves math.

I have light brown hair, and I mostly wear jeans and T-shirts. I'm an only child. And I hate math. But I have one big thing in common with all my friends: We love cupcakes.

That's why we were in my kitchen on a Tuesday afternoon, baking cupcakes on a beautiful spring day. We were having an official meeting to discuss our next big job: baking a cupcake cake for my grandma Carole's seventy-fifth birthday bash. But while we were thinking about that, we were also trying to perfect a new chocolate-coconut-almond cupcake, specially created for my friend Mia's stepdad and based on his favorite candy bar.

We had tried two different combinations already: a chocolate cupcake with coconut frosting and almonds on top and then a coconut cupcake with chocolate-almond frosting, but none of them matched the taste of the candy bar enough. Now we were working on a third batch: a chocolate-almond cupcake with coconut frosting and lots of shredded coconut on top.

I carefully poured a teaspoon of almond extract into the batter. "Mmm, smells almondy," I said.

"I hope this batch is the one," said Mia. "Eddie finally started taking down that gross flowery wallpaper in my bedroom, and I have to find some way to thank him. I would have paid someone a million dollars to do that!"

"You realize you could buy a whole new house for a million dollars, right?" Alexis asked. "Probably two or three."

"You know what I mean," Mia replied. "Besides, you know how ugly that wallpaper is. It looks like something you'd find in an old lady's room."

"Hey, my grandma Carole's an old lady, and she doesn't have ugly wallpaper in *her* house," I protested.

Emma picked up the ice-cream scoop and started scooping up the batter and putting it into the cupcake pans.

"We need to find out more about your grandma," Emma said. "That way we can figure out what kind of cupcake cake to make for the party."

"Right!" Alexis agreed. She flipped open her notebook and took out the pen that was tucked behind her ear. Sometimes I think Alexis must have a secret stash of notebooks in her house somewhere. I've never seen her without one.

"First things first," Alexis said. "How many people are coming to the party?"

I wrinkled my nose, thinking. "Not sure," I said.

Then I yelled as loud as I could. "Mom! How many people are coming to Grandma Carole's party?"

My mom appeared in the kitchen doorway. "Katie, you know how I feel about yelling," she said.

"Sorry, Mom," I said in my best apology voice.

"The answer is about thirty people," Mom said. "So I think if the cupcake cake has three dozen cupcakes, that would be fine."

"What exactly is a cupcake cake, anyway?" Mia asked. "Do you mean like one of those giant cupcakes that you bake with a special pan?"

"I was thinking more like a bunch of cupcakes arranged in tiers to look like a cake," Mom replied.

Mia nodded to Alexis's pen and notebook. "Can I?"

"Sure," Alexis replied, handing them to her. Mia began to sketch. She's a great artist and wants to be a fashion designer someday.

"Like this?" Mia asked, showing Mom the drawing. I looked over Mia's shoulder and saw the plan: three round tiers, one on top of the other, with cupcakes on each.

"Exactly!" Mom said, smiling and showing off a mouth full of perfect white teeth. (She *is* a dentist, after all.)

Alexis took back her notebook. "Excellent," she said, jotting something down. "Now we just need to decide what flavor to make and how to decorate it."

"What do you think, Mom?" I asked.

"Oh, I'm staying out of this. This is your project," Mom replied. "I think I'll let you girls come up with something. You always come up with such wonderful ideas, and I know Grandma Carole will love whatever you do."

"All done!" Emma announced, putting down the ice-cream scoop.

"Mom, oven, please?" I asked.

"Sure thing," Mom said, slipping on an oven mitt. She put the chocolate-almond cupcakes into the preheated oven, and I set the cupcake-shaped timer on the counter for twenty minutes.

Mom left the kitchen, and the four of us sat down at the kitchen table to work out the details.

"So what kind of flavors does your grandmother like?" Alexis asked.

I shrugged. "I don't know. She likes all kinds of things. Blueberry pie in the summer, and chocolate cake, and maple-walnut ice cream . . ."

"So we can make blueberry-chocolate-maple cupcakes with walnuts on top!" Mia joked.

"Hey, we thought bacon flavor was weird and that worked out well!" said Emma. It was true. Bacon flavor was a really big seller for us.

"You know, we don't know anything about your grandma," Emma said. "Maybe if you tell us something about her, we can get some ideas."

"Sure," I said. "Hold on a minute."

I went into the den where Mom and I keep all our books and picked up a photo album. We have lots of them, and there were pictures of Grandma Carole in almost all of them. I turned to a photo of me and my mom with Grandma Carole and Grandpa Chuck at Christmas. Grandma Carole looked nice in a red sweater and the beaded necklace I made her as a present at camp. Her hair used to be brown like mine, but now it's white.

"That's her," I said. "And that's my grandpa Chuck. They got married, like, forever ago, and they have three kids: my mom and my uncle Mike and my uncle Jimmy. She used to be a librarian."

"Just like my mom!" Emma said, smiling.

I flipped the pages in the photo album and found a picture of Grandma Carole in her white tennis outfit, holding her racquet.

"Mostly she loves sports and stuff," I said. "She runs, like, every day, and she won track medals in high school. She goes swimming and plays tennis, and skis in the winter, and she likes golf even though she says there's not enough running."

"Do sports have a flavor?" Mia mused.

"Um, sports-drink-flavored cupcakes?" Alexis offered.

"Or sweat-flavored cupcakes," I said, then burst out giggling.

"Or smelly sneaker-flavored cupcakes," Mia said, laughing.

"Ew, sweat and sneakers . . . those are so gross!" Emma squealed.

"But I guess she does like sports most of all," I said. "She's always trying to get me to do stuff with her. Because I am *soooo* good at sports." I said that really sarcastically, because the exact opposite is true. Now it was Emma's turn to giggle.

"Yeah, I've seen you in gym," she said.

"It's even worse than you know," I confessed. "When she tried to teach me to ski, I wiped out on the bunny hill—you know, the one for little kids? I even sprained my ankle."

"Oh, that's terrible!" Emma cried.

"And when I played tennis on a team with

Grandpa, I accidentally whacked him in the head with my racquet."

Mia put a hand to her mouth to try to stop from laughing. "Oh, Katie, that would be funny if it weren't so terrible!" she said.

I nodded. "He needed four stitches."

"So I guess you don't take after your grandmother," Alexis said.

"Well, not the sports thing," I admitted. "But everyone says I look exactly like she did when she was younger. And she's a good baker, too. She used to own her own cake baking business."

Alexis stood up. "You're kidding! Why didn't you tell us?"

"I just did," I said.

"But she's a *professional*," Alexis said. "It's not going to be easy to impress her."

"Yes, the pressure is on," Mia agreed.

I hadn't thought of that before. "Well, we'll just have to make a superawesome cupcake cake, then."

Alexis sat back down. "Okay, people, let's start jotting down some ideas."

We tried for the next few minutes, but nobody could think of anything. Then Emma looked at her watch.

"You know, I need to get home," she said. "It's my turn to make dinner tonight."

"We need some more time to come up with ideas, anyway," Alexis said. "Let's schedule another meeting."

"Let's do it tomorrow," I suggested. But Alexis and Mia had whipped out their smartphones, and Emma took out a little notebook with flowers on it—and they were all frowning.

"Alexis and I have soccer practice tomorrow and Thursday, and a game on Friday," Mia reported.

"And I have concert band practice on Wednesdays and Fridays," Emma said. Emma plays the flute, and she's really good at that.

"Sorry, Katie. You know spring is a busy time of year," Alexis said.

"Yeah, sure," I said, but really, I didn't. I don't really do anything besides the Cupcake Club, and it's not just because I have cupcake-itis. I'm no good at sports, and I'm not so great at music, either. When we learned how to play the recorder in fourth grade, I ended up making a sound like a beached whale. My teacher made me practice after school, after everyone went home.

Just then the cake timer rang. I put on a mitt and opened the oven door. All the cupcakes in the pan were flat. They should have gotten nice and puffy as they cooked.

"Mom!" I yelled.

Mom rushed in a few seconds later. "Katie, what did I tell you about—Oh," she said, looking at the deflated cupcakes.

"What happened?" I asked.

"This looks like a baking powder issue to me," she said. She put the pan of flat cupcakes on the counter and picked up the little can of baking powder. "Just as I thought. It's past its expiration date. You need fresh baking powder for your cupcakes to rise."

I felt terrible. "Sorry, guys."

"It's not your fault," Emma said.

"Yeah, and anyway, Eddie's not finished taking down that wallpaper yet," Mia said. "We can try again next time."

"Whenever that is," I mumbled.

Emma, Alexis, and Mia started picking up their things.

"We can talk about your grandma's cupcakes at lunch on Friday," Alexis said. "Everybody come with some ideas, okay?"

Emma saluted. "Yes, General Alexis!" she teased.

"Ooh, if Alexis is the general, can I be the cupcake captain?" I asked, and everyone laughed.

When my friends left, the kitchen was pretty quiet. Mom went into the den to do some paperwork, and all that was left was me and a pan of flat cupcakes.

As I cleaned up the mess, I thought of Alexis and Mia and Emma all going off and doing stuff—stuff that I couldn't do. They were all multitalented, and the only thing I was good at was making cupcakes. It made me feel a little bit lonely and a little bit like a loser.

In fact, it made me feel as flat as those cupcakes.

If you're not an expert baker like the Cupcakers, that's okay—here is a quick and easy-to-follow recipe that's just as sweet! (Ask an adult for assistance before you start baking since you might need help with the oven or mixer.)

Pineapple "Upside-Down" Cupcakes

• Makes 18 •

BATTER:
1 box of yellow cake mix
1 cup sour cream
½ cup of pineapple juice (use juice from canned pineapples; see topping)
⅓ cup vegetable oil
4 large eggs, room temperature
1 teaspoon pure vanilla extract

TOPPING:
8 tablespoons unsalted butter, melted
¾ cup firmly packed light brown sugar
1 can (20 ounces) crushed pineapple, drained (set aside ½ cup of the pineapple juice for batter)
maraschino cherries (optional)

Center baking rack in oven and preheat to 350°F. Grease cupcake tins well with butter or cooking spray.

CUPCAKES: In a large mixing bowl combine all of the batter ingredients. With an electric mixer on medium speed, mix the ingredients together until there are no lumps in the batter. Spoon the batter into the cupcake tins so that each tin is about halfway full.

TOPPING: Mix the melted butter and brown sugar together with a spoon. Sprinkle about a teaspoon of the mixture on top of the cupcake batter in the tins. Now add a layer of about a tablespoon of pineapple. If you'd like, put one cherry on top, pressing it into the pineapple layer so it's level.

Bake the cupcakes about 18 to 20 minutes or until a toothpick inserted into the center of a cupcake comes out clean. Remove from oven and place on a wire rack to cool for about 5 minutes. Carefully run a dinner knife around the edges of the cupcakes and invert the cupcake pan onto the wire rack. Let the cupcakes cool for about 20 minutes.

yummy! ♡

If you're not an expert baker like the Cupcakers, that's okay—here is a quick and easy-to-follow recipe that's just as sweet! (Ask an adult for assistance before you start baking since you might need help with the oven or mixer.)

Vanilla Cupcakes with Vanilla Buttercream Frosting

• Makes 12 •

BATTER:
½ cup unsalted butter, at room temperature
⅔ cup granulated sugar
3 large eggs, at room temperature
1 teaspoon pure vanilla extract
1 ½ cups all-purpose flour
1 ½ teaspoons baking powder
¼ teaspoon salt
¼ cup whole milk

FROSTING:
½ cup unsalted butter, at room temperature
4 cups sifted confectioners' sugar
⅓ cup of whole milk
1 teaspoon pure vanilla extract
food coloring (optional)

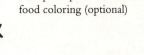

Center baking rack in oven and preheat to 350°F. Line cupcake tins with cupcake liners.

CUPCAKES: In a medium bowl, beat the butter and sugar with an electric mixer on medium speed until fluffy. Then add the eggs one at a time. Blend in the vanilla extract.

In a separate bowl whisk together the flour, baking powder, and salt. With the mixer on low speed, add the flour mixture to the butter-sugar mixture and alternate with the milk. Mix until there are no lumps in the batter.

Evenly fill the cupcake tins with the batter and bake for about 18 to 20 minutes or until a toothpick inserted into the center of a cupcake comes out clean. Remove from oven and place on a wire rack to cool completely before frosting.

FROSTING: In a medium bowl mix the butter with an electric mixer until it looks fluffy. Add in some of the sugar, alternating with the milk and vanilla until it is all blended. Add food coloring per package's directions and mix well to color the frosting. Then frost the cupcakes.

Want more

CUPCAKEDIARIES?

Visit **CupcakeDiariesBooks.com**
for the series trailer, excerpts, activities,
and everything you need for throwing
your own cupcake party!

Coco Simon always dreamed of opening a cupcake bakery but was afraid she would eat all of the profits. When she's not daydreaming about cupcakes, Coco edits children's books and has written close to one hundred books for children, tweens, and young adults, which is a lot less than the number of cupcakes she's eaten. Cupcake Diaries is the first time Coco has mixed her love of cupcakes with writing.

Are you an
Emma, a Mia, a Katie, or an Alexis?
Take our quiz and find out!

Read each question and circle the letter
that best describes you.

(If you don't want to write in your book, use a separate piece of paper.)

1. You've been invited to a party. What do you wear?

A. Jeans and a cute T-shirt. You want to look nice, but you also want to be comfortable.

B. You beg your parents to lend you money for the cool boots you saw online. If you're going to a party, you have to wear the latest fashion!

C. Something pretty, but practical. If you're going to spend money on a new outfit, it better be one you'll be able to wear a lot.

D. Something feminine—lacy and floral. And definitely pink if not floral—a girl can never go wrong wearing *pink*!

2. Your idea of a perfect Saturday afternoon is:

A. Seeing a movie with your BFFs and then going out for pizza afterward.

B. THE MALL! Hopefully one of the stores will be having a big sale!

C. Creating a perfect budget to buy clothes, go out with friends, and save money for college—all at the same time—and then meeting your friends for lunch.

D. Going for a manicure and pedicure.

3. You have to study for a big test. What's your study style?

A. In your bedroom, with your favorite music playing.

B. At home, with help from your parents if necessary.

C. At the library, where you can take out some new books after you've finished studying, or anyplace else that's absolutely quiet.

D. Anyplace away from *home*—away from your messy, loud siblings!

4. There's a new girl at school. What's your first reaction?

A. You're a little cautious. You've been hurt before, so it takes you a while to warm up to new friends.

B. You think it's great. You welcome her with open arms. (Maybe you can share each other's clothes!)

C. If she's nice *and* smart, maybe you'll consider being friends with her.

D. You'll gladly welcome another friend—as long as she really wants to be friends with you—and not just meet your cute older brothers!

5. When it comes to boys . . .

A. They make you a little nervous. You want to be friends first—for a long time—until you'd consider someone a boyfriend.

B. He has to be tall, trustworthy, sweet—and of course, superstylish!

C. He has to be cute, funny, and smart—and he gets extra points if he likes to dance!

D. He has to be loyal and true as well as good-looking. You look sweet, but you're tough when you have to be.

6. When it comes to your family . . .

A. You come from a single-parent home. It's hard for you to imagine your parent dating, but you will try to get used to it.

B. You come from a mixed family with stepsiblings and a stepparent. At first it was overwhelming, but you're starting to get used to having everyone in the mix!

C. You get along okay with your parents, but your older sister thinks she's queen of the world. Still sometimes you ask her for advice anyway.

Which Cupcake girl are you?
What your answers mean:

Mostly As:
You're a Katie! Your style is easy and comfortable.
You always look good, and you always feel good too.
You have a few very close friends (both girls and boys),
and you like it that way. You don't want to confide
in just anybody.

Mostly Bs:
You're a Mia! You're the girl everyone envies at school
because you can wear an old ratty sweatshirt and jeans
and somehow still look like a runway model. Your
sense of style is what everyone notices first, but you're
also a great friend.

Mostly Cs:
You're an Alexis! You are supersmart and not afraid to
show it! You get As in every subject, and like nothing
more than creating business plans and budgets. You love
your friends but have to remember sometimes that not
everyone in the world is as brilliant as you are.

Mostly Ds:
You're an Emma! You are a girly-girl and love to wear
pretty clothes. Pink is your signature color. But people
should not be fooled by your sweet exterior. You can
be as tough as nails when necessary and would never
let anyone push you around.

D. You live in a house with many brothers—dirty, sticky, smelly boys! You love them all, but sometimes would give anything for a sister!

7. Your dream vacation would be:

   A. Anyplace beachy. You love to swim and also just relax on a beach blanket.

   B. Paris—to see the latest fashions.

   C. Egypt—you'd love to see the pyramids and try to figure out how they were constructed without any modern machinery.

   D. Holland—you'd love to see the tulips in bloom!

Find out which Cupcake girl you are!